# THE
# MOON
## IN THE
# MANGO
# TREE

# Also by Pamela Binnings Ewen

**Fiction**

*Walk Back the Cat*

**Nonfiction**

*Faith on Trial*

# THE
# MOON
## IN THE
# MANGO
# TREE

A NOVEL

# PAMELA BINNINGS EWEN

Nashville, Tennessee

978-0-8054-4733-0


Published by B&H Publishing Group,
Nashville, Tennessee


Dewey Decimal Classification: F
Subject Heading: HISTORICAL FICTION \
BARBARA BOND—FICTION \ HUSBANDS AND
WIVES—FICTION


1 2 3 4 5 6 7 8 • 12 11 10 09 08

*Perhaps her faults and follies, the unhappiness she
had suffered, were not entirely vain if she could
follow the path that she now dimly discerned before
her . . . the path that led to peace.*

W. Somerset Maugham
*The Painted Veil*

To Barbara Jeanne Perkins Binnings
and June Perkins Anderson

And in memory of Muriel Carol Austgen

# Prologue

AT THE MOUTH OF THE MENAM—THE Chao Phraya River—fireflies covering mangrove bushes at the edge of the water sparkled in strange unison through the dusk, creating beacons of light that were seen for miles. The river flows to the Gulf of Siam from Bangkok. It is the key that unlocks the mysteries of Siam to weary travelers arriving by sea. As Harvey and I peered from the deck of the *Empress of Asia*, we saw each bush glimmer with light from the fireflies then quickly disappear into the gloaming—on and off together as if they were one, light, then dark.

Siam, as I knew it then, has disappeared as the light of those fireflies. Today it is known as Thailand, the land of the free people. It smolders beneath the white-hot glare of the sun, just a few degrees south of the Tropic of Cancer. When we arrived at the end of the year 1919, Siam was laughter, music, color. Many years later I fled the country and the rage of darkness that howled within me.

This is our story, my child—Harvey's and mine. These are the years that you can't recall. Sift for the truth. But look to the light and learn what those fireflies taught, what draws the moth to the flame and flowers to sun. It is this that I want you to know:

Darkness is only the absence of light.

# Part One

# Chapter One

**Siam**
**December 1919**

I SAT NAKED BEFORE A TARNISHED, old mirror in the middle of the jungle and contemplated the situation, letting my anger cool. Sunshine streamed through a window on the right, lighting my hair to a copper haze, burnishing my skin. Still damp from the bath, I patted beads of water on my neck and shoulders with a towel, trying to ignore the question that had begun to gnaw at my thoughts: Have I made a terrible mistake? I turned my eyes to the window. Across a clearing and past the little mission church, a ragged line of tall, twisted trees encroached. Dark shapes seemed to dance in slender bamboo that advanced before the forest, undermining the discipline of the mission, but I knew it was just the undergrowth that made those shapes—fern, creeping vines, and waxy dark-green banana leaves.

Downstairs, waiting for me with the force of morals and religion, were the missionaries, and, as of just two months ago, I was a missionary wife. Turning back to the mirror, I brushed back the damp, tangled curls with a flick of my hand, reliving the scene.

Harvey and I had only just arrived at this place, hot, tired, and hungry. After the two-month journey that began in Philadelphia on October 26, we had emerged this morning from the higher terrain of the forested range of mountains that circled the Nan Valley and rode our ponies across the rice fields in the blazing sun. When we arrived at our destination, the missionary house in which I now sat just outside the ancient walls of Nan—known as the Jungle City of Siam—I slid from the pony and whipped the hot, heavy sun helmet, the topi, off my head, reveling in the freedom from its weight. The motion loosened my hair, tumbling it across my shoulders, and the missionaries sitting on the veranda above had stared.

After a brief hesitation, a plump, elderly woman, followed more slowly by a dignified gentleman of about seventy years, descended the stairs to greet us. Reverend Ruckel and his wife, Dora, were the senior members of the mission. A young woman about my age, and a pale, thin man dressed in an immaculate white suit rose to wait for us at the top of the stairs. Emery and Amalie Breeden wore stiff smiles as Mrs. Ruckel introduced them, and Mr. Breeden's eyes strayed to my disheveled hair.

As Mrs. Breeden took her seat, Harvey and Mr. Breeden went off with the *syse*, the horse-boy, to see to the ponies. Mrs. Ruckel took my arm to show me to our room.

"Perhaps it would be best to tuck your hair into a braid or some such thing, Mrs. Perkins," Amalie Breeden had murmured from her chair, raising her thin eyebrows and giving me a cool look as we turned to go inside.

I stared back at her, bewildered.

"Ladies don't take down their hair in public, you know. At least, not in this mission they don't." She then lifted a cup of tea to her lips and lowered her lids, dismissing me.

I frowned at the mirror and shook myself from the rumination. Well, here we are, I thought, and like it or not, this would be our home for the next few years.

*The past is gone, closed up behind you now, warned my inner voice with a note of alarm. Turn your thoughts to the future, to action. Actions have power. Smile at the inevitable. A smile can turn regret to anticipation, to pleasure.*

The sound of voices drifted through the window, and I looked out to see Harvey striding across the clearing toward the house with Emery Breeden. Harvey's step was jaunty. As I watched, he laughed at something Mr. Breeden said and the sound contained all his hope, his great expectation for our future here at Nan, his intoxication with the country of Siam, and his new work as a missionary doctor. This is my husband, I thought with a surge of love and pride.

"That which is necessary," Nietzsche has said, "does not offend me." I took a deep breath and, holding every muscle taut, forced myself to smile while I thought of something pleasant, like Harvey. I closed my eyes and for just one minute . . . I let the past emerge.

On a crisp, cool day in Philadelphia three years before, a shout from the crowd drew my attention to Harvey Perkins.

"The vote won't help you clean out your sink spout!"

The taunt was accompanied by a pebble that landed in front of me and rolled under my foot, breaking my stride. My head snapped around and I glared at the gray wall of stern men in bowler hats wearing neat, dark suits, and workmen in baggy pants and loose shirts that jeered, their faces red with anger and disdain. They lined the narrow streets as we marched past, four columns of ladies straight as arrows. Streamers of yellow ribbon from our sashes fluttered in the breeze, and our white muslin skirts whipped around our ankles as we walked. Music played ahead of us, echoing against the tall buildings, two trumpets and a drum. The little band marched under a banner held high proclaiming, "The Vote For Women—NOW!"

This was the year 1916. The right to vote was long past due.

I scanned the crowd and my gaze fixed on an uncovered head of sandy-colored hair ruffled by the wind. Below, a pair of clear green eyes looked back in frank admiration. With a flicker of excitement and surprise, I recognized Harvey. Then I glimpsed the face beside him frowning in disapproval—his father, Penrose Perkins. I groaned and missed a step.

An elder of our little church in Germantown, Penrose was known for his stern views on temperance and the place of women in the home. Naturally, he and my father were acquainted. I would hear more of this, I knew.

But Harvey's wide, true smile dissolved the angry crowd. His father disappeared and all I saw was Harvey. I smiled to myself and, with a surge of new confidence, lifted my chin and marched on down the golden line with the other suffragettes.

"What are you going to tell Dad?" hissed my younger sister Evie, who walked beside me. She had spotted Harvey and Penrose standing in the crowd.

"I'll think of something," I answered with a shrug, still tingling from Harvey's smile. My eyes swept over the crowd to the wedge of bright blue sky visible between the buildings just ahead. Now my step was sure, the air sparkled, the banner blew in the breeze, the trumpet blared.

My father was not at all happy after Penrose Perkins spilled the beans. "Suffragettes!" he scowled. "You're so impetuous. And now you've created a spectacle." He shook his head. "What were you thinking?"

"I was thinking that it's past time for women to have the vote."

He continued to glare at me. I started to argue the point, but his lips twitched, then he rolled his eyes and shook his head. "You've always had a mind of your own." I heard him chuckle as he ducked behind his book.

The following Sunday I watched from the choir loft as Dad and Mummy and Matilda and Charles Otis Bond entered the cool, dark Summit Presbyterian Church, followed by my younger brothers, then my sisters. My father, confident and sure, an Annapolis man with a strong jaw and stern mouth, a man who tipped his hat when he spoke of Valley Forge, led the way down the middle aisle between the high brick archways, now holding that hat in both hands. He stepped aside for our mother just as he reached the family pew, number four on the right, behind the Melchiors. She tilted her heart-shaped face upward and gave him a warm smile that made apples of her cheeks before gliding in to take her place, followed by my four younger brothers in order of age, then by my sisters, Evelyn and Alice. I was the eldest daughter.

Harvey sat with his family on the opposite side of the aisle. His father stared up at me with puzzled eyes. Penrose was not fine-tuned; he saw things in the simplest light, black or white. No vague gray clouded his thoughts. As the choir stood to sing, his wife, Marion, put her hand on his arm, a gentle touch, but he started and began turning pages in the hymnal.

The service seemed to drag on for hours. I repeated the familiar prayers automatically and stifled a yawn, letting my idle gaze roam over the congregation while Reverend Bennett's voice droned through the long sermon. My eyes met Harvey's and I threw him a bold smile, then ducked my head when I felt Dad's look. I studied the prayer book as I mused on this new development.

Harvey came calling that afternoon. I watched from the front porch as he negotiated the walkway up the hill with care, stepping over spots where the tree roots had shoved through the bricks. When he reached the gate, he removed his hat. Our house, set off Greene Street by a narrow lawn behind a low iron fence, was in Pelham, the most pleasant part of Germantown. Old and snug, warm in winter and cool in summer, the small, two-story stone house was almost indistinguishable from those of our neighbors.

"How's the sink spout?" he said in a dry tone.

I gave him a sideways look and smiled when I saw that he was teasing. "There's not much chance that I'll be spending a lot of time in front of a sink spout when I leave school," I answered cheerfully.

"It's nice to see a girl who has beauty and spunk." He stood at the bottom of the steps and looked up at me. "You're not afraid of much, I imagine."

"Oh well," I said, pleased at his words. "Women mean to have the vote. There's no point in being timid when you want a thing." I smoothed my skirt with the flat of my hands. "Besides, I guess I can take care of myself."

A glint of amusement flickered in his eyes, and I invited him up. We sat on a slat-board swing that hung on the front porch and whiled away the time in the midst of a steady procession of brothers and sisters racing in and out of the house, shrieking, laughing, quarreling. Pale yellow sunshine slipped through the leaves of an apple tree nearby and we watched phantom shadows shifting shapes on the floorboards in the cool fall breeze as we talked and laughed.

Then Dad strode through the door and nodded and sank into a chair nearby. Harvey straightened, sitting upright as I braced the toe of my shoe on the floor, bringing the swing to a shuddering halt. Dad said hello and settled comfortably with his hands folded over his stomach, gazing with a pleasant expression across the street in front of our house.

"Studying medicine, are you?" he asked, knowing full well that Harvey was a student at Jefferson Medical School in Philadelphia.

"Yes, sir." Harvey looked Dad straight in the eye as he answered.

"Well, that's a fine thing," Dad said in a polite tone. "There's nothing in this world so interesting as science." Dad was an illuminating engineer for the United Gas Improvement Company in Philadelphia. "Some of my happiest times are in the laboratory."

"Dad's an alchemist," I interjected. "He turns coal into heat and light instead of gold."

Harvey leaned forward. "Is that so?"

Dad nodded. "It's a whole new world."

"You're right—we live in a very modern age," Harvey said. "Yesterday I saw pictures of the actual structures of molecules."

"You saw what?" Dad sat straight up and stared at Harvey. "You've actually seen *pictures* of them, have you?" he asked in astonishment.

Still leaning forward, Harvey gestured, demonstrating with his hands. His elbows were braced on his knees. "Yes, sir. They're done with X-rays—the molecules crystallize, like sugar, then the X-rays reflect off the crystals and create a picture of the structure of the cell."

"You don't say!" Dad thought about that a minute, then he bent so that his head was just inches from Harvey's. They began speaking in a language foreign to me—long scientific words with no vowels and just a smattering of English.

I leaned back in the swing with satisfaction while they talked, reflecting that Harvey would probably be around for a while. For years I had watched older girls flush and their mothers smile when Harvey Perkins passed them by and tipped his hat, tall and lean and self-assured.

Over the next few months we became inseparable and Harvey's quiet reserve gradually peeled away to reveal new facets of his personality, like stripping old varnish from a picture to expose complex and vibrant brushwork underneath—a kind word and a coin slipped to an old man in rags on the street when he thought no one was watching; a baby bird carefully slipped into his handkerchief to be returned to its nest with no human scent; a surprising sense of humor.

Medical studies absorbed most of Harvey's time while I attended Germantown High School, skipping mathematics and science and concentrating instead on the music that I loved, especially voice, and philosophy and poetry as well—Tennyson, Dickinson, Shelley, and Keats. Harvey's world was made up of tangible things, instruments and books read for instruction, not pleasure, and patients and blood and diseases, problems that could usually be resolved by hard work. Mine was full of melodies, trills, and scales, a world of gauzy dreams.

Grand opera was my passion. Every afternoon I spent two hours in the private studio of Miss McGregor learning the technique required to one day sing the great arias. I relentlessly practiced cadenzas and scherzi, controlling my breathing to release the simple, rounded tones—exercise the jaw, the mouth, open the throat, lower the larynx, let the sound come naturally, use the eyes, the face, the entire body. Sometimes Miss McGregor grew impatient and drew close enough to touch me, fixing her sharp, bird-like eyes on my throat, reading my expression, mouthing the words as I sang.

Like sympathetic vibration between two instruments, Miss McGregor sensed when I grew tired or bored, and I quickly learned to hide this, fearing that she'd lose interest in teaching me to sing. "Your voice is not yet made, Barbara," she warned at these times with a disappointed sigh. "You're young and music is hard work." Then I'd double my efforts as I was in awe of Miss McGregor, who'd had conservatory training in Europe and sang with Melba and Ponselle—small parts but on stage with the great divas. I wanted everything she had to offer. I wanted an opera career. I wanted her to shout to the world that she'd found a new silver voice. But dedication and discipline comes from the student, not the teacher.

And what of Harvey? Sometimes thoughts like ghosts crept in, dissolving images of things that, years from now, could turn into what might have been. It didn't occur to me then that Harvey was nowhere to be seen in those dreams of singing. But those were fleeting thoughts, and unwisely I let them slip away.

At home I accompanied myself on the piano and sang songs to drift on, tunes like "Melancholy Baby" and "You Made Me Love You." As I played, the scents and sounds of old Germantown breezed through the window: the fragrance of bluebells and roses, of fresh-cut grass, of velvet green moss on damp old stone; the hollow clop of hooves on the proud new asphalt street as draught horses pulled their wooden carts, and the vendors' sing-song calls—"Vegg–a–te–bals! Got–ch'er vegg–a–te–bals! Fresh, sweet melons, apples, and pears"—and urgent tones— "Ice! I–i–ice!"; shrieks of laughter from children hurrying home from school; soft, expectant cries from the new baby next door as he woke from his nap.

This small village was a refuge from the city, linked to downtown Philadelphia by the Pennsylvania Railroad that the men rode to work each morning, Monday through Friday, to sit at desks or teach or sell dry goods while their wives and children stayed behind. Entire families were born, grew up, and died within sight of the white peaks of Summit Church just up the hill. Even as a child I knew that change was in the air, that the world was on the cusp of something new and free. Possibilities stirred things up, like leaves on the breeze before a storm. But new ideas never took hold in Germantown, and the breeze never gathered more strength than a soft current moving through otherwise still water. Bohemian poets in Paris and New York, careers for women instead of love and marriage that lasted until death—these things were strange and remote, not really a part of us at all.

At times like these I thought of Harvey, not of opera. Harvey and I were the same note, just pitched in different keys. In the music of life Harvey picked out each chord one by one, until together they formed the melody, while I tended to hear the whole thing at once. But it made no difference to me; in the end, we both heard the same song. Harvey seemed to always know what I was thinking even before I told him. I adored this serious, gentle man.

When Harvey wasn't studying, we were together, skimming across frozen ponds in the white mist of winter on silver skates, lounging at picnics in parks that bloomed with small children and new spring flowers, going to silent pictures, riding the electric trolley up Carpenter Lane for ice cream. My youngest brother, David, who was eight years old, had formed a strong attachment to Harvey and often tagged along on these expeditions. But when we were able to slip away, Harvey's kisses lit a flame that warmed me long after he had gone.

# Chapter Two

THE SUN WAS ALREADY DROPPING TOWARD the horizon as I dressed and hurried down the stairs for tea, feeling refreshed from my bath and more cheerful now. We were guests of Reverend and Mrs. Ruckel until minor repairs could be completed on a house, I had learned. Thrilled at the idea of our own home, I resolved to see it as soon as Harvey was free.

The Ruckels were already comfortably seated on the veranda with Harvey and Mr. Breeden. Reverend Ruckel and Harvey rose as I appeared, but Mr. Breeden seemed distracted, looking off into the distance. Mrs. Ruckel's eyes lighted on my hair, neatly twisted into a knot, and she greeted me with an almost imperceptible smile of approval.

Reverend Ruckel and his wife both had hair the color of old iron, kind eyes, and warm smiles. He was a sturdy-looking man, about middle height and fit for his age, his skin was brown and weathered, whereas Dora Ruckel was plump, with a pale complexion and rosy cheeks. Her eyes crinkled at the corners; her smile ended in soft folds of skin.

Amalie Breeden floated about, arranging cups and saucers on a small tea table set up next to Mrs. Ruckel. I took a seat and watched her, masking my annoyance as her earlier remonstrance still rang in my ears. Mrs. Breeden had a deceptively delicate appearance. She was small-boned and petite, with pale, translucent skin like fine porcelain. A gauze dress fluttered as it hung from a frame that had a fragile, almost brittle look. Her plain features combined in a way that made her rather pretty, I admitted to myself, and her brown hair displayed glints of gold in the sunlight. She wore it braided and coiled neatly around her head.

She caught my eye as I studied her, then shifted her attention to Harvey. "How is it that you arrived ahead of your carriers this afternoon?" she asked.

"They were about an hour behind us," Harvey answered. "They're taking the road. Should be here any time."

"We took the shorter route and left them on the edge of the plain," I added.

"Oh?" She slanted her eyes at me. "Do you mean that you rode directly through the rice paddies?" She turned her attention back to the tea table. "That's a little foolish, you know. The ponies could have been hurt on the soft ground."

"They were brave little things," I said. "They've earned a reward, I believe."

"They've done what was expected of them," she answered in a crisp tone. "Out here, you'll find that rewards aren't so easy to come by."

Mrs. Breeden turned to Harvey. "There are no motors in Nan, I'm afraid. The ponies and a surrey are at the disposal of the hospital, however." She wore a bright smile for my husband. "So they'll be yours to use. Mind your wife doesn't spoil the ponies, though."

I bit back a quick retort, but Harvey chuckled, as though she had said something amusing. "Babs has a tender spot for animals," he said, and I softened at the look he gave me.

Emery Breeden knitted his brows. His face was long and his close-set eyes were ringed with shadows. Round glasses with thin, black rims gave him an intense, serious look. Hair of an indeterminate shade, somewhere between brown and dark blond, was parted in the middle and slicked back from his high, shining forehead. His mouth curled down at the corners in a slight pout, giving him a dissatisfied expression.

"It's easy to be soft, of course," Mr. Breeden said. "But I've found that trait sometimes indicates a certain weakness of fiber that we must guard against and tamp down." His voice was low and brusque. He leaned toward Harvey as he spoke. "The local people suffer somewhat from a lack of discipline. Our mission sets an example at all times. Keeping a firm hand on things is what the Scriptures require."

"Ah, well," I said. "I don't suppose a pony needs such a firm hand."

Mr. Breeden sat back, raised his chin, and gazed at me with an icy look. "The pony's not the point. It's really a fundamental question of character, Mrs. Perkins," he said.

Harvey, engaged now in conversation with Reverend Ruckel, had turned away and didn't hear his words. This is Harvey's work, I reminded myself, the beginning of his career. And first impressions are everything. I managed to curve my lips into a polite smile that took the reverend by surprise. He quickly glanced away.

❧

As the afternoon wore on, the air grew oppressive and fatigue made me listless. Through the haze I watched a constant stream of people moving past on the river road: farmers, vendors from the market outside the walls of Nan, women with babies on their hips. Two children strolled by pulling a water buffalo behind them.

Finally the carriers began to arrive with our baggage, straggling from the direction of Nan in twos and threes. Harvey rose to direct them and he, Mr. Breeden, and Reverend Ruckel disappeared around the back of the house where our things would be stored for a few weeks. Mrs. Ruckel rose after a moment and bustled inside to see to the preparation of tea, leaving me alone with Mrs. Breeden.

I spoke first, to break the uneasy silence. "How long have you been here?" I asked. From the interior of the house I heard Mrs. Ruckel giving instructions to her cook.

"About two years," Mrs. Breeden answered, covering a yawn with the back of her hand as her look traveled over the river road. "My husband is the pastor and also the headmaster of the school. Mission headquarters in New York asked us to take things in hand when Dr. Pitters became ill."

"Dr. Pitters is the physician that Harvey will replace."

"Yes. He and his wife founded the Nan mission about twenty-five years ago." She gave me a bored look. "The Ruckels joined them a few years later. But they're all well on now and couldn't continue handling things alone."

"Ah," I murmured, "to stay so long! That's encouraging. I suppose they must like Nan."

She pursed her lips. "Like?" she said in a brisk tone. "Yes, well . . . that's not really the point, is it?" She curled her hands and studied her nails. "They've accepted the burden that the Lord has laid upon their shoulders." She hesitated, then added, "As have my husband and I."

"I don't understand." I was puzzled. "Don't you enjoy living here?"

Her hands dropped to her lap. "I've never given it any thought," she said with a shrug. "We have food to eat, a place to sleep, a job to do." Her eyes wandered past me again.

"That's quite a sacrifice, I must say."

A faint smile flicked across her face, then disappeared. "Yes. I expect the home office will be grateful. It's difficult dealing with the Siamese, however. We're certainly giving them our best years. To tell you the truth, it seems as though we've been here a hundred years."

A small bamboo fan lay on a table nearby. I picked it up and fanned myself. "You certainly don't look that old," I said, smiling.

She shifted her look to me with an expression that was curiously blank. Minutes passed. Cicadas buzzed in the blazing heat. A large black bird circled lazily overhead.

"What is it you do for the mission?" I finally asked, straining to bridge the gulf that seemed to stretch between us.

"I teach the girls' classes at school. Everyone is expected to do their part. There's no room for idleness here."

"Well, I expect that I could teach music . . . or give singing lessons to the children."

Her smile was cold. "You'll find that this is a very practical place, Mrs. Perkins." She dropped her eyes and folded one hand over the other. *"Music,"* she gave the word an odd emphasis, "is not likely to have a high priority in the curriculum anytime soon."

"Oh." I paused, at a loss for words, then added, "Perhaps hymns?"

She sighed with patience, gathering energy to speak. "This is a poor country. Here in the north, you must understand, we're more concerned with things like medicine and food. The mission ladies *here* are not merely decoration for their husbands." Her look slid to my hair then flicked away.

"Why, that's wonderful!" I said, thinking that perhaps I had misjudged her. I leaned forward. "That modern view is causing changes long past due back home. In fact, you'll be happy to hear that it looks like the Nineteenth Amendment will soon be law."

"The Nineteenth Amendment?"

"Suffrage." I leaned back in my chair and smiled. "The woman's vote . . . the constitutional amendment is going to be adopted."

She looked startled, then laughed, a short, snorting sound. "Oh that. Heavens, that's not what I meant! Why in the world would women want to vote?" She drummed her fingers on the arm of the chair and her eyes again reflected boredom. "I was speaking of our duty as wives. The whole voting thing is non-sense, if you ask me."

I stared and reminded myself not to smudge the copybook so soon. "I suppose," I said amiably, while the former suffragette inside me cringed with each word.

"Women don't need to involve themselves in government matters," Mrs. Breeden went on with startling new energy. "We should concentrate our efforts on creating good Christian homes. Our power is to set the example."

Her words stopped me. The silence grew. From inside the house I heard Mrs. Ruckel humming as she clanked and rattled plates and glasses and pots and pans. Mrs. Breeden's eyes roved lightly over one thing after another in a preoccupied manner. A group of boys kicked a woven rattan ball back and forth across the clearing in front of the church, and Mr. Breeden and Reverend Ruckel, rounding the corner of the house, stopped to watch.

I was relieved when Mrs. Ruckel arrived with a tray that held tea and bread and sweet jam made, she told me with a proud smile, from local mangoes.

"The best jam you'll ever taste." Mrs. Breeden's voice took on a surprising lilt as she jumped up, reached for the tray, and set it on the table. Mrs. Ruckel gave her a grateful smile.

Reverend Ruckel walked slowly up the stairs to the veranda, seeming to pull himself along step by step on the railing. Mr. Breeden followed close behind the old gentleman.

"Where's Harvey?" I asked.

"Still explaining to the carriers where everything must go," Reverend Ruckel answered, sinking into a rattan chair with a sigh. He pulled a handkerchief from his pocket and wiped his brow. Mr. Breeden took a seat beside him, sitting stiff-backed, forearms braced on the arms of the chair.

As Mrs. Breeden poured the tea, a hearty voice hailed us from the river road where two ladies on old, worn bicycles careened toward us. The first to turn in the drive was somewhat stout, not overweight but built with heavy bones. Her face was round, but with a determined square jaw, and her hair—a mixture of brown and gray—was pulled back into a tight bun. She parked her wheels as her companion lagged behind. I rose and had to laugh when she stomped up the wooden stairs and stuck out her hand in greeting.

"This is Emma Mamsey," Mrs. Ruckel said by way of introduction, "one of our mission teachers." She nodded at the second cyclist, just parking her bicycle. "She and Lucy Best share the little cottage at the edge of the mission property."

I watched as Miss Best carefully removed her wide, ribboned hat and walked up the stairs, slapping the hat against her leg in an absent manner. She looked at me with curiosity. Her face was narrow and plain, framed by limp brown hair tucked behind her ears and hanging straight and loose to her shoulders. Miss Mamsey had begun to butter a piece of bread from the tea tray and, reaching for the jam, introduced us with a wave of her hand. Miss Best nodded and, with a furtive look, took a seat without speaking.

As voices hummed on the veranda and the sun sank below the trees, the sky turned slowly from blue to lavender to violet. At first I felt rather than heard the drums, low and rumbling in the distance. Then the tempo quickened as the volume steadily grew until at last the sound seemed to envelope us.

"The evening temple drums," Reverend Ruckel said when he saw my puzzled look. "This is a nightly greeting to the rising moon."

"It's lovely."

Mrs. Breeden gave me a sharp look. "Nonsense," she snapped. "It's a pagan custom."

But I ignored her as the drums brought to mind a deserted temple in Nan that Harvey and I had ridden past that morning. "We saw some interesting ruins on the other side of Nan-town, near the far gate," I said to Reverend Ruckel. "The building was shaped like a cross and looked as though it was built over carvings of two huge serpents."

"The shape is cruciform," Mr. Breeden corrected. "Buddhists don't honor our cross."

"That's the oldest temple in the area," Reverend Ruckel said. *"Wat Phumin.* The serpents are known as *nagas.* The local people believe that nagas are deities, an influence that's crept in from Laos. Inside are four large Buddha images, each facing one side of the building . . . representing the four directions in the universe."

"I'll ask Harvey to take me back to see it," I said, fascinated. "I'd like to go inside."

Mrs. Ruckel looked up abruptly at my words. Miss Mamsey's eyes widened and her gaze swung to Mr. Breeden.

Mr. Breeden spoke in a preemptory tone. "That wouldn't be a good idea, Mrs. Perkins."

I turned to him. "Why not?"

Reverend Ruckel shook his head. "It's probably not safe, the building is deserted. You could get hurt."

Before I could respond, Mr. Breeden added in a curt tone, "Explanations shouldn't be necessary. It's a house of idol worship. That's enough reason for anyone in this mission."

I felt a chill at his words and shivered despite the heat. Just then the rumbling drums were joined by the chanting of temple monks inside the ancient walls of Nan. Across the field, the little mission church stood sentry.

As I curled into the crook of Harvey's arm that night, our first at Nan, I could feel his body moving gently with each breath. He had already fallen into an exhausted sleep. We lay together in a four-poster bed made of dark wood. Mosquito netting hung from a brass ring on the ceiling directly above, and I had pulled it back on one side, hoping for a breeze.

In the moonlight I gazed at his fine-boned face—his straight nose and firm mouth, his eyes that turned down slightly at the outer corners—and smiled to myself, remembering how handsome he had looked at our wedding a year ago, standing strong and confident in his uniform in the little walled garden behind our house on Greene Street. Harvey had just graduated from medical school and immediately enlisted when the United States entered the Great War in Europe.

I did my best to keep him with me, but everywhere we went young men were called to duty, stirred by the flags that pulled them along in the draft, by the call of the bugles, the brass buttons that flashed in the sun. I clung to his arm as uniformed soldiers filled the streets of Philadelphia, singing as they marched, bright-eyed, excited, full of energy. *"Johnnie get your gun, get your gun, get your gun . . . show your grit, do your bit."*

"The suffering never ends," he had written from Base Hospital Number 120 at the battlefields near Tours, France. "As far as the eye can see, the ground seems to smolder. The grass, what's left of it, is gray, like ash, and dry, and there's no horizon. The sky is gray as well. Sometimes we have to operate without chloroform, Babs. Some of the wounded are just boys and some are older, but when there's nothing for the pain they all cry out for their mothers, or their wives. Then, we stiffen our spines and have to bury the pity, otherwise we couldn't go on."

Streams of soldiers, tired and wounded, bandaged, missing limbs, bruised inside and out, began to return to Philadelphia. The excitement was gone from their faces now, eyes dulled and haunted, their steps slow. *"Hoist the flag and let her fly, like true heroes do or die,"* we sang as they returned. It seemed to me that the men who made it back were harder. Even their smiles were grave. But those were the lucky ones. Our own Summit Church lost six and gained six gold stars.

"I tell you, Babs," Harvey wrote again. "You have no idea of hell until you've seen war. I miss you so. But it could have been worse, I suppose. There might have been no doctors or medicine or base hospitals over here at all. It certainly makes one think."

While Harvey was gone I waited for him in our house on Greene Street, trying not to think of that savage, ashen place on the other side of the world. Evie, Alice, and I shared a bedroom. Mornings were spent helping Mummy with ordinary chores and doing volunteer work with the Red Cross. But every afternoon from three to five was spent with Miss McGregor.

One day I arrived to find her thumbing through some old music scores. I took off my hat and coat and gloves, hung them on the peg near the door, and turned to find her watching me with a sly smile. My heart skipped a beat and I paused, looking at the music in her hand.

"What's that?" I asked.

She shrugged and continued flipping through the scores. "We're going to try something new. Ah! Here it is." She pulled a slim, brown booklet from the stack in her hand and dropped the others to the floor by her feet, then flipped her hand in my direction. "Come, come! This will suit you. Let's get started." She walked to the old piano that dominated the room, then, realizing that I had not moved, turned back to me and raised her eyebrows. "Are you coming?"

"Cara Nome." It was Gilda's song from *Rigaletto*.

"Now, don't get carried away," Miss McGregor said, reading my face. "This will be hard work."

Lessons were stretched to three hours every day to provide time for the basics as well as practice. Miss McGregor said that vocalizing is the only way to master the music, to discover what a singer is capable of. Careful repetition of a single sound would strengthen and train the muscles of the mouth. Day after day we worked, first on the vowels, gradually learning to blend the sounds into words, then into harmony. We worked relentlessly, developing a sense of timing, of contrast and control. Although I was learning only one aria, Miss McGregor insisted that I must understand the entire role. I must learn how to stand, how to move when singing, how to express the music with every part of my body.

"Here, like this," Miss McGregor said one day, and breathed a high note that was tremulous, fragile, like wind blowing glass against glass. I strove for that sound, labored for it. While we worked I was exuberant, but when we stopped each day I longed again for Harvey, torn between the sheer exhilaration of singing, of perfecting the music, and terror that my husband would never come home. *Johnnie get your gun, get your gun, get your gun.* The words echoed in my mind.

# Chapter Three

IN JULY OF 1919, HARVEY WAS finally returned to me, a full lieutenant, proud of his work on the battlefield but bearing grim lines around his mouth and eyes. I met him in New York, and, as he disembarked from the transport *Marica*, I ducked under the ropes that separated the crowd on the wharf from the soldiers and raced to him, falling against his long, lanky body. He grinned but his eyes reflected something new, like sorrow; but, wrapped in his arms once again, I didn't want to think of that. I felt his warmth as he held me and I sank against him with a contented sigh.

Mummy and Dad set aside some space for us on Greene Street, cramming all of the boys into one room. Now, for the first time, we were faced with the practical decisions that must be made in a marriage—where to live, what path our lives would take. Harvey spent most of his days at Jefferson Hospital and with an odd, expectant feeling I continued my singing lessons, concentrating now with heightened focus on each note of the aria, working to make it bloom and swell, to make it perfect. Wonderful things lay ahead, I knew.

One bright afternoon during lessons, the door to Miss McGregor's studio swung open and a lovely lady drifted into the room, followed by a gentleman in a dark suit and a bowler hat that he swept from his head as he stepped in. When my voice sailed unnaturally high at the intrusion, Miss McGregor glanced up without surprise. The lady waved her fingers at us and took a seat near the window, while the gentleman nodded and stood nearby, holding his hat in his hand.

"Let go—open your throat, Barbara," my teacher scolded in a low voice. "You're singing like you're on a bumpy road. The notes must flow together. Smooth. *Legato, legato*!"

I shifted my attention back to Miss McGregor. For the next hour the visitors didn't say a word. After a while Miss McGregor seemed content to let me sing my aria, my treasure, with only occasional interruptions. The new freedom was exhilarating and I soon forgot the strangers.

"Rest now, Barbara," Miss McGregor finally said, her signal that we were through for the day. She looked past me, then rose and extended both arms toward the visitors. "Come," she said to me.

I followed her as she crossed the room to embrace the strangers. An aureole of sunshine gave the lady an ethereal quality, but as she moved from the window and bright light, I could see that her age was about fifty years or so. My breath stopped as I recognized Mary Garden, Miss McGregor's former teacher, the *prima donna* of the Chicago Opera who had recently appeared in Philadelphia. She was mesmerizing on stage, a glorious coloratura soprano.

As Miss McGregor introduced me, first to Miss Garden, then to the gentleman accompanying her whose name I barely heard, I found myself speechless. Every mistake I'd made during the afternoon lesson repeated itself in my mind. Miss Garden tilted her head back and studied me for a moment.

"Yes," she said slowly to Miss McGregor. "The girl has a natural gift." Miss Garden pronounced each word very clearly, as if taking particular care. Her voice had a slight tinge of Scottish brogue. She seemed to catch herself after an instant and gave me a steely, focused look. "But that's not enough, my dear." She took my hand, patted it on top with hers. "What I must know is this: Are you strong enough? Willing to work? Will you give up everything for the music?" Her eyes locked with mine.

The gentleman beside her watched me.

I nodded in confusion. She studied me again. "Good, good," she finally said, dropping my hand in dismissal. "Let us talk with your teacher."

Miss McGregor steered me toward the door then. Reluctantly I put on my coat and left the studio. My feet barely skimmed the ground as I walked home along the broken sidewalk. I stretched my arms above my head and danced a few steps. Wait until Harvey heard this! And Mummy and Dad. I had actually met Mary Garden, the Sarah Bernhardt of opera! And she'd said that I had talent . . . a *gift*.

"What did she mean?" I immediately asked Miss McGregor upon greeting her the following afternoon. "About working hard . . . and being strong?" The past night and day had seemed endless as I'd rehearsed the question to myself and imagined the answers.

Miss McGregor did not wait an instant to respond. "She will take you on, Barbara!" Her voice shook with suppressed excitement. The words burst out as she looked at me with pride. "You made quite an impression yesterday."

"But what does it mean?" I asked, trying to contain my impatience.

"I've been writing to her about your progress. This is the beginning." She took a deep breath. "You'll sign a four-year contract with the Chicago Opera and debut with Miss Garden in a few months. It's a minor part," she added as she saw my expression, "only a small part, but she thinks you have promise."

My heart pounded, I backed into the chair near the window and sat.

"What are you doing?" Miss McGregor laughed. She whirled and headed for the piano. "We have work to do."

"Chicago Opera!" I was still, trying to breathe in the shallow air.

"Yes. You're on your way, my dear. You're on your way. It's every singing teacher's dream."

My head spun as I thought of sharing this news with Harvey. Chicago wasn't so far from Philadelphia by train. And surely the city had major hospitals and medical schools just as good as those in Philadelphia. Of course it did. This thought calmed me and I took a deep breath, filling my lungs. I resolved to wait for exactly the right moment to discuss the move with Harvey.

*My debut*. I straightened my back and lifted my chin, loving the word.

But the oriole sang too soon. On Sunday afternoon, before I spoke with Harvey of the Chicago Opera, the church that had sheltered us beneath its wings lifted those wings just a bit and

Harvey caught a glimpse of the opportunities awaiting a young medical missionary in the exotic Far East. In Siam.

Harvey's face had glowed as he told me of the proposal.

I took a deep breath when he had finished. "Missionaries," I said, feeling my way, treading on glass. Miss McGregor's face loomed before me and all that I could lose—the studio, the contract, Miss Garden.

I forced myself to smile and said in a casual tone to mask my growing turmoil, "Somehow, Harvey, I have never pictured myself as a missionary."

"But think what we might accomplish, Babs," he said, grasping my arms. His fingers pressed into my flesh and his expression was grave. "Until the war, I'd never realized how people suffer without doctors and hospitals and medicine." His eyes clouded as he spoke. "Can you imagine what that would be like?"

I shook my head, puzzled by the sudden urgency I heard in his voice. A wave of alarm rushed through me. I struggled with images of a velvet-curtained stage . . . the lights . . . the orchestra below, and knew that this was the wrong time to tell him of Chicago. Not now.

I leaned against him to hide my face. "Missionaries!" I repeated, surprised to hear my voice was steady. "Where is this place? This is all so sudden." As I spoke into his chest, his arms slid around me. I looked up and his eyes shone down at me. "How far away is it?"

"Eight thousand miles. I looked it up."

I closed my eyes and in the silence felt panic rising from my chest, up through my throat, and then, before I could stop myself, the words rushed out. I told him of Chicago, of the contract and Mary Garden, and of all the hospitals that city surely housed . . . but even as I told him all these things, I saw the shadow cross his face and my voice trailed off.

"I heard stories today of people who've never even seen a doctor," he said, releasing me and stepping back. "Babs, every single day children die in countries like Siam from lack of basic medical care." He paused, then added in a firm tone, "I'm a doctor. I *have* to go where I'm most needed."

I grew cold. "But Harvey . . ." I began to argue, then caught his puzzled look. Music can never compete with medicine and life, his eyes said. I needed time to think. "Let's talk about this later," I said with a false smile and a growing sense of loss.

He nodded. "Certainly I won't go without you, Babs," he added quietly. "But I have to say I've never given any thought to practicing medicine in Chicago. Couldn't singing wait a bit? This is a chance to really *do* something and make a difference. To change things for people who have nothing."

"What do I do?" I cried to Mummy later that day. She held me as I wept. "He doesn't understand."

"You're Harvey's wife, Babs. Let him think things through a bit," she answered, smoothing my hair. "He'll discuss it with you when he's clear about his decision."

I lifted my head abruptly. "It's my decision as well," I argued. "It's my life also."

"That may be. But he's a man and it's his career that will be affected if he goes off to Chicago with you." A line appeared between her eyes. "God forbid that you should go without him. You're his wife . . . you must support his decision."

"What about my singing? What about Chicago?"

"What about it?" she laughed. "Do you think that you can feed a family with music?" She gave me a hard look, but her voice was gentle. "Grow up, Barbara. Harvey's home now and he's your husband. Your duty is to be a good wife and support his decisions."

I froze and stared, but she had already turned away, ducking her head toward the mending she held in her lap with a strange, tight expression on her face.

Evie thought I was mad when I told her the news. "Do you really expect Harvey to follow you around Chicago while you sing?" she asked, taking a long drag on a forbidden cigarette. We sat near an open window and she fanned the smoke while she studied me from the corner of her eye. "What will he do, hold your coat?"

"Perhaps I'll go without him," I said obstinately.

"Hah!" She looked at me and laughed. "For heaven's sake, Babs. Where would you live—in a tenement?" Grinding the cigarette into a small ashtray she held in the palm of her hand, her voice turned sober. "Look . . ."

I averted my eyes and stared through the window at the garden.

"Be serious," she said. "Harvey has strong feelings about this. He's not going to ignore his responsibilities so you can prance around a stage. And think what your life would be like there without him, alone and poor . . ."

"Not necessarily."

"Yes, *poor*." She emphasized the word. "You'd just be one more singer. A lonely girl without a man, with no home, no family nearby . . . no pretty clothes, no babies." With a shake of her head and shoulders she glared at me. "A career woman!" She turned away with disdain. "I don't even want to think of it."

That night Harvey brought up the subject again. "Perhaps you could sing in Bangkok, Babs." His voice was low. We were alone in our bedroom in the dim light of late afternoon, that magic time of transition. He pulled me down into his lap and smoothed the flesh beneath my chin with his fingers as he spoke. "Or you could sing in Chiang Mai, if we're posted there—it's in the north. I'm told they're both large, lively cities. Lots of Europeans, ambassadors and such."

His fingers tickled. I ducked my head and smiled. "Is that where we'd live," I asked, "*if* we go to Siam?"

He nodded and his fingers moved down into the hollow of my neck. "Sure," he said into my ear, raising the hair on my arms. "Where else would the hospitals be?"

His lips traced the edges of my ear, slid like feathers to my check, and brushed over to the corner of my mouth. He turned me to him as his lips covered mine, caressing, and then I grew soft and warm and could no longer think. For a brief moment he drew back and looked at me, and I gazed at him, feeling the love balloon inside. When at last we lay together on the soft bed, thigh touching thigh, his heart beating in my chest, and dissolved into each other, there was no room left for anything but Harvey.

Later, as we rested in the dark room, he said in a low, pleading tone, "Please say yes, Babs. You'll love Bangkok, or Chiang Mai."

In his mind we were already there, and I knew that I would agree. The price was too high otherwise. It wasn't a question of choice—there *was* no real choice. Even if I convinced Harvey to stay, he would always wonder what he had missed. A knot of sorrow lodged in my chest and my throat constricted. Tears threatened but I squeezed them back. I told myself to forget about Chicago—Chicago was hard and cold and hostile. Forget the music and the contract. We were young and there would be time for that someday. We lay quiet in the darkness for an hour and each time a forbidden thought shimmered into my mind, I stopped it. *There's nothing you can do to change this*, whispered my inner voice. At last, after an hour, Miss McGregor and the studio and "Cara Nome" and luminous Miss Garden all sank into the shadows. And so, I locked the grief away, deep inside, and trembled with the effort.

"Are you cold?" Harvey pulled me closer to him.

"No," I said, putting a smile in my voice and trying not to think of the ladies in drab brown dresses that from time to time visited our church in Philadelphia with their missionary husbands. Their hands were rough, their faces tired and pale. But I wouldn't have to wear such clothes, I knew, in Bangkok or Chiang Mai where the hospitals were. "I'm just thinking what an adventure this will be."

"You'll love Siam. And we'll be a good team," Harvey murmured.

We talked late into the evening of our plans, our future, and the excitement of foreign places.

The moon was full and it hung low, a flat silver sphere in the sky. In the soft light, the straight white lines of the little mission church stood against the forest, invisible now in the dark. Here in Siam, hundreds of miles from the golden salons of Bangkok and Chiang Mai, I was more conscious of the moon than in any other place.

Suddenly annoyed with Harvey, I pushed away from him, rolling onto my back and staring into the darkness of the room.

Would I have agreed to come if I had known that we would end up in the jungles of northern Siam? Despite my earlier resolution, thoughts of what might have been taunted me. *Foolish, girlish dreams*, whispered the fierce voice. *You're Harvey's wife and he's made a choice. Singing, Chicago—those were mere amusements. This is his profession.*

*All right! All right*, I told myself. *You're here, Babs. Don't wallow in self-pity.* But Amalie Breeden's face rose in my mind and an undercurrent stirred, an ominous frisson that prickled my skin. I closed my eyes, took a deep breath, and banished the gloomy thought, trying to recall some of the exhilaration I had felt when we first arrived in Bangkok a few weeks before.

# Chapter Four

AFTER CROSSING THE PACIFIC ON A vessel of the Empress line, the *Empress of Asia*, we stopped at Yokohama and Singapore before reaching the Gulf of Siam. At the mouth of the Menam we waited for the tide to wash the ship over the sandbar before starting slowly upriver for Bangkok in the wake of the pilot boat. As the ship began to glide up the watercourse, fireflies on the bushes in the mangrove swamps lit our way, one bush illuminating the river's edge, only to be veiled in darkness a moment later and immediately replaced by another.

At dawn we docked at the port of Bangkok. From the deck in the morning mist, Harvey and I reveled in a skyline of glittering parapets rising at intervals from a wide expanse of dark-green vegetation and low roofs. Gilded spires of palaces and temples reached fairy-like toward the sky, but these were everywhere contrasted by tired wooden buildings and small bamboo huts suspended precariously over the banks of the river. Long-tailed boats and canoes bustled around us, while steamships flying the flags of nations all over the world were anchored farther upriver.

Men and women on the landing stage and wharf below were dressed in colorful cotton tops and the *panung*—a perfectly straight piece of cloth several yards long and about a yard wide that, when gathered below the knees in front and pulled well up in the back, looks like a pair of knickers. The women all had straight, black hair that gleamed in the sun, cut short like a man's. My own long hair, even twisted into a knot, seemed heavy and impractical in the heat.

The journey had taken almost two months and both Harvey and I were weary of life on board ship. I had grown tired of seeing the same people at dinner each evening, tired of the cramped quarters and of waiting, waiting, waiting for our new life to begin. The burdens of travel were forgotten in the tremendous excitement of arrival, however. As I turned my face up to catch the warmth of the Siamese sun, I laughed for sheer joy. It was almost impossible to believe that across the globe in Philadelphia winter was in full force, dark and gray, with snow crusty from rain and trees too heavy and stiff to wave their branches. Here the air was sultry; trade winds blew warm and moist with a slight salt tang of the sea. The light, quick movements of people darting below us on the landing and riotous colors gave the impression that we were looking at Bangkok through a kaleidoscope.

Harvey and I hurried down the gangplank, eager to reach solid ground. A portly gentleman dressed in a baggy blue-and-white-striped seersucker suit, a short-sleeved white shirt caught with a bow tie under the starched collar, and a white straw hat, began to wave in our direction.

"Duncan . . . M.D.," he introduced himself as we reached the landing. "I'm with the mission." He smiled and his mouth disappeared into jowls that lined his face like punctuation marks. His skin sagged, his hair was white, but his eyes were clear and his gaze direct.

After accounting for baggage, we started for his motor. Dr. Duncan grasped my elbow because my legs were still unsteady, being used to the rolling motion of the ship. Porters followed with our trunks as we were led briskly through a crowded market, dodging baskets of fish and carts full of bright-colored fruit and vegetables, all the while pushing past constant throngs of people milling about, then down alleys that separated the *godowns*, long buildings housing goods for export.

People made room for us in a friendly manner as we pushed through the congestion. We rounded a corner and I stumbled over a vendor squatting on her heels near a large basket of rosy mangoes and bananas. Flashing a smile, her hand shot up, holding fruit, and I found myself staring at two rows of perfectly black teeth. Startled, I halted and Dr. Duncan's arm slipped from mine. He turned and followed my gaze.

"Come," Dr. Duncan whispered, checking a smile as he shook his head at the woman. With an imperturbable look she shrugged and put the fruit back into the basket.

As we walked on I saw many black holes where mouths should be. "It's caused by chewing the betel," he explained.

"They chew insects?" I gripped his arm.

"Betel is an areca nut," he said with a chuckle. "It's grown on a palm tree, usually right next to the house, and to chew, it's wrapped in a leaf spread with red lime paste that looks like blood." He glanced at me. "The nut blackens the teeth so that at first sight they're almost invisible."

Harvey was unmoved by this strange sight, but I clung to Dr. Duncan's arm as he pulled me through the crowds. "The more educated people in Bangkok and Chiang Mai no longer chew the betel, but you'll find that almost everyone else does, particularly in the north."

"Well then, thank heavens I don't have to get used to it."

He shot me a puzzled glance as we continued to navigate our way toward his motor.

As we drove away from the wharves and godowns, we passed shop-houses with sloped roofs and crossed high bridges raised over *klongs*—that is, canals—filled with more long-tailed boats picking up passengers or hustling to market. Some of these boats housed entire families.

The klongs that wound through the city seemed to provide the main concourse for transportation in Bangkok. They were lined with small, sometimes dilapidated wooden houses often set right beside beautiful large buildings decorated with fantastically colored tiles, many of Italian architecture topped with golden domes. We passed palaces that spread across several city blocks behind scrolled iron gates and high walls, government buildings and consulates, and temples made of stucco covered with intricate gilded designs that flashed gold in the sun.

Rickshaws ran alongside automobiles, and bicycles cut in and out of traffic. Dr. Duncan ignored warning bells from streetcars and the honking of horns as we raced through the tumultuous city. Everywhere we were met with a cacophony of laughter and music. Chinese fiddlers, bamboo flutes, card players, music halls and cabarets, market women, and well-dressed gentlemen in the silk panung and jackets, with white stockings and buckled shoes, who Dr. Duncan said were government officials. Bangkok sizzled with movement, sound, and color.

We turned onto a serene, tree-lined boulevard, partially obscured by dense, lush green foliage. A few blocks farther brought us to the Duncans' home. The large wooden house, built off the ground with louvered shutters covering the many windows, was reached by wide stairs that rose to a long veranda stretching across the front. Tall, feathery trees that looked like they were of the pine family clustered close around the house, and in the wind they made a lovely sound like distant running water.

Mrs. Duncan was waiting and she greeted us both with a warm smile. Despite gray hair pulled into a severe bun, she looked much younger than her husband. Her skin was soft but still firm and smooth, and she had an easy demeanor that immediately made us comfortable. Her dress of light blue linen was starched and pressed and billowed to just above her ankles. She wore thick white stockings and solid, chunky shoes with a low heel.

Here was a plain and sensible woman, I reflected. A feeling of apprehension came over me at the thought that I was now also a missionary wife, but I brushed it aside as I pictured the new dresses in my trunks. I'll never wear such unfashionable clothing, I assured myself and hid my thoughts with a bright smile.

"You will only be with us a few days," she said, as she led me through the cool, dark rooms. "The mission office in Chiang Mai has been told of your arrival."

"Chiang Mai is the capital city of the north?"

"Yes, it's a beautiful old city near the border of Burma. If you're posted there, you'll love it. Everyone does."

Although the Presbyterian Mission Board in New York had hired Harvey, we knew that the decision of our final posting was left up to the local mission authorities. "Before we left home there seemed to be some confusion about where we were to go," I said blithely, thinking privately that I would prefer Bangkok to Chiang Mai, no matter how beautiful the northern city was. Besides, I was certain that any European community was centered in Bangkok.

Our bags were placed on an enclosed porch shaded by trees. Two narrow beds hung with sheer, white mosquito netting looked cool and inviting. After pushing aside clothes hanging in a locker, Mrs. Duncan left me to unpack. When this chore was finished, I longed for a bath and soon found my way to a large room with a shallow zinc-lined enclosure at one end. Standing in the makeshift tub, I ladled cool water from a large earthenware jar and poured it slowly over my shoulders. A small window was open and while I bathed, birds of every cast flitted in and out of trees nearby, their iridescent colors flashing as the sunlight through the leaves caught their feathers. Small frogs, glossy and dark green, wandered up and down the drainpipes and sat in corners, staring at me curiously. I was delighted with my first impressions of Siam.

The realization that things were not at all going to be what I expected emerged only gradually, taking me by surprise. It began innocently enough. While Harvey and I waited in Bangkok to learn our posting, Dr. Duncan told us a little of the secretive, mysterious country and its rulers who still held the power of life and death over their subjects. King Vajiravudh, Rama VI in the reign of the Chakri dynasty and son of the great Chulalongkorn, was the present monarch of Siam.

"Buddhism, of the more conservative Theravada school, is the pervasive influence here," he said. "It encourages a calm, passive view of life that allows the monarch's absolute power. Until recently Siam was closed to the outside world, except for a few tolerated missionaries and limited trade."

"What's happened recently?" I asked.

"Western influence is inevitable," he shrugged as he puffed on his pipe, regarding us.

"The people have so little," Mrs. Duncan interjected. "The king is trying to open up Siam and modernize a bit. In fact, he just completed a new railway to the north, the first in Siam."

"Does it go all the way to Chiang Mai?" Harvey asked.

Dr. Duncan nodded. "It's a few day's journey, but not altogether difficult from here."

"Not difficult if you stay with the train until it reaches Chiang Mai," Mrs. Duncan added cheerfully. "It's in-between that's the problem."

"What do you mean?" I asked, conscious of the look of interest that had appeared on Harvey's face. I decided to press my case for Bangkok over Chiang Mai with Harvey at the first opportunity.

"The railroad links Chiang Mai and Bangkok, and the two cities have accepted some of the king's new ideas. But in the countryside, especially in the north, there's great resistance and," she shrugged, "people merely continue in the old ways."

And then Harvey asked the catastrophic question: "Are there hospitals in any of these smaller places?"

I had leaned forward to say something to Mrs. Duncan when I heard her husband's answer. "Certainly, there are. They've been established by the mission all over the country, even in the most remote areas of the jungle in the north near Laos."

I froze, then turned my head toward Harvey. "Uhmm," he murmured as he gazed out the window, avoiding my eyes.

I stared at him as the significance of the answer crystal-lized. The mission had constructed hospitals throughout the country—not just in Bangkok and Chiang Mai, as Harvey had thought.

Dr. Duncan didn't notice my concern. "Yes," he drawled. "In those areas even some of the simplest things that we take for granted have yet to gain a toehold." He chuckled. "Electricity, ice, motors. A few years ago His Majesty issued an edict commanding that everyone adopt surnames." He tapped the pipe on the corner of the table and stuck it back into the corner of his mouth. "You must understand that this was a startling concept in Siam. He even went so far as to personally name hundreds of families, but in the rural areas this idea is still bewildering to most people."

I smiled, trying to ignore the new suspicion that nagged at my thoughts.

One morning, not long after, Harvey rushed up the stairs. He was breathless and flushed as he entered the study where I sat with Dr. Duncan, and it took a minute for him to make the announcement. Finally he managed to get the news out. We had received the decision of the mission board. Doctor and Mrs. William Harvey Perkins were assigned to the station at Nan, an ancient walled town in the north of Siam.

I stared at him, speechless.

Dr. Duncan had a large map of the country, and now he spread it out before us. "Here, this is Nan." He waved vaguely to a remote area near the Laotian border. "Chiang Mai will telegraph Reverend Ruckel of your arrival. He's the senior member of the mission in that area."

I took a deep breath. "I don't see it," I said, bending over the table.

"It's not on the map."

"*It's not on the map?*" I repeated the words in horror.

Dr. Duncan didn't seem to notice my consternation. "No," he said in matter-of-fact tone, concentrating on the lighting of his pipe. "It hasn't been charted yet, I suppose. The whole area was an independent principality until just recently. Even today, though the province is a part of Siam, local princes govern it. They pay tribute to the king in Bangkok, but not much is known about the area."

I felt Harvey's eyes on me as I continued to glare at the map in silence.

"There are no roads to Nan," Dr. Duncan went on. "It's quite isolated—the town is known as the Jungle City of Siam."

"Then how will we reach it?" I asked, already dreading the answer.

He shrugged. "Overland, through the forest from Phrae, the point where the new railroad turns northwest toward Chiang Mai. The only other route is by river, upstream against the current." He leaned forward and traced the meandering line of the Nan River with his forefinger as it headed north. "Through the jungle it only takes about five or six days. You can see that the river route is much longer; only heavy things are sent that way."

I looked up at Harvey, stunned, waiting for him to tell me that this wasn't true, that it was meant to be a joke. He spread his hands and shrugged apologetically.

"Perhaps there's been a mistake," I said, turning back to the map.

Dr. Duncan regarded me with curiosity and shook his head.

"No mistake, Babs," Harvey said in a mournful tone.

I fell back into my chair with a thud. The room swam before me and suddenly I felt limp and weak. I *will not* faint, I resolved, holding myself taut and still to preserve strength for the effort.

Harvey's voice echoed from a great distance. "Would you like some water, dear?"

"Yes. Yes I would . . . please," I stammered, and closed my eyes as I thought of the fashionable expatriate community that would continue life without us in Bangkok—and then of the dark jungle.

Dr. Duncan hurried out while Harvey knelt before me with a worried look. "Just give it a chance, Babs," he whispered, cradling my hands between his. "Think what an adventure this will be."

I opened my eyes and in that instant my thoughts had spun round as fast as monkeys on a circus wheel, but I wasn't able to think of a single solution. I pictured the look of disappointment on my father's face if we returned so soon with our tails between our legs. I could not go home, I realized. That wouldn't do even if Nan were the very end of the earth. By the time Dr. Duncan returned, I had composed a smile and Harvey was engrossed in the map, fascinated.

# Chapter Five

TWO WEEKS AFTER WE ARRIVED IN Bangkok, Dr. Duncan drove us through the city at dawn while Buddhist monks in robes the color of marigolds glided silently through streets, hugging their begging bowls to their chests. They went from door to door, receiving rice from devout householders.

We were put into a long day coach and took seats on a bench near the open window, but the car was airless, the heat already fierce. Mrs. Duncan had prepared for us a basket of bread and fruit and Harvey slid it under the bench. I fanned myself with a palm-leaf fan given to me by Mrs. Duncan as I listlessly watched the car fill up with Siamese, Chinese, and Hindu travelers who disposed themselves and their packages, bundles, suitcases, and food boxes over every inch of seat and floor. Most sat cross-legged in the position of the Buddha and seemed comfortable that way. Our train left the Hua Lam Pong station, emerging slowly from beneath a high-arched glass roof into the surrounding city. Soon Bangkok, the Menam, the gleaming temples, and marble palaces were left behind.

Harvey and I had already begun learning Siamese, a tonal language that I thought of as music. Occasionally we attempted conversation with our fellow passengers who responded with infinite patience and gleeful smiles. After about an hour the heat and noise and rough motion of the train defeated us, however, and we lapsed into silence. The day now stretched endlessly before us.

At midmorning we began crossing the immense rice plains of central Siam. The fields themselves were neat patches of criss-crossed green and gold. As the sun continued to climb in the sky, white light covered everything and the glare became intense. The seats were hard, uncomfortable benches made of wood, long and covered with thin cushions. Despite the open windows, the heavy air, already laden with dust, became stale with cigarette smoke. The crowded carriage was close, fetid, and hot.

The rhythm of the wheels on the track and the rocking of the train lulled us through the long afternoon, and I became somewhat disoriented by the haze of heat and rancid odors and constant chatter, most of which was unintelligible to me. By the time we finally stopped for the night at the town of Phitsanulok, I had lost all track of time. We'd finished the fruit and bread by early afternoon and, as the train rolled to a stop, my stomach churned and my head throbbed. We left our baggage on the car and, taking with us only the overnight essentials, stepped down onto an open, dark platform.

The town was small, but we saw with relief that a rest house for passengers adjoined the station. The rooms, lit with lanterns, were partitioned with half-walls of rough board. After a hurried meal of rice and curried chicken, we sank into our bed-mats on the floor and covered ourselves with mosquito netting—and immediately fell asleep.

The next morning the train rolled slowly over rails that split a trail through great rice plains and tobacco fields before beginning a long, slow climb to the high terrain of north Siam. Here the air was light and dry. Finally, at mid-afternoon we ground to a halt at a railroad station we were told was near the town of Phrae. I felt a jolt of anxiety mixed with sudden excitement: This was to be our point of departure to Nan over a forested, mountainous range.

As the train pulled away and continued on to Chiang Mai, Harvey and I found ourselves standing on a small platform surrounded by our baggage in the middle of a flat, dry plain. No town was in sight—only a dusty road through brown fields that appeared scorched. The ground was dry and cracked. The sun beat down unmercifully and waves of heat shimmered above the hard dirt road. In the distance we could see small clusters of bungalows scattered over rolling hills across the horizon. I suddenly ached with longing for the little house on Greene Street.

I adjusted my hat so that the brim provided shade from the blazing sun. Irritable, I felt dirty and hungry and completely at the mercy of fate. Harvey fanned me with his straw hat, then walked to the other side of the platform and back again. I examined my hands, wishing that I had brought gloves to protect them. Where was Phrae? Had we come so far for this? Perhaps there was no such town.

A curious swirl of dust and dirt moving far down the road caught my eye. Shading my eyes, I nudged Harvey and we watched anxiously as an old motorbus emerged from the cloud, careening in our direction. Bulging with people and bundles, it finally rattled to a halt beside us. Harvey lifted me into the front with the driver and climbed in after, leaving our baggage to be picked up later. With assurance of transportation, my spirits rose. As soon as we were seated, the old vehicle wheezed and bolted away from the station. Periodically the engine sputtered.

Sometimes it completely rebelled, at which point the driver got out, opened the hood, and admonished it gently while he banged on various parts of the engine until it gasped and started up again.

Late in the afternoon, we arrived at Phrae, glazed with perspiration and dirt. The town was small and nondescript. People moved about on foot and on bullock carts and bicycles. Harvey and the driver reached an arrangement and we were deposited at the door of the mission compound, composed of two residences, a small church, and a hospital with a dispensary. The Phrae missionaries were expecting us and welcomed us with excited smiles and handshakes and questions of news from home. Porters were sent for by word of mouth through the locals and were dispatched to retrieve our belongings from the bus station.

To my surprise the mission at Phrae had already telegraphed for two ponies to be sent from Nan for us to ride the rest of the trip through the jungle.

"Ponies," I remarked apprehensively to one of the mission ladies. "How big are they, do you suppose?" I worked to keep my tone casual.

"Not very large," she assured me. "Ponies from the northern areas are smaller than ordinary ones."

"I've never ridden a horse," I confessed. "And I have no riding clothes."

She threw me a knowing look and scrutinized my long dimity dress. "Don't worry—it's easy. All you have to do is balance on top."

I was skeptical, but the next words from our hostess cheered me considerably. "Let's have some sturdier things made up for you." Immediately she called for a local Chinese tailor, who took measurements then quickly agreed to create two khaki riding habits for the journey.

"Very nice," our hostess said the next day as she looked at sketches of the clothes. "But you'll need a topi."

The tailor disappeared and returned minutes later with a sun helmet.

I placed it on my head and turned to the mirror. "It looks like a mushroom." I grimaced at my reflection, then swooped it off and handed it back to the tailor.

Our hostess pursed her lips in disapproval. "You'll get heat-stroke without it," she warned.

Another of the mission ladies took the topi from the tailor and tucked it under her arm. "Don't be absurd," she said to me in a no-nonsense tone, settling the matter. "You cannot travel in the daytime in this country without one."

I bristled at her tone but swallowed the retort, knowing that she was right, as serious older ladies generally are. Later, when she had gone, I tied a bright ribbon around the brim and the ugly thing was transformed. Much better, I concluded, satisfied with the change. That night Harvey exploded with laughter when he found me sitting in our bed wearing nothing but the topi.

Our porters came from various outlying villages. Each man was to carry a load of forty-five pounds in two baskets balanced on the ends of a bamboo pole. The baskets must weigh exactly twenty-two and one-half pounds when packed, I learned, so that by placing the pole over the shoulders the weight was evenly distributed. Our heavier things, including my books, had been consigned to river boats, but the forty baskets required for immediate necessities would be carried through the jungle, and a large steamer trunk full of cooking utensils, tinned food, dishpans, bed linen, and mosquito netting would be carried as well. In addition, the carriers were to haul mats for sleeping, chairs and tables, live chickens in coops, rice for the ponies, buckets for water—everything we might need for five or six days in the jungle.

The carriers wore scanty clothing, not much more than a loincloth and a scarf wound around the waist to serve as a belt and pockets. All of them carried large knives, cigarettes, and chewing paraphernalia, as well as small objects in the fold of the sash. Many were tattooed from waist to knees with intricate designs of animals—monkeys, birds, and monstrous, dragon-like creatures.

"It must save an enormous amount of laundry time," I remarked to the mission ladies, indicating the porters' lack of pants.

As the women gazed back at me, silent, I blushed.

These ladies were not the little brown sparrows I had expected. Mrs. Duncan had told us that just a few years before our arrival, Phrae was invaded by a rebel army of the Northern Shan from Laos. When the town was taken, the rebels ordered that every Siamese person in Phrae be hacked to pieces, even women and children. A bounty was offered for each mutilated body. Missionaries at Phrae, including some of these same ladies, risked their lives to hide a small group of locals, spiriting them into the jungles nearby. For more than a month the missionaries slipped from town under cover of darkness each night to feed the refugees, until rescue troops finally arrived from Bangkok.

My face grew hot as I quickly changed the subject.

On the day of our departure from Phrae the sun was a great golden globe ascending as if by special command. Perched precariously on our ponies, Harvey and I started in single file across the dry, cracked plain that divided Phrae from the jungle. Our caravan was composed of thirty carriers, the guide, a local teacher, the cook, a boy who assisted the cook, and an assorted group of local travelers who joined us for safety. Only the guide spoke English, but even so, fear of mountain bandits made us grateful for the large company.

My pony was small and brown, with white spots and a peculiar gait. As we bounced along I felt every jolt of his hooves on the hard, packed dirt. The guide's eyes watched me with concern, and I was grateful when he began to halt the caravan at frequent intervals for rest. The afternoon strung out, a long, hot, and grueling affair. At sundown we reached our first camp just inside a line of trees on the perimeter of a forest. A large platform with a thatched roof but no walls was perched on poles about six or seven feet above the ground in a clearing. The structure was made of split bamboo tied together with rattan. These platforms, or rest houses, reached by loose, swinging ladders, were left in place permanently for the use of officials or other travelers making the trip between Nan and Phrae.

Our baskets were lifted onto the platform, and the chairs and table were quickly set up for dinner. The carriers dispersed in small groups to prepare rice for their evening meal, while the cook prepared our food. As darkness descended, Harvey and I sat at the table by the light of a lantern and dinner was served by a small boy. Fires burned beneath rice pots here and there on the ground before the rest house, throwing circles of light

around the figures squatting near them. The faint glow illuminated the faces, making them appear more angular and bronze
than they were. As time passed voices faded, campfires flickered
below, and stars gleamed in the clear sky above.

Harvey left to tend to blistered feet and administer quinine
in the camp against the constant threat of malaria. Suddenly
immobilized by the lack of privacy, I sat for a moment holding
a toothbrush and powder, a bar of soap, a cloth, a hairbrush,
and a nightgown. Finally I blew out the lantern and began to
undress. Protected only by darkness, I moved behind the baskets
and dipped water from the bucket, pouring it over myself and
listening to it drip through the cracks in the bamboo floor. As
the cool water caressed my skin, I felt tension slowly release and
my mood brighten. In the pale light of the moon I could see
that the mats we would use for beds were already framed and
hung with mosquito netting. I patted myself dry with the cloth,
slipped on the gown and crawled under the net, onto my mat,
for a deep, exhausted sleep.

We were awakened before dawn, still early enough to allow
me to dress in the darkness. The sun rose as I began to brush my
teeth, however, and as I stood on the edge of the platform and the
tooth powder began to foam, I suddenly realized that I was an
object of great interest. The carriers who had been laughing and
chattering among themselves as they worked in the camp, froze
and watched me in utter silence. I swallowed the tooth powder. It
was inconceivable to spit it on the ground in front of this group.

Embers from last night's fires still sent curls of smoke through
the camp. Morning dew shone translucent as it dripped from the
foliage, and sunlight filtered through the canopy above. The air
was fresh, pungent, and cool. Orchids and sprays of fragrant
orange and yellow flowers wound through green tangled vines

and hung from limbs of trees like ribbons and party streamers. Small, bright-colored parrots perched overhead and sang their songs, ignoring our intrusion, and great dark birds with curved beaks swooped through the clearing.

After a hurried breakfast, my pony was led forward to me. I greeted him with a smile and a piece of fruit that he nibbled from my hand. I stroked his soft, thick neck while he ate and thought happily that things would be much improved on this second day. As we prepared to leave, I composed a description of the surroundings in my mind for a letter to my father and imagined its effect, picturing his proud smile as he read. Word by word, phrase by phrase, my adventure would unfold to him across the globe, at home in Philadelphia, each letter adding a strong new thread to the tapestry.

At a signal, the company formed again into a single file that straggled along the trail. As the sun peaked above the trees, we began our ascent into the higher country that divides the provinces of Phrae and Nan. A stream with its source in the hills above bubbled as it wound its way round the range, the current gradually increasing as it flowed downward.

After two days we crossed over the apex of the range and began our descent. The change was subtle as we made our way amid taller trees, greener foliage, deeper shadows. Darker soil emerged. The jungle loomed around us, secretive and brooding. This was not the gaudy rainforest that we had left behind. Occasionally colors penetrated the heavy bush, but the leaves were thick and dark and the colors were subdued here.

The shadow and darkness were foreboding. We kept to our narrow path and disturbed the jungle as little as possible. Time after time the ponies stopped, trembling, and we were forced to dismount and gently urge them on.

"What's wrong with them?" I asked our guide.

He gave me a long look then seemed to make up his mind. "Tigers, Mem. The odor is distinctive. They stop because the spoor crosses their path."

Startled, I peered into the dark between the trees, then nudged the pony forward, keeping a close eye on the thickets around us. No one lagged behind now. For the next few days we continued a fast pace, stopping only for meals and rest at night. Voices were hushed because the jungle around us was so silent, as if the foliage absorbed all sound. Each day the bamboo and leaves in the undergrowth seemed thicker, even darker, than the day before.

Finally, as we moved down into the Nan Valley in the early morning light of the last day, the jungle was left behind. We emerged onto a broad, level rice plain covered with tall plumes of pampas grass that rustled in the warm breeze. Mist was heavy and distorted our world—nothing seemed as it should.

When the sun reached its zenith, it began to burn off the fog and the full beauty of the fertile valley was slowly revealed. The effect was magical, like no place I'd ever seen, and I gazed around with a sense of new discovery. *This must be how explorers feel,* I thought. The fields seemed to stretch forever, carpets of silver and gold, green and blue, all edged with feathers of dew-damp betel-palm glistening in the light.

The carriers were eager to rest, but Harvey and I were now fired with the anticipation of our arrival and eager to continue. "Nan is straight ahead," said the guide. "Just across the rice fields." He pointed in a northeast direction.

"How long will it take?" Harvey asked, squinting into the haze, trying to see the town.

"About one hour if you cut straight over," the guide said. "About two if you take the road."

Harvey looked at me and I nodded, eager to see what lay ahead.

"We'll go on," he decided. "The men can use the road and meet us there." The guide looked relieved as he gave us directions to the mission compound. Across the fields would be a difficult trick for the carriers burdened with the weight of our baggage.

"Keep to the raised paths along the sides of the paddies," he warned as we urged our ponies forward, onto an embankment.

As we rode slowly through the rice fields, the sun beat down on us. Perspiration rolled down my neck and the topi was oppressive. Suddenly in the distance, through the bright light and tall grass, we glimpsed the small town of Nan. Like a mirage it rose foursquare from the plain, enclosed by a high red-brick wall that was crumbled and decayed. As if Joshua had blown his trumpet, the gates of the wall on one side were collapsed, forming a rough-hewn entrance. We rode up to the jungle city and through the opening.

Ahead was a wide avenue, covered with grass. To our right were the ruins of a temple built in the shape of a cross, with huge carved dragons underneath. It was enclosed by a low, meandering wall, the whole overgrown with tangled vines. Pointed spires were glittering golden shafts in the bright sun, the light reflecting across the blue tiled roof that curled up at each corner. The entrance seen from the road was covered with heavy wooden doors carved in intricate patterns of flowers and animals. The whole thing was deserted.

Without a word we sat on our ponies, surrounded by eerie silence. An elephant moved slowly toward us through the white haze, as if in a dream, and passed with no sign of interest. The animal's *mahout*, its driver, threw us a mere glance. A yellow-robed priest appeared for an instant far down the avenue then disappeared, leaving only shimmers of heat. Now the old city was perfectly still and no living thing was in sight. It seemed that we had slipped centuries back through time.

The ponies sensed that they were near home so we let them have their heads as we rode on through Nan in the direction given us by the guide, past a palace covered with slabs that looked to me like marble cake. Everywhere there were fantastic temples, many left in ruins, palaces, and occasional smaller teakwood houses built off the ground among the trees. Some of the buildings were old and decrepit, while others appeared to be sleek and new, their brighter colors illuminated by the blazing sunlight.

After about twenty minutes we emerged through the elephant gates in the wall on the other side of Nan and found ourselves in a tumultuous market, a sharp contrast to the silence just left behind. Beyond the market the jungle grew, lush and green. Here the avenue narrowed into a dirt road that was filled with rickshaws and bicycles, bullocks pulling big-wheeled carts, and small boys leading water buffalo. Vendors hurried between stalls, chattering in the musical dialect of the north and carrying baskets heaped with vegetables, fruit, and dried fish. Lengths of bright cotton material were on display, and on a table jumbled with bric-a-brac, I even glimpsed a few bars of Palmolive soap in faded wrappers.

Small shops constructed of bamboo had doors tied back with rattan so that they opened directly onto the well-worn road. In an open restaurant, the door was folded back and men squatted on a dirt floor, eating from steaming bowls of rice. To our left, behind the market, the Nan River snaked past.

Here the women wore long skirts, instead of the panung we had seen in Bangkok, and a scarf tied across their breasts or cotton blouses cropped at the waist. Most had long shining dark hair brushed into low, flower-studded chignons that were twisted into a coil at the nape of the neck. More delicate and graceful than the ladies of Bangkok, these were slim and small-boned, with fine features and skin the color of caramel gloss, like hot brown sugar with butter and cream.

"You see, Babs," Harvey said in a jovial tone. "There's a good side to things after all. This is going to be a great adventure."

"It *is* an interesting place," I had agreed, smiling to myself as the ponies headed down the river road to the Ruckel home in the mission compound. "Ah, well," I added. "It's just too bad we're so far from Bangkok and Chiang Mai. But, I suppose we can't have the palm leaves without the crucifixion."

For an instant Harvey had looked shocked, then he burst into laughter.

The pleasant memories disappeared as a monkey hooted in the forest—hollow, haunting sounds that rose from the great cathedral of trees and drifted over the Nan Valley. It was midnight. The house was quiet, but outside the jungle was alive with a chorus of croaking frogs and crickets that seemed to take on a distinct rhythm as their sounds mingled with the muted chanting of the monks inside the ancient walls of Nan.

Harvey moved, then reached across and pulled me to him. I nestled against his body, feeling his heartbeat, and resolved once again to forget about my music and Bangkok and Chiang Mai, and make him proud of his wife. *We'll be a good team.*

"The woman is the spirit of a home," Mummy had always said. As my limbs grew heavy and my eyes began to close, monkeys and elephants and temples and kings tumbled through my thoughts, and the glow of the moon covered us in its pale white light.

# Chapter Six

I WAS EAGER TO SEE WHERE we were to live, but on the first morning after our arrival at Nan, we woke to find several people waiting for the new doctor on the Ruckels' doorstep. Harvey pulled on his clothes and, without eating breakfast, went out on the porch to tend to them. He listened quietly as each person struggled to describe what was wrong. Then he cleaned wounds, applied bandages, and dispensed medicine from the supplies he had carried in his bag from Bangkok.

Soon a steady stream of patients began arriving. Even before we had seen the hospital, his new medical practice began. As was his way, Harvey treated each person with great respect, standing to greet the women and stooping down to speak to children. He could be stern, but the kind smile never left his eyes as he worked all that first day without rest.

I stood at a window in the parlor watching Harvey with his patients when, suddenly, I heard exclamations from the room in which Reverend and Mrs. Ruckel slept. I found Mrs. Ruckel rummaging through a pile of clothing pulled from shelves.

"White ants!" she exclaimed, holding up one piece after another against the light from the window. I could see that every piece of clothing was neatly drilled with holes. The ants had invaded during the night, devouring everything in their path from bottom to top.

"Where on earth did they come from?" I asked.

"Our house is built too low to the ground," she grumbled as she tossed the ruined things into a pile in the middle of the floor. "The local people are much smarter than us about this sort of thing. They protect themselves from the little beasts by building their huts on high poles, then they slick the poles with black oil from the sap of the yang tree."

I winced as I held a shoe up to the light. "They've bored right through it," I marveled.

"It's almost impossible to disrupt the file once they burrow through the floors." The ants were lightning quick and, because they attacked from below, were difficult to spot.

Mrs. Ruckel was a warm, comfortable person. Like an elderly aunt with the privilege of age, she addressed all the mission ladies by our Christian names. But although she was kind and practical, accepting the hardships of her life without complaint, I did not think that she was efficient. Several local people were employed in the Ruckel household to handle domestic chores, but each day I watched her bustle around the house behind them, polishing and cleaning, laundering and cooking, repeating the work of her staff.

"Why does she hire these people if she insists on doing the work herself?" I asked Miss Mamsey.

"It's expected," she told me. "The wages we pay are nothing by standards at home, but here a day's wage is a small fortune. The jobs are highly prized by the local natives."

"But it seems such a waste of time—to do everything twice."

"Yes. But they don't know how we do things, and it's expected." She studied me. "Anyway, time moves slowly here. Unless you're specially trained, like your husband, you may find that it helps to complicate things."

Mrs. Ruckel also managed the mission while the old Reverend disappeared for days into the jungle to preach in the villages of the Nan Valley and mountains north, near the border with Laos. She knew the local people well and constantly visited their fragile homes, counseling in her gentle way when problems threatened to overwhelm them. Mrs. Ruckel had a special concern for young women who had lost their husbands and raised children alone. Often she sat with these widows, listening intently as they spoke in murmurs, her hands clasped quietly in her lap, her gaze never wandering.

I worried that I wouldn't fit in and Harvey noticed my discomfort.

"Everyone seems to have a purpose here," I told him. "Miss Mamsey and Miss Best and Mrs. Breeden all teach at the school, and they seem to agree that there's no need for another teacher just yet. Mrs. Ruckel manages the mission's accounts, and you're busy from sunrise to sunset with your patients."

"Don't worry, Babs. Just watch Mrs. Ruckel. You'll find out what's expected of you soon enough."

"I'm certain of that," I said, giving the words a wry twist. But thoughts of the gay life that I had envisioned among the Europeans and diplomats of Bangkok and Chiang Mai slipped through my mind. I veiled my eyes and looked away. "Perhaps I'll preach."

Harvey laughed, an easy, happy sound.

Mrs. Ruckel had a piano made of wood that felt like fine satin when I ran my hands across the top. It was slightly out of tune, having endured the hardship of a journey upriver from Bangkok some years before on a boat built specially for its transport. At one of the rapids, the boatmen got out to pull and the ropes had broken under the strong current. Only by extraordinary effort had the boatmen prevented the piano from overturning in the water. The special piano boat now rotted on the riverbank at Nan, as the boatmen finally concluded that the spirits were angered by this use of the water and would exercise their wrath on anyone foolish enough to try it again.

I began playing the piano every morning. It was placed in the parlor near a large window and, as I played, I gazed down the river road through the open shutters, singing along and sometimes just making up words when I forgot a song. The words are not important anyway; it's *feeling* that makes the music. Occasionally someone walking past on the road would turn and smile, and then I'd shift to something like "Alexander's Ragtime Band." It seemed to me that the unfamiliar western sounds made the local people happy, and once a farmer walking to the market just outside the walls of Nan laughed and broke into a surprising jig.

When thoughts of home crept in, I played pensive tunes—sonatas and nocturnes, music by Chopin, Beethoven, Liszt. I banished thoughts of the look on Miss McGregor's face when I'd told her of my decision to leave with Harvey, to abandon my chance to sing with the Chicago Opera. But "Liebestraum," my father's favorite piece, always conjured bittersweet memories as the notes drifted through the window and over the steamy rice fields and jungles of the Nan Valley. *Home.*

In Philadelphia my family's house was filled with books, but instead of the neat embossed rows in the Perkins library, our books at home were worn and scattered, filling shelves, piled on tables, stacked on the floor near favorite chairs. My family fascinated Harvey, I knew. Unlike his own, we were unruly, passionate about ideas and music and art, but careless about practical things that make life run smoothly. The furniture was tattered, but the house had a pleasant musty smell, and Mummy ruled with vague discipline. She was small and plump and smelled of lavender. My throat grew tight as I thought now how far away she was.

We had left our families standing together in two small, tight groups on a platform at the Broad Street station in Philadelphia months ago. My father had hugged me to his chest and I rested there one moment, my head snug beneath his chin. I had wanted to hold onto him forever.

"You are marked for something special, Barby," he whispered as he stroked my hair. "You've always had a special spark, an independent way." His voice grew tight. "Just remember, now. At night in Siam, look to the stars. We'll be watching the same stars here at home and thinking of you, Mummy and I." His voice caught. "We'll pick one out for your own while you're gone, so make it shine. Shine out for us!" The warning whistle blew just then and he thrust me away, holding me stiff-armed before him for a moment before turning me toward Mummy.

Mummy ran her fingers along the crease of my collar, as if to make it crisp, then smoothed my long hair, pushing it back from my face. Giving me a significant look, she whispered, "Time to drop the schoolgirl dreams. You're a grown woman and a wife now." She softened the words with a smile, then looked away and fumbled for a handkerchief. My throat was thick, but I nodded to let her know that I understood.

The train station was stark, gray, and cold. The wind chan-
neled down the platform and wrapped around us. We had shivered and lingered with them until the last possible moment,
climbing up the steel steps of our car only at the warning of the
final whistle. Whether from the chill or because of the knowledge that we would not return for many years, my mother and
father huddled against each other as they waved good-bye.

As soon as we boarded, the train gave a sudden jerk forward
and began to move, rattling down the tracks, gaining speed.
I hurried to the nearest window and leaned out, waving until
Mummy and Dad and all of my brothers and sisters slid away
behind us and finally disappeared. For an instant my heart
constricted and blood surged to my head, pounding in my ears.
I was dizzy, breathless, and consumed with terror at the rup-
ture. Then Harvey folded me into his arms and I let myself rest
against him, fighting back the tears.

Gently, from habit, he smoothed my curls. "Marmalade
hair," he had murmured, looking down at me. His green eyes
were bright with excitement and as he cupped his sturdy, reliable
hand behind my neck, I felt his strength. Slowly the terror had
dissolved, to be replaced by a spark of new courage and excitement. For a fleeting moment Miss McGregor's face flashed into
my mind, but I stopped the thought.

I lifted my hands from the keyboard and drew back, letting
the memories go—as I had resolved to do, as we all must sometimes do when we marry. As my mother had taught.

But it was hard, so *difficult*. I forced the shadows from my
thoughts before they grew too long and dark and fell on Harvey.

"Mrs. Perkins." The voice startled me. I swiveled to see
Mrs. Breeden entering the parlor behind me.

"Good morning," I said cheerfully, glad for the diversion. I swung around on the piano bench to face her—any port in a storm, they say. "Have a seat. Would you like some tea?"

"No, thank you," she answered, smoothing her dress as she sat. She wore a broad-brimmed straw hat that she removed and placed carefully upon her lap. I waited, but she merely gave me a long look.

"Beautiful weather," I said.

She nodded and agreed, and for a few minutes we talked of the weather, how warm it was, how dry, for now. "But just wait a few months when the rainy season starts," she said in an ominous tone.

When we'd exhausted the subject of weather, she fell silent again. I waited with the uneasy feeling that she'd come here for some particular purpose.

"My husband has asked me to have a word with you," she finally said.

With sudden trepidation, I swallowed.

She shifted to a more comfortable position in the chair and gave me a deprecating smile. "I'll just come right out with it," she finally said with a dismissive flick of her hand. "It's about all of this." Her mouth tightened as she spoke and her eyes darted past me to the piano.

"About what?" I asked, glancing back over my shoulder.

"The music," she said, with a drawn-out sigh. She spoke with sharp little jabs of her chin as she went on in a lecturing tone. "We're here to witness, not sing, Mrs. Perkins. Popular music has no place in this mission. It gives people ideas." My stomach plummeted as I listened. She folded her hands and rested them on the hat. "We have rules to obey," she said. "My husband is concerned that proper discipline be maintained at all times, particularly for the children."

Seconds ticked by as she looked past me, took in the open window, and slowly shook her head. When her eyes turned back to me, her voice rose an octave and she added, "The children are right across the way." She paused and arched her brows.

"I beg your pardon," I said, with what I hoped was a cool, deliberate look, "but I don't believe I understand."

Her expression hardened. She rose, picked up her hat and set it on her head, then adjusted it delicately with the tips of her fingers. "Oh, I think you do," she said, drawing out her words. "We're not a frivolous group, Mrs. Perkins. We're concerned with *souls* out here, not votes for women and songs and such."

She wheeled around and stormed toward the door, heels clacking on the wooden floor, while I stared after her. As she reached the door, she halted, bracing her hand on the frame for an instant. With a heaving breath, she turned and choked out her final words: "You know *nothing* about this country or these people. How dare you wander into this mission and try to change things?"

"Give it time," Harvey advised when I raged later. "You'll have more freedom when we move to our own home. We're guests right now, and the mission school is right across the field."

He held me and stroked my hair while I sobbed. "Babs, Babs." His voice was low and soothing. "Just put it out of your mind and wait until we move. You can sing all day long in our own house."

# Chapter Seven

MOVING BECAME MY PRIMARY CONCERN, BUT two long days passed before Harvey's stream of patients slowed and he could take time to visit our new house. Reverend Ruckel told us that it was about one mile farther on down the road, directly across from the Nan River, near the hospital. "House first. *Then* the hospital," I announced.

"No, Babs," Harvey said. "Dr. Pitters is waiting for us. It's arranged. Besides," he added when he saw my frown, "he'll be able to direct us to the house."

Harvey and I were eager to meet Dr. and Mrs. Pitters. We had learned at Phrae that when the elderly couple first arrived in the Nan Valley, it was untouched by Christianity and they began by living in native huts that barely held back the rain and heat and ants, the scorpions, centipedes, and other such creatures. Harvey's new hospital was established by Dr. Pitters, but now, after bouts of illness and the passage of time, he was unable to continue. Because of this, the Nan mission had been without a physician for some time, so word of Harvey's arrival had spread quickly.

We hitched the ponies to a small surrey that looked like an apparition from the nineties and rolled down the Ruckels' drive and through the gate. Behind us, as we turned onto the river road, was the mission church that I had seen from our bedroom window. It was a prim little building of New England style that stood on its own small piece of ground carved from the jungle. Like the Ruckel house, it also looked as though it didn't belong.

Headed away from Nan, we passed two small, white buildings on our right, the little school and the dormitories for the students. Across a playing field behind the buildings, the thick jungle continued, tall trees, dark-green creepers, bamboo. Children milled about and some waved as we rolled past. At the end of the picket fence that separated the mission compound from the river road was the cottage in which Miss Mamsey and Miss Best resided.

Past the cottage at the edge of the compound area, a wall of jungle again crowded the road. Occasionally we passed small clearings carved from the forest and occupied by raised huts, some quite large, and here and there a more traditional occidental house built of local wood.

On our left the Nan River curved, flowing into a course parallel to the road. A narrow strip of land bearing trees spaced well apart, with spreading branches providing shade, separated the road and the river. The ground here was bare, hard, as if the area was well used. Clumps of reeds grew in the shallows of the brown water. Across the river were rice fields stretching toward more jungle and the mountains.

The day was clear and sunny. As we bounced along, we laughed with excitement and talked of our new house, trying to guess what it would look like, how big it was—probably small,

Harvey warned—where it was located, whether it had a yard
or gardens. The river road leading out from the mission and
Nan was well used, rutted with cart tracks and potholes. It was
always busy with the traffic of bullock carts, bicycles, and small
carriages, like ours, that were similar to rickshaws but pulled by
a pony or two.

About one mile from the Ruckels' house we came upon
a small, whitewashed wood-frame building with a sign that
announced it as the hospital. As the surrey slowed and pulled to
a stop in front, our laughter died away. We were stunned into
silence. Scrub bushes surrounded the hospital and a tangled
growth of vines covered the walls, even creeping in between
the wooden planks and invading the windows. The paint was
chipped; the thatched roof sagged. My dream of a large, airy
hospital vanished as I looked from the building to Harvey and
then back again.

"Harvey," I said hesitantly, "this is just a shack."

He was silent and we both stared at the little building. A
brown bird fluttered from beneath the eaves. I watched as it
soared up with the heat and over the river road, then into the
tops of the trees.

The front door creaked open and I was startled from the
reverie. A fine-looking, dignified old gentleman stuck his white
head out to greet us. He shouted, "Hello-o-o," like someone who
is partially deaf, and gestured us in.

"This must be Dr. Pitters," Harvey whispered. Instantly, he
hopped out of the surrey and, as I composed myself and climbed
down, he was already mounting the stairs.

Dr. Pitters looked to be in his late seventies. He watched
our progress with sharp eyes. As I approached him, I noticed he
was slightly unkempt. He wore a white suit and bow tie, but the

jacket and shirt were wrinkled. And, although his mustache was neat, a day's growth of whiskers darkened the bottom half of his face, as though he had forgotten to shave.

"It's been a long time since we've had a doctor on duty here, young man," he told Harvey as he showed us in.

Harvey towered over him. Dr. Pitters was thin and frail and it was evident that disease and long years of hard work had taken their toll. Even so, although he was no longer active in the mission work, Dr. Pitters told us that he still did what he could, handling simple cases with the help of his wife, who was a nurse, and two local men he'd taught to assist. Quinine and iodine were their basic supplies.

We entered through the wing of the hospital containing the surgery and dispensary. Everything was covered with dust and mold. Instruments and large jars that appeared to contain medicines lay askew on shelves lining the walls, but we could see that the labels had been eaten away by insects or else had simply dropped off during the rainy season.

Stepping through a back door, we found ourselves on an open porch that provided a bridge to another small building. As we entered through the only door, I glanced at Harvey. His eyes were round.

"The ward," Dr. Pitters announced. "Children are kept over there." He nodded to a corner where several wooden cribs lay empty.

"Only one room?" I asked.

"Yes," his voice had an edge of bitterness. "We have the dispensary, the surgery, and one room for patients. Chiang Mai would never fund an expansion." He looked at Harvey. "Mission headquarters, you know . . . Nan is small." His voice trailed off.

I looked around. A few older patients, men and women covered with thin and dirty cotton cloths, lay on mats on the floor among empty bottles and filthy rags. They looked at us without expression as we walked into the ward. The whole area was layered with dust and insects. Sunlight flicked like darts through parts of the thatched roof ceiling. As we stood in the middle, small bits of thatch drifted down onto the wide, rough plank floor. The ground was visible through large cracks between these boards. Except for the empty cribs, there were no beds other than mats—no linen, no furniture of any kind.

Without hesitation Harvey squatted down to speak to the patients in a reassuring tone, just as if he were making rounds in the most modern hospital in Philadelphia. Slowly he moved from one person to the other until he had spoken to each one, sometimes brushing away flies that hovered around their wounds. Dr. Pitters watched with a thoughtful expression. Harvey did not seem discouraged. Any disappointment that he felt was carefully hidden. He had treated soldiers on the battlefields of France under much worse conditions, he later said.

I was dejected and light-headed from the heat and dusty quarters. Excusing myself to Dr. Pitters, I walked back through the dispensary and outside to the surrey. The afternoon sun blazed as I fanned my face with the hem of my skirt and waited for Harvey to finish inside. Trickles of perspiration ran down my neck and soon my clothes were damp. Squinting through the bright haze reflected from the white building, I pulled my hair back with both hands and twisted it into a knot atop my head.

When Harvey returned, I tried to hide my disappointment. Dr. Pitters gave us a cheerful wave. "He certainly seemed happy to see you," I commented as Harvey settled in his seat behind the ponies.

Harvey glanced at me with a placid expression. "It seems that the mission board has had a hard time filling this post," he said. "In fact, Dr. Pitters let it slip that everyone else turned it down before it was offered to me."

I frowned, trying not to think of Bangkok and Chiang Mai, or Miss McGregor and Chicago.

"I suppose this assignment is so difficult to fill because of the isolation—probably only the newest doctors end up in places like this," Harvey reflected as he picked up the reins. He glanced over at me.

"Now, Babs, don't worry about this," he said in a hearty tone. "Once I get everything organized, it's going to look much better . . . and maybe we'll even do some remodeling if things go well." He reached over and patted my hand. Quickly I withdrew it, unable to hide my dismay.

"Let's go look at our house," he urged.

I watched him from the corner of my eye. "Did Dr. Pitters give you directions?"

"Sure he did," Harvey said, flashing a smile. "It's right next door." He snapped the reins, turning the ponies back onto the river road in the direction of Nan. But immediately we took a sharp left turn away from the river. My pulse quickened as we rolled onto a dirt drive and through an opening in a low hedge. We passed a small cottage on the left just inside the entrance, then the long drive continued until it finally ended in a curve in front of a large, raised, two-story house with a low sloping roof. The surrey stopped with a clatter.

"This is it!" Harvey announced.

Before us were wide stairs that led up to a broad wooden veranda that stretched across the front of the house. Green vines and blooming jasmine trailed over the railing and the fragrance drifted to us as we stared. A large fig tree sprawled in front and the branches of a mango tree at our left provided shade. Vivid wild roses, hibiscus, and bougainvillea grew in disarray along the front of the house and down the edges of the drive, their riot of colors exploding in the heat against the dark green foliage.

Oak and laurel trees clustered along the sides and in the back of the wide yard that had been cleared from the surrounding jungle. A banyan tree had a wide, twisted trunk and spread over a great area, and this tree and a tamarind nearby provided shade for a small shed that I later learned was for laundry. Far behind the house there was a sparse-looking chicken coop and a small outhouse of painted wood as well. Tall bare trees that Harvey said were teak grew along the edge of the property in a thicket of bamboo and banana trees and bush. Farther on, behind a barely visible low cement wall, the thicket dissolved into the jungle.

As I turned around, looking back at the river road, to my right and just beyond the small cottage, I could see a corner of the hospital under its cover of vines and trees and shrub. The front of the property, split by the long drive, was separated from the road and the river only by the hedge.

I was astonished. "It's so big . . . I had no idea we'd have such a large place," I said, turning back to Harvey.

He fixed his eyes on mine. "Do you like it?"

I nodded, smiling. "It's a lovely house," I said. His face flushed with relief, then he leaned across the seat and kissed my cheek.

"Come on," he said. "Let's go have a look." He fished a key from his pocket while I smoothed my hair, then we scrambled down from the surrey and walked up the stairs.

The front door opened into a cool dim hallway. The house was spacious, with stairs at the end of the hall that led to a second floor. Wide doors on each side of us opened into large rooms that, from my vantage point, resembled somewhat the inside of packing crates. But I gazed around and didn't care. We could make it beautiful, I knew. A door at the back, to the right of the stairs, opened into a large kitchen.

I stepped into the room on the left, shoes echoing on the wooden floor. The walls and floor were made of dark, rough bare planks with nails clearly visible. Many lanterns hung from the ceilings and in corners. "I suppose we knew there'd be no electricity, didn't we?" Harvey said, with a quick, worried look at me.

"Of course," I said, glancing at the lanterns before slanting my eyes at him. "The light from a lantern is soft—flattering. And romantic, too."

He smiled and linked his arm in mine. Two walls of the room were lined with windows covered with closed wooden shutters. They had no windowpanes or glass, I knew, but the slats in the shutters could be opened for light and adjusted for a breeze. Four chairs were arranged around a large round dining table permanently affixed to the floor. An empty cabinet for china stood against the inside wall.

The parlor on the right side of the hall had a wall of bookcases and one window in the front overlooking the veranda. A comfortable looking chair and a footstool stood nearby. I smiled as I imagined Harvey relaxed in this chair, reading and surrounded by his books. A small table that held a lantern and two straight-back chairs were the only other furniture in the room.

After a quick trip through the kitchen, Harvey and I climbed the stairs to the upper floor. In the largest room at the top of the stairs, a solid wooden bedstead with no springs was placed opposite a row of windows. I threw open the shutters and found myself looking into the upper branches of the mango tree that shaded the veranda. Through the leaves I could see across our lawn to the cement wall that held back the encroaching jungle. I smiled and turned to Harvey. "Our bedroom," I announced. In one corner I was thrilled to find a large armoire for storing clothing. And there were two extra rooms.

"One for the nursery," Harvey said, with a chuckle at my surprised look.

I gazed around, picturing the house clean and filled with our things, washed with light. "It's all wonderful," I said, smiling. And babies could compensate for many things.

Harvey immediately shifted his practice from the Ruckels' front porch to the hospital, and I began preparations for our move. He was learning tropical medicine on the job, so to speak, and sometimes it seemed that Harvey just dropped right through the firmament to some other place. He wasn't absent-minded in a conventional sense. In fact, he was steady as a rock. But Harvey was completely absorbed in his work. One evening when we were still at the Ruckels, I walked into our bedroom to find him reading a shabby old book.

"Harvey," I said. "Dinner's on the table. We've been waiting some time for you."

"Hmmm," he murmured without looking up.

"Harvey?"

He started. "Babs! You must hear this. I've found the answer to a most interesting case. An old gent came to me with hardening of the eyeballs. Just listen." He proceeded to read out loud a paragraph on a medical condition that might have well been Greek, then looked at me with glee. "Isn't that just something?"

"Must be a miracle."

He thumped the book. "Pulled this off a shelf in the dispensary today. I suppose it belongs to Dr. Pitters. Imagine how strange—to find the treatment in an old dusty book in a hospital in the middle of the jungle."

"Certainly is," I said, raising my eyes to heaven.

He caught the expression and laughed, putting the book aside as he rose. "Well then. Let's go see if we can forage up something to eat. I'm starved."

"Ask and you shall receive, Dr. Perkins. Right this way."

"Swell!" With another glance at the book, he rubbed his hands together with satisfaction.

Workers were hired to scrub everything down and paint the walls and floors of our new house. Cabinets were cleaned, lanterns refitted and hung in every room. Mrs. Ruckel said that mattresses could be made locally and these were promptly ordered.

Fresh foods were purchased in the local market. But Mrs. Ruckel advised me to order a large supply of dry and packaged groceries to be sent up the river from Bangkok. Heavy freight was transported by riverboat that began at the junction of river and rail traffic near Phrae to avoid the shorter, though more arduous, trip through the jungle.

"What an interesting way to do marketing," I commented.

Mrs. Ruckel laughed. "Keep that attitude and you'll do fine," she said in her gentle way. "A home that is orderly and shining, surrounded by gardens and fruit trees, is how a missionary wife shows the local people that Christianity is meant for life, not death and nirvana as Buddhism teaches."

I smiled, but privately I was not optimistic that this peculiarly Anglo-Saxon view of Eden would impress the local people, given their constant battle with nature. After all, I reflected, look what a single file of white ants had accomplished in only a few hours.

*Perhaps, instead, we could find some black oil from the sap of the yang tree.*

# Chapter Eight

THE SUN SHONE AND THE SKY was bright on the day that we moved into our first home. Harvey and I left the Ruckel house in the surrey in high spirits, swaying down the river road as we passed bullock carts loaded with fruit and goods hurrying in the other direction to market. The little ponies hauled us slowly and laboriously up small hills, then hurried down the other side in a desperate rush away from the impending weight.

As we rolled up the drive and stopped in front of the house, I was surprised to see a Siamese man of about middle age and medium height, dressed in panung of soft cotton and a cropped white jacket, waiting on the veranda. Supple brown skin stretched across his thin face over prominent, high cheekbones; black eyes watched us impassively. His dark hair was neatly combed back from his forehead. His look was friendly, but his eyes said that he had seen others like us before.

"This is Kham Noi," Harvey explained. "Our new cook. It seems Mrs. Ruckel sent him to us." He gave me a knowing look. "His name means something like 'a little piece of gold.'"

Kham Noi smiled and made obeisance. "Mem," he said, moving aside for us to enter.

"How do you do? Do you live nearby?"

He brightened at my attempt to speak his language and nodded. "Near the old city."

Harvey explained, "He lives with his family just outside the walls, near the market."

Kham Noi gave me a frank look of curiosity that held no hint of subservience as we entered, saying that he had learned English but that it wasn't very good. His tone was confident and sure. "I am happy to work for you," he added. "And if you will teach more English words, I will teach my language."

As we walked into the hall, sunlight streamed in through the open shutters. Newly painted walls and floors gave everything a fresh, clean look. I smiled to myself with excitement. Harvey had been busy at the hospital and had not yet seen my renovations. He looked around with surprise. "Why you've transformed the place, Babs."

I took his hand and pulled him into the parlor on our right. Harvey's medical books were neatly arranged by size in the bookcases. My own books, considerably less useful, were still being shipped up the river with our heavier things. Fresh-cut flowers held loosely in a pretty vase sat on the table next to the comfortable chair and on the dining table in the room across the hall.

Kham Noi disappeared into the kitchen while Harvey and I roamed through the house that now looked like a home. Finally we climbed the stairs to the upper floor where our locally-made kapok mattresses lay on the beds, covered with clean, pressed linens. I pushed open all the shutters and the sun tossed patches of light into the room through the branches of the mango tree. Harvey closed the door quietly behind him and, with soft laughter, we tumbled onto the bed.

Harvey left for the hospital at the first light of dawn on the next morning. As I lay gazing through the open window at the mango tree almost bursting with ripe fruit, I sensed a delicate throbbing in the air. It was the merest pulse of sound, a clear silver timbre that seemed to come at once from every direction. As the lovely unearthly sound came closer, it drew me down the stairs and onto the veranda.

For as long as half an hour nothing was visible to explain what I could hear. I waited in a comfortable rattan chair in a shaded corner of the veranda. Finally, over the hedge along the river road a bullock train appeared, the animals wearing bells that filled the air with a musical shower of notes. The bells were so beautifully matched that the waves of sound seemed to blend and magnify one another, carrying the tones across the entire Nan Valley. Around the neck of the lead ox was a collar made of widespread peacock tailfeathers. As the animal lumbered along, the sun played on the deep, iridescent colors.

These bullocks were of a small Indian variety with a hump on the shoulders and large, soft brown eyes. With them were hill-men from the Northern Shan states, dressed in embroidered blue costumes, turbans, and heavy silver jewelry.

Later Kham Noi told me the meaning of the decoration of the oxen. "The feathers on the first animal will protect the caravan from evil spirits. The bells warn travelers and help their owners find them when they are grazing."

The train created a long procession, filling the width of the road.

"What happens when someone comes from the other direction?" I asked him.

"They must move. Even the mahout moves his elephant aside when he hears these bells."

"Do you know them, Kham Noi?"

His eyes flicked away. "No one knows them, Mem," he finally said with a shrug.

The bullock train moved slowly past our drive and stopped at the hospital. Each time they passed through the Nan Valley, iodine was purchased because the people were subject to thyroid deficiencies. After we had lived in Nan for many months, these Northern Shan became friendly with Harvey and sometimes brought us large potatoes from China, a rare treat in Nan. However, I was never comfortable with them, as the haunting story of the Shan uprising told by the missionaries at Phrae still lurked in the back of my mind. Later Miss Mamsey told me that the true purpose of their journeys was the trading of opium grown high in the hills near the border with Laos.

Each Sunday Harvey and I attended the mission church. It was always filled with students from the boys' and girls' schools, the teachers, and a smattering of Siamese guests. About twenty or thirty local people attended the services regularly, but each week some dropped away and new guests arrived. It occurred to me that perhaps they came merely as a mark of respect for the efforts of the American missionaries. The Siamese were extremely courteous.

The small church was plain, somewhat austere. We sat in hard wooden pews placed in rows divided by a center aisle. The children, dressed in their uniforms, sat stiff-backed, shifting uncomfortably on the hard seats. Girls sat on one side of the aisle, boys on the other. Even with rows of windows on each side, the room was dimly lit. In front, two steps up to a raised area, stood a pulpit and an old organ that looked as though it had never been used.

After church one Sunday, I met Mrs. Pitters for the first time. The missionaries in Bangkok and Phrae had spoken of her with reverence, and I had looked forward to this meeting with anticipation, knowing that she was a pioneer in the Siam mission.

"Mrs. Pitters is an extraordinary woman," Mrs. Duncan had told me before we left Bangkok. But when I asked for more details, she seemed to avert her eyes and changed the subject.

When Dr. Pitters introduced us, my delight turned to wonder as she gazed at me without returning my smile. She was a tiny, bird-like woman, wrinkled and weathered from her years in the north. Her lips were thin and colorless, and her hair and clothes were severe.

"I am happy to finally meet you, Mrs. Pitters," I said, despite my sudden trepidation. "I've heard so much about you that I feel we're already acquainted."

She studied me for a moment. "I've wondered where you've been keeping yourself, Mrs. Perkins," she finally said. "We live nearby, you must know." She tilted her head to one side and said in a caustic tone, "Just on the other side of your husband's hospital, as a matter of fact."

I flushed. "I should have called, but . . ."

She interrupted, raising her hand to stop me. "Explanations aren't necessary, young lady. I know you must be very busy. Mrs. Breeden's been to visit and told me that you've been moving into your house." Her tone was brisk and dismissive. "How do you find the hospital?" she asked, turning from me to Harvey before I could say another word.

"It's coming along, Mrs. Pitters," he said with a smile. "But it needs some work."

"Yes. Well, we've turned it over to you now, Dr. Perkins. You and Mrs. Perkins," she corrected. Her lips pressed into a thin line. "We weren't consulted when you were proposed by New York and, as I say to Dr. Pitters, we aren't the ones expected to carry the burden now. He's ill, you know." She gave Harvey a sharp look, peering up at him with her small round eyes. She then turned and walked away, with Dr. Pitters trailing behind. We stared after her.

"She speaks her mind," I said uncertainly. I was unused to such sharp-edged disapproval. Medicine in our house on Greene Street had always been dispensed with a bit of sugar. One morning when I was seven or eight, Dad caught me out on some infraction. He'd given me a stern look as he warned that he'd use the day to determine the consequence. By the end of a long day clouded by my sense of doom, I was worn out from worry. He'd returned from the city that evening with a package wrapped in brown paper and a long, brown strap hanging out. "Here," he'd said gruffly.

I'd opened the package with dread, carefully avoiding the strap that I guessed would see my backside soon. But inside was a brand new pair of ice skates. His eyes had twinkled when I'd looked up at him, and he'd swung me into his arms. "The day was punishment enough for you, Barby," he'd told me, patting my back as he hugged me.

Harvey took my arm as we walked toward the surrey. "Looks like you'll have to use all your charm, Babs," he said. "Old ladies will have things their way."

Kham Noi was paid fifteen *ticals* a month, about three dollars. He quickly took charge of the house and, within a few days of our arrival, Harvey and I found that with no discussion we had acquired a rather large number of helpers. Kham Noi hired a boy for heavy work like hauling water and scrubbing floors, and also a shy young man, known only as the "cook's boy," to wait on table.

A watchman, Tip, lived with his wife, Ma Ping, in the cottage at the entrance to the river road, and they appeared to share it with the syse, although I was never certain of the arrangement. Tip was a small man with a quick smile and a jolly sense of humor. Ma Ping was taciturn and her eyes were sly. A laundress also arrived and set up tubs and a small charcoal burner to heat water in the shed near the house.

"Who are all of these people?" Harvey demanded one evening.

I thought for a moment as I counted silently. "We seem to have acquired a staff of six so far."

"Babs," he exclaimed, "we can't afford such extravagance."

I gazed at him. "These are mouths that we're expected to feed, Harvey. How would it look if we turned them out?"

"Oh, good heavens!" He grimaced and shrugged. "What does Mrs. Ruckel think of this?"

"She says that we have a responsibility to help the local people—they need the work." I smiled, thinking that this was certainly a civilized development. Harvey threw me a suspicious look.

Each evening I gave Kham Noi money for the next day's food. He arrived early with his helper, then left at dawn, walking to the market and returning in time for breakfast with a basket of very small eggs, a hunk of meat hanging on his finger by a string, and the season's vegetables and fruit. The vegetables were tasty and the fruit was sweet and so full of juice that it sprayed into your mouth at the first bite. I was never able to identify the meat, however. At first I waited with apprehension for it to appear, but after several weeks it became clear that the strange food was not meant for our table. Once I asked Kham Noi what it was, but he pretended not to understand the question.

Occasionally a hunter arrived at Nan with venison, or peacocks and wood dove that Kham Noi cooked slowly over an open fire. But chickens that were so small each person could eat a whole one generally supplied the main course at our dinners. The small coop in our backyard was the source of the constant supply. These birds had very little flavor. With monotonous regularity, they appeared after soup, along with sticky rice, string beans, and egg custard.

Kham Noi's habit was to tear through the kitchen in short bursts of speed as he prepared breakfast and lunch, then collapse in a heap. About mid-afternoon each day he issued instructions to his helper to begin preparations for dinner. I could almost set the clock by the commencement of furious squawks from our coop, signaling that, once again, chicken was on the menu. I learned not to think about this too much and avoided the coop, not wanting to become too fond of the little birds. The stock was constantly replenished by Tip from a mysterious source.

Once I asked Kham Noi how the boy, who was a Buddhist, could bring himself to kill the chickens. Kham Noi was unperturbed. "The Buddha teaches us the middle way, Mem. He saw that in nature animals do not kill for pleasure, but it is right that they kill for food."

"But the boy won't eat the chicken."

"Yes. But he must work so that he may live and his family will eat. This is his work."

He saw my discomfort. "Do not worry, Mem. He is fortunate to have this work. The wages feed many small brothers and sisters."

The chicken problem was never resolved, although once we did endure a memorable variation. One night just as Harvey and I drifted off to sleep, we were wakened by a terrific crash, followed by squawking from the direction of the chicken coop. We both leaped from the bed and Harvey grabbed the nearest weapon, a bamboo cane. In our nightclothes, we rushed downstairs and out of the house just as Tip, the watchman, ran up with a lantern in his hand. There was no moon and the area beyond the lantern's light was covered. I let Harvey and Tip take the lead as we stole quietly through the yard, not knowing whether we would encounter a tiger or a chicken thief.

As we reached the coop, not far from the cement wall at the edge of the jungle, Tip exposed his lantern and the light caught the scoundrel. Surrounded by feathers, a huge weasel was just beginning to feast on one of our little chickens. The sudden light blinded him and, confused, he abandoned his prey, scampering straight toward us into the chicken wire. Harvey slammed him on the snout with the cane and he fell, rolled over, and lay still. The thief looked quite dead, but Harvey finished the work with a knife to make sure.

"Never saw such a big one," Tip said, looking at the weasel.

"It's too bad we got here so late," I replied, thinking of the poor chicken.

"Don't worry, Mem," he chuckled. "Chicken inside weasel . . . tomorrow weasel inside you." He seemed amused by this joke. We ate curried weasel for three days, although Kham Noi swore that it was chicken. I never did get used to the Siamese sense of humor.

A few weeks after we were settled, my thoughts wandered to the old temple ruin that Dr. Ruckel had called *Wat Phumin*. Mr. Breeden's warning came back to me and my heart swelled with indignation at his cool dismissal—as if it required no explanation. The depressing reprimand simmered in the back of my mind for several days as a constant annoyance.

One morning I drove Kham Noi to market in the surrey. The air was clear and the day was bright. I gave a cheerful wave to Mrs. Ruckel as we rambled past without stopping. She stood in the front door of her house with several students from the school. Arriving just outside the walls of Nan on the outskirts of the open market, we climbed down from the surrey and Kham Noi led the ponies to a shady spot beneath a tree where a large bucket of water was kept for the animals.

As I waited for him to return, my thoughts wandered again to the temple ruin. Mr. Breeden's stern face hovered, then disappeared. When Kham Noi reappeared, I made the decision. "Kham Noi," I said in a matter-of-fact tone. "I have something to do in the old city. I'll meet you at noon under the tree where the ponies are." He nodded his understanding.

Winding my way through the market, I entered Nan through the elephant gates, then started down the same broad, grass-covered avenue that Harvey and I had traversed on the day we arrived. I sauntered on for about twenty minutes, past the old teak houses and palaces and several temple compounds, now alive with the movements of yellow-robed monks and their helpers.

The day grew warmer and as I walked, my dress, which reached to a length just above my ankles, became damp and limp and clung to my legs. Occasional puffs of dust kicked up from under my shoes when I came to patches of dry dirt in the road. Finally I reached my destination, the ruins of Wat Phumin. A tingle of excitement ran through me.

The temple was overgrown. The area in front of the building was tangled with weeds and dark-green vines that crept over the small, crumbled wall and up along the sides of the building. The gnarled roots of a fig tree had broken through the wall near the entrance. The *nagas* reared and coiled before me, guardians of the old ruin. I hesitated, somewhat reluctant to walk through the wild growth. Suddenly I realized that I had given very little thought to this excursion.

The front door and windows were closed and shuttered, but a door on the side was ajar. Taking a deep breath, I stepped gingerly through the overgrowth around the building until I came to a heavy wooden door decorated with the delicate carvings I had noticed when we first arrived. I walked up the steps and the door swung open easily as I pulled it toward me.

Inside was shadowed—cool and dark. I hesitated before taking a cautious step into the room. Ribbons of pale light slipped in through broken slats on the shutters. The sunlight filtered dreamlike through motes of dust that hung in the air. The room was very large and spare, but carved pillars painted black and dark shades of red gave the space a secret feeling. The uneven brick floor was patched with dark areas of mold and mildew, reminding me of the brick on shaded sidewalks in Philadelphia on a morning in October before the sun absorbs the night moisture. And the air in the room was redolent of the same damp, musky smell.

On a raised dais in the center of the room sat four large gilded Buddha figures facing north, south, east, and west. They were identical; each wore a detached, almost languid smile. The eyes appeared to be fixed on something far away, and even in the dim light they gleamed. Except for the sound of my shoes on the floor, the room was silent.

As my pupils adjusted to the darkness, I noticed pictures on the walls, painted murals of rich, vibrant color. Some were of small boats filled with men and women, of three-masted sailing ships and a variety of monsters. Several scenes depicted a particular man who, I thought, could only be the Buddha. His followers surrounded him and the figures were painted above smaller ones of men and animals, as if one group were in heaven and one in hell. Serpents, like the sculptured nagas that cradled the base of this temple, rose from the sea and attacked a man.

As I began to follow the pictures from wall to wall, I saw that they told a story. Some images were horrific, some benign, and some were radiant with joy. The bright, colorful pictures were an exquisite contrast to the stark simplicity of our little mission church.

"It is *Jataka*," a voice said in accented English.

I jumped and whirled around. In the far corner, sitting on his heels, was an elderly monk, head shaved, wearing faded yellow robes. Near his bare feet were a small bucket of water and some old rags. I had not noticed him before.

My heart pounded, but he didn't move as he watched me with mild interest. He looked harmless enough and, after a moment, I began to recover. "You speak my language?" I asked with surprise.

"Some," he said. "The pictures are from the lives of the Lord Buddha . . . Siddhartha. It is a history called Jataka." A quiet smile stole across his face. "Look." He stood, adjusted his robes, and walked to a wall.

I stood behind him, careful not to move too close since he was a religious man. He directed my attention to a portion of the painting that seemed to depict torture and anguish.

"The Buddha had many lives before he was born into our world as Siddhartha," he said, pointing to these scenes as he spoke. "Until that time he was caught in *samsara*, the cycle of suffering, of birth, death, and rebirth. These pictures are of the lives shaped by the *karma* that he created as he passed through."

I inspected the mural. "What is karma?" I asked, having only a vague understanding of the concept.

"It is like the wind. It is a force moving through our lives like the wind moves through the branches of a tree." He paused, staring at the pictures. "The word means action—action that creates energy. The actions that we take now will have consequences when we are reborn into another existence. Our own moral choices, even our thoughts, determine our rebirth." He returned to his corner, adjusting his robes, and squatted again on his heels.

"How many times is a person reborn?" I asked, dropping to the floor at a respectful distance from him. I folded my legs to one side when I sat and tucked my skirt under, as I had seen the local Siamese women do, hoping that the close proximity of a female would not make the man uneasy. Mrs. Duncan had warned me that a monk must keep a distance of at least three times his height from any woman.

He seemed unperturbed as he answered. "We have many rebirths. Maybe ten or one hundred or one thousand or many thousands of lives as we make our way toward enlightenment."

"That's very different from Christianity," I said. "In my religion, we only have one chance to get it right."

"Yes," he nodded, speaking in a careful tone as he dipped his rag into the clean water in the bucket beside him. "Perhaps that is why your God sent his son to you—a savior would be necessary if you believe that you must get things right in one lifetime. But the Buddha teaches that each of us must save ourselves."

"Is the Buddha your god?"

He began to rub dirt and mold from the wall in front of him, using tiny circular motions. The colors brightened as he rubbed, almost as if lit from within. I thought he was not going to answer my question, but finally he said, "No, but this is sometimes difficult for foreigners to understand, particularly missionaries. Buddha is a title—it means 'the enlightened one.' The Buddha taught us a way to achieve enlightenment. It is something that each person must do alone." He glanced at me. "We have no god that we worship."

I was confused. "Then why does every temple have an image of the Buddha?" As I spoke, I thought of the plain lectern at the front of our own church.

"The image is only an object that helps us to identify our thoughts with the Buddha nature, to meditate." He watched, to see if I understood. I nodded, and he went on. "It helps us to see ourselves in his universe and to escape thoughts of this world."

"Escape thoughts of this world?" I asked. "Why should you want to do that?" I smoothed my skirt and gazed at the spot of picture that he was cleaning. The philosophers that I had studied were all consumed with thoughts of this world, as were the teachings of my own church. This didn't sound like a very practical religion to me.

He hung the rag on the edge of the bucket and smiled to himself. "Because once you recognize that everything in this world is temporary and will pass away, you find that you must begin to detach yourself from those things, that they only cause suffering. Craving springs up wherever there is the prospect of pleasure, the desire for enjoyment. It is craving that causes suffering. But you can learn to stop the craving; that is the Buddha's method."

"This focus on suffering—it's a rather harsh view of life," I said.

"When you realize that things you see and touch and hear and think are empty, then you will stop clinging to them." He reached for the rag, dipped it into the water, and twisted it dry as he said, "Think of a rainbow. It appears to stretch before you, but it is really an illusion—it exists merely because of the play between light and drops of water and your own point of observation . . . your own perspective. If you move . . . if you take away any one of those things, the rainbow vanishes."

He began to make small deliberate circles on the wall with his damp cloth again. "Everything in life is like the rainbow. It is all illusion—we arise, abide, and then die. Nothing is permanent."

I reflected on his words as he continued his work. The circular motion moved into an easy rhythm. The monk was elderly, but his face was smooth and unlined. It was easy to believe that he was unaffected by the cares of this world.

"My husband would tell you that the *nature* of the rainbow is permanent," I finally said, "because of the conditions of the atmosphere . . . refraction and such."

"And is that what you believe as well?" His voice was friendly.

I thought about the question. "No," I answered. "I don't know if the rainbow is an illusion—but it's beautiful." I paused and gave him a wicked look. "And I'd certainly like to know if the pot of gold at the end is real."

He looked startled, then chuckled, and I smiled with him.

"Do you live in Nan?" I asked, watching as he continued his meticulous cleaning of the wall.

"Yes. Not far." He told me of his temple in the old city where he was a teacher for young novices who must learn the teachings of the Buddha, the *Dharma*—the way to achieve enlightenment—before they were permitted to enter the priesthood.

In a soft voice, as if he did not wish to offend, he said, "Many people choose to continue their existence without denying all earthly pleasures . . . like your pot of gold." He glanced over his shoulder at me. "And some will make *merit* by their good actions in this life." He hesitated and his face grew solemn. "But they will not escape the wheel of life and suffering."

"Merit—like the giving of alms? Or building a temple?"

His eyes remained focused on his work. "Exactly," he murmured and gestured to the wall in front of him. "The colors have faded and the pictures are covered with dirt. I am cleaning them to honor the Buddha."

I nodded, understanding. "Then you will make much merit."

He worked in silence and after a few minutes I stood and ambled again around the room, studying the picture-stories with my new information. He seemed to have forgotten me as he went on dipping the cloth into the water over and over, twisting it dry, and rubbing away the dirt. Finally, in silence I left, closing the door quietly behind me.

To step from the temple into the blazing light of day was like waking from a pleasant dream. The sun was now high and cicadas buzzed in the overgrown garden, reminding me of the sweet summer days of childhood. As I walked from the temple onto the avenue, I turned back to look. The serpents still roiled beneath the ancient building, and the shuttered windows in front hid the secret of the old priest who worked alone inside. I walked on through the heat, exhilarated, finding a sense of freedom and beauty in his Buddhist teachings.

The thought flicked through my mind that this visit to the temple might be perceived by the Ruckels and the Breedens as reckless, perhaps even as rebellious, but the worry vanished instantly as soon as it appeared. The day was too beautiful for brooding. As I swung along, my spirit bubbled. Harvey wouldn't care, I knew.

Kham Noi was waiting when I returned. He had already piled our baskets of vegetables and fruit and some fresh-caught fish on the floor of the surrey. As we clipped along, bouncing over the worn dirt road, he held them firm between his bare feet. Harvey was sitting on the veranda in the shade of the mango tree as we barreled down the drive at home. The time for lunch was past.

"Where have you been?" he asked as he met me on the stairs with a sweet hug.

"Oh, just burning off karma," I replied. He gave me an uncertain smile.

# Chapter Nine

I WATCHED HARVEY, TALL, STRAIGHT, AND lean, walking from our house down to the hospital early one morning. Beyond him I could see the traffic on the river road. Young women glided by with a peculiar swinging gait. They balanced baskets on either end of a pole across their shoulders, sometimes also carrying a baby in one arm and produce in the other. Merchants calling to each other appeared and disappeared behind our hedge. Occasionally, a cart pulled by water buffalo crept past on creaking wheels.

Almost every family in the Nan Valley owned at least one water buffalo. During the dry season small boys walked these poor, fawn-colored creatures to the river every day to wallow in the muddy water. Nature had failed to provide them sweat glands, so this was the water buffalo's only means of cooling off in the searing heat. As the heavy animals sank into the river, sometimes leaving only noses above the water, like alligators, the boys grabbed their tails, planted a foot on the hind legs, and hoisted up onto their broad backs.

This morning, after Harvey had disappeared, I continued to watch as the children splashed in the water with their buffalo.

Suddenly a harsh scream pierced the air, followed immediately by loud shouts from every direction in the river. I stood abruptly, shading my eyes from the sun and strained to see what had happened. A great commotion ensued. The animals splashed in confusion and children scattered, scrambling up the riverbanks.

Over the hedge I saw people erupting from the hospital, running toward the noise. Just then Kham Noi rounded the corner of the house, headed at a full run toward the river. I gathered my skirts to follow him. Ahead I could see Harvey already plunging into the water, heading toward a young boy who seemed to be struggling in a muddy swirl. As I grew close, I could see that he was hurt—blood gushed from an open wound in his side.

Harvey gestured to his assistant, who had followed him into the river, and together they carried the boy from the water. He seemed to be taller than the children around him. Holding the boy awkwardly between them, they climbed up the bank of the river, hurried across the road, and disappeared into the hospital. I continued on to the river's edge and joined Kham Noi and Tip, who were listening as the excited children massed around them, chattering. A crowd began to gather as word of the accident spread along the river road.

"What has happened?" I asked Kham Noi, breathless as I caught up with him. His eyes were grave.

"A buffalo gored the boy, Mem," he answered.

"Was he badly hurt?" I asked. "Could you see him?"

Kham Noi shrugged.

"Terrible beast," I said, staring at the buffalo standing alone and still in the shallow water. I gasped as a young boy splashed over to it and grabbed the rope strung through a ring in its nose. "Leave him!" I called out. "He's dangerous."

Kham Noi touched my arm, then pulled his hand away. "Not dangerous," he said in a calm voice. "He shook his horns to rid him of flies. The boy was in the way." I stared, and seeing that I did not understand, he added with a shrug, "It is the buffalo's way."

I stared in disbelief at this placid acceptance of the goring of a child. As I watched, the buffalo was led away.

Harvey didn't appear for lunch. When he finally returned, it was dark and he was worn and hungry. Kham Noi had kept the dinner warm.

"Ai Mah is his name," Harvey said, as he sat down at the table, leaning his head against the tall back of the chair. "We had to operate. He'll be all right, but he'll have pain." His face was grim.

Harvey had just begun performing surgery, but with great trepidation because of the poor hygienic conditions. So far results were encouraging, however. Each time he worried for days that infection would set in, and each time his success seemed to us to be miraculous.

Kham Noi brought hot soup and ladled it into large bowls. Cook's boy, who usually served, had already left for home. Harvey took a spoonful and swallowed before he continued. "The boy's name means 'dog boy.'"

"That's a strange name," I said.

"Children are given poor names that will not attract the spirits to them," Kham Noi said. "When they are safe and grown, the name can be changed if they wish."

"Do you know Ai Mah?"

"He lives in the Village of the Beautiful God," he said. "About a half-day's walk into the forest on the edge of the rice plain. He is no longer a child." Kham Noi wrinkled his forehead and shook his head. "His parents died when he was very young. His grandfather raised him and left him the buffalo and a rice plot when he was gone. The boy plants and harvests it by himself every year."

"Have you been to his village?" Harvey asked.

Kham Noi nodded. "It is very poor."

"What will happen to the buffalo now?" I asked.

"His village will care for it until Ai Mah returns." Kham Noi removed Harvey's empty soup bowl, with a glance at mine, still full.

"I'll tell him that," Harvey said, as Kham Noi left the room.

Early the next morning I dressed and walked down to the hospital. Kham Noi had prepared a basket of rice with herbs and spices for Ai Mah, and I had added three plump mangoes. The branches of the slender trees along the way seemed to trace a pattern against the bright blue sky. Their leaves dripped from a recent light rain. Beneath the hedge, brilliant hibiscus were sprinkled among the fern and the long shining leaves of the banana plants. The air was soft and warm and smelled of flowers and the damp earth. I walked on sunbeams, feather-light as I turned onto the rough river road. My thin cotton skirt fluttered around my ankles in a gentle breeze.

This was the time of day that local men and women came to bathe in the river. I watched the men stalk into the opaque water, most in their blue tattooed shorts and little else, but the ladies were much more clever. As they waded in, they loosened their skirts at the waist and gradually lifted them, always keeping the hem of the skirt just above the waterline. By the time that the water reached their necks, the skirts were twirled onto the tops of their heads like turbans. As each one left the water, the process was merely reversed so that the skirt was gradually lowered, covering the woman as she stepped back onto the shore.

Reverend Ruckel had told us that the blue tattoos of the men were very painful to obtain and sometimes opium was used to blunt the pain. "The body is tattooed from immediately above the navel to the tops of the knees," he said, "including some very sensitive areas. It's a long process; sometimes it is repeated several times before it's complete."

I grimaced. "Why do they put themselves through that?"

"It's an old custom among the Siamese-Laos of this area," he answered. "It shows that a boy has entered manhood, that he has great courage."

The hospital was now in front of me. Beside it, on the far side, was the home of Dr. and Mrs. Pitters. I had visited her once since our meeting after church, but she was no friendlier in her own home, and the conversation was strained. She remained a mystery to me, although Harvey told me that she was quite fond of Mrs. Breeden. I sighed, tucking the worry away.

Harvey already had a great variety of patients, including Buddhist priests and local officials, in addition to native villagers and people who lived inside the walls of Nan. Many mothers had begun bringing their babies to the hospital for medical care. Mrs. Ruckel confided that this trust on their part was something new—a great compliment to Harvey as it showed unusual confidence on the part of the families.

As I opened the door to the dispensary on this morning, I was surprised to see the room so orderly and clean. Harvey had told me that his assistant, Sawat, and Nai Lueng, the dispenser, were organizing things, but the last time I'd visited, the place had looked nothing like this.

Dr. Pitters was resting in a chair, with his cheek propped on his hand as he gazed through the window at the river, lost in thought. Over his wife's objections, the elderly gentleman still spent several hours each day assisting Harvey, until someone else could be trained to do the work.

"Sawat and Nai Lueng have done a wonderful job getting this place in shape," I exclaimed.

He lifted his head, smiled, and rubbed his eyes. "Not them, Mrs. Perkins," he said.

"Who then?" I asked in surprise, halting my stroll through the room.

"Mrs. Breeden," he replied, yawning. "I don't know what we would have done without that angel. As busy as she is, she still finds time to help. She arrived one morning last week with some of the girls from the school and they spent several days scrubbing floors and walls and cabinets." His gaze swept the room. "It looks fine, don't you think?"

Mrs. Breeden? I looked about and my stomach knotted. Harvey had never mentioned this. But the place sparkled. The floors shone with polish. Each bottle had been cleaned and set in its place on a shelf. Even the walls were freshly scrubbed.

Dr. Pitters didn't seem to notice my consternation. "She's a fine Christian example, Mrs. Pitters likes to say," he murmured, almost to himself. "Dr. Perkins is fortunate to have her."

His words burned in my mind. I recalled several times that Mrs. Breeden's look had lingered on Harvey. And why hadn't Harvey mentioned this to me? I raged inside, even as I grew conscious that I should have organized the cleaning of my own husband's hospital. We were supposed to be a team. My face grew hot at the humiliating thought.

Dr. Pitters had returned to his watch over the river and I hurried away. Before opening the door to the porch that separated the dispensary from the patient ward, I paused to get my bearings. Then, with a deep breath, I lifted my chin, stretched as much of a smile as I could manage across my face, and crossed to the ward.

The ward was much too crowded. Several children scrambled about on the open porch and climbed on window seats. Inside, mats that substituted for beds covered almost the entire floor. Patients confined to their beds tossed impatiently. Several babies shared the rough, unpainted wooden cribs in the corner of the room, and men and women that I took to be parents squatted on their heels nearby. Despite the chaos, however, the atmosphere was cheerful and the room was exceptionally clean.

Harvey was kneeling next to a mat on the floor when I entered. From across the room, I heard his low murmur, steady and consoling, as he lifted bandages to inspect his work. I watched him for a moment.

"The hospital looks wonderful," I said in a bright tone as I went to him.

"Yes," he answered in a distracted manner without looking up as he began to clean the wound. "It's all the work of the girls from the mission school. Mrs. Breeden brought them over."

I put my hand on his shoulder. "That was kind of her," I said, still brooding. He threw me a quick smile as he continued his work.

"This is Ai Mah." He nodded at the patient.

The boy lay on a mat, the odor of chloroform still clinging slightly to him. He was no longer a child, but not yet a man. Eyes like black berries, framed by graceful curving brows, peered up at me from a thin face. Glossy dark hair was swept back from his forehead. He did not appear to be afraid or shy, even when my eyes caught and held his, but his face was tight with pain, his lips pressed firm against his teeth.

As I looked at Ai Mah, thoughts of Mrs. Breeden vanished. He was an orphan, Kham Noi had said. The boy was alone. I put the basket down on the floor and Harvey lifted the lid.

"Rice is fine, but no spices yet," he said. "And no mangoes." He replaced the lid of the basket and moved on to the next patient. I nodded and dropped to the floor next to Ai Mah's mat to stroke his forehead, which was hot to the touch.

"That's good, Babs," Harvey said from across the room. "It will let him know that someone cares."

The boy wasn't interested in the rice, so I began to sing to him, sweet, childish songs he could not of course understand; but I knew that the melodies alone were soothing. As he watched and listened, Ai Mah lay without moving. After an hour the lines in his face softened and the tension melted. Before I left, his eyes were closed and his breathing was deep and even.

When I entered the transformed dispensary to leave, Sawat and Nai Lueng were waiting. I was surprised, as they seemed to expect my visit. Nai Lueng showed me to a small cane chair. Dr. Pitters had disappeared.

"Please sit, Mem," they urged.

"Thank you, Sawat, Nai Lueng," I said. They beamed as I sat down to wait, expecting Harvey to arrive. After they had assured themselves that I was comfortable, Sawat and Nai Lueng disappeared through the door to the surgery at the side of the dispensary.

A few minutes later they returned pushing a hospital table on wheels before them. On top lay a patient barely covered by a ragged sheet. One leg was bare and two dirty feet dangled from the end of the table. Mrs. Breeden's invasion of the hospital still lurked in my mind and I mulled over the problem, watching in a distracted manner as the two assistants carefully maneuvered the table around to position it in front of me. So, when the patient groaned, I was startled.

I watched, puzzled now, as Sawat brought out gauze and bandages. Nai Lueng took instruments down from the shelves and handed them to Sawat to be arranged neatly on a low table next to my chair. The patient gave me a frightened look and began to chant in a low monotone and I glanced at the door with growing apprehension, wishing that Harvey would hurry along. When Nai Lueng and Sawat came to stand beside the patient and looked at me, I looked back at them and raised my brows. Another groan rose from the patient lying prone before me. "What is all this?" I asked, spreading my hands.

Sawat glanced at Nai Lueng and they conferred. Sawat stepped forward and bowed, hands folded together before his face. As he straightened he announced, "Missus Doctor, Mem. The man is ready for you to dress wounds."

I stared at Sawat and he gave me an anxious look. "You must dress wounds, please." He lifted the sheet, then the makeshift bandage on the patient's thigh, displaying an open and bloody gash in the flesh. I gazed in horror and a feeling of nausea rose to my throat as it slowly dawned that I was expected to care for this poor man. The thought flicked through my mind: *I'd bet a hat Mrs. Breeden has done this before.*

Fighting the sickness I shifted my gaze to the strips of gauze and instruments that Sawat had arranged on the low table.

With an encouraging smile, Nai Lueng moved forward, picked up a thin silver instrument from the table and held it out to me. Paralyzed, I let him place the instrument in the palm of my hand, and with this, the patient emitted an even louder groan. His head began to thrash from side to side and the chanting increased. I sank back into the chair, overwhelmed.

Nai Lueng scrutinized me and his grin slowly disappeared, to be replaced by a look of confusion, then utter disbelief. My face grew hot as I watched him turn to Sawat to confer once again, and after a minute of hushed talk, avoiding my eyes, they shoved the table and patient back through the door without a backward glance.

I stormed down the river road toward home in shame and fury. Again Mrs. Breeden's face formed in my mind with her tricky smile, that tight, straight line that should be a frown, but that curled up at the ends just at the last moment, turning it into something else. I banished the image, but immediately it was replaced by visions of Sawat, Nai Lueng, and the patient. As I remembered Sawat's name for me, "Missus Doctor," slowly I understood. The misunderstanding arose from Mrs. Pitters, who had been her husband's nurse. Harvey's two assistants thought that doctors and nurses came in pairs, I realized.

As I reached the driveway to our house, I stopped to watch two elephants coming toward me. Their wooden clackers sounded as they turned and walked with ponderous steps from the road down to the edge of the river. The mahouts, dressed in loincloths and turbans, sat on the animals' heads as they waded into the Nan River and lowered themselves, then rolled from side to side in the cool water. The gloom slipped away as I watched the mahouts running across the elephant's backs shouting to each other and laughing, as if they were balancing on huge rolling barrels. The elephants allow this, Kham Noi later told me, because in Siam the mahout and his elephant are usually together for life.

They're a team, I thought—like Harvey and I will be. The entertainment changed my mood and thoughts of Mrs. Breeden's interference and the disasters of the morning faded. Walking up the drive to our house, I bent to pick a pink hibiscus from a bush and stuck it in my hair. I'll find my place here, soon, I told myself. Every spider spins its web a different way, Dad always said.

One Sunday Mr. Breeden rose as usual to give the sermon. In a fitted and pressed seersucker suit with his hair parted in the middle and slicked back with tonic, he looked like a Philadelphia lawyer as he walked to the pulpit at the front of the church. Then looking hard at our Siamese guests, he frowned and began to speak.

"God has given us a written revelation—the Bible," he began. He held his Bible up. "This revelation is our truth. It is not a myth . . . it is not a mere stepping stone to the truth. It is literally and absolutely true. We dare *not* add anything to this truth—no worship of spirits, no determination by church councils, or teachings of Buddha or monks, or priests or popes." His glance slid to me as he stressed the word "Buddha" before continuing. "The Bible is the whole, entire truth."

His voice droned on, and I recognized the catechism of *The Westminster Confession of Faith*, the doctrine of the Divines and John Calvin and our Presbyterian church. I sighed and Mr. Breeden's voice receded into the distance as my eyes fixed on him. He stood straight, almost rigid, but his eyes and eyebrows worked in a fury while he shifted from one foot to the other to emphasize his words. He seemed to grow smaller as I gazed at him, until at last he was far away and flat—gesturing like a puppet—or perhaps an actor in the silent pictures.

I had never given much thought to religion—just accepted what I was told Sunday after Sunday in Summit Church. My faith was unexamined, based on something comfortable and reassuring like a warm blanket. On the *Empress* I had intended to engage in serious study to prepare for my role as a missionary wife and brought a copy of the *Confession* along for that purpose.

"They don't expect us to preach, you know," Harvey had laughed. And with the sun glittering on blue water during the day, caressing, warm enough to make us drowsy, and with moonlight sliding through our cabin window at night, the newlyweds never quite got around to lessons of Calvin and the divines.

In the little church, Mr. Breeden's voice continued in a monotone. A mosquito flitted onto my arm and I swatted it. The slap of my hand rang through the room and Miss Best, who sat just in front of us to the right, jerked her head toward me at the sound. Her thin, colorless face wore a slight frown as she turned back toward the front of the church. Her dress of plain muslin, lank hair, and flat straw hat were all the same dreary, earth-colors. As Mr. Breeden ranted on, the heat in the church seemed insufferable.

Suddenly his voice rose an octave and he slammed his hand upon the wooden pulpit. I jumped at the noise and looked up. Now his tone grew loud, emphatic. He pronounced each word with a hard beat.

"God has created us in his image. He has given us the ability, the power, to understand the revelations of truth set forth in the Scriptures, and he expects us to read it, to grasp the meaning, and to believe it!"

The congregation gazed at him dutifully. Mr. Breeden preached in the simpler dialect of Bangkok. Some nodded, but I was sure that many of our guests did not recognize a single word that he said. I fanned myself in the heat, recalling the beauty of the Buddhist teachings—the story of the rainbow. Music might help, I thought, as my gaze stopped on the organ in the front of the church.

Harvey caught my eye as Mr. Breeden began a closing prayer. I bowed my head, remembering my resolve to become a good missionary wife. But, as Mr. Breeden prayed for our souls, I stared at the organ from underneath my lashes. Maybe I could liven things up a bit with some hymns, I mused.

As soon as the service concluded, I sought out Mr. Breeden. His wife nodded to me without speaking but smiled when Harvey joined us. With the Breedens, we followed the Ruckels down the aisle of the church toward the front door.

"I will be happy to play for the Sunday services if you'd like," I said to Mr. Breeden, who was in charge of the service, with a nod back to the organ. "The congregation might enjoy singing a few hymns."

Mr. Breeden looked annoyed, but before he could answer, Mrs. Ruckel turned to us. "What a wonderful idea . . . don't you think so?" she said to Mr. Breeden in her soft voice. Harvey glowed as he glanced at me.

"Why yes, I suppose," the headmaster replied. Small muscles at the outer edges of his eyes flexed. "But nothing about sinners and wretches, Mrs. Perkins. Nothing like *Amazing Grace*, you understand."

I nodded, speechless.

Mrs. Breeden gave me a surprising, but almost imperceptible smile. "Are you planning to have them sing in Siamese?" she asked. She tilted her head. "Or will they sing in English?" And, with a sharp little laugh and without waiting for an answer, she was gone, followed by her husband and the Ruckels. Harvey and I stared after them in silence.

After a moment he shrugged. "Some of them can read. But most don't speak English," he said. "They'll have to sing in Siamese."

"That won't work, either," I muttered.

He looked at me. "Why not? I'm certain the hymnals have translations. That's provided by the mission in Chiang Mai."

"They will have them," I said, shaking my head. "But the Siamese musical scale is different from ours. And if that's not enough, their language depends on tone." He raised his eyebrows and waited. "The variations in tone will interfere with the melody," I explained, wondering how Mrs. Breeden had thought of this on the spot. "So they can only sing our hymns in English."

Harvey grimaced and put his hat on, with a glance at the fence where the ponies were tied. "Don't worry, Babs," he said. "We'll figure this out. Wait here and I'll get the surrey."

As he retreated, I crossed my arms to wait, looked down at my shoes, and began tracing small circles in the hard-packed dirt of the path to the church.

"Wake a cat and it will scratch," a voice said behind me.

Recognizing the laconic tone, I turned to Miss Mamsey. "I've got a problem," I told her.

"I heard," she said, smiling. "But I know a way to solve it." Seeing my expression, she gave me a mild look and added, "You'd know too, if you'd grown up in revival tents. Call me Emma, by the way. This *is* 1920 after all."

I had never played an organ, but years of study had made me quite proficient at the piano. "Surely this old thing can't be much more difficult," I told Harvey later.

"I said you'd find the right work for this mission soon enough," Harvey said, with a proud look. "And here it's music after all! It may not be a piano, but it's the next best thing."

*It isn't a piano, and this little church isn't a drawing room in Bangkok either,* I thought crossly, but the words did not escape my lips.

With fresh resolve I rose early on Monday morning and left our house after breakfast, spinning an old bicycle down the river road to the mission church to practice on the organ. The church was open and Emma had said she'd find the hymnals. They'd been stored away, she thought. The portable organ was ancient and made of carved dark wood, with chipped gold paint scrolled across the front above the keyboard. It had not been used for several years and was covered in dust. A hymnal was waiting on the bench in front of the organ. I picked it up and took a seat.

The keys resisted when I first tried to play, making laborious, groaning sounds as the music wheezed from the instrument. At first it took all my strength to pump the bellows. After a few days of practice, everything loosened up, however. Then it was wonderful to play alone in the cool, dark building.

On the following Sunday in the middle of the service, Reverend Ruckel announced that we would sing a hymn and the rest of the hymnals were passed around. Mrs. Breeden watched with a smug look as I walked up to the front of the church and sat down on the organ bench, while her husband took a seat beside her. When I heard Emma rise and walk to the platform,

I turned to watch. Mrs. Breeden gaped while Emma explained to the congregation what would occur.

At Emma's signal I played the first stanza through, stopped at the end, and started again. This time while I played, Emma shouted out the first line of the hymn in English, pronouncing each word with care, loud enough to be heard in the back of the church. When she'd finished, she raised her hand and I repeated the tune, but now she sang the words, leading the congregation along with her, and emphasizing each word with a downbeat stroke of her hand.

At first the voices, accompanied by occasional, smothered giggles, were hesitant and low and didn't resemble at all the hymn that I played. But "The Church's One Foundation" has an easy melody and a natural rhythm, and it goes on forever— long enough to give everyone time to understand. Soon their voices combined in passable harmony.

I was thrilled. Toward the end of the last line, I glanced over my shoulder and saw broad smiles throughout the little church as the congregation sang with gusto, eyes riveted to Emma in the front. The Breedens sat stone-faced and silent. But never mind that, I told myself. This was going to work! I glanced over my shoulder at Emma as I played, and she gave me an I-told-you-so look. So I hid my smile, but sunshine rose inside as my hands struck and held the last chord of that first hymn.

Mrs. Breeden was waiting for Harvey and me as we exited the church after the service. I hid my surprise and greeted her with what I thought was a fairly gracious smile, under the circumstances. But she said nothing of the music. Instead, with a brief nod to me, she tilted her head up to Harvey. "Dr. Perkins," she said in that lilting voice, with a hint of a smile. "We need a fourth for tennis this afternoon and I understand you're quite good at the game. Would you do us the honor?"

The Breedens had built a grass tennis court on their property. I flushed as Harvey accepted the invitation with obvious pleasure. "I'm sorry you don't play as well, Mrs. Perkins," she murmured to me. Her eyes swept past me as she turned away.

# Chapter Ten

THE MISSION ENTERTAINED LOCAL OFFICIALS SEVERAL times a year, and one day this became a point of discussion among all of the ladies, with the exception of Mrs. Pitters, who, I'd begun to notice, was seldom around when I was present. We were sitting on the Ruckels' veranda, and Emma said that we should try, for once, to have something other than a tea.

"I agree," Mrs. Breeden said to everyone's apparent surprise. "We've had them for tea too often. A tea is somewhat boring, don't you think?"

"I've always enjoyed them," Miss Best said hesitantly. "Perhaps we could invite our guests for tea, but add something to make the party a little more interesting, if you think it's dull otherwise."

"If we have it at the Ruckels, I'll be happy to play the piano," I offered, flush with my recent victory with the hymns. "Something classical," I added hastily, thinking of Mr. Breeden's dislike for popular music.

"That's very nice of you, dear," Mrs. Breeden said in a dismissive manner. "But these people are really tone deaf,

I think. They don't enjoy our music." She turned her attention to Mrs. Ruckel as though the subject was closed.

I took a deep breath to steady my voice. "They seem to enjoy our music in church. Perhaps their wives would like something lively, some of the new songs from home." I directed my words to Mrs. Ruckel.

"Hardly," Mrs. Breeden said.

Mrs. Ruckel's smile was kind. "They won't bring their wives, Barbara. They never do. In fact, they will not even mention their wives."

I was shocked and forgot my irritation with Mrs. Breeden. "How terrible!"

Emma laughed. "Not so terrible for them. They're not the ones that have to attend."

"Really, Emma," Mrs. Ruckel said impatiently. "You know perfectly well how important it is for the mission to keep friendly relations with local officials."

"Perhaps we could have a separate tea for the wives, then," I suggested. "It would be nice to get to know them as well."

Mrs. Breeden scrutinized me with a cool look. "This is a different culture, Mrs. Perkins. You really can't expect to suddenly impose your own views on the Siamese . . . or upon the mission, for that matter." Her patient, studied tone grated.

Before I could respond she turned back to Mrs. Ruckel. "We'll invite them for tennis at my house." She arched her brows and a smile played around her lips as she glanced past me, fixing her attention on something over my shoulder. "The Doctor is an excellent tennis player, Mrs. Perkins. I find him quite a challenge . . . on the court."

"Well, Amalie," Mrs. Ruckel said, with a puzzled look. "I never realized you had such strong opinions about our teas."

"I'm certain our guests will prefer tennis," Emma murmured. "But surely only the gentlemen will play?"

"Well, I suppose I would enjoy—" Mrs. Breeden began, but Mrs. Ruckel interrupted her.

"Only the gentlemen," Mrs. Ruckel said firmly.

It was settled. The tea party became a tennis party to be held at the Breeden's home. The Siamese officials, it seemed, were excellent tennis players.

"What does one serve for refreshments at a tennis party?" Miss Best asked.

"Tea," Emma said, with a mischievous glance at me.

On the afternoon of the party, I sat with Mrs. Ruckel, Miss Best, and Emma on the shaded veranda of the Breeden house, listening to the plunk of tennis balls being swatted back and forth. The court was off to the side of the property, not far from the road, and from where we sat we could watch the game. Intermittently the sounds of play were interrupted by the thin voice of Mrs. Breeden issuing orders to her houseboy from somewhere inside the house.

The players were dressed in white clothing that reflected the afternoon light. Harvey and Mr. Breeden teamed up with two of our guests, while Reverend Ruckel sat with several others on a bench beneath a large shade tree. Dr. Pitters was in poor health and so, to my secret relief, he and his wife had declined the invitation. I still found Mrs. Pitters somewhat aloof, difficult to engage in conversation.

The veranda was decorated with fresh-cut flowers set in small pots along the flat-topped railings. A long table covered with a crisp white cloth was placed at one end of the veranda and, on it, pretty china surrounded several more vases of flowers. A young boy emerged with a tray of small cakes, followed by Mrs. Breeden, who carried a large covered teapot that she placed on the table. She looked fashionably cool in a soft cotton gown of buttercup yellow. It fell loose to her ankles, hugging her ethereal form, and was trimmed with a wide satin ribbon around her small waist.

"She is a perfect hostess," Miss Best said in a tone of admiration.

"Would you like some help?" I asked Mrs. Breeden.

"No, my dear. I have things under control."

My gaze wandered as I hid a yawn with my hand. The sun was white hot. I reached for my handbag and pulled out a fan. Conversation had died in the heat and humidity; no one spoke as the plunk of the ball on the court continued with monotonous regularity. Mrs. Breeden fluttered around us, in and out of the house, around the table and back again, rearranging spoons and cups and cakes.

Mrs. Ruckel remained placid with her attention fixed on an embroidery hoop. I watched as she pushed the needle threaded with dark-blue silk through fine fabric, lost in her thoughts. Miss Best and Emma followed the activity on the tennis court beneath sleepy lids.

With loud shouts the sportsmen finally ended their game and joined us, flushed and perspiring. The Siamese officials were men of slight builds, all sinew and muscle with no fat, and immaculately groomed. Smooth, unlined skin made them look younger than they probably were. Mrs. Breeden pulled out small Turkish towels and the men wound them around their necks to soak up the dampness. I watched with envy as she conversed fluently with our guests, smiling as she filled each cup to the brim with hot tea before handing it over without a spill, adding milk first for Harvey, as I knew he liked it. Each of the officials bowed as they received the cup and saucer with both hands. Mrs. Ruckel had been right; none had brought their wives.

Harvey mingled with our guests while they drank the tea. The officials looked comfortable with him and at times the conversation grew quite lively. Once, he stumbled on a Siamese word, stopped short, and laughed at himself. Mrs. Breeden joined in the laughter and gaily supplied him with the correct one. Our Siamese guests looked at her with admiration as Harvey repeated the word and finished his sentence.

"Go on over and speak to them," Emma said.

I jumped and realized that I had been staring.

"Go on," she urged again, nudging me. "You already speak the language as well as anyone here. You can't just sit like a lump all afternoon. If you want to fit in, you'll have to make some sort of effort."

I had grown friendly with Emma since she'd helped with the hymns. She had come to the Siam mission in 1918, she'd told me, and although she was a few years older than me, was still unmarried. Once, she'd mentioned, with a hint of bitterness, that she did not miss her home. Here she was a missionary; back home in Georgia she was just an old maid. Ironical at times, she seemed to have a clear view of what she expected from life and, despite the Breedens, was settled and comfortable in the Nan Valley and with the local people, especially the children that she taught in the mission school. I admired her seeming ability to take the true measure of every situation.

Mrs. Breeden moved to Harvey's side and was now fully engaged in the men's conversation. "You're right," I said. "I'll give it a try."

Just then Harvey turned, caught my eye, and gestured for me to join him. As I rose, the Siamese gentlemen bowed and one, who had been speaking with Harvey and Mrs. Breeden, gave me a friendly look.

"It is so very nice that you and the Doctor have come to us, Mrs. Perkins," he said. He spoke in slow, halting English, pronouncing each word with care. "We hope you will enjoy your stay in Nan."

"I'm sure that I will," I told him. "Your country is fascinating. I am sorry I haven't had time to explore Nan yet. We've been getting settled in our new home."

He looked puzzled. "But I thought that you visited our temple, Wat Phumin, a few weeks ago." His voice rang in the sudden silence on the porch. My heart gave a little jolt and from the corner of my eyes I saw a cat-like smile forming on Mrs. Breeden's face. Harvey gave me a sharp look.

I mustered my response in a low voice, hoping that Mr. Breeden was otherwise occupied. "Why yes," I replied with a smile. "It is lovely. But I don't recall seeing you on that day."

He chuckled quietly. "No, of course not," he replied. "Someone mentioned it to me. It is an honor to the people of Nan to have an American lady visit our poor temple."

I was conscious of Harvey's stare and refused to meet his eyes. "Why has it been left in ruins?" I asked. "The pictures on the walls are wonderful."

"It is too costly to repair. But we are pleased that you thought it beautiful." He bowed again. I raised my eyes to meet Mr. Breeden's glare.

As the afternoon wore on, I braced myself for the harsh reproof I knew was coming. Suddenly my visit to the temple seemed foolhardy, an impetuous mistake. I searched my memory, trying to think of a plausible reason for the visit, but none came to mind.

"Prepare yourself," Emma drawled in an undertone. "Breeden is going to land on you like an avalanche of brimstone." I gave her a haughty look to hide my growing embarrassment.

As the Siamese officials rose to depart, they moved in a synchronized motion, almost as if they had received a signal. Harvey sidled up next to me. "Did you really go to Wat Phumin alone?" he whispered. When I didn't answer, he sighed. "Babs, how could you do such a thing?"

"It was perfectly safe, Harvey."

"That's not the point, as you know."

Our guests bowed low, expressed their gratitude, and rode away on their bicycles. I watched them depart, staring after them until only a cloud of dust was left on the river road. In the calm that precedes heavy weather, I observed the curiosity that they seemed to pump their pedals in unison.

I drew myself up and turned to Harvey. Just then the head-master's voice rolled across the veranda, ominous, low, cold, and smooth as butter. "Mrs. Perkins."

My mouth grew dry. "Yes?" I said, turning my head toward him. I was surprised that my voice sounded even and unconcerned.

He looked at me with flinty eyes. "It is unseemly for a member of this mission to be seen visiting a temple, a place of idol worship, much less to be wandering alone through an old ruin."

"Barbara!" Mrs. Ruckel sounded shocked. She dropped her embroidery into her lap and looked up at me. She hadn't heard.

I wrestled with feelings of contempt and, yes, I acknowledged to myself, a growing sense of dislike for this man and for his wife. I wanted to tell him what I'd learned from the old monk—that the figures of the Buddha were not idols in the sense that they were not worshiped at all, that Buddhists have no god to worship, that they were no threat to our Christian church. But my tongue stuck to the roof of my mouth.

Just then Harvey moved to me and slipped his arm around my shoulders. "I believe that I'm quite capable of deciding what is seemly for my wife," I heard him say. Surprised and weak, I leaned against him.

Mr. Breeden stiffened and his eyes narrowed. "I must insist for the sake of the mission that your wife try to comport herself within the boundaries of behavior that we've already established," he said to Harvey through tight lips. "You're both new here. You have no real understanding of these people or what effect your actions can have."

Mrs. Breeden gave me a scornful glance as she followed the houseboy into the kitchen with a tray of cups and saucers and leftover cakes. Her husband turned away, still angry, and stalked off behind them. Reverend Ruckel frowned.

I glanced up at Harvey, but he puffed away on his pipe with a calm, pleasant expression on his face and patted my shoulder. If Harvey was upset he hid it well. He never mentioned the incident again.

Harvey grew quite fond of Ai Mah, who was making a steady recovery from the surgery. At first he returned to the hospital each night after dinner to check on the boy, worried that the assistants would not recognize a sudden change in his condition, or that Dr. Pitters would be too stern with him.

When he was finally able to walk, Harvey began to teach him how to assist in very simple medical procedures, cleaning and bandaging wounds. Ai Mah was fascinated by the work and asked for permission to live at the hospital after his recovery. He slept on a mat in the corner of the ward at night.

"He's naturally intelligent," Harvey said, pleased with Ai Mah's progress. He developed a plan to get the boy into the mission school. "He would do very well there," Harvey said. "Perhaps he can learn enough to provide basic medical care for his village."

Ai Mah's dark eyes widened when Harvey first introduced the idea of attending the school, then he shook his head no.

Harvey went on to describe the school and the dormitories, but Ai Mah remained firm. He was not interested in attending the school. Harvey was bitterly disappointed. "Ai Mah!" he exclaimed. "This is a good opportunity. Don't pass it up."

Again the boy shook his head. His expression turned gloomy as he fingered a dirty skein of cotton threads tied about his wrist to protect him from the spirits. He would not let anyone remove it.

Harvey was not defeated by Ai Mah's rejection of his idea. One day a young girl from Ai Mah's village, who was a student at the mission school, arrived in the surrey with Harvey. She had come to visit Ai Mah at the hospital. His eyes lit up as he saw her walk into the room. She was Boua Keo—Crystal Lily—a childhood friend.

Boua Keo was lovely, as were most of the women of North Siam. She was slender, her skin smooth and golden, and she had dark, almond shaped eyes that looked down when Harvey introduced her to me. Her hair was shiny and straight, pulled back in the customary coil with flowers. When she spoke, her voice was like soft bells.

We left the two friends alone to visit. When Harvey came home that evening, he chuckled as he announced that Ai Mah had changed his mind. He would attend the mission school. I was happy for Harvey, and for the opportunity that this would give Ai Mah, but as we listened to the temple drums rumble through the valley in salute to the rising moon, I thought of the charm that Ai Mah always wore, the threads about his wrists. He was a true child of this country, where the teachings of Buddha were blended with worship of the spirit gods, and Mr. Breeden, the headmaster, was rigid, uncompromising in his religious zeal.

Night birds called from the jungle bush around our house and a monkey screeched in the distance, as if to ask, *What is it you think you can change, that for thousands of years has remained unchanged?*

# Chapter Eleven

ONE OF HARVEY'S PATIENTS WAS THE granddaughter of the *Chow Luang,* the ruler of the province of Nan. The Chow Luang, a royal prince, was a cheerful, amiable gentleman of about sixty-five years. He was short and thin, with a thatch of soft hair that sometimes stuck straight out from the sides of his head like goose-feathers. His little granddaughter was afflicted with a mild case of eczema that Harvey was able to treat with an ointment, and for this the Chow Luang was grateful.

One day Harvey and Dr. and Mrs. Pitters and I received a special invitation from the Chow Luang to attend a local Buddhist festival as his guest. It was held every year at *Wat Phra That Chae Haeng,* a temple compound on the other side of the river about two miles away. Harvey and I did not hesitate to accept the invitation. "It's good diplomacy," he said.

I went around to the hospital the next morning to find Mrs. Pitters. Harvey said that she was worried about her husband and had begun a project in the dispensary to keep her eye on him. As always, I was conscious that the elderly lady still reserved her friendship, but perhaps, I thought, this might break the ice. I found her marking labels and placing them on small bottles standing in groups on a table in front of her.

"What do you think we should wear?" I asked casually, after greeting her.

"Good morning, Mrs. Perkins," she responded in her high, reedy voice without looking up from the work. After a moment she raised her head and frowned. "Wear to what?"

"Hasn't Dr. Pitters told you?" I was surprised. "We are invited to attend the festival tomorrow across the river as guests of the Chow Luang."

She retained the frown as she clucked her tongue and bent her head over the bottles again. "Why would I want to attend a pagan festival? We're here to discourage these practices, not encourage them."

"Don't you think that the Chow Luang will be offended if we don't attend?" I asked with chagrin. With my index finger I traced figures on the top of the table while she worked. "Besides," I added, giving the figures all my attention, "it should be interesting."

Mrs. Pitters carefully wrote the name of a medicine across a small piece of paper without looking up.

"It will be fun," I went on, feeling like a child asking for an extra portion of candy. Still she ignored me. Overriding my intuition, I added, "We may never have another chance to see such a thing. There will even be fireworks."

She looked up at me and I saw the scorn in her eyes. "*Fun* is not the object of this mission, young lady," she said in a sharp tone. We stared at each other in silence, then wearing an expression of remote disinterest, she turned away and set the newly labeled bottle on a shelf behind her.

That afternoon, Dr. Pitters informed Harvey in a regretful manner that they would not attend.

The next morning Harvey and I crossed the river and rode the medical ponies on a narrow raised path that ran through a stretch of rice fields. The sun tipped its hat that day and the weather was beautiful. Streams of people, dressed in their gayest clothes, laughed and called to each other as they flowed with us toward the temple. The men were dressed in the panung or in Chinese trousers of brilliant colors, most predominantly bright cerise or pink and apple green. The long skirts of the women were of the Laotian style, a blaze of blue, lime green, cerise, red, yellow, sometimes shot through with ribbons of silver stripes. Most wore loose white jackets edged with red or purple trim. I wondered what Mr. Breeden would think if he knew that many faces on the way to the Buddhist ceremony were familiar from our Sunday mission service.

Across the field, while still a long way off, we could see the temple and a high golden tower that the Siamese called a *chedi*—a building to house and honor sacred artifacts. It threw off flashes of light in the bright sun. The temple compound rested on top of a small hill. As we came closer we saw that an open pavilion, decorated gaily with colored streamers and flags, had been constructed next to the temple. The steep, smooth incline to the top of the hill was guarded on either side by two enormous nagas that almost seemed to glide down its full length, their heads resting on the bottom.

We entered through the main gate and found ourselves standing in a raised courtyard shaded by a huge bodhi tree, its branches spreading over a great expanse, its roots punching through the earth. Now we could see that the roof of the *viharn*, the hall that usually holds the Buddha image, was layered in multiple tiers in the Lao style. Brightly painted stucco sculptures that looked like lions stood near the high golden chedi. The tiered base of the chedi, we were told, represented heaven, hell, and earth.

The Chow Luang was seated in full glory at the center of the pavilion on top of the hill, overlooking the plain. He wore a cocked hat with long white plumes. Upon our arrival he gestured us up with a great smile. The floor of the pavilion was covered with rugs, and on a table before him lay his gold-and-ruby sword and several exquisite little gold boxes containing cigarettes, betel nut, and other essentials. These were the symbols of his rank, and his attendants, walking behind him, carried them everywhere. The Chow Luang sat on large velvet cushions embroidered with silver and gold.

"Ah, the Doctor and his beautiful lady," the Chow Luang said in a gracious tone as we arrived. One of his attendants indicated that we should take a seat on a rug nearby.

When we were settled, he offered drinks of cool water in silver cups, which we gratefully took. The day was extremely hot and we had been riding for more than an hour so we drained the cups quickly.

The Siamese women of the party, the Chow Luang's many wives and daughters and granddaughters, were gathered and seated in one corner. They were dressed in royal purple and silver skirts, fine, soft silk jackets, and many gold bracelets.

A pretty young girl bowed her head and approached the Chow Luang on her knees. I watched as she waited for him to speak to her, then, with her head lowered and still on her knees, she asked a question in a shy, quiet voice. I was suddenly conscious of the fact that no female present was standing other than Harvey's patient, the young granddaughter. In Bangkok the custom of prostration, the prohibition that no head may tower higher than the head of royalty, had been abandoned, but here in the north it seemed to have persisted, at least where women were concerned. Although I was grateful that there appeared to be no such expectation with regard to me, the distinction was a curious one.

During the afternoon the Chow Luang turned to me and pointed to the colorful stucco lions below. "Do you know what those are?" he asked.

I looked at the sculptures. They were formidable with their gaping mouths and long, snakelike tongues. "No," I answered. "What are they?"

"They are the *Rachasee*," he told me. "The king of all animals, the most magnificent of beasts. From the beginning of time the *Rachasee* ruled all animals from the top of a large mountain. At the foot of the mountain flowed a crystal stream. For many years he protected his subjects from enslavement by men. But one day he looked from the edge of a cliff down into the stream and saw his image reflected in the crystal water below . . . What do you think that he did?"

I answered quickly. "He liked what he saw and was pleased."

The Chow Luang smiled. "No. That is a woman's answer."

"Then what did he do?" I asked, curious now.

"Ah. He became enraged at the intruder and leaped toward him from the high cliff. He was crushed upon the rocks below."

I laughed and said slyly, "*That* . . . is surely a man's answer."

The Chow Luang smiled again. "He was a wise king, however. He appointed his authority to the albino animals in the event of his death. That is why the white elephant became the king of all elephants."

Suddenly great popping noises shot from the rice field below, and I heard the sound of rockets whistling through the air. The fireworks had commenced, even though the sun was still high in the sky and bright, making them somewhat difficult to see. The Chow Luang told us that even though daylight competed with the fireworks, their presentation was a great offer to the Lord Buddha.

"It's a beautiful, extravagant gift," I said.

He nodded, but added, "Here it is not safe to offer them at night when animals are on the prowl." We watched for a long time as the fireworks traced intricate patterns of faint color against the clear blue sky.

When the festivities came to an end, the Chow Luang turned to me. "Would you like to ride home on an elephant?" he asked.

I was delighted. A great elephant was led to the pavilion and it slowly knelt before us. The Chow Luang's first, or superior, wife and his granddaughter, Harvey's patient, entered the red and gilt *howdah* filled with cushions and I followed. A band of musicians all dressed in scarlet played flutes made of bamboo, gongs, tom-toms, a strange kind of guitar, and other musical instruments as they led the way. The Chow Luang rode before the elephant on a small horse under a red-and-gold umbrella eight feet tall, its silver handle held straight aloft by the royal umbrella carrier, followed by Harvey on his pony.

On top of the great pachyderm, we swayed gently from side to side as it lumbered across the plain. Behind us glided hundreds of monks in robes the color of marigolds, holding delicate yellow parasols. As the afternoon light shimmered through the thin silk, they were illuminated like many small suns. Festival guests with sleepy children on their shoulders trailed the monks.

Bears, lions, and leopards lived in the northern forests, but tigers were everyone's great fear at Nan. The villagers set out shrines in the form of tiny wooden houses and offered food to the spirit gods for protection against these strong, intelligent predators. Sometimes Harvey was summoned at night to care for patients in the villages, and on these night calls he was usually forced to travel alone. On occasion he would be accompanied by Ai Mah, for which I was always grateful. Ai Mah showed Harvey how to hold his lantern aloft and swing it from side to side to make shadows that flickered and danced against the foliage when moving through the dark jungle. "This confuses the tigers," he assured Harvey, "so they do not know where to pounce."

The jungle sprawled on both sides of the River Nan. The trees grew close together with great, gnarly trunks, and the ground was almost hidden by tangles of bamboo and creepers and brush, so that even in the daytime the light was dim. In the rice fields, foliage on the banks of irrigation canals sometimes grew so dense that it covered the canals and, when they were dry, formed hidden tunnels, perfect hiding places for predators.

At dusk the cunning tiger crept in the narrow furrows under the green canopy to stalk its prey in the fields and at the edge of the forests. Ai Mah offered Harvey charms to protect him from the ever-present threat, worried that Harvey's God would not understand the tigers' habits. Tigers in the area had killed many men and boys, sometimes even the huge water buffalo.

One morning Harvey rushed home from the hospital with Sawat and Nai Lueng in tow. Mr. Breeden hurried up the drive shortly after. While we waited for Harvey to change into a loose shirt, long pants, and boots, they told me what had happened.

"A farmer stayed in his paddy too long last night," Sawat said. His eyes narrowed and his lips were white and he spoke in a small, tight voice. Sawat would say no more.

Mr. Breeden hesitated, then continued the story in an even tone. "He was working along the side of the canal and the tiger must have surprised him. His body lay in the rice field all night after the animal ate its fill." He watched me for the effect of his words. "His son found the remains this morning."

As Mr. Breeden spoke, I pictured the tiger hunched, gliding through the pale green light that filtered through the leaves, its muscles rippling beneath the skin, undulating with the smooth rhythm of its silent prowl. Suddenly the tiger stops, its paw frozen midway to the earth as it peers through an opening in the canopy. Ahead it spots the man, bending as he works, digging, pulling on some weeds, wiping the sweat from his face and ignoring the slant of the afternoon light that warns of the coming of the dusk, the tiger's feeding time. The tiger lowers its paw and slowly crouches, black-and-yellow eyes fixed on the foolish man. Hunger slices through the animal and its tail flicks from side to side as the beast waits and watches. The farmer is hungry also and straightens, thinking of the rice and curry waiting for him at home, of his pretty wife and children. Suddenly his sinewy tendons tense and bulge; sweat bubbles form on his smooth brown skin. He turns his head slowly, now staring into the leaves that cover the canal. For one brief moment he's suspended in time as his muscles twitch in recognition. Then the great cat springs, bursting through the foliage— no more than a streak of gold and yellow before the farmer feels blinding pain and all turns dark.

Nai Lueng said that the doctor knew the farmer. He had been treated recently at the hospital. My heart sank as I heard this, realizing that Harvey would go with them. *How can you be so hard?* I admonished myself. *Think of the poor man's family.*

Men from a nearby village and from Nan began gathering in our yard above the river road. In small groups they hunkered down on their heels, murmuring and gesturing as they waited for the tracker to arrive, the man who would find and shoot the tiger. As soon as Harvey returned, he and Mr. Breeden and Sawat and Nai Lueng joined them below the veranda.

The tracker seemed to appear from nowhere, and the men listened silently as he told what he had found so far. The animal had retreated to the jungle in an area about one mile away. Now I noticed for the first time that only the tracker, Harvey, and one or two men who constituted the local police force at Nan had guns. The rest carried bamboo sticks and knives. One man held on to a pretty checkered umbrella.

"What are you going to do with that thing?" I questioned, pointing to his umbrella.

"Mem?" he asked. Then suddenly understanding, he grinned and answered that he would use it to beat his way through the bush.

"You'd better stick close to the tracker then," I warned.

Harvey came toward me and I grasped his arm. "Why must you go with them?" I demanded in a low voice. "Have you ever even shot that gun? You don't know any more about hunting tigers than that man with the umbrella over there!" I clung to him. "Can't you wait here?"

He unwound my fingers from his arm with a wry smile. "Now how do you think that would look, Babs?" he asked.

I tightened my lips and frowned. He pulled me close and as he hugged me he whispered, "There are just some things that have got to be done, you know."

"What do we care about what these people think?" I hissed fiercely. "You're a doctor, not a hunter." He gave me a steady look and my throat constricted. I swallowed the rest of my words.

Just then, with a great shout, the villagers, led by the tracker, struck out like a herd of rogue elephants headed for water. I rushed to the railing to watch as Harvey and Mr. Breeden hurried down the drive to join them. Soon they had all disappeared from sight on the river road. Still I stood looking after them, as if I could will them to reappear. My arms and legs were leaden.

"Would you like something to eat, Mem?"

I turned abruptly to see Kham Noi's worried look. I didn't want him to know how afraid I was. "Thank you, Kham Noi," I said lightly, crinkling my eyes. "That will be fine. I'll have it here on the veranda."

I sat in the shade of the mango tree and tried to read, but the words blurred as my thoughts rushed ahead to the rag-tag group of hunters. I tried stitching, but after looking at the results I gave it up and fixed my distracted gaze on the entrance to the river road. Kham Noi brought lunch, which I ate absently as I continued to stare into the distance, trying not to picture Harvey or the forest or the tiger.

About mid-afternoon Emma appeared, wheeling her bicycle furiously around the bushes that separated our yard from the river road and pedaling toward the house. My heart twisted and I stood abruptly, fearing the worst. With a deep shudder, I willed myself to be still and waited for her to arrive.

"I just heard," she said breathlessly, as she leaned the bicycle against a tree and joined me on the veranda. Her hair was damp with perspiration from the ride and she brushed it back from her broad forehead with one hand. "Mrs. Ruckel knew the farmer's wife. She's just gone down to the village to be with her."

I nodded, wondering if she had come all this way to tell me that.

"Mrs. Breeden's very upset. We can't calm her down. Miss Best and Mrs. Ruckel have been with her all morning. Mrs. Ruckel sent me down to see if Dr. Perkins could come."

I regarded her as my fury rose. "He's gone tiger hunting," I finally said, keeping my voice level. "Mrs. Breeden will just have to pull herself together on her own."

Emma gave me a startled look, then a smile crept across her face. "Well, then," she said, removing her hat, "I'll just wait here with you for the hunters to return. Have you got some tea?" I called for Kham Noi. When he had left us with refreshments, we sat in companionable silence, looking out at the river road, now deserted.

In the late afternoon the hunters returned, exhausted but noisy and jubilant. From far down the drive we could see that some of the men carried a large burden." It must be the awful beast," I murmured. We strained to watch them through the twilight.

"What's that man doing with an umbrella?" Emma exclaimed, as they grew closer.

But I found I couldn't answer. I had just spotted Harvey's sandy-colored hair in the midst of the group, and as I watched him approach I felt the tension ease from my body. My heart swelled as he walked with an easy gait, chortling with the others around him. He seemed to be intact.

Emma and I ran down the stairs to greet the hunting party. I bumped into the umbrella man and, laughing, gave him a jubilant hug that left a stunned expression on his face. Then I whirled to meet Harvey. Over his shoulders I saw the soft gold and black coat of the tiger. The strong muscles in the lean body were plainly visible and the eyes, still wide open, stared back at me with resigned, frozen dignity. Startled, I forced myself to remember that this was a man-eater.

Since we were the only audience available, everyone was eager to talk with Emma and me, to describe the hunt. At first they had followed the trail across the rice fields where the farmer was found, then the tracker led them into the jungle.

"The jungle is a very different place when you are following an animal that refuses to stay on the path," Harvey said.

"You must know him to find him," the tracker said.

The forest was so thick and dark that they could only see a few yards ahead; the hunters were often forced to stop and cut their way through clumps of bamboo and heavy, choking vines. Time and again the tracker's dog scented tiger spoor, and several times they spotted the animal's paw tracks in the soft banks of a shallow stream.

"The silence was unearthly," Harvey said, "as if the jungle held its breath. No birds sang. Every crack of a breaking branch echoed through that stillness like a shot."

"Weren't you afraid?" I asked.

"Of course we were," he said. "We knew that soon the tiger would turn to defend itself."

A sharp-eyed boy from the village had suddenly spotted the animal through a clump of trees, cornered against a rocky ledge. At a signal from the tracker, the hunters spread themselves into a wide crescent and moved slowly toward the ledge. The tiger sat on his haunches with a regal air, watching them approach, the movement of his tail gaining momentum as they grew close. The beast seemed to gaze at them with disdain, Harvey said, these men who were so slow and clumsy, who needed sticks and guns and umbrellas to hunt. Then the animal's tail stilled.

"I expected him to fight," Harvey said in a quiet, puzzled tone. "But instead he just sniffed the air, as if to take one last breath, then gazed into the forest behind us."

"He was thinking," the tracker interrupted. "He knew his time had come."

"He was saying good-bye to the forest," Nai Lueng said simply.

We all looked at him.

"What happened then?" I finally asked.

"I killed him with one shot," the tracker said with a shrug.

The tiger was hung in our backyard on a pole braced between two crossed bamboo sticks. Rope around its neck and under its middle and haunches gave it a very life-like appearance suspended there. Its legs swung loose and the amber eyes still gazed off into the distance. Even the tail was stretched out and tied to the pole.

Emma and I ventured close for a good look. "It's somewhat scrawny," she observed.

The eyes seemed almost alive. The fragile balance that existed between life and nature in North Siam struck me as I looked at the dead tiger. I pictured the big cat watching the hunters approach, taking that last deep breath. I pictured the farmer in his last fleeting moment. "I wonder if it's possible they could both be reborn," I murmured, suddenly feeling depressed.

Emma gave me a surprised look. "I think you've mixed up your religions," she said. "Come on. Enough of that," Emma said briskly. "This animal *killed* a man."

But after that day, when shafts of sunlight began to slant through our windows in the late afternoon, often I caught myself gazing at the jungle on the edge of our property, thinking of the tiger. I saw it crouched low beneath the foliage, slinking in slow motion through the pale green light in the rice fields, gliding through the tangle of dark forest toward our home. When it turned its yellow eyes on me, I saw . . . arrogance. And majesty. And death.

*Is it really possible to make a difference in this wild country?* I wondered. Somehow, for an instant, it seemed a shadow had drifted between the sun and me.

# Chapter Twelve

DR. PITTERS WAS ILL WITH TUBERCULOSIS. HARVEY
diagnosed it. The older doctor was pale and weak; his hands
shook and he had trouble walking. Every time we were around
him I tensed as though bracing to catch him when he finally
collapsed.

Ai Mah remarked that Dr. Pitters was so irritable now that
he must be the most difficult patient Harvey had ever treated.
Harvey, Reverend Ruckel, and Mr. Breeden all tried to convince
the elderly man that he should retire to mission headquarters
at Chiang Mai, but both he and Mrs. Pitters refused to hear of
it. Periodically Dr. Pitters declared himself under quarantine
and disappeared for a few days. But the rule never stood for
long. He always reappeared, and then I worried that we were all
vulnerable to exposure. Ai Mah now became Harvey's primary
medical assistant, but he'd begun attending the mission school
each day, and his absence during that time was taking its toll
on Harvey.

"Things are much more difficult with Ai Mah in school,"
Harvey volunteered one evening. "Mrs. Pitters has begun helping out, but it's not enough."

"I'll come around and see what I can do," I offered, secretly pleased. I would even brave Mrs. Pitters for this chance. "If you don't have time, perhaps Mrs. Pitters could teach me some simple things, cleaning and bandaging and such."

Harvey looked happy. "That would be a big help."

I was excited. Harvey and I had come to Siam to work for change. Playing the organ for service on Sunday was not enough. The music was not part of Harvey's work. Now, I reflected, I could learn to assist Harvey, and perhaps at the same time I could melt some of Mrs. Pitters's icy exterior. I brushed off the flutter of apprehension.

Upon arriving at the hospital the next morning, I found Mrs. Pitters seated at the big wooden desk in the dispensary. I put on a smile and, keeping my tone casual, asked if she would like some assistance.

For a moment she didn't raise her head or answer. I stood near the desk, waiting, feeling my smile grow tight. Through the open window in the front of the room, I heard a pony cart rattle past on the river road. Finally she looked up. She turned to me and, with a cold look, asked why I had never thought of this before.

I was taken by surprise. "Pardon me?" I said in a high, foolish voice.

"Mrs. Perkins," she said, without blinking, "you are a spoiled and careless child. How Dr. Perkins can put up with your selfishness is beyond me." Her voice trembled with her dislike.

I stared, unable to think of a suitable reply.

She continued to look at me with her sharp old eyes. "Well, young lady? I don't believe in beating around the bush. You don't seem to have any understanding at all of such things as duty and sacrifice . . . qualities that made this mission strong enough to survive long before you arrived." She shook her head and picked up a notepad and a pen. Looking down, she began writing as she went on, "You act as though hard work is an imposition. I'll say it again: You are spoiled and selfish. My suggestion is that you take a lesson from young Mrs. Breeden and learn what it means to be a good Christian wife, instead of flitting around amusing yourself at Buddhist festivals and such."

I gave her a furious look but checked myself in time to stop the rush of acid words. Mummy's face wavered, slowly emerging through the angry haze. Suddenly I found that I had an absolute inability to be rude to the old lady.

"I had thought . . . perhaps . . . that you could use some help," I stammered. But when she remained silent, I turned to go. As I reached the door I hesitated, took a deep breath, and turned back to her. "Perhaps some other time?" When she didn't answer, I closed the door behind me with a bit more force than necessary.

I wanted to disappear, to be any place but Nan. Missionaries in Phrae had spoken of Mrs. Pitters with such reverence. But I suspected that she would never like me.

Later, Mrs. Ruckel held me as I sobbed. There was no one else that I could tell, certainly not Harvey. He'd try to fix things and would only make them worse. "I don't know what to do. I just can't seem to fit in," I cried.

"Shush," she murmured. "You must try to understand. She's had a hard life. They've given everything they have to this country."

I sank against her, thinking that Mrs. Pitters's spirit was as dry and shriveled as her parchment skin, and I didn't care what had squeezed her dry. As if she could read my thoughts, Mrs. Ruckel rested her hand on my head; it was comforting.

"They raised their children over here under the worst circumstances," she went on, "in bamboo huts without any of the things that you took for granted back home. They've lived through drought, famine, monsoons, and all sorts of petty persecution by local authorities."

With a wet shudder I straightened and wiped away the tears, using the heel of my hand and smearing my face in the process. Mrs. Ruckel pulled a handkerchief from her pocket and handed it to me. Then she went inside and soon returned with two cups of tea and a plate of small cakes.

I eyed the tea and wished that it were whiskey.

Mrs. Ruckel took a seat and sighed.

"They're made of iron, those two, and they expect a lot from everyone around them," she said. "About twenty years ago their son—only a toddler at the time—became deathly ill. He needed to see doctors in Bangkok. So they bundled the boy into a small boat, no more than a canoe really, and for six days in torrents of cold rain and wind they tossed down the river, through an absolute tempest of water—waves so big that they broke over the banks of the river and washed huts away."

She handed me a cup of tea and took one for herself. "It was the rainy season," she went on, "and we all knew that the river currents were too swift for travel. The boatmen warned them not to go." She sipped her tea and looked off. "We begged them not to go. A few days before, a boat headed down to Phrae had capsized and seven were killed."

She gave me a wondering look. "But somehow they made it. The child lived. And when they returned," she shrugged, "Mrs. Pitters went right on with her mission work as through nothing out of the ordinary had happened."

❦

On my way home I stopped at the mission church to play the organ. The enclosure of the small room was strangely comforting, even though the dim light enhanced my melancholy mood. I felt a need for familiar Western music, something from home. "Liebestraum" doesn't sound right on an organ, but slowly, gradually, I lost myself in the music.

That evening when Harvey returned, my eyes were still red.

"What's wrong?" he asked, putting his arm around me as we walked into the parlor. Suddenly I was terrified that Harvey would find out about the disastrous afternoon. I writhed inside as I thought of Mrs. Pitters's rebuke and realized that I would have to handle this on my own. I could not bear his pity.

I shrugged from under his arm. "I was a little under the weather earlier on, but I'm fine now," I said in a cheerful tone as I reached for his pipe on a nearby table. By the time I turned around and handed it to him, I'd managed a bright smile. "I haven't been much use to you, though," I sighed, dropping into one of the wooden chairs. Sprawling, I stretched out my legs and crossed them at the ankles. "I stopped in at the hospital this morning, but Mrs. Pitters has her own way of doing things and . . . I thought it best not to interfere today." With a wry grimace, I added, "So I'll try again tomorrow."

"Well, perhaps you're right." he said. "Give it time." He dug through his pockets for a light, cupped the bowl of the pipe with his hand and lit it. He sat down, drew on the pipe, and looked off. "Mrs. Breeden seems to get on with her quite well. Perhaps she could give you some advice," he added, speaking from the side of his mouth as smoke drifted out with his words.

I lowered my eyes to veil the flash of anger I knew they must reflect.

❧

One afternoon when we were all sitting on the Ruckels' veranda, Mr. Breeden mentioned that he was reconsidering Ai Mah's admission to the school. The boy was spending too much time at the hospital, he complained. And he wasn't doing well in his religious studies; it was becoming obvious that he would never make a good Christian.

Harvey's lips grew tight. "I didn't know conversion was a requirement for learning."

Mrs. Breeden leaned toward her husband and touched his arm. "I think the boy will be fine, dear," she said. "It just takes time." She glanced at Harvey and slid her eyes to me. "And Mrs. Pitters says that he's a tremendous help at the hospital."

*She knows*, I realized.

"I'll be the judge of the matter, Amalie," Mr. Breeden said in a sharp voice. He shifted his arm, dislodging her hand in the process. I was surprised to see a flush crawl up her face. She settled back in her chair and gave her husband a covert look as she folded her hands on her lap.

"He's a difficult boy," Breeden went on.

Harvey disagreed—told how quick Ai Mah had been to learn some basic medical procedures, how helpful at the hospital, and how the patients took to him. "We're understaffed," he said.

Emma's head swiveled from Harvey to Mr. Breeden and back again as their voices rose. "Perhaps Mrs. Perkins could make herself useful," Mr. Breeden finally said, with a glance in my direction.

My face grew hot. With an angry slap on his knee, Harvey leaned forward to respond, but Mrs. Ruckel interrupted. "Let's just see how things get on," she said, with a mild look.

I told Emma that Mr. Breeden constantly seemed to whittle my soul, chipping at it until one day I'd have nothing left. "I'm beginning to think I'm hopeless as a mission wife," I admitted.

Emma said that she had seen the careers of a good many missionaries done in by their wives. When I grew concerned, she added in a dry tone that I should not worry. "Dr. Perkins is of such strong character that he will eventually pull you up to his level," she said.

I gave her a sharp look, not certain how to take such advice, but her expression was inscrutable.

Sickness was pervasive in the Nan Valley this time of year, and it seemed that the hospital was always full. The hospital had its own laundress; however, lately she was somewhat overwhelmed. With Mr. Breeden's words still stinging, I steeled myself to face Mrs. Pitters once again. Each morning cook's boy and I walked down to gather dirty sheets, towels, rags, and children's clothes from the ward for laundering, returning them the next day, clean and folded. I mended the rags that passed for linens and sang songs to the children in the ward when space permitted. The old lady continued to hold court in the dispensary and occasionally acknowledged my presence with a regal nod, thin lips pressed together in disapproval.

As more patients appeared with dysentery and nausea, their faces rosy with fever, Harvey began to suspect that we were in for trouble. His suspicion was confirmed a few weeks into December when a young man with dark, sad eyes came to our home looking for the *farang*, the foreigner. He had run a long way, he said, without food or water. His village and others nearby were raging with fever.

Reverend Ruckel accompanied Harvey to the village and they were gone for three days. Ai Mah went along even though it meant missing school, partly because he knew the trails that meandered through the jungle, but also because he could vouch for them to the villagers. I was glad he was with them, as Ai Mah was young and strong, and I worried over what reception Harvey would encounter. Many in the forest did not trust foreign missionaries.

Ai Mah told me later what had happened. As Harvey and Reverend Ruckel entered the village of the young man who had come for help, a wizened, yellow-robed priest met them. After pleas from the young man, the priest struck a gong to call the people of the village to the temple courtyard to hear what Harvey and Reverend Ruckel had to say. They stood with the priest on a raised porch in front of the temple. Reverend Ruckel told them about the Bible and our God, and Harvey told them about his medicine and how he could care for them. He showed them his medical bag, holding out the quinine and bandages as he explained. They murmured and watched with interest.

While Harvey and Reverend Ruckel spoke to the villagers, Ai Mah noticed a small dark man sidling up to the priest. His eyes were narrow and glittered with contempt as he listened. This was the spirit doctor.

When Harvey finished, the spirit doctor began to harangue the villagers, warning them that the spirits would be angry if they put their trust in the farang.

Harvey grew angry. "Would you let them die, then?" he asked the man.

The priest remained silent as the spirit doctor pushed his way in front of Harvey. Lifting his fist, he shook it at the villagers. "The gods will punish you!"

Enraged, Harvey grasped the spirit doctor and holding him by the shoulder, twisted the man's arm behind his back and forced him to the edge of the porch, where he shoved him to the ground below. The spirit doctor, sprawling on the ground, muttered something in his fury, pointing his finger at Harvey, and the crowd began moving forward.

"The people were angry at the Doctor when they saw," Ai Mah told me. "Very angry. They were afraid, Mem. But I saw them coming and moved to stand beside him." He fingered the threads he always wore around his wrist as he spoke, but his eyes glowed, and I smiled at him. I knew that he, too, had been frightened of the spirits and yet he'd stood with Harvey. "Doctor Ruckel stood with us also," he added as an aside.

"You had courage," I said to him. He gave me a puzzled look, and I added. "You were very brave." He smiled with pride. "What happened then?" I asked.

"Then, Mem, the old priest began to speak. He told the village that your God must be very powerful to pick a battle with the spirit doctor."

"And . . . ?"

Ai Mah shrugged. "He said the farang could stay but that the village must make a special offering to the forest spirits . . . to show respect."

How ungrateful these people were! They were so difficult to help. And even a success in one place did not guarantee Harvey's welcome in another. Each village in the jungle was an isolated community, separate and distinct from those around it. Harvey was forced to start anew each time he visited a different one.

Poverty and illness were considered fate by the people of North Siam. As for the future, it seemed to me the villagers cared only for enough rice to get through each day, for a bamboo house, a few blankets, and banana and papaya trees. No one worried about the future. The future would take care of itself.

Letters from home began to leave me with a vague sense of anxiety, but I couldn't quite identify the problem. Sometimes I thought that underneath the words were hints that Dad was ill. A mention here, an omission there, but nothing clear.

"Something's wrong," I told Harvey one day after a letter arrived.

"Why do you say that?"

"I just feel it. Sort of a premonition."

He looked disgusted with this reasoning process. "You certainly can't get all worked up over a vague feeling."

"There's something wrong, I tell you. I know it."

"Babs," Harvey said with a patient look, "when a doctor makes a diagnosis that something is wrong, it is based upon facts, not feelings. Be practical. You can't operate on premonitions. Now look at this," he took the letter from my hand and scanned it. "Your father writes about Harding and Wilson and Hoover, the new prohibition law, your brothers' antics, Alice's new beau." He paused and gave me a look, "There!" and tossed the letter on the table beside me. "Everyone's fine at home. How ordinary can you get?"

I picked it up and read it through again. "He doesn't mention the stars," I said.

"What?"

"The stars, Harvey! He always ends with that." I frowned. "'*Shine out, Babs!*' he always writes. It's in every single letter, but it's not in this one."

"Perhaps he forgot."

But a wave of apprehension settled over me. "Something's wrong . . . I can't put my finger on the trouble, but I wish we weren't so far away."

"It's hard to believe we've been here a year already," Harvey said, as he picked up his book. "It seems like just yesterday that we arrived, don't you think?"

I didn't answer. But Mrs. Breeden's words when we'd first arrived came to mind. It seemed to her they'd been at Nan for a hundred years, she'd said. I glanced down at the letter in my hand and the sense of foreboding lingered. A dull ache spread through my chest and I longed for home. For Dad and Mummy and lights and music and motorcars and movies and ice. It seemed to me that we had been here forever.

# Chapter Thirteen

THE RUCKELS' DAUGHTER, JUDITH, ARRIVED JUST before Christmas at the end of our first year in Nan. She had spent the last few years teaching at a girl's school in Bangkok. Judith blew into the mission like fresh air, bringing with her some sheets of new music. "For you," she told me. "Mother wrote that you love to sing."

Judith and I were about the same age. She was calm and self-assured, traits that I admired. I thought this came from having lived on her own in Bangkok for several years. But she was also independent, with high spirits that were somewhat surprising given her background as a missionary child.

Shortly after the New Year, Judith proposed a trip to Chiang Mai. To my delight, Harvey suggested that I keep her company even though he could not get away. Dr. Pitters was still ill. The details of the trip consumed us for several weeks, during which Harvey sat with Judith and me at night, going over maps and lists that Mrs. Ruckel prepared and laughing at stories Judith had to tell. We were to travel overland through the jungle to Phrae, then catch the train north to Chiang Mai. The mission there sent word that we were welcome, and we were invited to stay with Dr. and Mrs. Cord, old friends of the Ruckels. With travel time of approximately ten days each way, we planned to be gone for six weeks.

Riding two of the mission ponies, we departed with an entourage of fourteen carriers bearing food, clothing, bedding, chairs, and a small table. In addition, one cook, one cook's boy, one guide, and one syse accompanied us. Mrs. Ruckel left nothing to chance.

Near dusk on the first day of the journey, we came to a village where we planned to stop for the evening. To our dismay, we found a royal prince on a tour of inspection from Bangkok traveling the same route. The prince, his advance guard, and his carriers took over the rest house for travelers, as well as all huts, animal pens, and clearings in the village. We were forced to move on, traveling through the dusk—tiger time—until finally we found a small village that could accommodate us.

For the next few nights as we arrived at each scheduled stop in the forest, we found the royal entourage already decamped and filling every available space. As a result each night found us scrambling for a place to sleep. I was perplexed by the fact that our guide seemed continually surprised at this.

One evening we came upon a cluster of small bungalows that belonged to a British lumber company. The English employed many natives throughout North Siam to work the giant teak forests under a concession from the king. Hundreds of elephants were used to move cut timber to the river where the huge logs were tied together with rattan and floated down to Bangkok.

As we rode our ponies into a clearing near the bungalows, a gentleman with skin like brown leather and hair the color of corn leaned against a tree, watching. We dismounted while he observed us without expression, chewing on a Burmese cheroot that hung from the corner of his mouth. He was a large man, tall, with chiseled muscles and a firm, square jaw, but not an extra ounce of loose flesh.

Finally he seemed to come to a decision. He dropped the cigar, ground it into the dirt with his foot, and ambled toward us. Judith and I stood aside as he took the reins from our hands without a word and led the ponies, followed by our guide, in the direction of one of the bungalows at the edge of the clearing. The carriers milled around and, after a few minutes, the guide returned for them, asking us to wait.

After the ponies were tethered, the man returned and introduced himself as the manager of the camp. His eyes ranged over the two of us while we talked. He was from Denmark, he said, but he spoke English with only a slight accent. His crew had been working these jungles for more than a year.

Judith and I freshened up in our bungalow, scrubbing our faces and arms with water brought by a carrier. When she wasn't looking, I bit my lips to make them red, then we returned to the clearing where the Dane waited under a tall, solitary tree in the middle of the clearing. Our carriers were nowhere to be seen. He built a fire and we settled near him on the ground and waited for dinner to be served.

"The fire discourages tigers," he said, poking the wood with a bamboo stick, shifting the logs until finally the flame caught and flared.

It was a hot night. I fanned myself with the hem of my dress as the heat reached us. "We've gotten quite used to tigers," I said looking off.

He looked amused and tossed the stick aside. "If a tiger has such poor judgment as to turn up here tonight, my wager's on you."

I smiled, feeling confident.

He gave a high, shrill whistle, then settled back against the tree. After a moment a young brown man emerged from the forest. The Dane gave him instructions in a low voice. The young man's eyes wandered toward us, then he nodded and disappeared. Soon he was back with two cups of tea, two teaspoons, and a small bowl of brown sugar on a tray. Also on the tray were a large bottle of gin, a smaller one of vermouth, a pack of English cigarettes, and three glasses.

I hadn't had a cigarette since Harvey and I arrived in Siam. He lit two and handed one to me and one to Judith. I closed my eyes and inhaled slowly. As the smoke slid down my throat, I began to feel languid and relaxed. I shrugged off my riding jacket and yanked out the ribbon that held my hair off my neck.

We laughed and bantered while the smoke rose from the fire, drifting to the tops of the tall hardwood trees. His eyes were the color of lapis lazuli, and they lingered on mine as the hours passed. When the tea was gone, we drank gin and vermouth and smoked more of his cigarettes. The bitter drink burned, but soon I began to enjoy the blend of alcohol and smoke. By the time we realized that we had not eaten dinner, it was past nine o'clock.

"Where is the cook?" I asked.

The Dane shrugged. "You were a surprise," he said. "We've made no arrangements."

"Can you try that whistle again?" Judith asked.

He grinned and hooking his fingers in the corners of his mouth, gave out a loud blast. We waited, but no one came. I gazed through the trees, into the empty darkness where fireflies danced. *Oh well,* I thought, *who needs food?*

The Dane poured another round, an inch or two of gin and a few drops of vermouth. Judith rose and began to dance, moving slowly, dreamlike to secret music. A shower of sparks shot from the flames and, as I watched and smoked and sipped my drink, the fire blurred to streaks of copper and gold, and the heat from the flames felt good as it sank through my skin, dissolving each muscle and sinew one by one. With a pleasant feeling of fatigue, I lounged back against the wide trunk of the tree.

The Dane moved aside to give me room, stretching length-wise on the ground and twisting toward me as he propped himself on one elbow. I glanced down, startled to see how close he was but too tired to move.

He gave me a lazy smile. "You have a bit of the devil in your blue eyes," he said in a low and husky voice.

"I've been told that before," I said with a chuckle that seemed to come from someone else.

"What are two young women doing alone in this god-forsaken place?"

"We're on our way to Chiang Mai," I replied in a careless tone, "to visit friends."

"But where is your husband?" He glanced at the gold band on my finger.

In a flash I knew I would not tell him that Harvey was a missionary. With a vague feeling of guilt, I veiled my eyes and drew on the cigarette. "My husband is in Nan on business."

"What is his business?"

"He's a physician." I tilted back my head to let the smoke drift from my mouth and glanced at him.

He cocked one eyebrow. "Ah—a medical missionary. But why isn't he with you? I wouldn't let you out of my sight."

I was flustered. "At the last moment he was unable to leave," I murmured while I inspected the tip of the cigarette.

"I'm surprised to find the wife of a missionary sitting at my campfire without her husband." He paused. "That's a little unusual, you must admit."

I looked at him and frowned. "I can't see why. Perhaps you've been here too long." The sudden reminder of the Nan mission was irritating. "These days ladies seldom require chaperones."

He puffed on his cigar. I watched it glow, then dim. "I see," he said. "Well. Things have certainly changed in the world." He looked at me and grinned. "If I were your husband, I think I might take better care of you."

"Harvey is a conscientious man," I snapped. The cigarette had lost its taste. I flicked it into the fire and added, "It's a matter of responsibility to his patients."

"Hmmm," he drawled. Now the grin stretched, creasing his rugged face, and a spray of wrinkles appeared at the corners of his eyes. "Somehow, my conscience disappears after sundown and a few good drinks. But missionaries can keep their morals. I prefer to take my rewards here on earth."

He was a handsome man. I looked down at him, and looked away, fixing my eyes on the flames.

"Would you like another?" He nudged the bottle toward my glass. His voice had grown intimate. Surprised, I glanced down to see the glass already empty. Perhaps I'd have one more . . .

"Oh . . . no, thank you," my conscience said instead.

"*If you were the only girl in the world, and I were the only boy* . . ." Judith's voice drifted from the other side of the fire. It was a song that Harvey liked, one of his favorites.

". . . *we would go on loving* . . . whoop!" Judith stumbled and laughed. "I wish we had a phonograph," she called as she swayed. I watched as she stretched up her arms and returned to her dance. Shadows from the flames danced with her. "Bring on the band! Where's the Victrola?"

The Dane was silent. He cupped his hands to light another cheroot. When he looked up he caught my eyes. His were indigo now, deep and dangerous. The back of my neck pricked, but I could not look away. He plucked the cigar from his mouth and leaned close, reached up his hand—with the cigar—and caught a curl of my long hair between his fingers. He held it up to the light. It was the color at the center of the fire.

Suddenly I heard Harvey's voice, as if he were sitting next to me. "Marmalade hair," he whispered. The Dane brushed my cheek with the curl. Harvey's face shimmered into a quiet smile, and with a sudden movement, I twisted my face from the hand with the curl. The lock of hair dropped from the Dane's fingers as the trees whirled.

Avoiding his eyes, I placed my hands, palms down on the ground beside me and pressed them into the earth while I tried to order my thoughts. I felt the Dane shift his weight, leaving a space between us now, and I took a long, slow breath. Then watching the fire and Judith and the trees, I exhaled and began to push myself up. "We had better get some sleep," I called to Judith, to seal the decision.

"*There would be such wonderful things to do . . .*" Judith's voice faded as she turned away, still dancing, arms stretched to the sky.

"It would be a shame to waste such a night," the Dane whispered, pointing his cheroot toward the stars that sparkled through the lacy branches of the trees.

His voice was deep and sensual. For an instant—for one split second—I felt lovely and soft and I wanted to stay. I turned and looked down at him, but with a long, slow smile, I shook leaves and grass from my skirt, turned and swayed around the fire to Judith. I grasped her arm, and, still singing, she let me lead her away from the fire and the danger and toward our bungalow.

"I was worried about tigers," he said in a lazy voice behind us. "If I had known that all I had was rabbits, I could have done without the fire."

I jerked my head around and he chuckled. "It's a dangerous game you're playing, Mrs. Perkins," he said softly.

"I don't know what you mean," I said, turning back toward the bungalow.

"Oh, I think you do."

I tossed my head and steered Judith—still humming—toward the bungalow, but now my back was straight and stiff. When we reached the door, I hesitated for a moment, then, feeling his eyes on me, I turned. The tip of his cheroot still burned in the darkness, a red glow, solitary and brooding. From the interior of the cabin, Judith finished her song, a raw, fatigued sound, drawing out the last words. *"And if I were the only boy . . ."*

I shivered and pushed myself through the door.

In the morning we were again delayed. The Dane, now somewhat cool, informed us that protocol required us to wait for the prince and his entourage to pass before starting out. This was royalty from Bangkok, and they were somewhat unpredictable, he said. An attendant in the royal party arrived to make sure that we understood the warning. He told us that the caravan was made of three hundred ponies, thirty elephants, fourteen hundred carriers, and one thousand guards. Judith looked at me and raised her eyebrows. That sounded somewhat extravagant to me, as well, but we waited for an interminable period before we were allowed to fall in behind the royal train.

We proceeded on the narrow trail through thick undergrowth of bamboo beneath a canopy of tall hardwood trees. Some trees had shed their leaves and these lay on the ground, brown and dry, crackling under the pony's hooves. After a few hours Judith had moved well ahead, and I found myself left alone with only a few of the carriers. Our path followed the curve of a hill that dropped to a stream on our left.

We were picking our way through a clump of bamboo that encroached on the path when I heard rustling in the thicket below. My pony tensed and pricked his ears. As I tightened the reins the carrier nearest me stopped dead. "Mem!" he said in a hushed voice, and pointed.

Following his direction I saw branches and leaves rippling below at my left. As I watched, through the foliage a large gray snake slowly reached up. I stifled a scream and held onto the reins while the pony danced. But the snake dropped, coiling around a batch of green leaves on a low branch. My thoughts churned, then slowly it dawned that this was not a snake—it was too thick and rough skinned for that. It was an elephant's trunk.

Sensing the carrier's eyes on me, I assumed a neutral expression and leaned forward once more, peering through the bushes. The path was on a rise and below I could see the elephant standing near the stream. The pony quivered when I pulled back, stunned at the size of the animal—much larger than the ones kept at the Philadelphia Zoo. "Hold steady," I begged the pony in a whisper.

The din of an iron bell shattered the silence. I flinched and fear shot from my spine and spread as I recalled a warning at

Phrae that bad-tempered rogues were tagged with these iron bells when they were released into the jungle by logging crews. The pony tensed under my legs. The Dane's face rose before me and I fumed as the clang reverberated again through the forest.

The carriers halted at once, recognizing the sound. I looked back at them, poised and listening, and knew that they would melt away into the trees. My thoughts scattered. *Oh help*, I thought, with the sinking feeling that I was on my own. Judith and the rest of our caravan were long gone.

Hollow bamboo cracked as the big animal moved closer. Paralyzed, I watched the movement of the trunk in the thicket. It seemed to have developed a life of its own now, cleverly and neatly reaching for each little leaf. Beads of perspiration formed at my temples. I lifted the reins to snap the pony into a run, when a shadow moved between the rouge elephant and me. A small brown man took the pony's bit in one hand and placed his other hand on the pony's neck, stroking it.

"He is too close, Mem," the carrier warned in a low voice. "If you frighten him, he will charge." I nodded. With a grave look he inspected the path before us. Following his eyes, I could see that the trail dipped down to the stream not far from where the elephant stood, then ascended on the other side. The spot was dangerously close to the rogue, but as I twisted in the saddle and looked back at the bamboo thicket, I knew there was no other way to go.

*Hold steady, Babs,* I heard my father say. My heart pounded in my ears, but I lectured myself: *You're a suffragette,* I told myself, *and Harvey's wife.* A missionary's wife cannot run away.

I closed my eyes, and when I opened them again, the other carriers were gliding up around us, forming loose lines on either side of my pony. The carrier holding the bit glanced back and nodded once, then began to lead the pony slowly forward while I sat immobile, gripping the reins. I sucked in my breath as we moved toward the stream, the pony and I, surrounded by the barefoot guard. I looked down at the carriers and one smiled up at me. Despite his missing teeth, and his skeletal, tattooed frame, I was filled with affection for him, for all of them. They could have left me there alone.

I had been wrong about them, I realized as we moved down the trail together. What I had assumed was apathy, a passive view of life, was really a different sort of courage. These jungle people of Siam had learned to take things as they came, to enjoy life and deal with hardships one at a time instead of giving in.

As we moved closer to the stream, the rogue elephant came into full view. Huge, gray, and leathery, the behemoth shifted its weight, ringing the bell as it swayed slightly from side to side and watched our approach through hooded eyes. Its long ivory tusks gleamed in the half-light of the jungle.

"Don't look at him," my guide whispered. "He senses fear. You must think of something . . ." He used a Siamese word for joy, or happiness.

Despite my terror, I smiled, remembering a song . . . *with rings on her fingers and bells on her toes* . . . we reached the stream and the pony hesitated . . . *she shall have music wherever she goes* . . . *and elephants to ride upon* . . . the carrier gave a gentle tug and the pony followed him into the water.

The bell again sounded behind us, but I didn't hear the great rogue move. As we reached the other side of the stream and ascended toward a turn in the path just ahead, I felt the release of tension and looked down to my guards. The brown man gazed back at me, grim-faced, then he raised his elbow straight out in front of him, clenched his fist and, with an almost imperceptible

motion, gave a slight pump of his arm in the universal sign of triumph. As I looked at them all, I remembered something I'd once
read: Cowards die many times, but brave men only die once.

We rounded a bend in the trail and a copse of trees, and my
guide dropped his hand from the pony's bit. With a flush of pride
I flicked the reins, nudging the pony on while I imagined the
letter I'd write to Dad about this, and about what I'd learned.
The path ahead was broad and straight, and further on were
Judith and the rest of the caravan, waiting for us to catch up.

It was seven in the evening when we finally arrived at Phrae,
where we thankfully put ourselves in the hands of the missionaries in residence. Traveling from Phrae to Chiang Mai by train
was most comfortable after several days on the pony. The railroad to Chiang Mai was still fairly new. Until its completion, all
travel to that remote city was overland through the thick, harsh
jungle, or by river, as it remained for Nan. The train stopped for
the night at a rest house.

About ten days after our departure from Nan we arrived
in Chiang Mai, the glorious city of palms. The city sat in the
shelter of an immense mountain rising from the rice plain.
The slopes of the monolith were covered with tea gardens that
provided a living to the people of Chiang Mai who picked the
leaves. I had it from good authority that at the pinnacle a temple
marked the location of a true footprint of the Buddha.

The city, overflowing its ancient vine-covered walls, was
located about one thousand feet above sea level on both sides
of the Mae Ping River. The mission compound, including a
boys' school, the mission press, a dispensary, and a hospital, was

located on the riverbanks. The hospital and dispensary did a brisk business—Dr. James McKean and his wife, who managed the mission, had been in Siam for more than twenty-five years, and thousands of patients were under their care. The printing press had fonts of Siamese and Laos, as well as English, and the mission translated and printed Bibles, catechisms, tracts, textbooks, reference works, and hymnbooks for the entire northern part of the country, as well as for Burma and Laos.

Our mission hosts immediately set about making Judith and me comfortable. Dr. Cord was a kind and gentle man, loved by everyone in the province. Most of his patients were unable to pay for his services, but he never turned down any request and seemed to obtain great joy merely from the doing of the thing. "Healing the sick is a good opportunity for spreading the gospel," he said, smiling as he tucked Scriptures and tracts into packages of medicine distributed at the dispensary.

In Chiang Mai we were showered with golden sunshine. The days faded into lovely nights full of stars that peeked through the branches of cocopalm trees. From my bedroom window I had a view of the river bustling with traffic and lined with small, graceful houseboats. Large teak logs lodged on the sandbars, and women pounded the family wash against them. Small children with light-brown skin bathed in the cool water, and occasionally an elephant joined them.

On the other side of the river stood a large golden temple. Judith said that a rich Burman had earned much merit by covering the gabled ends of each of the four roofs and the pagoda with an enormous quantity of gold leaf and blue Chinese tiles. As it rose to the sky, each roof was smaller than the one below. The temple blazed in the sun and gleamed in the moonlight, a splendid sight.

Judith and I spent hours wandering the wide, well-kept streets and narrow alleys, strolling through markets stocked with beautiful silver work, woodcarvings, lacquer-ware, and fine fabrics. There were many people of Chinese, Laotian, and Burmese descent, as well as Siamese, in the marketplace, which bustled with activity in the cool mornings. Surprisingly the bartering and buying was orderly and calm. Voices were held to a murmur, laughter was low, soft, and gentle.

The Cords lived next to the palace of another Chow Luang who, like our own in Nan, was a royal prince in his own right. This flamboyant prince, called the king of Chiang Mai, was the most powerful in the north. But Mrs. Cord told us that even this Chow Luang paid tribute to the king in Bangkok, sending a procession of emissaries once a year with gifts of shimmering gold and silver fashioned into the shape of delicate trees of intricate design.

The king of Chiang Mai owned many well-trained elephants that he posed in strategic spots throughout the gardens when he entertained. The enormous lawn that surrounded the palace blazed with electric lights for these festivities almost every evening. Drums rumbled through the night, and stringed instruments provided music that had the peculiar resonance and cadence of Scottish bagpipes. Judith and I peeked from our windows, mesmerized. Through the wide-spaced trees we saw sylphs, young dancers from Laos who had caught the king's fancy, we were told, wearing sarongs made of gold cloth with jewels that caught the light and flashed as they darted among the guests.

"I'd give just about anything to be at that party," I whispered to Judith one night, tapping my hands on the windowsill to the sultry beat of the drums.

One day we came upon a festival of flowers. A procession of lavish floats made of flowers wound its way through the streets inside the city walls. Market women bobbed up and down in coordinated rhythm, carrying baskets balanced on each end of the bamboo sticks across their shoulders. They spread out their sweets and cigarettes and rice cakes for sale under the shade of an occasional palm tree.

A Chinaman walked past with a portable restaurant on his shoulders. On either end of his pole was an entire cupboard containing steaming rice, hot curry, and blue and white dishes to serve in. He swung along easily with his load, his big straw hat tilted at a rakish angle and his black silk trousers flapping around his legs. Another blew fascinating little animals out of red and green taffy, much like a glassblower would fashion figures out of glass. The children danced around him, squealing with delight as he created pigs, dogs, and horses for them with great speed and fastened them onto bamboo sticks.

One night a tall, gilded pavilion with multilayered roofs appeared like magic in the middle of a rice field. Even though a temporary structure, it was carefully painted with flowers of blue and gold. Streamers of white gauze hung from each of the four corners, curtains edged with tinsel that were tied back with garlands of flowers. A cremation ceremony for the high priest of Chiang Mai was held and fireworks exploded through the darkness every night for several nights, their brilliant colors bursting into patterns shaped like trees, then slowly they expanded and branches grew from the center until, finally, from the tips they appeared to shoot forth flames. The deep sound of temple gongs and drums rolled through Chiang Mai all the days and nights of the long funeral ceremony.

On the day of the cremation, a procession of thousands pulled a glittering *catafalque* raised high on top of a funeral sleigh to the rice field. Priests in yellow robes scattered roasted grain to the crowds, a symbol of great blessing. A priest at the head of the procession held high a long white ribbon of cloth, the Thread of Life, which stretched over the crowd and at the other end was attached to the gilded catafalque, so that the virtue of the priest would help him lead the deceased into a future of joy and peace. When the ceremony was over, only the pavilion remained in the rice field, its four white streamers fluttering in the breeze. I was told that with each movement of the gauze a departed soul can pull itself into rebirth by grasping the tinseled edges.

I looked at those streamers and the silver tinsel flashing in the sun and fought a sudden urge to grasp one for myself. I knew that when we returned to Nan, I would think of the sparkling city of Chiang Mai as one longs for sunlight from deep within a cavern. As the time drew near to leave, each day cast its shadow on our lives at Nan. For the first time in a year, I had breathed free of the harsh judgments, disapproving faces, the sheer tedium of endless days alike. In Chiang Mai we had ice, music, electricity, and the view of life was so gay. Even fashion magazines from Europe appeared from time to time.

But when a letter arrived from Harvey asking when I would return, we made plans to leave. My heart was torn at the thought, pulled between my love for Harvey and the new sense of freedom I had discovered in Chiang Mai. Gloom settled around me like a heavy dark mist. Sometimes when I thought of Nan, I found I almost couldn't breathe.

# Chapter Fourteen

JUDITH AND I RETURNED TO NAN in March of the year 1921. Several letters from my father, dated back to January, waited for me. Bits and pieces of family life tumbled from these missives, but somehow the picture they sketched was melancholy. Mummy scribbled a note on the bottom of one that Dad wrote from a sickbed, but Dad added not to worry—he was merely enjoying a brief respite from the hurly-burly of the usual winter problems.

My father had always walked to the train station for work each morning, but now he wrote that on the days that he was able to work, Poley the milkman gave him a ride in his cutter because of the snow and frigid weather. An old artillery horse pulled the sleigh and, Dad wrote, he seemed to brace himself for battle each time the locomotive came in sight. I frowned and returned to the paragraph. Why had he used the words "on the days that I am able to work," I wondered. After a moment I continued to read.

"I'll take the cutter over any motor in bad weather," Dad wrote. "No need to stick to the road. If you were here, Babs, I would add bells to the thing, and with a crack of the whip, we'd scud across the snow."

A lump formed in my throat. I put the letter down on my lap and looked away. The uneasy feeling had returned.

Since returning to Nan from Chiang Mai, I had a new awareness of how completely we were cut off from the rest of the world in our little valley—isolated, surrounded by thick jungle and mountains and people who did not speak our language. Judith had returned to Bangkok. Never before had the days seemed so long, the hours so difficult to fill. Except for visits to the hospital to collect laundry or to sing to the children, I found myself with absolutely nothing to do. Despite my resolve to find a place in the mission, to fit in and make Harvey proud, I felt shut out, unable to be useful or productive.

Harvey decided I was lonely and to the great delight of the children on the river road, brought home a pet monkey, a gibbon. He was covered with glossy, light-brown fur that was wooly and thick. The monkey was always up to tricks, and when I scolded him, his eyes locked with mine and he almost seemed to smile. The assistant commissioner of Nan had given him to Harvey. We just called him "Gibbon."

At first I kept Gibbon tied to a pomoloe tree. The watchman's wife, Ma Ping, took a great interest in him. She was a tiny woman with dark spotted skin concealing delicate birdlike bones. She didn't smile much, but Gibbon seemed to amuse her. Gibbon was soon free and following one or the other of us everywhere. He was a lovable little monkey and often perched companionably on the limbs of the mango tree above my head when I sat outside.

Small boys sometimes came into our yard to throw rocks at ripe fruit in the tree, hoping that it would fall. The mango tree was Gibbon's preserve and this caused him great agitation. After much chatter and hopping back and forth between the tree and the veranda, he would launch himself through the air, swinging through the branches and drop with a thud in front of the surprised children. Usually they turned and ran, and at this lucky turn of events, Gibbon would give chase.

Since returning from Chiang Mai, I woke each morning with dread, thinking of the long empty day ahead, the time that I had to fill. One day I came to realize that my entire frame of reference was dependent upon Harvey—my days were measured by Harvey's schedule, the time that he would be home for lunch, the time when flowers must be picked or arrangements made for dinner. It was all Harvey's time, I thought with surprise.

Harvey accused me of brooding. "What is it you'd like to do?" he asked one night.

I thought about that. "I suppose I'd like to go to a dinner party in a room that's lit with electric lights, with dancing and music—Western music, not Siamese—and we'd have champagne that's cold, on ice. I'd like to wear beautiful clothes and sparkling things in my hair and have people to talk to other than missionaries. People with interesting ideas and conversation about something other than religion." I folded my hands on the table in front of me with slow, deliberate movements to camouflage my restless mood.

❧

On the next Sunday after church, while Harvey chatted with the Ruckels, I cornered Mr. Breeden. "I *must* take on a regular job in this mission," I told him, struggling to keep the sound of desperation from my voice. Amalie Breeden stood by his side and one brow slowly rose at my words. I ignored her and went on. "I'd like to organize a children's choir for service. Learning our hymns might help their reading skills."

He gave me a wintry look. "That's not necessary, Mrs. Perkins."

I faltered.

"We feel the children's time is better spent on studies and Scriptures," Amalie Breeden said. "Music is *such* an indulgence."

"That's a foolish statement." My voice grew heated. "Music has always been used in worship; it's a way of communicating that's not limited by differences in language." I looked at her and frowned. "Even in illiterate cultures music expresses shared emotions. It arouses us. Just think how jungle tribes use instruments, conch shells or drums and flutes in warfare."

"Emotions should be directed toward the Lord, Mrs. Perkins," Mr. Breeden said in a bored tone, wiping his forehead with a handkerchief. He glanced at the blazing sun while he added, "It's a grievous error to mistake emotion for truth."

I was shaken by his words. But the idea took hold. Mr. Breeden hadn't *forbidden* a children's choir, he'd merely said that it wasn't necessary. That afternoon I found Ai Mah working in the hospital ward. We sat together on the open porch between the small buildings while I explained my idea to him. He listened and nodded as I talked and when I left, he wore a smile that probably had more to do with the possibility of agitating Mr. Breeden than the promise of a children's choir.

The children whispered to each other in excited tones as I passed out the music sheets. It had taken me several days to copy on paper the songs they would learn, but I knew if I tried to remove that many hymnbooks from the mission church it would be noticed. I wasn't quite ready for a full confrontation with Mr. Breeden.

Ai Mah had rounded up ten of the younger students for the choir, and including himself and Boua Keo, that made twelve in all. We gathered in the shade of the mango tree and started with songs that I'd already introduced in the Sunday services. They all seemed proud to have been chosen and threw themselves into the work of singing as a group with great energy. Three days a week the boys and girls walked down the river road to our house for practice after school. The children's voices were clear and sweet, and more often than not Kham Noi and Tip and Ma Ping stopped what they were doing to sit on the veranda steps and listen.

"It's good to hear you singing again," Harvey said one evening. He gave me a small hug and smiled.

"Just wait until you hear the children," I told him. "They're wonderful. The voices harmonize perfectly. Ai Mah certainly chose well."

"I've been a little worried, Babs," Harvey said. He sat and pulled me down onto his lap. "You've seemed at loose ends for a while, but this little choir is your own unique contribution to the mission. I'm very proud of you."

I leaned against him and dismissed a frisson of worry, knowing it had not occurred to Harvey that the choir was not yet officially sanctioned.

"Are they going to sing this Sunday?" he asked.

"Not yet. We'll give a surprise performance in a couple of weeks." I skimmed my finger up his neck and circled his ear. "But we can explore the rhythm and harmony of the music right now if you'd like."

The isolation at Nan was interrupted one day by the arrival of Dr. Kerr, a British citizen employed as a botanist for the Siamese government. To celebrate the occasion, the Ruckels invited everyone in the mission to dinner to meet him. Our visitor told of a mysterious gentleman reported to be on his way to Nan. "No one knows anything about him," he said. "He arrived in Bangkok from the Middle East and, before we knew it, had gone. That was a month ago."

"How interesting!" I exclaimed with delight. Mr. Breeden knitted his brows and his wife glanced at Mrs. Pitters and rolled her eyes at my words.

"It doesn't take a month to get to Nan from Bangkok. Perhaps he's lost," Emma said.

"Ah, but I haven't finished, Miss Mamsey," Dr. Kerr teased. "On my way through, I heard from the mission in Phrae that he actually arrived there but then disappeared alone into the jungle."

Mrs. Ruckel's eyes widened and everyone looked disappointed.

Visitors were rare at Nan and Emma took the opportunity to help herself to another piece of bread. A line appeared between Miss Best's eyebrows as she watched—the mission frowned on second helpings.

"Do you think he's really headed for Nan?" I asked.

Before he could respond, Emma interrupted. "Not unless he's lost," she said, buttering the bread. Mr. Breeden scowled, but Emma remained unperturbed as she popped the bread into her mouth.

A few weeks later the routine of the mission was once again interrupted by the arrival of a package marked "Holiday Bookshop." It was addressed to Joshua Smithers "in care of the missionaries" at Nan and delivered directly to Mrs. Ruckel. The box was torn and shabby. Through tears in the corners, we could see that it contained books.

"Perhaps it's for the mysterious Englishman," I said.

"Maybe he really is on his way here," Mrs. Ruckel said as Emma pushed back a corner of the cardboard exposing the name of an author, a philosopher named William James. I wanted the book desperately, having read everything I had brought with me from Philadelphia several times by now.

The book did not interest Emma. She pushed back into her chair with a puzzled look. "Why would someone wandering through the jungles of Siam be shipping books ahead?" Emma asked.

Mrs. Ruckel was perplexed as well. She shook her head. "I could certainly understand medicine or clothing," she murmured, "but books?"

I thought privately that books were a good choice. Later when Mrs. Breeden arrived, to my chagrin Emma showed her the package. She glanced at the spine of the book I wanted, visible through the tear in the box. "William James is hardly appropriate reading for this mission," she said with a frown. I changed the subject quickly, hoping to distract her. Once Mr. Breeden learned of the book, I'd have little chance of reading it, I knew.

Every day I found an excuse to visit the Ruckel house, hoping that the owner of the books would appear, but as the days passed with no sign of him, slowly my interest waned. Once Emma rode out on her wheels to announce that a visitor had arrived and I rushed to the Ruckels' in a frenzy of excitement, but it was only a British diplomat wandering through. Gradually we all began to forget about the mysterious Englishman and turned our attention back to the concerns of the mission.

The children's choir was becoming quite proficient. On practice days I waited on the veranda, watching the boys and girls run up the drive from the river road. Sunlight gleamed on the tops of their small heads and, as they neared, faces turned up with their excited smiles. Ai Mah sometimes excused himself to work in the hospital, but Boua Keo always accompanied them. When the children's voices rose in song, it seemed to me that the music brought us together, united the little group in a new form of friendship that had not existed before.

After several weeks of practice, I announced to the children that the choir would sing in church on the following Sunday. "You will sit in the front row, together, on the left, just beside the organ," I told them.

"Boys and girls together, Mem?" one of the older children asked.

"Yes," I said firmly. "We certainly can't have a decent choir if we're scattered all over the room, can we?"

They giggled. Ai Mah's eyes flicked toward me, then away.

With some reticence Emma agreed to help arrange the children on the first row according to plan. "If nothing else," she said in a dry tone, "this may shorten the service."

On the way to church in the surrey on Sunday morning, Harvey was unusually quiet. "Don't worry, it's going to be wonderful," I said, patting his hand. "Just wait and see. Even the Breedens will have to appreciate the effort these children put into their songs." My eyes skimmed over a pretty flock of small green parrots perched on bushes near the bank of the river as we rode by. "Besides," I added, "they're singing hymns, not popular songs."

"Hmmm," he murmured, concentrating on the ponies.

We arrived early and I busied myself with arranging the hymnals. Books were in short supply and had to be shared.

The children arrived on schedule and Emma managed to steer the choir members properly to the first pew on the left side, boys and girls together. Miss Best stood immobile while this took place, and I saw her hiss something to Emma before they each took their seats. I ducked my head and hid a smile.

Reverend Ruckel, who usually enjoyed modest success in moderating the tone of things, was absent from the church service that morning. Mr. Breeden rose to preach. He must not have noticed the choir before, because as he opened his Bible and looked out over the congregation, he suddenly coughed and seemed fixed upon the sight of the little boys and girls sitting together in the front row. After a moment his head swiveled toward me and back to the congregation. Then he slammed the Bible shut.

As he began to speak, I realized with astonishment that he had abandoned whatever it was he had planned to say in favor of an impromptu sermon. My stomach churned as I heard him describing what Mummy always referred to as "the horrible decree," the idea that everything—*everything*—in life is predetermined by our own God according to Christian rules. There's no saving grace to change that.

"No one can deny that God knew eternal damnation would be our fate when he created Adam and Eve and they sinned." Mr. Breeden's voice was hushed as he preached. "No man can doubt that certain nations and people and *even children* are condemned to eternal death because of this sin."

As he ranted on, from my perch at the organ I glanced around the church. Ai Mah's face was closed, except that his eyes were narrowed and hard as he gazed at Mr. Breeden. The choir sat on the edge of their seats with a row of big, round eyes. They had not yet sung a note, yet somehow they were fully aware that they'd inspired this sermon.

Mr. Breeden gazed out over the congregation. Then his voice began to rise. "Our God is a *jealous* God. The number of those condemned to the *lake of fire, to burn for eternity*, is fixed and certain. You may be one of these!" His voice thundered now as he reached a crescendo.

*"This is the will of God!"*

The words echoed through the church. I was so shocked that I almost missed the cue for the first hymn when he'd finished. The little voices in the front row rose dutifully, in shrill, strained harmony. I looked down at them from my perch in front of the organ and smiled encouragement, but it was no use. They were terrified.

No mention was made of the choir as Harvey and I walked down the aisle in front of Mr. Breeden after the service. The congregation was unusually quiet as we made our exits.

I commented to Harvey that perhaps the sermon was a bit harsh for our guests.

"It's written in the *Confession*," Mr. Breeden said over my shoulder in a tone of withering scorn.

"I have always thought the Scriptures joyful," I answered. "But those words were dreadful."

At first I thought that he had not heard me. I turned and he leaned down and thrust his face into mine, speaking in a low, harsh voice that trembled with rage. "Suffering is part of God's plan, Mrs. Perkins. It is fear, not joy, that leads us."

I stared at him in disbelief.

He clucked his tongue and shook his head as he straightened. "You would be wise to spend some time on our teachings, Mrs. Perkins. Our fates—yours, mine, *theirs*"—he gave a nod toward the choir scattering across the lawn—"have already been determined." He wheeled away, then turned with a parting shot. "In fact, I've often wondered if you weren't brought here exactly to test that very point." He wagged his finger at me. "Fate, Mrs. Perkins. Fate! There is *no such thing* as karma to change fate, despite what the Buddhists may believe."

He was gone before I could retort.

As Harvey and I rode home, I thought of the expression that I had caught on Ai Mah's face. Everything Mr. Breeden said in his sermons conflicted with the religious experience and philosophies of the Siamese people. In Siam, lives revolved around Buddhism and were structured by it. Temples formed the center of life in every town and village; even the smallest village had one. Most young men served some time as Buddhist monks, if only temporarily. The people of the country were completely immersed in Buddhist principles. Buddhist thought gave them a sense of peace in face of the ravages of nature. *"It is fear, not joy that leads us."* Trying to capture the minds and hearts of these people with Mr. Breeden's fiery sermons seemed as futile as trying to imprison the wind.

Perhaps music could still give them a few brief moments of happiness. I resolved to round up the choir members and try again. But in my heart I knew that the children were frightened now and my idea had failed.

Ai Mah's face rose before me and I glanced at Harvey with sudden fear for the disappointment that I knew would come. The boy would never convert. Mr. Breeden's threats of hell and damnation would fail in this regard. Ai Mah was a Buddhist through and through. In addition, although they had no place in Buddhist teachings, the spirits, the *phis*, also governed Ai Mah's life and those of his people. Despite pervasive hunger, the tiny shrines that stood on bamboo poles before almost every house in the Nan Valley were kept filled with offerings of rice for these spirits. Ai Mah believed that the spirits brought good fortune—not Harvey, not his medicine, and certainly not Mr. Breeden or his God.

Ai Mah once told Harvey, "When my buffalo dies, I will cut into his liver and look for a stone that will protect me from all harm."

The choir regrouped and I personally led the children into the church each Sunday morning under Mr. Breeden's glare and sat them in the front pew on the left. This small rebellion in his church seemed to astound the headmaster, but neither Dr. or Mrs. Ruckel, nor Harvey, appeared to be perturbed by the presence of the mixed choir, and everyone else seemed to enjoy the music. Mr. Breeden kept silent week after week, and my pride grew each time the children sang. And I let down my guard.

Then one early morning I was playing the organ in the empty church when the front door opened and a razor of light split the altar. Startled, I turned my head to see a tall silhouette, backlit by the sun. Mr. Breeden was hatless and stood still and quiet in the doorway, even after my hands lifted from the keys and the music died away. The hair on my arms rose in spite of the heat.

"Good morning," I said, struggling for a confident tone and thinking how strange it was to see him standing there, motionless and silent. My voice seemed to echo through the church as I waited. He didn't answer. "Good morning," I repeated, thinking that he probably hadn't heard.

Still, Mr. Breeden said nothing and an ominous chill ran through me. From across the field in the distance, I could hear the voices of the children at the mission schoolhouse. A door slammed somewhere, then thick silence while I waited for him to speak. Staring, I watched as he stepped inside the church without a sound and closed the door behind him. The latch clicked in warning, and with disbelief I watched Mr. Breeden moving slowly down the aisle toward me.

"Are you looking for something?" I asked, conscious that my voice was strained. I braced my hands on the bench and gripped it as he advanced. "I'm almost finished here if you need for me to leave," I added, putting a lilt into my voice and watching him with sharpened senses as I picked up the hymnbook I'd been using. To my eternal regret, I tried to smile. Weaker monkeys in a pack will smile when they are frightened, Harvey had once said.

He drew closer, and even in the dim light I saw the contempt in his eyes. With a pounding heart, I pushed myself up from the bench and stumbled. The floor rushed toward me and I threw out my hands, landing on all fours, with the hymnal spread open beside me.

Scrambling to my knees, I grasped the bench to rise when a weight pressed me back down to the floor, a hand upon my head that bowed my neck. I struggled against the weight of his hand, struggled to look up at him, to look him in the face, but his fingers gripped my skull, holding me down in a steel vise, and I found I couldn't move. Fury rose with sobs into my throat, and pride choked them back while I fought against the weight of Mr. Breeden's hand.

When he spoke, his voice was unearthly, hollow—like the man inside. *"Those that refuse to understand . . . those who refuse to ask forgiveness . . . those are the hopeless ones, the condemned."* Bending before him, my teeth ground together with fury and I struggled again to rise. But with each movement, he shoved me harder, holding me before him and grinding my knees into the wooden floor so that the pain knifed through my bones. Tears spilled then—tears of hatred and terror and fierce humiliation—but I would not let him see me wipe them away, would not give him that satisfaction.

A hiss escaped his lips as his grip tightened on my head. "Better men than me have said this—but I say it once again to you, Mrs. Perkins: *The pit is prepared . . . the fire is made ready . . . the furnace is hot to receive you . . . the flames already rage and glow."*

He waited, seeming to expect some response, and I gave him none.

He leaned down and put his mouth to my ear. "Perhaps you don't understand," he whispered. His voice was monotone now, flat and cold. "The authority of this mission will *not* be undermined by your disobedience. Do you understand?" He forced my head from side to side in the vise. "If you continue flouting propriety, your husband will pay the price. Or Ai Mah will pay the price. *Do . . . you . . . understand?*" He shook my head with each word.

Enraged, with all my might I reached up and, circling his wrists with my hands, tore his from my head. He flung mine off, as if my touch burned, and with that I twisted from under him, gasping. Lifting my eyes to his, I sucked in my breath and stared as I rose and backed away from him.

He raised his hand—I thought—to slap my face, but I looked back at him, breathing hard and lifted my chin, daring him with my eyes to touch me again, prepared to scream. Slowly he lowered his arm and stood rigid, his face turned to stone. Seconds passed as his eyes burned into mine, and then he turned away and walked back down the aisle to the front door. I watched him go, hardly daring to breathe as he pulled open the door and stepped into the blinding light without a backward glance. When the door closed behind him, I released my breath.

Still watching the door, I dropped to the bench and wiped the tears from my cheeks. The drum in my chest finally slowed. *He's insane*, I thought. Another wave of terror turned my eyes to the door, expecting to see it open once again. After a few moments I came to my senses, lurched from the bench, and tore down the aisle, leaving the hymnal on the floor where it had fallen.

All I could think of was Harvey! I wheeled down the river road on my bicycle through the dust and heat, swerving blindly around carts and animals and people, wanting only to reach home and Harvey. Harvey would hold me and I'd be safe— he'd know what to do. But as I turned in at the hedge and raced up the drive, Harvey rushed through the front door with his medical bag, trailed by Ai Mah. I had reached the steps and dropped the bicycle when Harvey stopped to wait. Ai Mah flew past, breaking into a run.

I looked at Harvey and heard the hiss of Mr. Breeden's voice: *Your husband will pay the price. Or Ai Mah*. In that moment I realized that a confrontation between Harvey and Mr. Breeden on my account would finish his career here.

Harvey's eyes swept past me to Ai Mah, who was halfway to the river road. "I have to go, Babs," he said, turning to me, his eyes narrowed with tension. "It's urgent. There's fever in a village up in the mountains."

*Hold steady, Babs*. I tried to smile as I fingered the collar of his shirt. "How long will you be gone?" I asked, surprised to hear that my voice was steady.

Hefting the medical bag into the crook of his arm, he leaned over and kissed my cheek. "Two days, maybe three," he said. His eyes traveled over me. "That must have been some bicycle ride," he said, touching my disheveled hair. He looked at me again. "Is something wrong, Babs?" he asked. "You look upset."

I smoothed my hair and tucked stray strands behind my ears. "Well, yes, something is wrong," I said in a careful tone. "I have to talk to you. It's about Mr. Breeden."

He glanced over his shoulder and I did the same. Ai Mah stood just outside the hedge. I could see that he was waiting. Harvey shifted his weight from one hip to the other. "Can it wait?" he asked, giving me an intent and searching look.

I opened my mouth and found that I couldn't speak. His eyes flicked to the road and back again. How could I describe the humiliation, the violation—the spiritual rape—that I'd just endured in the seconds that I had left, with Harvey ready to bolt. I took a breath and tried. "I was in the church, practicing on the organ . . ."

"Look here, Babs," he said, shifting the medical bag back into his hand. His voice was kind, but I heard the note of impatience. "If it's about the choir, I'm afraid you'll have to handle it yourself right now. I've got to hurry." He squinted at me when I didn't answer, and his voice held a slightly peevish tone as he added, "Can't it wait a bit?"

I needed time to think this through. "Yes. Of course," I said with a tight smile. As I watched him hurry down the drive toward Ai Mah with his long loping stride, I thought of Mr. Breeden's warning again and slowly realized that this would have to be my secret.

And as I'd expected, when he returned several days later, Harvey became engrossed in his medical practice, his patients, the hospital, Ai Mah, and all of Siam, and he never raised the subject again. Or else he had forgotten. I learned to live with my fear of Mr. Breeden after that by avoiding the church when it was empty and by avoiding him. We were mutually cold from that day on but polite—when it was necessary. *But if he touches me again*, I resolved, *I'll fight and he'll have to kill me.*

A new and curious thought flicked through my mind occasionally after that day: Just what *is* the price of love—and faith?

# Chapter Fifteen

ON THE VERANDA ONE NIGHT IN early spring, I leaned back against Harvey and watched the moon. As the evening salute of temple drums rolled around us and joined others far across the Nan Valley, amber light from the rising moon gleamed through the mango tree. The tree seemed to capture the glow, as if the thick, dark branches were dusted with gold. Harvey's arms tightened around me. While we watched the moon rise the drumbeat grew until finally the cadence of the drums and the beating of my heart seemed to merge. When at last the moon emerged, hanging like a globe over the tree, I realized that the drums had stopped.

The air was soft and sultry, filled with the white fragrance of jasmine and the sparkle and dark mystery of a warm tropical night. In the new silence we heard only the songs of tree frogs and cicada. Harvey's fingers ran through my hair and drifted down my neck, brushing my flesh and sending shivers through me. He lifted my chin and explored my eyes. Love swelled inside, and then his face disappeared as the silk of his lips covered my own. His lips were soft when they moved, caressing mine, and as we kissed a warm mist embraced us. We were a part of each other, Harvey and I.

One Sunday, weeks later, as I pumped the bellows in the mission church, a flush of warmth came over me and suddenly I felt faint. It took every ounce of my strength to finish. That afternoon as I sat listless on Mrs. Ruckel's porch complaining of fatigue, she gave me a close look and her soft face lit with a smile.

"You won't be lonely much longer, little Barbara," she said. I was perplexed at her words, but she did not explain.

A few days later we learned that our first child was on the way. Harvey pressed me to him and kissed my forehead, radiant at the discovery. As months passed the joy settled around us, but once in a while when I thought of the babe that grew within me, a new rush of excitement surged through my chest—*exhilaration*—an ephemeral flash of pleasure, like sliding down a moonbeam.

In the fall of 1921 a thick envelope arrived from home. Mail had not come in a long time, so I opened it with great anticipation. Two letters fell to the floor, one from my father and one from my sister Evie.

*Ah-ha!* I thought happily as I bent down to pick them both up.

I took a seat in my old cane chair on the veranda and read the one from Dad first, dated last April. He still seemed to be somewhat ill and spoke of neighbors sending up delicious meals for him, and sweet oranges and grapefruit sent by friends in Florida. He said that he was loafing in bed and thought that he might have a touch of malaria, described as a six-inch chill, by which, he wrote in an amusing aside, he meant the amplitude of the vibrations in which his body engaged. Copious quinine doses were being administered, however, and surgical X-rays at great expense were scheduled in a few weeks.

Malaria? I stopped reading for a moment. How on earth could he get such a thing in Philadelphia? I shrugged and read on.

The peach tree was in bloom, he wrote. Small white stars had blossomed at the tips of its thin branches and tender shoots of leaves were appearing. And, Evie and Alice had slicked up a spot for flowers in a sunny patch of the garden near the old stone wall. I pictured our house, solid, comfortable, unchanging, hewn from the same gray stone glistening with mica.

I could almost feel the soft spring air in Philadelphia as I set his letter aside. The baby moved within me, strong little kicks and punches coming first from one side, then from the other. My due date was only a few months away. I laughed to myself as I thought of how the baby sometimes seemed to jerk to attention, standing straight up in my womb when I sang. Content, I picked up Evie's letter. My glance skimmed the date in the upper right hand corner; about a month after the one from Dad, I noticed.

I began to read, and in the twinkling of an eye my world began to spin. The words seared my heart. I read them twice before I understood.

"Dad is gone," Evie wrote. He had passed away.

*Dead*, said my inner voice, using the harsher word.

I doubled over, then grasped my head with both hands, covering my ears while I squeezed my eyes shut. *"No!"* I breathed. For a moment everything froze. I gasped but couldn't fill my chest with air. Bright spots danced in darkness behind my lids, and then my limbs grew cold and I began to tremble, until finally I could only hug myself and rock and let the keening escape.

Time passed before the rocking motion calmed me; I did not know or care how long it was. I lifted my head and, at last, the truth sliced through me with its sharp, burning pain. I looked down again at the letter, this time with fury. The "malaria" had in fact been cancer, and I could hardly take this in. How could they not have told me this? And, for an instant, I hated all of them, Mummy and Evie and Alice, and even the little boys. *It's not true,* I shouted silently at them. *Charles Otis Bond is too strong, too solid to just disappear!*

Hours passed while my rage turned to anguish and dusk settled. The air grew thick and stale, as if infected by my grief. At last, drained and listless, I forced myself to pick up Evie's letter once again. The one from Dad had been found after his death, she wrote, and the two were sent together in the hope that Evie's would be read first.

As I grasped the paper in my hand, I wondered what I was doing at the moment of his death and the thought consumed me. It's not right that I might have been happy on that day, I cried, breathless with my own betrayal. Perhaps I was laughing on the day that he had died. I turned hollow with the thought, and my eyes burned with the fresh onslaught of tears.

The sun began to set and temple drums rumbled deep and ugly, like thunder in the distance. I looked up and gazed through the twilight at the river road, resentful that the usual traffic still moved past. Clattering carts, foolish people trudging past the hedge, going nowhere, continuing their lives as though nothing had changed! The colors in our yard and on the road were dull, as if the vibrant parts of life were gone, absorbed into a vast, terrible gray cloud.

The river road faded as the gray cloud sank through me and expanded, filling my heart, my chest, my throat, rising into my mind. Dad was my listener, the one who caught my smiles and thoughts and dreams and made them real. In some part, I mused, all of us live in the reflections of those we love. The simple things I wrote in letters home were glorified, interesting, and beautiful to Dad; when I saw them through his eyes, they became adventures. I imagined him as he'd read my words, smiling and proud, shaking his head when something I had written surprised him.

And now, here was his own letter to me—it lay in my lap and spoke to me as if he were still alive. That was the terrible thing. I looked at the words he had written not knowing that they would be his last. Such ordinary, trivial things he had talked of! If he had guessed, what would he have written to me instead, I wondered. A cold, lonely feeling gripped me then, as I realized that never again would I be able to lay my head upon his shoulder, or hear his voice, or see his smile. I wept with the longing and the yearning and the longing . . . wept to have him near.

"I cannot bear it," I sobbed when Harvey arrived. "We're halfway around the world."

Harvey pulled me onto his lap and cradled me against his chest in a grip of iron, as though both of us would shatter if he moved. He'd loved my father, too. After a while he stroked my hair and whispered consolations, empty words, false and full of promises that he could not keep.

"How is it that I didn't know?" I cried. But he had no answers. Finally I collapsed with deep shuddering sighs and he carried me to our bed, where we lay together quiet in the gloom. I fell asleep at last with my face buried in the crook of his arm.

Reverend Ruckel sat beside me when I awoke. "You must pray for strength," he urged gently. "When life becomes too hard, God will help you bear the burden. Just ask."

"I should have known," I wept. "I should have guessed." I looked up at him, stricken at the knowledge that I could have said good-bye. "How could I not have known?" Suddenly I was overcome with the *nothingness*, the bleak fragility of life. "What if death is the end of things?"

"Pray," he said.

I prayed, but no one answered. Instead, a strange detachment took hold. As if my world had faded, the days were dull and flat, passing before me like scenes in a silent film while I waited for each scene to give way to the next. Gibbon watched from the mango tree with a grave, curious look, one arm grasping the branch above, the other stretched across, curling over his shoulder.

One day a few weeks later, everyone in the mission embarked upon a picnic to look at birds in the jungle, but I refused to go.

"Please come, Babs," Harvey urged. His eyes held a worried look. "I need you, too."

I shook my head. "You go along," I said.

"I'm not going without you."

"Leave me alone!" I flung the words at him and turned away, longing for solitude, unwilling to return to the ordinary things of life, to diminish my grief. Finally I heard his angry steps on the wooden floor, the door slammed, and then the bicycle wheels crunched over the hard dirt drive as he rode off.

*Good*, I thought, but the stillness of the room now depressed me. After a moment I wandered out to the veranda, gazing in

the direction of the river. The afternoon was overcast. Across the
road the Nan River was the color of mud. *Funny that I'd never
noticed that before*, I thought absently.

Gibbon watched impassive from his perch in the mango
tree.

And then the baby moved, a sharp little kick that jolted me.
A small red bird swooped down and settled briefly on the rail,
then off it went, lifting, circling up among the branches of the
trees, calling sounds so peculiar that I have never heard again.
The baby moved once more, as if to say, *Here's something new—
I'm here with you.*

Slowly a wave of peace rose, flooding me until it filled each
hollow limb. When it reached my heart, I felt it warm and
soften. A wisp of strength, delicate but strong, like a silver strand
of cobweb in the sun, began to spin its way into my thoughts.
I'm a mother now, I realized. I remembered my father's pride in
me, his love. And then I heard his voice, a whisper in my mind,
gentle now, but firm. *Come, Babs—this won't do for a missionary
wife.*

I straightened in the chair. "Are you there?" I called out.
My voice broke. No answer came, but then . . . somehow he was
there. I had to pick myself up and be strong, I knew. I was made
of tougher fiber now.

I drifted in the stillness for one moment, feeling my father's
presence, then squared my shoulders and recalled again my
mother's words: *The woman is responsible for the spirit of a home.*
For the first time, it occurred to me that her advice was a heavy
burden. But I shook off the thought. Grief is a private thing,
I told myself. Set it aside and don't look back.

Just then a light shower fell, a mist of rain, fine and soft; it
washed the air, fed the flowers and the river and the rice fields.

A gust blew a spray against my skin, cooling the burning anger, cooling the sorrow, and cleansing my parched spirit. Plump drops of water fell from the leaves of the mango tree that sheltered me. As the water touched my skin, my senses sharpened. The babe moved. I pulled myself up and took a deep breath to gather my strength. And then I said good-bye to Dad.

The cobweb shimmered and took hold. The web was spun. Hours later, when Harvey returned, I greeted him with a smile.

He hugged me to him, then said softly, "Welcome back."

Harvey was tense as time passed and the baby grew. One evening he confessed to me his fear of delivering our child alone at Nan. "What if something goes wrong?" he asked. "Not that it will, Babs," he was quick to add. "But we shouldn't take a chance. It's not good practice for a physician, even a medical missionary, to do more than the simplest thing on a patient where emotion is involved."

So when the time came in November, Harvey and I left our home in charge of Kham Noi and journeyed down the Nan River to Phrae, and then by rail to Bangkok for the birth of our child. On the boat I was placed like fine china in the middle of a pile of comfortable cushions. Our boat was little more than a raft made of bamboo and logs. It had a small hut at one end and straw mats on the roof to shield us from the sun.

We traveled with the current, so the boat moved swiftly and our boatmen had a fairly easy job. They wore loincloths over their tattooed legs and loose rags tied around their necks that they used to wipe off perspiration. When the current slowed, the boats were rowed and sometimes even poled, which involved one man at a time moving to the bow and thrusting a bamboo pole ten to twelve feet long into the water and swinging his body around it with all his weight to move the boat forward. The boatmen took turns poling while the captain watched the stream for rocks and logs and other obstacles.

Occasionally we came upon rapids and then Harvey and I climbed out to walk as the carriers hacked our way through the bamboo thicket and the boat was pulled over the dangerous water with heavy ropes. I tired easily, so we stopped frequently and took our meals resting under trees that grew out from the banks of the river. We had to travel slowly this time so the trip from Nan to Phrae, even traveling downstream with the current, took almost six days.

My condition was held in great reverence, and the boatmen took pains to make me comfortable on the journey. Carriers and the cook always preceded us to each stop in a separate boat, so that at mealtimes we found hot food waiting. Water came from the river, but it was purified in a long process. The cook scooped it into huge jars where it was first allowed to settle, then it was boiled and strained for drinking.

We passed villages on the banks of the river and, occasionally, other boats traveling in the opposite direction. Sometimes we glided through thick clumps of trees where bright-colored birds flitted and sang among the branches that stretched out over the water.

Periodically the forest gave way to rice fields and plains, and without the shade of the trees, the heat became intense, searing our skin. All of us were wet with perspiration, and the muscles of the boatmen gleamed like carvings in bronze as they poled and rowed and steered the boat down the river. Sometimes the heat became too much to bear and the boatmen wet down the roof of the hut. Harvey dipped his handkerchief in the river water and laid it over the top of my head.

At night we slept in *sala nam* near the rivers, village rest houses for travelers, no more than platforms and usually situated near small temples. I was huge and clumsy with the baby so it was difficult for me to sleep on the boat. Most of the villagers welcomed us amiably, particularly when they saw my condition, although we encountered a few who proved somewhat surly.

"Perhaps we're an intrusion," I whispered to Harvey at one place where the headman was openly hostile.

"They're afraid of us," he explained. "If the spirits are angered by our visit, they believe they will pay a heavy price. It's easier for them to think that bad things happen for a reason."

One night we lay on the open platform of a sala looking out over a village in the darkness. Yellow light from pitch pine candles flickered, shooting droplets of burning pitch into the gloom.

"We're in the middle of a shower of shooting stars," I murmured.

Harvey laughed softly. "You're such a romantic, Babs. I don't think there's a practical bone in your body."

I bristled. "What a terrible thing to say!"

"I meant that you have a dreamy sort of nature." He gave me a sly look. "It's a feminine trait that I love. I never said that you're weak," he hesitated, then added. "You're strong, but soft and fine at the same time. Like a strand of silk."

"Silk?"

"Yes. Haven't you ever noticed how difficult it is to break a silk thread? And the finest cloth is made from silk."

I was mollified and moved closer. "I *am* a little frightened, Harvey," I admitted. "About the baby. What if we've waited too long? Do we have enough time to reach Bangkok?"

He nodded to assure me and brushed his hand over my stomach, feeling the baby. "We're fine. Once we reach Phrae, it's just a two-day trip by train. Don't worry . . . there's plenty of time. You'll have a few weeks in Bangkok to catch your breath before it arrives. And I'll be with you every minute."

His voice was soothing and I relaxed. Harvey was my rock. Surrounded by the fragrance of flowering acacias and the night sounds of the jungle, I drifted off to sleep.

It was November and the mornings were slightly cool. As the sun rose, the villages came to life. Jungle fowl in cages screeched. Wicker pails were lowered noiselessly into shallow wells, their ropes held by strong girls sent to fetch the day's supply of water. Small boys herded animals, mostly buffalo, out from under the houses, and then their younger sisters occupied the space to husk rice. Men left for the paddy fields that were never far away, and women began their weaving, moving with the rhythmic sound of the rise and fall of the pounding stakes of the rice huskers.

We arrived in Bangkok only one day before the birth of our daughter. "Just in time," I noted to Harvey, who had the good grace to blush. Dr. Duncan had made arrangements for us at the Bangkok Nursing Home, a hospital that catered to expatriates. With shuttered windows of a traditional style in Bangkok, a breeze kept the large, clean rooms cool. Mrs. Duncan and Harvey stayed by my side through the entire ordeal. Afterward, when the nurse had cleaned the baby and wrapped her in a soft, tiny blanket, Mrs. Duncan brought her to us.

At first sight of the little bundle, I immediately forgot the pain of the delivery. "Here's your daughter," Mrs. Duncan said with a happy smile, placing her in my arms.

"She's perfect!" I breathed, cradling her against my breast.

"She looks like you, Babs," Harvey grinned. "And that's as good as it can get."

We called her Barbara Jeanne. Harvey and I watched her flutter and listened to her sweet little sounds for hours. Her skin was like satin, her voice fine and high—the softest sound that I have ever heard, like the sound of a *hoa pee-a*, a hollow coconut with strings across the opening. When the strings are lightly touched it brings forth a delicate fairy sound, like music borne from the distance on a breeze.

Harvey called on Judith and brought her to me as a surprise. While she rocked the baby, I filled her in on things at Nan. We stayed with the Duncans when I was able to leave the hospital, and Judith took me on whirlwind tours of sights in Bangkok. Sometimes wistful thoughts of Dad intruded, of how he would have loved this child, of what he could have taught her, and I grew melancholy. But I had learned now to push these thoughts to the recesses of my mind and hold them there. A new mother has no place for morbid feelings, I told myself, and I resolved not to dwell upon anything depressing.

When the time came for us to return to Nan, the carriers built a small cage, a box made of bamboo with screening stretched across the front, to carry Barby Jeanne. The cage was similar to those used to transport captive animals. She would be carried in it on poles through the jungle.

"Why do we need this?" I complained to Harvey. "I'm perfectly healthy and capable of holding her on the trip. She'll be frightened in the cage."

"It's necessary, Babs," he said in a manner that left no room for argument. "It will protect her from animals and insects . . . and curiosity."

I sighed. During the arduous journey she bore up well, however. "Such a brave, tiny thing," I breathed in wonder.

Harvey beamed in agreement.

# Chapter Sixteen

BARBY JEANNE BECAME AT ONCE THE center of attention upon our return to Nan. Everyone hovered and bustled around her until she grew quite spoiled. While we were gone, Tip had made a cradle and a large table for the nursery as a gift. His worn, brown face crinkled with smiles when we laid her down on the soft pillows that he and Ma Ping had prepared for the little bed. Ma Ping sucked on her teeth without smiling, but I could see that she was pleased.

Ai Mah came to visit the baby and he brought Boua Keo with him. He stared at Barby Jeanne with amazement, holding out his finger to let hers wrap around it. Dr. and Mrs. Pitters gave us an old rocking chair, and Boua Keo held the baby in her arms for hours, rocking gently back and forth, singing sweet songs in her melodic language.

Kham Noi could not pronounce Barby Jeanne's name and began to call her "Ot Dee." Ai Mah soon adopted the name as well, so Ot Dee she became. Ma Ping found a big basket at the market that we filled with pillows and kept downstairs. Barby Jeanne fit into it perfectly and, as we moved it from room to room and out on the veranda, her eyes roved over the bright new world with fresh wonder. Ma Ping came to see her every day. She held the child for hours and rambled on with stories in Siamese that seemed to have neither a beginning nor an end. Even Gibbon was fascinated—he danced around when I held the baby, chattering with excitement, sometimes pulling on my sleeve or skirt for attention.

But Mrs. Breeden was a different story. One evening at the Ruckels' house, I noticed her staring at Barby Jeanne with an odd expression. She seemed almost transfixed. I watched her for a moment, then, on an impulse I picked the baby up, cradled her in my arms, and walked over to Mrs. Breeden. She started and looked at me.

"Would you like to hold her?" I asked.

Her hand slid to her throat and she adjusted her collar, tilting her head to the side with an almost imperceptible jerk of her chin. "No, thank you, my dear. Babies and I don't mix." Her words were quick and sharp, like splinters of glass.

*They're both insane,* I thought, watching as she stood, brushed off her dress with brisk little slaps of her hand, and glanced around for her husband. "Shall we go, my dear?" she called to him. "It's growing late."

He glanced at his wife and ignored her as his eyes slid to me. Amalie Breeden started toward him, but without a word he turned and strode away, leaving her behind. He walked down the steps and disappeared among the trees into the dark where the surreys were kept, and with a stricken look, his wife trailed behind.

I thought that Gibbon loved her.

And Barby Jeanne was fascinated with Gibbon. She watched him with great interest, her blue eyes stars of excitement as they followed his clownish antics. Each time he became aware of her attention, however, he doubled his momentum, chattering as he swung up and away into his favorite spot, the mango tree. Sometimes he even kept his eye on the baby from the branches that spread just outside the nursery while she slept.

One day, as I held Barby Jeanne, Ma Ping watched Gibbon for a long time with a thoughtful expression.

"He is jealous of Ot Dee," she finally said.

I was astonished. "Gibbon?" I watched him fling himself through the branches with his long arms as she spoke. "Don't be silly, Ma Ping," I laughed. "He's just a little pet."

She clucked her tongue and her expression turned inscrutable.

Other creatures had become permanent lodgers with us, too. From time to time there were white mice, lizards, a flying squirrel, several dogs, and of course, the ubiquitous frogs. But we also had unwelcome guests—scorpions in odd corners, centipedes lurking on shelves, and spiders in the bathroom. One day I heard noises in the attic. I asked Kham Noi what it was, but he just looked at me with a solemn expression, seemingly struck dumb. Ma Ping promptly informed me that the sound was the movement of snakes, and my blood ran cold.

Our most unwelcome boarder arrived soon after. I spotted it on the wall one day—a large lizard, almost two feet long. After that, the creature materialized in various rooms, slithering in and out of ventilation grilles and peering over the top of pictures. Suction pads on its feet enabled it to walk upside down on the ceilings. Once I tried to remove it from the high ceiling with a long-handled broom. Its tongue flicked toward me and spat. I leapt back in horror, almost stumbling over Ma Ping who had just walked in. Following my frozen gaze, she commented slyly that if the lizard fell on me, the suction pads would stick until one of us died. My skin crawled and I backed away.

"It's horrible," I said later to Kham Noi, trying to control my trembling voice. The reptile still hung motionless on the ceiling and its long, spiked tongue flicked out from time to time. The face was ferocious and the thick hide was covered by wart-like bumps.

"He's catching his dinner," Kham Noi laughed carelessly. He went off and returned with a large stick that he poked toward the lizard. It fixed its eyes on him and spat again. I gasped.

Kham Noi just laughed some more and poked the stick again toward the ceiling.

"Stop that!" I scolded, frightened now. The reptile's eyes remained on Kham Noi.

He stiffened at my tone.

"I'm sorry, Kham Noi," I said quickly, realizing that I had offended him. "It's just that I'm a little afraid of the creature." I worked for a reasonable tone as I backed away and was stopped by the wall. The lizard stared at Kham Noi while I spoke.

"It's about the most horrid looking thing I've ever seen," I said to Harvey that night as I related what had happened. "It had huge eyes with slits in them."

"It's a *tokay*—a primitive lizard. Some think it's a type of chameleon," he said in an off-handed manner. "They're the only reptiles that can focus their eyes on a single point for long periods of time."

I shuddered with disgust. "It seemed to be staring at Kham Noi."

"Well, I suppose it has to stare; it has no eyelids. But their eyes are very powerful. They can see in the dark as well." Harvey's voice took on a patient tone. "But see here, Babs, it's not going to hurt you. Just leave it alone."

At night the fiend emerged from his hiding places and threw us into utter confusion by croaking "Doc-tuh, doc-tuh . . . doc-tuh." The first time this occurred Harvey leapt out of bed and hurriedly dressed, running downstairs to see who needed medical aid. We could never pinpoint the direction of the call, however, so each time we heard it, I lay awake for hours wondering if the tokay was on the ceiling, ready to drop on us.

We hired a young girl to act as an *ayah*, or nurse, for the baby. She was the first Siamese person I had met who was sullen by nature. She walked with her eyes cast down and refused to look into mine when I spoke to her. I argued vehemently against hiring her at first, but Harvey dissuaded me, and Mrs. Ruckel was of the opinion that we would find no one better. Gibbon, too, took an instant dislike to her, however, and consequently she was terrified of the poor monkey.

One morning I was daydreaming on the veranda when a piercing shriek erupted from the interior of the house. I leapt from my chair just as a longer scream, even louder, followed the first. The noise continued, growing in intensity as I raced through the front door and up the stairs, followed on my heels by Kham Noi. As we rounded the top of the stairs and flew into the nursery, the shrieks turned into a steady crescendo of wailing.

I stopped cold. Near the open window Gibbon hugged Barby Jeanne to his chest, his long arms wrapped about her tiny form. The ayah was huddled in the corner, her voice rising and falling as she covered her eyes. The thick branches of the mango tree brushed against the windowsill, easy access for Gibbon and his little bundle.

Gibbon shifted his gaze from the ayah to me. I saw his fear, and—Ma Ping was right—from the dark interior of his animal being rose raw hatred and jealousy. For an instant he was still, uncertain, then he tensed and I somehow knew that he would bolt for the open window and the tree. With no time to think, I leapt toward him, reaching the window just as he began to move. I reached out frantically for the baby, he loosened his grip in surprise, and she dropped into my arms.

Shaking, I cradled Barby Jeanne in disbelief. The worthless ayah remained curled in the corner of the room, her voice now lowered to an incessant whimper that attacked my nerves.

"*Quiet!*" I ordered in a fury as I stared at Gibbon. Her cries were reduced to a low keening sound.

Gibbon hopped from one foot to the other in agitation, moving rapidly from side to side as he chattered. I held the baby, hypnotized. The small sharp movements that had so recently amused us all were no longer so. In his excitement his mouth drew back into a grotesque smile and he bared his teeth. Then suddenly, inexplicably, he grew still, almost as if he knew that Barby Jeanne had won. He gazed at me in what I imagined was sorrow. His lips were thin and tight, his face contorted. Later I knew that this was his good-bye—then he whirled and leapt through the window onto the branch, swinging out of sight.

I pressed Barby Jeanne to me. For the first time I looked over to Kham Noi. His face was flushed and he was out of breath. "Ot Dee," he wailed in a strange, high voice. "Ot Dee, Ot Dee." Then he began to shake and Barby Jeanne began to cry.

Tip and Ma Ping rushed into the room, having heard the commotion all the way to the river road. Neither Kham Noi nor I nor the ayah was capable of speech, but Ma Ping looked at the window and seemed to understand. She took the baby from my arms in a gentle way, quite unlike her, and I followed her to my bedroom. I lay on the bed, stretched out with my head on the pillow, and Ma Ping carefully placed Barby Jeanne beside me, in the crook of my arm against my breast. The baby whimpered for a moment, then settled down as I cuddled her. I was overcome with fatigue. As I drifted off, I could hear Kham Noi speaking to the ayah in angry, rapid bursts.

When I awoke, Harvey was sitting in a chair by the side of the bed in the dim light of late afternoon, holding Barby Jeanne. Tip had run all the way to the hospital for him. Gibbon was nowhere to be found. I never saw our little monkey again. Later I learned that Tip had found him, and, although he was vague when asked, I suspected that he had been returned to the forest rather than given to another family. Gibbon's eyes and contorted face haunted me for months afterward.

Ma Ping brought spirit charms to the nursery when she thought I wasn't looking, and placed them here and there in odd places.

# Chapter Seventeen

ONE EVENING WE JOINED THE BREEDENS, Miss Best, and Emma at the Ruckels' house for dinner and stayed late into the night. The air was torrid, oppressive. It was a bright evening; the moon was full, bathing us in pale light as we sat on the veranda.

"There's been another sighting," Emma said casually.

"Sighting?" I asked, rising to the bait.

"Of the mysterious Englishman," she said.

"How do you know, dear?" Mrs. Ruckel spoke without looking up. She went on working her needle through a thick piece of material that she was mending.

"A traveler in the market mentioned him," Emma said. "The missionaries at Phrae say that he emerged for a day or two from the jungle, then disappeared again."

Mrs. Breeden frowned. "I certainly hope that he's not going to arrive on our doorstep."

"He *will not* arrive on our doorstep," Mr. Breeden said.

"That would be poor judgment on his part," I snapped, unable to hide my dislike.

"It surely would," he agreed.

Harvey threw me a warning glance. Emma looked amused.

In the distance the last of the evening temple drums rumbled through the valley, punctuated now and again by the clang of gongs and a soft distant drone of voices. "The monks seem to chant ceaselessly," I complained, fanning myself against the heat.

"It's a way to detach themselves from worldly things," Reverend Ruckel said. "The repetition focuses their thoughts, helps them attain a high state of contemplation."

"That would not be a bad thing for Christians to learn," I muttered, fanning harder. My skin was damp with perspiration. "Perhaps without distractions it would be easier to understand just what is expected of us in this life."

Mrs. Breeden looked shocked. I lowered my eyes and hid a smile. "But I do love the sound of those drums—they add a certain pizzazz."

"May the day come when they are replaced with the bells of a Christian church," Mrs. Breeden said under her breath.

I composed a pleasant, neutral expression.

Mr. Breeden spoke with condescension. "Christianity doesn't need tricks like drums and meditation. Our Scriptures are enough."

I studied him for an instant, then made up my mind. We hadn't spoken since the day we'd been alone in the church. "Our church in Philadelphia had a beautiful choir," I said in a careful tone. "And other religions use music and art and poetry as tools, as guides, so to speak, to enhance the meaning of Scripture. Perhaps we should learn from them."

"Buddhist drums are not. . ."

"Buddhists, Catholics, Muslims," I went on, raising my voice, "they all have beautiful temples, cathedrals, and mosques filled with great art. Think how music like that of Bach or Verdi or Mozart expands one's thoughts."

Mrs. Breeden's eyes swung from me to her husband.

"You are speaking of flights of fancy, not Christianity," he spat. His complexion darkened and, when he spoke, he seemed to wheeze. "The words of the Scriptures are plain in themselves. The Holy Spirit will help us to understand them, but the tools are the teachers who have been trained in the Christian community. This type of understanding requires earnest study, Mrs. Perkins, not tricks like those drums."

I'd overestimated my self-control. A red rage rose, but as I opened my mouth to answer, Harvey interrupted. Smoke from his pipe wisped from the side of his mouth as he spoke. "Regardless, it seems to me that the real test of Christianity is not what we say, but what we do. How you *act* on your belief."

"I agree, Harvey," Reverend Ruckel interjected. "The Scriptures must always be interpreted by the rule of love. That's the only way to cause change in the lives of those who need us." But then he glanced at me and frowned. Although his voice was soft, the tone was firm. "But that is very different from Buddhism. The ultimate goal of the follower of Buddha is indifference and, ultimately, the highest stage of indifference—nirvana. Christianity, on the other hand, is not about indifference; it's about acting."

I felt Mr. Breeden's eyes on me and wouldn't let it go. "But even so, isn't that search for nirvana very similar to our own longing for heaven?" I asked Reverend Ruckel.

"Nirvana is nothingness," Mr. Breeden said.

"Well, I must say that there's certainly something wrong with a religion that has *nothingness* as the ultimate reward," Mrs. Breeden declared.

The Nan mission was always short of funds. Harvey and I began to notice the gradual deterioration of buildings and supplies, not to mention spirits. Once as I walked with students near the school, a shower of dilapidated brick rubble fell perilously close, barely missing one of the little girls. But our pleas for assistance from mission headquarters were ignored in Chiang Mai.

"It appears that we will have to suffer an injury before any-one at Chiang Mai will pay attention," I said to Emma, who had registered numerous complaints about the inadequate condition of the school.

"Well, you and Dr. Perkins may be the only ones around to see it happen," she said. Her voice was curt.

"What do you mean?" I asked.

"I've requested a transfer."

I was stunned. Aside from Harvey, Emma was the only per-son at Nan that I counted as a real friend. Mrs. Ruckel was kind, but she was of another generation. "Where will you go?"

"To Chiang Mai, I hope," she said. I could think of no response to this depressing news. "Dr. Pitters's health will force them to move to Chiang Mai soon, as well, I imagine," she went on. "And it seems the Breedens are hoping for an administrative position in Bangkok. It would be a promotion."

This was good news. I gave her a sharp look. "Is that right?" I asked, holding my breath.

She nodded. "They're expecting it. We'll all know soon. Mrs. Breeden is thrilled."

But the brief happy feeling disappeared as I suddenly real-ized that Harvey and I would be left with only the elderly Ruckels and Miss Best for company. Visions rose in my mind of spending year after empty year at Nan, with Harvey off at the hospital or a village, myself left alone with Barby Jeanne and Kham Noi. "Good heavens!" I blurted, as miasma set in, a foreboding, a terrible new sense that this was all there was and all there'd ever be.

After that day I began to notice things that I had not seen before. Now as I walked in the marketplace or along the river road, where once I had seen bright colors and heard carefree laughter, I was conscious that hunger shadowed the dark eyes of the children. Even the smallest ones had swollen stomachs and boils on their skin. Had the children always looked this way? I wondered.

"Breeden's God is mighty silent when it comes to sickness and hunger in the Nan Valley, it seems," I said one day to Harvey. "Why are we here? Who are we to preach religion to these people?"

Harvey's eyes turned hard, surprising me. "I'm not here to preach," he said. "I am here to teach them basic medicine, how to care for themselves." I watched as he began to massage the back of his neck in small circles with the tips of his fingers.

I picked up an old *Atlantic Monthly* that Evie had sent and flipped through the pages. "Even so," I murmured. "It certainly seems unjust, but they don't seem to notice. Perhaps that's the blessing of the Buddhist teachings. It lets them rise above the misery of their lives. By cutting themselves off from desires and emotions they transcend the sorrow—defeat it and destroy it."

"Perhaps that is the *cause* of the problem," Harvey answered wearily.

A sudden sense of hopelessness washed over me. "Everyone who escapes should be thankful," I said without thinking.

Harvey turned his eyes to me and I felt him watching while I read.

Kham Noi found a new candidate for me to consider as an ayah for Barby Jeanne. Ai Mah told Harvey that he knew the girl. She lived with her mother and father and many brothers and sisters in a small house about a mile farther down the river road. They owned one buffalo and the entire family worked two small plots in a rice field.

"Do you recommend her?" Harvey asked.

Ai Mah was puzzled. "What is recommend?" he finally asked.

"It is what you do for me in the villages," Harvey answered. "When the people are worried about the farang, you tell them that I am your friend and you trust me. Then they are no longer afraid."

He nodded, comprehending, then screwed his mouth into a grimace while he thought about the question. After a moment he said, "Yes . . . I will recommend her for Ot Dee."

Kham Noi put out the word and the next day, when I came down for breakfast, she was waiting for me in the kitchen. Her name was Seewana. She was very clever, with a sharp sense of humor. Seewana was heavier than the average woman in North Siam, plump and healthy looking despite having grown up in the Nan Valley. I quickly grew to like her.

"She has been blessed by the spirits," Kham Noi said one day. I noticed that his eyes followed her as she entered and left the room.

One day Seewana and I were bathing Barby Jeanne with enormous amounts of soap when I heard Emma's hearty shout from the river road. I looked up and watched as she peddled up the drive, looking frantic, then dropped the bicycle onto the grass and clattered up the stairs.

"What's all the excitement?" I asked, handing Barby Jeanne to Seewana, who wrapped her in towels and took her away.

Emma's face was flushed from the exertion. "He's here!" she announced.

I stared at her without comprehension. "Who?"

"The Englishman . . . he's come." She chortled with glee. "He just walked right out of the bush at the back of the mission school, like a specter."

She collapsed into a chair and watched as I hung a wet towel over the railing to dry. "Amalie Breeden almost had a fit," she added happily. "She looked out a window at the school and there he was."

I laughed as I imagined the scene. "Where is he now?" I asked.

"At the Ruckels' . . . reclining in state."

"What does he look like?"

"Like a bony pauper," she said. "Lordy! I'll bet a hat he doesn't have a cent. His shoes are almost gone, he was practically barefoot. He's extremely dirty," she went on, it seemed to me, with awe. "Mrs. Breeden wouldn't go near him."

That evening when Harvey returned from the hospital, I told him the news and we hitched up the surrey for the short trip down the river road to the mission compound.

When we arrived, the visitor was sitting on the veranda with the Ruckels, Mrs. Breeden, and Emma, drinking tea.

"Joshua Smithers," he said without a smile, lifting from his chair as he spoke. Then he fell back into the seat.

Harvey gave him a wide smile and extended his hand. Mr. Smithers looked startled, as if he had been removed from polite society too long. Harvey was perplexed and withdrew his hand. Reverend Ruckel pulled up some chairs and we sat down.

Our mysterious Englishman was small, thin, and bald on top with wispy gray hair around the edges that flattened against his head. As I studied him, I sensed something different about him. He had an almost ascetic quality, yet he looked like a beggar. His face was drawn; his bones were etched clearly beneath his skin. The Ruckels had found sandals and clean clothes for him, but he wore short pants and the flesh on his legs was covered with raw, painful-looking boils. His joints had the appearance of hard knots on a pine tree.

"Mr. Smithers has been traveling through the mountain villages between here and Phrae," Mrs. Ruckel told us in a cautious tone. We all turned our eyes to him.

"Yes," he said, speaking slowly, as if he had not heard the sound of his own voice for a long time. "I've spent so much time in the villages that this house seems luxurious."

"How long since you left Bangkok?" Harvey asked. "We heard it was some time ago. We've been looking for you to arrive."

"Five or six months." His tone was vague and he seemed somewhat confused. "I'm really not sure. I had the fever and lost track of time."

"Jungle fever?" I asked.

He nodded. "I was too ill to travel after that. Some villagers took care of me."

"That was kind of them," Reverend Ruckel said. "Are you here with a church?"

"No." His tone was abrupt.

"Why in the world would you want to wander through the jungle all alone?" I asked.

"I thought I might find something there," he said, looking off.

"What were you searching for? Gold? Fossils?"

He shook his head and gazed down the river road at nothing. "Something more elusive."

"Well?" He didn't answer. "Did you find it?" I pressed, curious now.

"Really!" Mrs. Breeden said.

Mr. Smithers looked at me and his eyes seemed to focus for the first time. "No," he finally answered. It was not a casual look he gave. He seemed to look *into* me. I shivered but couldn't think why.

While Mr. Smithers, looking fatigued, leaned back in his chair and rested, Reverend Ruckel brought out the box of books that had arrived weeks ago and placed it on a table. Harvey opened the box and I leaned forward to inspect the contents. Inside were three pamphlets that appeared to be tracts of some sort of the Roman Catholic religion. Harvey put them aside and pulled out the book I had wanted, *The Varieties of Religious Experience* by William James. I took it from him and flipped through the contents, finding chapters on such things as "The Reality of the Unseen." When Mr. Breeden leaned forward to inspect the title, I covered it casually with my hand and with a twist to the side, shuffled the book to another table, determined to sample this forbidden fruit without his interference.

I turned back to Mr. Smithers and our eyes met. I flushed, but he gave me an imperceptible nod with a glance at the book. Then suddenly he turned pale. Beads of perspiration formed on his forehead and along his upper lip. He swayed, lurched forward, and covered his eyes with his hand.

Harvey looked alarmed. "You're ill," he told the man. "And those open sores need to be treated right away." While Reverend Ruckel and Mr. Breeden helped Mr. Smithers inside, Harvey hurried to the surrey to retrieve the small medical bag that he kept with him at all times, then disappeared into the house.

"I think it's the fever returned with a vengeance," Harvey told me later. Jungle fever, sometimes meaning dengue and sometimes malaria, could turn into dysentery and spread from one village to another with lightning speed. But when I worried that one of us would catch it, he brushed off my concern, already fully occupied with the care of his new patient.

The fever raged for days. At times when he was lucid, Joshua Smithers talked of the deaths in the village that had sheltered him. "The noise . . . was terrible," he rasped to Harvey. "Constant funeral drums, pounding, pounding." He held his head in his hands. "They never ceased."

When Mrs. Ruckel told me this, her voice was low and mournful. She frowned and gazed into the distance. I gave her a close look, surprised at her strong reaction to a stranger's stories.

"I've seen too much," she murmured.

With a surge of pity, I reached over and cupped her soft hands in both of mine, feeling the delicate bones just beneath the paper-thin skin, spotted with age. I stroked the flesh on the top-sides gently for a moment; it was dry, silky, like powder.

Then she grew flustered, drew back her hands, and reached for a fan.

She was as strong and soft as Mummy, I thought to myself.

As the mysterious Englishman tossed, muttering and sometimes raving, he seemed to waste away before our very eyes. Mrs. Ruckel and Harvey took turns nursing him through the long days and nights. At times his forehead was so dry and hot to the touch that Harvey wondered aloud how anyone could live with such a fever. At times he shook with chills and grew damp from a cold sweat. Hot potions were poured down his throat by the glassful, but this seemed to have little effect. When the fever was at its highest, he raved of buffalo dung and sulfur, burnt hair and straw.

"Do you think he really smells those things?" I asked Mrs. Ruckel, wrinkling my nose.

"No," she answered. "He's remembering poultices that the spirit doctors use. They plaster foul-smelling mixtures on a sick person's head to keep the life-spirits from escaping through the whorl of hair on the crown." She shook her head in wonder. "Sometimes they massage the victim's sore muscles to force the devils down the limbs and out through the toes. They've learned from their fathers and grandfathers how to deal with these ravages."

"A massage certainly seems more practical than buffalo dung," I said in disgust.

Finally, one morning Harvey came home wearing a smile. "He seems to be pulling through," he said, handing me his medical bag. I guided him to a chair in the parlor. He looked exhausted but relieved. "His fever dropped today. I left him drinking a bit of Mrs. Ruckel's tea."

I pushed a footstool over to him and he lifted one foot, then the other, and dropped them onto it. Had it been me, I would have slid down in the chair, closed my eyes, and given way to sleep.

"I'll get a pillow for you," I said, turning to leave the room.

"Don't bother, Babs," he yawned.

"I'll put it under your neck so that you can rest."

"I don't need it."

"You need sleep."

"No. I'm not at all tired. I'd really like to eat."

I observed him for a moment, then nodded. "I'll tell Kham Noi." When I returned to tell him that breakfast would be ready soon, Harvey was sound asleep, sitting upright in the chair.

As he began to recover, Mr. Smithers told us of an old woman who cared for him in one of the villages. She had blown softly on his brow, intoning long incantations to the spirits as she brushed her fingertips across his eyelids. "With the touch of butterfly wings," he said. He'd tried to help the villagers when the fever first struck, but he had no medical training and did not know what to do. "Anyway," he shrugged, "I tried to pray with them, but it was useless. They trusted only in their spirits. When a patient improved, they thanked the spirits. If not, they blamed our God."

"You prayed with them?" I interrupted. "But you said you aren't with a church."

"There are many ways to experience religion," he said vaguely.

"Why did you finally leave?" Emma asked.

As the fever spread and grew worse, he told us, the villagers looked at him and wondered if their spirits were angry at the presence of the farang. Their gods were jealous gods, too, I thought. The eyes of the villagers followed him with hostility. Finally, fear had driven him from the jungle to Nan.

Slowly Joshua Smithers improved. His breath was still ragged and he was wracked with a cough, but the fever cooled and his dreams disappeared. He began to eat, a little at a time—at first, just a bit of rice softened in buffalo milk. Mrs. Ruckel prepared a daybed for him on the veranda so that he could lie in the warm sunshine. He was pale and thin, but Harvey announced that the worst had passed.

I waited in silent fear through the next two weeks to see if any of us had caught the fever, but no one became ill. Lulled by the sweet fruit of the lotus, I finally concluded that, after all, the pestilence had done its worst.

# Chapter Eighteen

ONE EVENING IN LATE SEPTEMBER, AI MAH arrived at our doorstep, breathless. It took some time to calm him. He was frantic and mixed his words as he attempted to speak first in English, then in Siamese. We couldn't make out a thing that he was saying.

"Slow down, Ai Mah," Harvey said, resting his hands on the boy's shoulder and pushing him down into a chair.

"Kham Noi!" I called. I heard a clatter in the kitchen, then bare feet shuffling across the floor. Kham Noi appeared in the door looking disheveled and sleepy. It was late—time for him to leave.

"Mem?" he asked. Catching sight of Ai Mah, he closed his mouth and stared. Ai Mah still struggled for breath. His light-brown skin had taken on a flushed, ruddy tone. It seemed he had run all the way from the school.

"Can you bring some water for him before you go?" I asked Kham Noi.

"Yes," he said. "Right away, right away." He hurried to the kitchen, muttering.

When Kham Noi returned with the water, Ai Mah gulped it down. "The brother of Boua Keo came to the mission school tonight," he said in a trembling voice. "She has left with him. Our whole village is ill—everyone is ill. Her father is near death." He looked pleadingly at Harvey. "I told her that you would come."

My throat grew tight. Harvey's eyes narrowed at Ai Mah's words. This is what he had feared, I knew. The fever had spread.

He rose and, without a glance at me, told Ai Mah to wait while he readied himself for the trip to the Village of the Beautiful God. At his words, the boy visibly relaxed. Harvey went inside but soon reappeared with his medical bag.

"We'll stop at the hospital for a few things, and then at the Ruckels' to let them know."

Ai Mah nodded and rose. Waves of fear washed through me, and I found I could not speak. Harvey brushed my cheek with a hurried kiss. "I may be gone a few days, Babs," he whispered.

I remembered the stories that Mr. Smithers had told. "Can't someone else go?" I cried, grasping Harvey's arm even as he pulled away. My thoughts raced. "Perhaps Reverend Ruckel . . . he knows almost as much as you about treating these things."

I hesitated before adding, "And he doesn't have a new baby." My voice sounded strange and shrill and desperate, but I could not seem to stop myself.

Harvey looked annoyed. "He's not a physician. Besides, it's Ai Mah's village. I have to go." He gave me a quick hug and they were off.

A strange premonition prickled my thoughts, but I could not find words for the vague concern. Jungle fever was noth-ing new, I told myself. I stood motionless on the veranda as

I hugged my shoulders and watched Harvey and Ai Mah trot quickly down the drive to the river road, then turn and disappear from sight into the shadows. The air was hot and humid; not a leaf stirred on the mango tree. For a long time I stared at the deserted river road.

The next morning I drove the surrey down to the Ruckels' house. Mrs. Ruckel was cooking and I took a chair in the kitchen. After an unsuccessful attempt at cheerful conversation, I lapsed into silence.

"Where's Mr. Smithers?" I finally asked. The house was unusually quiet except for the clatter of pots and pans. I was tense and nervous.

"He left with Ai Mah and the Doctor," Mrs. Ruckel said. She glanced around and patted me on the arm in a distracted manner as she bustled past on her way to the pantry for some sugar. "Don't worry yourself. He'll help. He understands how these people think."

I nodded, not at all reassured by the thought that the mysterious Englishman would assist Harvey and Ai Mah.

The next day I woke earlier than usual. The light filtering through the bedroom window was dim, the air heavy and damp. I gazed around with a vague, ominous feeling. After a moment I turned over and tried to go back to sleep, but thoughts of Harvey and jungle fever spun in my mind. Finally I gave up, rose and dressed, and headed down the stairs for breakfast.

The dining room was empty and dark. Kham Noi peeked his head around the corner when he heard me, and soon reappeared with breakfast. "Where's the boy?" I asked as he set down the plates and began arranging the silverware. This was normally the job of cook's boy.

"He will not be here today." Kham Noi moved around me to place an empty cup on the table as he spoke.

"Why not?"

His eyes flicked to the window. "Rain is coming," he finally said, pouring coffee into the cup. He set the pot down on the table, avoiding my eyes.

"How can you tell that, Kham Noi?" I asked.

"The air, Mem—I can feel it. The birds and animals know this as well."

Suddenly I was aware of the strange silence around us. No sound came from the river road; no birds sang outside the window. "Well, it's not here yet," I shrugged, as I began to eat. We'd endured the rainy seasons before. "I really cannot understand why the boy has not come."

Kham Noi was silent. When I looked around, he had gone.

Late in the morning, the wind began to blow. Barby Jeanne was moody, whining constantly. I hiked her onto my hip and stalked into the kitchen. "Where is Seewana?" I asked Kham Noi with annoyance.

He glanced at me but didn't answer.

"Kham Noi." My voice rose with irritation. "I asked if you know where Seewana is this morning. She's never been this late."

"She will not be here, Mem," he said. He was preparing soup in an old iron pot as he spoke and didn't look up.

"The storm again?" I struggled to keep the sarcastic edge from my voice.

He nodded.

My nerves were frayed. Anger erupted. "This is ridiculous! How is it that suddenly the weather is of such concern?"

Kham Noi stopped his work and looked at me. "The rain will be hard this time," he answered in a low voice.

"Don't tell me," I said, with heavy sarcasm, "the spirits are angry."

He said nothing. Just then a gust of wind blew through the trees outside and branches scraped the edge of the kitchen window. Kham Noi reached over the counter and closed and bolted the shutter. I watched in silence. Barby Jeanne began to cry, and I bounced her gently on my hip.

Kham Noi began moving from room to room, securing the shutters. I waited in the kitchen for a moment, then wandered into the parlor with Barby Jeanne. With the shutters closed, the room was dark and gloomy. I set her on a blanket on the floor with some toys and then lit the lamps to brighten things up. Taking a seat, I realized that Ai Mah would also be aware that a storm was coming. Harvey would be making his way back through the forest just now, back to Barby Jeanne and me.

Kham Noi came into the room and looked at us. His face was tense. "I will take you and Ot Dee to Missus Ruckel," he said after a moment. "It will be better there."

"No," I said. "If a storm is coming, the Doctor will just make sure the village has food and medicine and come right back. He'll be home soon. Barby Jeanne and I will wait here, but you can leave if you like."

He hesitated. I hid my relief when he shook his head.

"He'll be home any time now, and then we can decide what to do."

Late in the afternoon the rain began. A soft, pleasant trickle soon turned into torrents that beat against the house. With the shutters closed and the heat thrown off by the kerosene lamps, the air inside was stale and fetid, even as the wind churned outside.

Kham Noi made a bed for himself in the dining room on the floor. I gave him a mat and a pillow. All through the night the rain came down in steady streams. Water overflowed the banks of the river, and we woke to see that puddles around the house had grown into small lakes. I knew that the river road must be a sea of mud, and every minute we became more isolated—Barby Jeanne, Kham Noi, and I. The rooms were airless and dreary as the walls closed around us.

About midmorning I opened the front door a crack, peering through the rain to watch for Harvey. He had already been gone for three days. The deluge hid everything in shadows, and I strained to see, expecting him to emerge from the darkness. After a moment I drew back in disappointment and moved to close the door. It was then I happened to glance down. Puzzled, I froze and looked away as my mind rejected what my eyes had seen. I squeezed my lids shut and slowly opened them again. Beneath me, the entire veranda heaved like a living thing.

Steeling myself, I took a deep breath and stared, gripped with cold revulsion. The veranda undulated with heaps of thin, twisting white worms. I gazed at them with horror as a part of my mind observed that the slender, wriggling things seemed almost translucent. For a split second I couldn't move. Then nausea rose to the back of my throat as I slammed the door shut, swallowed, and sank weak and breathless against it.

*Hold steady!* my inner voice commanded. *Steady.* Suddenly I shuddered. My throat convulsed and I began to sob. "Harvey!" I screamed, covering my face with my hands.

Kham Noi rushed into the hall but halted when he saw my tears. I gagged as pictures of the roiling worms on the other side of the door formed in my mind again. The room whirled, and I pushed off from the door, stumbling forward. Kham Noi caught me as I fell, then gently braced my arm and turned me to the parlor. He led me to a chair where I collapsed, still sobbing. I tried to speak, to explain the horror of the worms, but my throat was thick and tight. At last, when I was able to choke out the words, Kham Noi understood. To my surprise, he looked relieved.

"They come up from under the earth, from the rice fields, to seek shelter from the rising water, Mem. No poison," he assured in a gentle tone. "They will not hurt you or Ot Dee."

*Ah*, I thought with a shudder, wiping the tears from my cheeks, *the Buddhist mentality—every living thing must be respected*. Nevertheless, I asked Kham Noi to stuff towels and, if necessary, clothes on the floor against the crack of the door.

He gave me a strange look. "We're not sharing the *inside* of the house with them," I said. When he had finished building the barricade, I found him in the kitchen. "Perhaps we should try to get to the Ruckels' after all," I said, keeping the tone of my voice casual. Harvey would know where to find us, I thought.

He looked grave and shook his head. "We cannot go now," he replied. He pulled out a chair from under a small wooden table that was bolted to the floor and indicated that I should sit. I fell into it, stricken at the knowledge that we were prisoners of the rain.

For days relentless wind hammered rain into the wooden shell of our house, driving like nails until I thought that the walls would splinter and collapse around us. I wandered through the rooms, trying not to wonder why Harvey had not yet returned, trying not to think of the rising water, of the worms. With the shutters closed, days merged into nights until, finally, time seemed to stop and we were left with only the din of noise that prowled outside—a steady, lonely howl.

Now Kham Noi grew morose and silent, as if the rampage of energy must be appeased. The baby was fretful, and I struggled to hide my fear. But as the water rose around us, it seemed to saturate the air. I found myself gasping for breath—small, shallow gulps that caught in my chest.

*Why hadn't I listened to Kham Noi?* I berated myself a thousand times. But finally I faced the truth. I knew. It had never occurred to me that Harvey would not come home when the storm began, that his concern for strangers and his sense of duty could ever outweigh his love for Barby Jeanne and me.

Perhaps he was hurt?

*No,* I told myself, *he's with Ai Mah and Mr. Smithers. Someone would have come for help if he were hurt.*

Perspiration formed with the thought. We were stranded now, I knew. It was too late. I picked up Barby Jeanne, sank into Harvey's chair, and doubled over her little form. She curled up against me and sucked her thumb. If Harvey were here, he would find a way to get us out, I knew, before . . . before the worms . . . and the snakes . . .

All at once a thought took root and my arms trembled, even as they cradled Barby Jeanne. Ma Ping's words came back to me: Snakes are houseguests in North Siam. They live in the attic.

The trembling grew. Even in dry weather, snakes live in the attic, and with rain seeping through the roof and rising water . . . ? I tightened my arms, gripping Barby Jeanne, and she whimpered. *Steady!* raged my inner voice. *Babies sense fear. You must be brave for Barby Jeanne. Think of something else! Sing.*

I forced myself to be still. I took a long, slow breath and let the air fill my lungs before loosing my hold on Barby Jeanne. I leaned back, looking down at her, and tried a smile when she fixed her eyes on mine. But when I began to sing, my voice faltered and the sound came out a hum. Her mouth trembled. I stroked her arms and tried again. *"By the light . . ."* My breath caught. *"By the light . . . of the silvery moon."* Barby Jeanne's eyes watched mine while I sang and held her. Soon the simple melody and words carried me back to Philadelphia and our little house on Greene Street, freeing us for an instant from the storm. *"Your silv'ry beams, will bring love's dreams . . . we'll be cuddling soon . . ."* My voice was stronger now. She looked up at me and smiled. *". . . By the silvery moon."*

But still, at night I heard noises above while I lay in bed—the sound of movement overhead, beneath the roof.

*Snakes.*

I drew into myself, curling into the smallest space imaginable as I strained to hear. In my mind's eye I saw them uncoil and slither across the attic floor. Sleep became impossible. Where was Harvey? I wept night after night, pushing my face into the clammy pillow so that Barby Jeanne and Kham Noi couldn't hear, until my eyes grew heavy and finally closed. But the wet, coiling images hung in my mind. Even when I slept, I dreamed of them.

One night, after more than a week of the wind and rain, silence woke me. I lay in bed, motionless, pondering what was different. It was a minute before I realized that the wind had died and the pounding rain had stopped.

A sense of relief surged through me. Bracing myself on one elbow, I twisted toward the table near the bed, slid the lantern close, and felt around in the darkness for a match to light the wick. When I found one, the air was damp and the flame flickered before it caught.

As the room slowly brightened from the lantern's glow, I fell back onto the pillows and let my gaze wander, trying to enjoy the silence, struggling not to think of snakes in the attic or water or worms—or of Harvey—just yet. My eyes scanned the ceiling, the beams and cracks and the lantern hanging overhead, and then I inspected the angles where the wall and ceiling met. As my gaze traveled slowly down the wall across the room, I saw the shadow of the thing first, a phantasm at the edge of my vision, before its form and shape and substance emerged in my consciousness. And all at once I froze, staring at the tokay—its wart-like skin and grotesque mask—stretched across the top of a wooden picture frame and staring back at me.

The tokay's eyes locked on mine and I couldn't scream and could not look away. I held my breath as icy fear crawled through my arms and legs and chest and entered my bowels, and then I knew that he would jump. Seconds passed and the reptile was motionless in the silent room, feeding on my terror, fear creating an almost physical cord of tension that linked us. I watched, paralyzed, as it slowly lifted from the picture frame, hovering in space for one second . . . or for two . . . or ten . . . before gliding toward me as a lover through the damp and heavy air, floating, ballooning as it loomed, until at last it filled the room. My thoughts shattered into fragments and, eyes fixed on the tokay, I screamed and screamed and screamed. But still he watched, unblinking.

⟲

"Mem! Missus Perkins!" a frightened voice called to me from a great distance. I struggled up through the fog, into the light, and opened my eyes.

Kham Noi stood beside the bed. As my vision cleared, I saw that his face was contorted . . . with fear, perhaps, and with a flicker of something else that I couldn't name right now. I blinked, confused, and gazed at him, then past him to the window and, as the memory emerged, quickly to the picture on the wall across the room.

The tokay was gone.

"He is outside, Mem," Kham Noi said in a gentle voice. "Gone."

I shuddered, closed my eyes for a moment, then opened them and looked at him and forced myself to smile. His face relaxed.

"Is Barby Jeanne all right?" He nodded. "Is Harvey back?"

His eyes grew flat. "Not yet. But he will come. Ai Mah would come if the Doctor were harmed." I lay still, letting the words sink in. "I will get hot tea for you," he said in a tone of relief and disappeared.

Turning my face toward the window while I waited for Kham Noi to return, I was filled with a sense of desolation, a new feeling of terrible loss. Outside I saw the pale, washed-out film of sunlight through the mango tree. *Where is Harvey?* I wondered in despair. A thought slipped in. *He could have been here by now,* and try as I might, I couldn't fight off the feeling of abandonment, as if he'd chosen another love over Barby Jeanne and me. *Abandoned.* I said the word out loud. A bleak, empty feeling struck a chord, like dark, sorrowful music in a minor key that crept into my heart.

In the nursery Barby Jeanne began to howl.

When the rain finally stopped, the Nan Valley had turned to mud. Day after day, I stared at the river road, waiting for Harvey, but it was another week before he returned. I watched with disbelief when at last he turned in through the hedge at the end of the drive. Moving toward me while I stood waiting on the veranda, he looked unreal, distant and flat. He was alone and that was strange, I thought. Where was Ai Mah?

He walked with slow, heavy steps, neck bowed, looking down, arms dangling by his sides. His shoulders were curved forward, as if the medical bag he carried weighed him down. He was far too thin, I observed. The clothes he'd worn hung on him now, and as he came closer, I saw that they were wrinkled, filthy, and torn.

The woman is responsible for the spirit of a home, I reminded myself, starting down the steps. When he looked up and saw me, a flash of anguish crossed his face before a smile broke through, and he hurried forward with a fresh burst of speed. He dropped the medical bag on the ground and threw his arms around me, hugging me tight against his chest.

*Don't ask. Now's not the time to ask.*

When he released me, I stepped back and scrutinized his face, his clothes, his muddy shoes. Without warning, relief turned to anger. I fought it back, hid it with a smile. "If you were shoeless," I said lightly, picking up the medical bag and taking his arm, "I'd think you were Mr. Smithers." As we walked up the steps, his hand gripped the rail and, with a stab of alarm, I realized that he was pulling himself along, one step at a time. When we reached the top step, he swayed and leaned against me.

"Kham Noi!" I called. Between us, we helped Harvey into the house and up the stairs to the bedroom. After stripping off the damp, dirty clothes, he eased himself onto the mattress, fell back, and was instantly asleep. Kham Noi and I covered him with blankets. I dragged a chair from across the room and sat beside him while Kham Noi gathered his clothes from the floor and disappeared. From the nursery I could hear the hum of Seewana's voice—back the day after the rains ceased—as she spoke to Barby Jeanne. On the river road wagon wheels creaked as they were forced through the mud, pulled by an unfortunate buffalo, no doubt.

The room was still bathed in the strange light that had hung over us since the monsoon. Or was it already dusk? As Harvey tossed in his sleep, my thoughts returned again and again to the roiling worms, the snakes, and worst of all, to the tokay. Music streamed through my mind, "Cara Nome"—Gilda's song that I'd left behind for Harvey—and "Liebestraum." Resentment, anger, fear—the bitter feelings surged through me, and I fought them back because I loved him. I looked at Harvey, closed my eyes, and told myself that it was up to me to control these emotions. And then I balled my fists and clenched them, inhaled, lifted my chin, and willed the resentment and anger and fear to disappear. Willed. Them. Away.

*I willed it.*

Harvey awoke in the middle of the night with a violent head-ache. Kham Noi and I took turns stroking his hot forehead with a cloth dipped in cool water. He complained that his vision was blurred; then a few hours later every muscle began to ache.

Kham Noi looked grave.

"Do you think it's the fever?" I asked.

He was silent. Kham Noi would not speak bad news for fear of making it worse. Immediately I sent for Mrs. Ruckel. She arrived with her own bag of medicines and herbs that she had learned to use over the years. Brisk and competent, she sent me running in all directions for bowls and towels, clean hot water, and herbal tea, while Kham Noi raced down to the hospital for more quinine.

When at last Harvey slept, we sat in silence in the bedroom. The sun slipped above the horizon, then rose with a vengeance. The air was still humid, and water dripped from leaves on the mango tree.

"Have you heard anything from Ai Mah?" she asked in a hushed voice.

I shook my head, watching Harvey's chest rise and fall with uneven, shallow breaths.

Mrs. Ruckel dipped a small towel into a bowl of clean water, wrung it almost dry, and folded it into a long rectangular shape. "Mr. Smithers says they couldn't find him when they left the village. He must have stayed behind." She pressed the cloth against Harvey's forehead.

The thought of the Village of the Beautiful God depressed me. I looked away through the branches of the mango tree to the lawn beyond bordered by the unruly jungle that constantly encroached on the grassy expanse.

"Has Boua Keo returned?" I asked, feeling listless.

"Not yet," she said. "Her father died, after all. She was bitter." Mrs. Ruckel hesitated, adding, "Some others in the village died as well, Mr. Smithers said."

I watched as shimmers of steam rose from the wood panel on the windowsill. I was strangely uninterested in her words. "Do you think that she blames Harvey?" I finally asked.

"No." She glanced at him. "According to Mr. Smithers, Boua Keo blames our God."

Within a few days Harvey showed some improvement, but his recovery was gradual. I sent Kham Noi to the mission school to see if Ai Mah had returned, knowing that worry over the boy weighed on his mind. But there was no sign of him yet. Neither had Boua Keo returned.

Once Harvey began to talk to me of the Village of the Beautiful God. His voice trembled, but I interrupted him, feeling fragile. This was dangerous ground. "I don't want to hear about it," I said, working to keep my voice even, the tone light.

A surprising look of relief appeared on his face. I watched him carefully, conscious that he hadn't once asked how Barby Jeanne and I had fared while he was gone. For an instant I longed to tell him of the worms, of the tokay, of my terror, that we had waited for him day after day. I longed for him to hold me as he'd used to and to explain and soothe away my fears. But I busied myself instead straightening the table near the bed, ducking my head to hide my face as I tamped down the rush of anger and resentment that surfaced.

One week later Boua Keo arrived at the mission school, alone. Days passed, then weeks, and still Ai Mah was missing. Mrs. Breeden was beside herself. "Ingrate," she muttered every time his name was mentioned. *She must miss torturing the boy,* I thought.

"Perhaps he has stayed at the Village of the Beautiful God?" Emma asked Boua Keo. But she wouldn't answer.

Harvey's face took on a permanent frown as we waited for Ai Mah to reappear. Boua Keo would not speak his name. We searched for him everywhere, Kham Noi and the Ruckels and I. Harvey slowly recovered and returned to work in the hospital, where Sawat and Nai Lueng made sad little attempts to carry on. But everything had changed. And now Harvey traveled alone into the jungle.

Boua Keo was like a wilted flower. Her father's death weighed her down, and soon her grades began to suffer. I tried to talk to her, to show her that I understood her loss. "You must go on with your studies—that would make him happy . . . and Ai Mah."

Her face flushed and she bowed her head without speaking. I touched her shoulder and when she looked up, her eyes were filled with tears, but the sorrow was mixed with anger. "Ai Mah is gone," she whispered. She wept as she spoke.

Harvey seemed withdrawn, I noticed with new detachment. Sometimes I caught him watching me with a puzzled look before he glanced away, avoiding my eyes. The question simmered in my mind: *Why didn't you come home?* Sometimes, in weak moments, resentment slipped the lock and sought release. I longed to ask why, but I bit my tongue and we spoke of other things instead.

After a few weeks the raging thoughts settled, and I realized that perhaps after all some questions are better left unanswered. Harvey and I each remained on guard, however, silent on the subject of Ai Mah, the Village of the Beautiful God, and what had happened during the monsoon.

I visited Mrs. Ruckel one day and found Mr. Smithers sitting alone on the porch in front of the house. His face was always composed, without expression. I realized suddenly that I had never seen him smile. Mrs. Ruckel was occupied in the parlor with a group of local ladies, so I took a seat beside him to wait for her. After initial pleasantries, we lapsed into silence.

The rain had brought mosquitoes. I fanned them away; the buzzing hum of the insects was annoying. When they landed on Mr. Smithers, he ignored them. I struggled to keep a grimace from my face as I watched them feed on him.

"How can you bear that?" I finally asked as I reached over to flick them from his bare arm.

He roused himself, giving me a startled look. "I've gotten used to it, I suppose," he said after a moment.

"They carry malaria, you know. It's foolish to ignore them."

He shifted in his chair and pressed his elbows against his sides. Inside the house Mrs. Ruckel's voice rose and fell in the musical tones of Siamese conversation. From the corner of my eye, I glimpsed a movement below us in the yard. A long snake slithered across the hard, packed dirt at the end of the drive near the river road. It was brown and plump; the skin was slick and gleaming, giving it a wet appearance. I shivered, thinking of reptiles in our attic.

Mr. Smithers followed my gaze. As the tail flicked and disappeared into the tall grass that grew along the edge of the drive, he regarded me with a thoughtful look. "You've had quite a time here, haven't you?" he finally asked in a low voice.

I felt myself stiffen. "No more than anyone else," I answered carefully.

"Hmmm," he murmured, looking back down the river road. "I think that you are different from the others, though," he added after a moment. "You don't quite fit, do you?"

"I don't know what you mean."

His eyes dropped to my hands, clinched into fists. I unwound my fingers and spread them, splaying them over my lap.

"Are you strong enough now to hear what happened in Ai Mah's village?" he asked. "Would you like to know what kind of man your husband is?" His eyes bored into mine and I turned away. "But for your husband—"

"I don't want to hear about it." I smoothed my skirt and pressed my hands down, feeling my thigh muscles tense as fear crept through me. My stomach tightened. Harvey had been gone for weeks; it was better not to know.

He paused before speaking again. "You're looking for something," he murmured, almost to himself. "What is it you look to out here when your husband's gone, what with all these other perfect souls?"

There was a touch of pity in his voice. I drew myself up and tucked a stray curl into the knot of hair atop my head, giving this all of my attention. "I don't count on a blessed thing except myself . . . and Harvey," I said, conscious that my tone was cold. "What else would there be?"

"Wait here," he said, grasping the arms of his chair and pushing up in one smooth motion. "I have something to show you." He hunched his shoulders, tucking his arms to his sides again, and disappeared into the house. After a minute he reappeared holding a small wooden box in his hands. He sat back down and rested the box on his knees. Lifting the lid, he reached in and pulled out what appeared to be a small piece of stone and handed it to me.

I held it flat in the palm of my hand and looked at it, turned it, touching it carefully with the tips of my fingers. The stone was thin and gray, like a sliver of granite. It was slightly rough and cold to the touch. "What is it?" I asked, looking up.

"It's what I hold onto . . . a piece of the true cross," he said, almost whispering. With that he reached out for it, as if I might drop it. I handed it back to him.

"So you are a religious man, after all."

"That depends," he said placing the relic into the box, nestling it in among a wad of old crushed paper. "You must learn to define what it is you mean by the term, Mrs. Perkins, before you reject it. Everyone needs something to hold onto, something that endures."

"Why do you think I've rejected anything?"

"Perhaps it's your question—'What else is there?' I think that's what you asked. And perhaps, also, it's your interest in the philosophical thoughts of William James." He closed his eyes and leaned back in the chair. "You can keep the book, by the way."

Harvey knew about the piece of the true cross. "It was given to him by an old monk in a monastery at the foot of Mount Sinai," he said that evening. "When we were in the Village of the Beautiful God he showed it to me." At the mention of the village I turned away.

"Ai Mah was with us then," Harvey went on. "He was fascinated with the relic. Mr. Smithers told him that it was a very powerful charm."

Joshua Smithers was a madman, I decided.

# Chapter Nineteen

A ROYAL VISITOR FROM BANGKOK, PRINCE Nakawn Sawan, provided a brief escape from our dull routine. He arrived on a lovely day, and there was great excitement as a large retinue of guards, attendants carrying betel paraphernalia and special cushions, horses, and elephants preceded the prince in a spectacular, glittering procession across the rice fields and into town. All of Nan waited outside the gates to greet him, except Mr. Smithers, who declined to attend.

That evening the Chow Luang hosted a banquet for the gentlemen of Nan in honor of the prince. Ladies were not invited. For the first time since the monsoon, since he had returned from Ai Mah's village about a month before, Harvey and I laughed together as he dressed for the royal entertainment. For an instant the steamy weather, jungle fever, and even the Breedens were forgotten. It was a blistering night, but even so Harvey attired himself in full formal dress. He was elegant in his white silk suspenders and the white pique shirt with the collar wing up, all starched and ironed by the laundress. His vest was made of intricate brocade, and a butterfly tie of imported silk was at his neck. When he was fully dressed, he stepped back and posed, pretending to lean on his walking stick as he waggled his brows and laughed at my expression. He was so handsome that I caught my breath.

But when Harvey returned around midnight, the party was forgotten. He had spotted Ai Mah near the market just outside the walls of Nan. The boy was attending a monk, and Harvey caught a glimpse of him on his way to the reception, just before the crowd closed around him.

"Are you sure that it was Ai Mah?" I asked, amazed that he'd kept himself hidden from us.

"I'm certain," Harvey said, pulling off his tie. "It was him— he turned and looked right into my eyes."

"But why wouldn't he have stopped to speak with you?"

Harvey shrugged, but I could see that he was hurt. I rested my hand on his arm, wanting to comfort him, when he added, "During the monsoon . . . his village went through a terrible, senseless tragedy. Perhaps he's angry."

I turned cold. "Things were difficult here as well," I said and moved away from him.

Mrs. Breeden, Miss Best, Emma, and I had spiffed up the mission school for an inspection by Prince Nakawn Sawan early the next morning. Harvey was needed at the hospital, so I attended alone. We cleaned the school until it shone. On the morning of the visit, Mrs. Breeden cut some flowers, and these filled large vases in every room, still fragrant and wet with dew.

The royal entourage arrived with great fanfare, escorted by the officials of Nan and the Chow Luang and his favorite wife. The boys and girls in the mission school, in freshly laundered uniforms, lined up before the dormitories to greet them with deep bows and shy smiles. As he was leaving the schoolhouse,

Prince Nakawn Sawan halted, picked a rose from a vase, examined it, and handed it to me with a few words about the beauty of the roses in the north. From under my lashes, I caught Amalie Breeden's furious look.

I noticed one evening that Reverend Ruckel seemed to have capitulated to Mr. Breeden's acrid view of life. During dinner at the Ruckels', Harvey made a point concerning the humanity of Christ in the Bible, the very human way that he changed his plans from time to time according to circumstances. Reverend Ruckel promptly rebuked him.

"The Holy Spirit directs us," he said. "We're not required to make decisions about the course of our lives. . . . We have only to follow the guidance of the Scriptures and the elders of our church."

I glanced at him in surprise, then at Harvey.

Harvey just shrugged and looked away. His expression remained placid, but I could see that he was annoyed.

"God is immutable," Mr. Breeden interjected. "He is perfect. And since the Scriptures are his words, they don't contemplate mistakes."

"Not so," Mr. Smithers interrupted. All of us were startled. "Human nature being what it is, mistakes are taken into account in the Scriptures." He stared at Mr. Breeden as he spoke. "The prophet Jeremiah told of the potter who molded a lump of clay into a vessel. But when he realized that it was imperfect, he pounded it down and started over again."

"And what do you take that to mean?" Mr. Breeden snorted.

"That our lives are not predetermined," he answered, looking off. "We must each decide *for ourselves* whether the things that we do are good or bad or right or wrong, according to the teachings of the Lord, not elders. We make choices, but when we make mistakes, we can fix them, modify our course of action."

The headmaster bristled. "That's absurd," he said. "Our lives are fixed by the Scriptures and certain. And nothing ordained by God can be changed."

"But what's the point of that?" I asked. What he was saying made no sense to me. "We all have flaws. Why would God give us the freedom to make our own choices, unless it's to allow us to muddle our way through and try to make things right?"

He tilted his head back and inspected me. Seconds passed. Then he shook his head and said in a bored tone, "We cannot just *try out* each principle of the church to see which one works the best. We accept what has to be."

"Then how do you explain the story of the potter?" Mr. Smithers persisted.

Mr. Breeden pursed his lips. "I don't have to explain the potter," he said with an icy look. "The Scriptures are rules to live by, not conversation."

In the ensuing silence, Mr. Smithers glanced at me, then his eyes clouded over and he looked away. I had the strange impression that he had something more to say, something important. For several days I expected to see him walking up our drive from the river road to complete unfinished business. But then one day Emma rode out to tell us that Joshua Smithers had disappeared.

Later that evening I thought back to the conversation, and it struck me that perhaps Harvey should consider giving the story of the potter a bit more thought.

Harvey searched for Ai Mah in Nan. Whenever he had a brief time off, he took the surrey or a bicycle and traversed the streets, methodically moving from one to the other, crisscrossing the town looking for the boy. He waited in vain in front of temples and watched for the yellow-robed priests, but Ai Mah never appeared.

One morning Harvey was late leaving for the hospital. We sat at the dining table while I supervised Barby Jeanne's attempts to eat her breakfast of Horlicks, sweetened condensed milk, and papaya. We were amused by her antics; she had a cheerful disposition, even though she did have spots of temper.

Suddenly a shadow fell across the floor. Harvey and I looked up. Ai Mah stood framed in the doorway, stiff with tension. When we both started and exclaimed, a smile crept across his face then quickly died.

"Come in, my boy," Harvey said, rising at once. He crossed the room and, placing his hand on Ai Mah's shoulder, steered him toward us. Barby Jeanne spotted him and her face was instantly wreathed in smiles. She raised her little rounded arms to him. Ai Mah touched her hand and her fingers caught his. He laughed and Harvey beamed.

He had come to tell us of a great change in his life, Ai Mah said in a soft voice. I called Seewana to take the baby, and Harvey and I walked outside with him to the veranda where the sun shone and flowers bloomed. When I sat, Ai Mah sank into a chair beside me. I noticed that his smile was tight, as if he knew that we'd be disappointed at what he had to say.

"Soon after you left my village, I left also. There was nothing more that I could do." His still, dark eyes were fixed on Harvey.

Harvey gave me a quick glance, then turned to Ai Mah. "But where have you been?" he asked. "We've all been concerned."

Ai Mah dropped his eyes. "When I left the village, I did not know where to go. I knew that the mission school was no longer my home. For a long time I sat at the edge of the forest and looked at the school and the church and the house—then I left for the old city. I walked down the river road, past the market . . . then through the elephant gates." He paused, shaking his head. "I will never go back."

When Ai Mah looked again at Harvey, his voice wavered. "The mission has taught me much, and I am grateful for that, and to you, Doctor, but I do not need your religion." He knit his brows together. "The first night I slept against the city walls under a market stall. When morning came, I found some water but no food. I walked around the old city all day and I was hungry.

"Then I heard the chanting of priests, and my heart grew light. It was the sound of our village . . . before . . ." He seemed to catch himself and went on. "In my village travelers were given food and shelter at the temple. I followed the chanting and came to a temple almost hidden behind a wall, among some trees." As he spoke, his gaze wandered over the yard, the hedge, the road, on down to the Nan River. He hesitated and looked to the right, lingering on the little vine-covered hospital on the river road just behind Tip and Ma Ping's cottage. Harvey watched him with an intent look.

"The temple was so beautiful," he said, smiling now. "The fingers of Buddha beckoned to me. I knew the priests would give me shelter—this was my place. The priests were praying in the sacred language, familiar words, the same chants that I have heard in my own village."

Kham Noi padded silently onto the veranda and placed a small plate of fruit on a table next to Ai Mah. He had not heard all that the boy had said, but his face told me that he sensed our sorrow—that this was good-bye.

"An old monk . . . a priest . . . sat alone under a bodhi tree, reading," Ai Mah went on. "I watched him while I listened to the chant—as if the voices were one, pouring joy and sorrow into the prayers. The priest made me think of my grandfather.

"Then the prayers stopped. The old priest looked up and I fell before him on my knees, made obeisance, and asked for rice and a place to rest." He glanced at Harvey. "I did not tell him about the mission school. I said that I came from the Village of the Beautiful God. He had heard. I told him that I came seeking to forget."

Harvey's eyes grew dark as he watched and listened.

"They took me in," Ai Mah said. "At first they gave me small jobs—sweeping the compound, drawing water to fill the great jars for the dormitories—and while I worked I listened to the novitiates repeat their lessons, the simple thoughts of the Lord Buddha. And I began to understand."

"Ai Mah—" Harvey lifted his hand to interrupt, but Ai Mah continued.

"The old priest took me as a disciple. He has much learning. He has traveled and lived in the world and studied the thoughts of the Buddha all of his life. The Buddha has given us the key to a life of purity, to perfection of the body and mind." His voice held a strange defensive tone as he added, "I was with my teacher when you saw me."

"You must come back," Harvey urged. "The mission school is your home. The hospital is your home."

"I have decided to take the vow of constant service," Ai Mah said, ignoring Harvey's words, avoiding his eyes. "I will enter the priesthood forever."

Harvey looked with despair at his young protégé. Hands curled, he gripped the arms of his chair. An ache spread through my chest for Harvey; he'd had such ambition for the boy.

"Your village needs you now, Ai Mah," he said in a low, urgent tone. "You were learning how to treat wounds and jungle fever, how to keep the well water clean. Have you forgotten?"

"I have not forgotten," Ai Mah said, with a darting glance at Harvey. His lips pressed together in a grim, tight line. "But nothing will change in my village. It is *samsara*—the circle of life and death and suffering, the wheel of life. Your God is not strong enough to help us."

I flinched, surprised at the harsh words.

His voice crackled. "For two years I have stood and sung and prayed to your God every Sunday in the mission church. But the headmaster said that is not enough, that I must also give up the teachings of the Buddha, and I must no longer pray to the spirits. To be a Christian I must believe many things that I do not understand." He shook his head. "But your God did not help my village."

"You will never help your own people if you withdraw from life, Ai Mah," Harvey tried to reason. "The Lord Buddha does not show you how to make the sick well; he does not show your people how to farm, or trade. You were learning so that you could help them."

Ai Mah threw himself back in his chair and his voice rose, keening. "The Buddha was right—everything is suffering. My village is suffering, birth is suffering, death is suffering, friendship is suffering—life is nothing but sorrow and pain and grief!"

He seemed to check himself then, pausing, dropping his chin as he took a deep breath. "But Buddha says this is because of worldly pleasures and desires," he added. "The priests say that when I uproot the desires, suffering will cease."

"That is running away, Ai Mah. You cannot solve problems that way."

"This is the path that the Buddha has left for us to follow."

"You will give your whole life to this? You're going to hide away in a monastery?"

Ai Mah turned to Harvey. His forehead smoothed, the crease between his eyebrows disappeared, and his mouth relaxed. His face lost all expression. "It is not this life that is important," he said with an invisible shrug, but his voice shook.

Harvey leaned forward, eyes riveted to Ai Mah's. "This life is a beautiful gift. We accept it and do our best while we are here. Service, the good that you can do for your people— that's your answer, Ai Mah, not emptiness, not dreams of nirvana."

But Ai Mah was no longer listening. In a calm, resolute tone he ended the conversation. "With the priests I will be happy, Doctor. My life is simple now. One night, not long after I saw you in the old city, as I listened to the drums and watched the rise of the moon, I knew that the Lord Buddha's way is now my life. The temple is my home."

I hugged Ai Mah even as he pulled back from me, then Harvey walked with him down the drive to the edge of the river road. I watched them clasp hands. Ai Mah turned to the left toward Nan, and Harvey turned right, toward the hospital.

After they left, I sat alone on the veranda until the moon was high, pondering what Ai Mah had said. Something truly terrible must have happened at the Village of the Beautiful God.

Ai Mah had asked us to attend his ordination ceremonies at the temple. Outsiders were permitted to visit and watch, and sorrowfully, we agreed to go.

Three months later, on the appointed day, we walked between tall trees through the winding, twisting streets of Nan, until we reached the temple compound. The sun reflected off the blue and white tiles of the roof. The rounded pillars at its eastern end extended to the sky, pointing to the glory above.

We walked through the gates into a small park. It was late afternoon and the sun already slanted low beneath the trees. The whole area, surrounded by low stone walls, created a sanctuary for hundreds of colorful birds that flocked and sang undisturbed in the open.

The ceremony itself was starkly beautiful, simple, meditative, and as unadorned as the life Ai Mah would henceforth lead. Candles lit the temple. His head was shaven and his body clean and purified after seven baths through which he had to pass. Standing beside three other young novices taking their vows this day, he looked straight ahead with a face like stone at the Abbot and the Buddha behind him. His lack of expression reminded me of the first time that I had met Ai Mah in the hospital—his eyes were dark pools of curiosity, but he had watched and waited to see what would occur.

Now, as Ai Mah prostrated himself in obeisance and chanted the words that would make him a priest of his people, he seemed to drift from us, farther and farther with each word. My eyes filled with tears, but I squeezed them back. I took Harvey's hand in mine and pressed it. He gave me no response; his eyes were fixed on the ceremony.

The novices had finished the chant, and the temple grew silent as we waited. The stillness was broken by a clear, bell-like tone, the chant of the three refuges—the Buddha, the priesthood, and the law. As the abbot intoned the words three times, the chorus of priests, their voices merging into an echo that seemed to multiply itself tenfold, repeated them. Finally, after Ai Mah had repeated with the others the basic precepts of abstinence by which he now promised to live, he bowed three times before his Buddha, and without rising, crawled to a place prepared for him among the priests. As the monks began the closing incantations, Ai Mah's voice joined theirs for the first time. Now his eyes were focused far into the distance, far beyond Harvey and me and the little mission school.

As I watched, my gaze fell upon an old monk who sat behind him. I caught my breath in surprise; here was the old monk from the ruins, the one I had met at Wat Phumin when we first arrived at Nan. His face was still, serene and impassive as he chanted, looking past me with no sign of recognition. Somehow I knew that this was Ai Mah's teacher.

Harvey and I were thoughtful as we left the temple proper. It was dusk; the sun was low, almost at the point of horizon. As we walked in silence through the violet shadows, Harvey stopped abruptly and, placing his hand upon my arm, nodded to a place beneath some trees. There a novice stood ready before five drums set side by side on a platform just slightly raised from the ground. Two were very large, at least two spans across, with hide covers held in place by laced leather thongs that stretched all the way back down the barrels. All of them, large and small, were decorated in carved geometric patterns and scrolls painted with bright-colored lacquer. The young beater's feet were braced wide apart to permit him to stretch to the farthest drum on each side. He was poised, tense and still, the muscles in his arms and back standing out as if they were carved from amber. His arms were raised high above each shoulder, waiting for a signal to begin.

As the sun flashed and disappeared below the horizon, the beater's arm stretched up, swung far to the side and down, and the first deep note of the big drum came rumbling through the trees. The sound seemed to sink through me as I watched, entranced. Recoiling from the force of the tense drumhead, the young man threw his arm back and stood taut, motionless and waiting. Ten seconds passed, and as the echoes of the first beat faded, his arm stretched high, whipped down, and the second blow was struck. Now blow followed blow, slowly at first, then gaining speed as the intervals grew fleeting—faster and faster, until at last the drumbeats rolled together, blending as the air around us throbbed.

The beater flayed the drums wildly now. Sweat flicked from his arms as he struck the cadence. As the tempo increased, he hit the tenor drums, punctuating the deeper throbbing sounds with riotous high notes. Urgent it came, the wild call throughout the north at sunset to greet the rising moon.

When the drums reached a thunderous roll, a new understanding began to form, hovering just at the edge of my conscious thoughts until it emerged. I could hear the drums of distant temples merging with these and rolling on, united, over the plains of the Nan Valley, through the jungles and across the land. The throbbing beat carried with it the spirit of the country, enveloping its people—the men, women, children, priests and kings, farmers and thieves—in this beautiful symbol of reverence for nature and their own strength and their Buddha.

Ai Mah's decision was clear to me now. Just as each drumbeat lost its identity in the thunder of the whole, so were the people of this country one, linked by the teachings of the Buddha and their spirit lore. At even-time the farthermost villages of Siam were bound to ancient precepts of their culture by the message of the drums: that the endless cycle of unfulfilled desire, of misery and disappointment, of restlessness—the wheel of life—can only be broken by each person from within. Our mission's teachings were meaningless to them. All that Ai Mah had accepted in the priesthood was contained in the eternal roll of the drums. They continued for a half an hour more.

I felt the silver cobweb tremble—the threads of wisdom and sorrow, a pattern woven at the death of my father, the birth of our daughter, the sacrifices we'd made to our marriage for this mission, the new distance between us, and I thought again of the music that I'd left behind as one after another the delicate fibers shivered with the beat of the drums. More than three years of our married lives were gone, spent trying to change the people of Siam, to teach them our ways.

*Who are we to tell Ai Mah that he should change?* I wondered. *Perhaps there is no wrong way or right way to think and live.* The thought struck like a blow as the potter's tale came to mind. With a fierce and sudden movement, the beater slammed both sticks down upon the large drum and emitted a long, deep roll of thunder that seemed to sap him of strength. With a series of slow pulsing beats, the drums slowed and finally stopped, leaving us in silence.

We never saw Ai Mah again.

# Chapter Twenty

IN THE SPRING OF 1923, AS the sound of the drums rolled across the Nan Valley each evening, I had a new awareness of the spirit of Siam and our place as the farang, always on the outside looking in. One morning on my way to visit Mrs. Ruckel, on an impulse I stopped at the mission church. Across the adjoining field, small boys scampered back and forth kicking a ball. I left the surrey on the side of the road with the ponies tied to the white wooden fence, and walked up the path to the front door. Flowers had been planted in neat rows along the way by the school children.

The door was unlocked. I turned the knob and, when it creaked open, I entered and walked softly to a pew in the front of the room. My heels made hollow clacks on the wooden floor, and I lifted them to muffle the sound. As I took a seat on a bench near the front, laughter from the children tinkled in the distance. The room was silent, cool, and dark.

I closed my eyes, trying to conjure the cheerful pictures of heaven that I had imagined as a child, but as the pictures formed they slipped away. Instead, the musty smell of the closed room made me long for Summit Church, Mummy and Dad, my sisters and brothers in our family pew, the youthful confidence that things exist beyond our physical world—and the certainty that death is years away. A feeling of loss washed over me. The pleasant, childish memories were there, but all I felt was sorrow. No. The feeling was wistful; it was nostalgia.

Leaning back against the pew, I grew conscious that every muscle in my body was drawn tight. I released the tension with a sigh. For an hour I waited alone in the mission church. "If you're there," I whispered, surprised to find my throat filled with tears, "just give me a sign. Some little thing that I will recognize."

Silence was the response.

I closed the door of the church softly as I left, realizing that I no longer wished to visit Mrs. Ruckel. With no particular plan I let the ponies ramble, following the river road on to Nan, then I snapped the reins, urging them into a brisk trot. We wound our way through the streets of the old city to Ai Mah's temple, where I sat for a moment before climbing down from the surrey. With the ponies tied to a post beside the gate, I entered the courtyard. The old monk, Ai Mah's teacher, sat on a bench under the thick, spreading branches of a tree nearby, just as Ai Mah had said he did every afternoon. He held a book, which I took to be Scriptures, but he glanced up over the top as if he had been expecting me. I stood silent.

"So you have returned," he said. "I thought that one day you would come."

I nodded, chose a spot, and settled on the ground, keeping a distance between us that would not make him uncomfortable and tucked my legs under my skirt and to the side in the Siamese fashion. A small bird's song rippled and played in the air around us. Flecks of light danced on the ground as a breeze rustled the leaves above. My thoughts were clouded with puzzling despair.

Finally the old man spoke. "The one you call Ai Mah is now free from the bondage of desire . . . free from suffering. . . . He will have a holy life that is utterly pure."

"I hope this won't offend you," I said. "But we were not happy to lose Ai Mah to the priesthood. I don't see that it is a good thing . . . overall, you know. He was learning medicine; my husband thought that he would make a difference to the lives of the people in his village, and in many other villages."

"The Buddha taught that what he gave up is nothing. Everything in life is an illusion—happiness, good health, pleasure. There really is no Ai Mah. He is unreal—an empty vessel, a temporary being of form, feeling, perception, concepts, and consciousness—as are we all."

He looked at me and his voice was gentle. "We call these forms, feelings, and so on, the *skandas*—that is, what you perceive as a person. But each person is a mosaic, constantly shifting, changing. Once you realize this, you cease to cling to things that were formerly important. Then the heart is liberated—you will be truly free."

I picked up a leaf from the ground and turned it in my hand. "If what you say is true, then life means nothing."

"It means nothing," he agreed in a placid tone. "There is no 'I am' . . . there is no self. There are only beings that move around particles of space, creating the wind of karma that flows through life after life. It is the *cumulative* effect of the pieces in the mosaic that matter. As we move from moment to moment, day to day, life to life, our actions and thoughts shape our existence."

I fingered the leaf and thought about that. "Aren't you really saying that our thoughts and actions have consequences?" I asked after a moment. "If so, what good does it do Ai Mah to withdraw from life and refuse to think or act at all? What good does it do for him to repudiate the things that he was learning from my husband that could help his village—to spend the rest of his life instead merely purifying his mind?" I shook my head. "It sounds like a waste to me."

"This is the Way. It will free him." The old man smiled. "The Buddha told a story," he said. "A monkey was captured in the jungle and imprisoned in a square cage with four solid walls—a cold, rigid place. He longs for his old life, yearns to fly from branch to branch through the trees, yearns for the beauty and freedom of the jungle, for the wind and sunshine, the ever-shifting shapes and colors, the flowers and vines and twisting trees." He paused and looked off. "Life was fluid and free before the monkey's capture," he went on in a reflective tone. "Now his life flow is still, like cascading water will freeze in winter in your country." His eyes met mine.

Ghostlike I saw myself, trapped inside the frozen waterfall. I nodded.

"Ai Mah was that captured monkey before he met the Buddha. His mind was frozen, imprisoned by this earthly illusion. He was trapped in endless rebirth by attachments, by his desire and suffering." He smiled. "But by cutting those ties, his thoughts will expand; his mind will become one with the universe. His thinking will be fluid. He will be free."

"Our mission church is not much interested in free thinking," I said. Mr. Breeden's face loomed in my imagination. "We don't probe beneath the surface—we learn from our holy Scriptures. The Bible is God's word, our source of truth."

His expression did not change. "How do you know that the Bible is really the word of your God?" he asked. "I do not mean to be impolite. I would like to understand."

I thought for a moment. "The Scriptures are like a first principle. You must have the gift of faith. There is no way to prove it."

"Ah . . ." he murmured. "I understand." He watched a leaf tumbling over the grass on a breeze. "Then the first principle of the Buddha Dharma would be personal experience," he said, turning back to me. In his dark eyes, I saw the reflection of my own bleak thoughts. "The Lord Buddha only asks us to find the truth for ourselves."

"And what is it that Ai Mah will be seeking?"

"Enlightenment," he said, then added, "nirvana—escape from the wheel of life. It is like blowing out a candle. When enlightenment is achieved, all suffering ceases, as a flame is extinguished."

I picked up a twig on the ground nearby and rolled it between my hands. "How do you know when you've reached nirvana?"

"You know because you experience it. You need no one else's word."

"Ah," I said. Seconds passed. "No faith is required," I murmured.

He smiled.

The days seemed endless. Everything was unsettled, gone to smash. The weather was hot and muggy, and we were constantly threatened with malaria and dengue fever. Reverend Ruckel said that he could not recall another year as bad. I moved about in a deliberate fog of angst, holding off the nagging thought that we were wasting precious time. Once in a while slivers of life from the world outside slipped into our isolated valley through letters or news from an occasional visitor, and then I yearned for home.

The old monk's words lingered. It seemed useless to me now to wonder whether or not life is an illusion, since either way this is the hand that we've been dealt. But I had come away from him with a new thought that slowly took shape: Buddha said that enlightenment comes by repudiating the things of this world. We are to chip away the dross of life—our dreams, desires, emotions—and at the end, find the universal truth for ourselves through experience and rebirth. But the church insists that moral law is something else. It's found outside of our *selves* and written in the Scriptures. And a priestly caste—priests, pastors, or preachers like Mr. Breeden—must mine the Scriptures for the gold and pass on to the rest the rules to live by. *But what if both are wrong?* I asked myself. I looked around. *What if this is all there is—right here, right now, and nothing more, nothing that endures?*

And there it was. Either way, under the teachings of Buddha or Christianity, everything depends on a belief that something else, something vague and undefined, transcends this world we live in. Life is the means in either case but not the end. But I had changed in these years at Nan, and now, I realized, the only things I knew to trust were those that were concrete and known, things that we could see or feel or touch. As frightening as it was, I came to the conviction that life is just the end of things. Nothing endures.

I tried explaining these new thoughts to Harvey. "And where does that leave you, Babs?" he asked when I had finished—not, I realized, where does that leave "us." I looked at him, feeling alone.

"Where?" After a moment I laughed, mugged a face and said, "Well, I'm left with one philosophy, I suppose. *Carpe diem*, Harvey. I'll just have to seize the day."

He shook his head as he looked back down at his book. I envied him, I thought, watching him. Because of his work, his life had meaning. Nothing slowed him down.

As if watching two strangers, I observed the span between us increase week by week. But when I opened my mouth intending to tell him that I was lonely and afraid, I told him instead of the funny things that Barby Jeanne had done that day, the vegetables that Kham Noi found at market, the flowers in the garden, the children on the river road.

One day Mr. Breeden announced that they would be leaving shortly for Bangkok. His face glowed with pride and satisfaction. He'd been given an important post with the mission in Asia. This was a great success for the Breedens.

"Of course, this is your triumph too," Mrs. Ruckel said to Mrs. Breeden when she heard the news. We were gathered at the Ruckels' for dinner. "Such a promotion can only have happened so quickly because the two of you work together well. You're an effective team." The words pierced me, knowing that she would never describe Harvey and me that way. I had never been a part of Harvey's work at Nan.

Harvey looked at Mrs. Breeden with admiration. She laughed happily and slanted her eyes at him, while envy wormed its way through my thoughts.

The men excused themselves, and Mrs. Breeden trailed Mrs. Ruckel into the kitchen where the cook waited with his helper. I wandered out to the veranda and leaned on the railing, fighting a sudden desperate feeling that I could not understand.

"There's no need to feel sorry for yourself."

I whirled to see Emma standing behind me. I straightened and smoothed my hair. "I was just looking at the stars," I said.

"No you weren't." She leaned on the railing next to me. "Did you know that she can't have children?"

I stood by her and gazed out across the field at the mission church that still stood sentry.

"No," I finally said. "I didn't know."

"It's a cross that she bears. That's one reason they came here in the first place. She was desperate to get away from the sisters and cousins and friends and continuous birthing of babies."

I was surprised, then remembered Mrs. Breeden's reluctance to hold Barby Jeanne, and an image drifted through my mind— the expression on Mrs. Breeden's face that evening. I thought of all the small rejections that I'd seen Mr. Breeden inflict upon his wife, subtle but humiliating actions. Suddenly an unexpected wave of pity washed over me. I could not imagine being committed for life to anyone as rigid and angry as Mr. Breeden. Turning my face from Emma, I looked up at the watery moon skimming the tops of the trees.

"She told me they were sent here because of Dr. Pitter's illness and because the Ruckels were getting on in years."

"Yes," Emma said. "That's what she says. But Miss Best says otherwise."

Not long after this, Emma received permission to transfer to the mission at Chiang Mai. When he learned that she was going, Dr. Pitters decided that he and Mrs. Pitters would travel with her. His health required more intensive treatment. A mission house near the hospital in Chiang Mai had recently been vacated, he told Harvey, and Dr. Cord urged them to come.

As everyone prepared to leave, I was overcome by the thought of being left behind. We might be isolated here for years before replacements arrive, I thought with despair. "I'm ill," I told Harvey one evening after I had spent the day helping Emma pack up her things in baskets for the carriers. I shivered, feeling cold through and through. But despite the cold, a sheen of perspiration covered my throat and chest.

"Cold sweat," he said as he wrapped me in a blanket and held me.

"Now I'm hot," I complained a few minutes later. The sudden heat was sickening. Not the pleasant searing of the sun but a radiating burn that rose from the center of my body and spread. I held the back of my hand against my forehead. Just as I had guessed, my skin was hot.

Harvey unwrapped the blanket and fanned me as I lay in our stifling bedroom. I was dizzy; things seemed to whirl around me. Harvey's eyes were dark, drooping more than usual at the outer corners.

"Aren't you being somewhat melodramatic, Babs?" he asked once. His voice, usually gentle and full of concern, was brusque with impatience.

"Yes, I suppose you're right," I murmured. But my limbs were heavy. My body sank into the mattress. My eyes remained fixed on the mango tree, and I couldn't look at him. Then, taking a deep breath, I forced myself to rise from the bed. My skin was tight as I smiled.

Harvey sighed, looking at his watch. I concentrated on each movement.

Christmas came and went. In February 1924 the Breedens departed in a great flurry of carriers and boxes and good-byes. As they readied themselves to mount their ponies, Mrs. Breeden brushed the side of my face with her lips and I saw the flash of triumph in her eyes. Then out of nowhere came a thought: These small triumphs are all that she has. I thought of Barby Jeanne, of Mrs. Breeden's cold, hard husband, and on an impulse I threw my arms around her, drew her to me, and held her, wanting to start over, to change things somehow.

After a moment she released herself, leaned back, and studied my face. With a wry smile she shook her head. "I guess I'll just never understand you," she murmured.

Behind her Mr. Breeden's icy look scanned past, as if I no longer inhabited the world that he occupied. Then he held out his hand to Harvey.

Emma left soon after, taking Dr. and Mrs. Pitters with her to Chiang Mai. The elderly couple rode astride a pair of mules in the middle of the carriers, with Emma in the lead. Mrs. Pitters was already haranguing a man who had the misfortune to be walking beside her. Dr. Pitters slumped on his mule in resignation.

"I don't know how they'll ever make it," I said as we watched them depart. I waved to Emma one last time, thinking how I would miss her dry humor.

"He's too ill now to make the trip," Harvey said.

As we stood watching the departure, the bamboo growth on the edge of the forest crept around us, closing in. Miss Best stood nearby. Her look of disapproval as she tucked her limp hair behind her ear foreshadowed the joyless years ahead. I turned my face from Harvey and shut my eyes. *How much longer?* I wept inside—bitter, silent, invisible tears. *Hold steady, Babs,* warned my inner voice. I dried the tears before they reached my eyes and fought for control. After a moment I glanced up. Harvey was studying me with a worried look.

Months passed, each one seeming like a year. I sat by the window in our bedroom, filling my days with the most ordinary, mundane tasks: replacing buttons on Harvey's pajamas, mending, ripping seams and sewing them back again with tighter stitches. In and out the needle slipped, a rhythmic, comforting routine. Sometimes my hands trembled, but the four walls were a shelter from disapproving eyes, unwanted visitors, decisions. I no longer sat on the veranda to watch the river road.

We were in the tag end of the dry season now, when the air turned to steam as the heat persisted despite the early rains. Leaves and grass were brown, so parched they almost crackled. When the rain began in earnest, once again we found ourselves awash in mud. On some nights when the rain fell in solid sheets, the patients in the hospital ward moved from place to place in the room, seeking a dry spot in which to rest.

One day in July, Harvey returned home early. The crease between his eyes had deepened. "I have to go into the villages for a week or so, Babs," he said, in a casual tone with a sideways glance at me.

I stared at him in disbelief, not certain at first that I had really heard the words. Even with Harvey's presence the constant rain was already unbearable. Barby Jeanne and I were unable to leave the house for days at a time as the seasonal torrent continued. White translucent worms crawled through my mind and turned to snakes. The tokay grinned and spat. A sharp pain gripped my chest. "Must you go again?" I cried.

"I have to, Babs," he answered. He took me in his arms and gently stroked my hair. "These people need me." Then he added. "That's what we came here for."

The words fractured my thoughts. Flecks of light danced before my eyes. I held myself stiff in Harvey's arms, struggling to control the panic that threatened to crush me while the lights turned to sparks, and—at last—the sparks burst into flames.

Fury shook me and I pushed away from Harvey, lifting my eyes to his. "*I* need you . . . your *daughter* needs you!" The rage surged from my core and emerged as a scream, harsh and unforgiving. I grabbed a book from the table nearby and hurled it at the wall, wheeling back to Harvey. "Whether you go or not will change nothing in those villages!" I clenched my fists. "We're all like that wretched *Rachasee* leaping from the cliff to destroy his own reflection. We look at the people around us and see only ourselves."

"Babs!" He reached for me.

I sobbed and held him off with stiff arms. "We're *wrong*, Harvey. Don't you see? We've made a mistake. They're not like us . . . *they don't want to be like us . . . they don't want to change!* They'll *never* change and maybe they're right to feel that way. We're wasting time. We've wasted years and years for nothing."

As the tears rolled down my cheeks, my thoughts swam with visions of coiling snakes, spitting tokays, and white worms; of Gibbon grasping Barby Jeanne; of Mr. Breeden's steel grip upon my head . . . pressing . . . pressing down and down . . . toward his lake of fire; of Ai Mah; of Dad—gone; of my music, the chance to sing that I had missed. And the price we paid for all of that, the price exacted by Nan and the mission, was our marriage. Suddenly I couldn't breathe.

I gasped for air and my heart throbbed. Like a drum it pounded in my chest, in my ears. *I'm suffocating!* I thought. Sobbing I sank to my knees through air that was thick and viscous, like heavy water. "Help me!" I cried. "Harvey, help me! I'm drowning . . . I can't breathe . . . *can't breathe* . . . " My arms flailed as I reached for him, unable to see.

"*Harvey!*" I screamed.

I felt him kneel beside me, felt his arms as they slid around me, felt the warmth of his chest as he pulled me close, murmuring, cupping the back of my head with his hand as I strained to hear his voice. As we knelt together, slowly a dark mist descended, enclosing us, separating us from the rest of the world. I remember the peace that came with that mist. I remember the quiet and the calm, and then . . . Harvey disappeared . . . and I floated weightless and alone in the black, and the only sound left in the universe was the ticking of a clock.

I woke to find myself in bed. Days had passed, I later learned. Harvey sat beside me. He was gaunt. I watched him from beneath my lids at first. His eyebrows were drawn together into a permanent frown as he stared past me out the window. The clock still ticked and the sound filled the room. I turned my head but could not find it. Harvey glanced down at the movement. When he saw that I was awake, the lines around his eyes smoothed and he drew himself up with a smile. But beneath the smile I sensed anguish. As he bent to stroke my forehead, the muscles in his face worked. His mouth moved, but I could not hear the words over the sound of the invisible clock. I frowned, fixing my eyes upon him, but still I could not hear a thing.

He leaned close, pressing his lips to my cheek, kissing the lobe of my ear, resting his lips in the curve of my neck. I heard his voice at last. "It will be all right now, my love. We're going home."

"How?" I whispered, drawing back to watch him.

He stroked my forehead. "Reverend Ruckel has asked Chiang Mai to send a temporary replacement. He'll be here soon." His voice broke on the last word, but all I heard was "home."

It was two months before we could leave. On the day of our departure, the sun rose big and bright as it had in Bangkok almost four years before when we rushed through the city, eager to meet the train that would take us to Phrae. The Ruckels and Miss Best gathered with Kham Noi, Seewana, and Tip and Ma Ping to see us off. Kham Noi's face contorted as he struggled against tears when I handed him Ot Dee for the last time. But I knew that tomorrow his sorrow would be only a memory. He stood next to Seewana, and I could picture them together years from now. They seemed unreal—ghostlike, as if they would always exist in that house on the river road, never growing older, never changing while the years rolled past and our replacements came and went, as the farang had always done at Nan.

Mrs. Ruckel hugged me, holding me in her arms for a long time. Then she kissed my cheek and backed away. As I looked into her eyes, for a flash I saw my failure. Then she veiled the look and smiled, a wistful smile.

Harvey took Reverend Ruckel's hand to say good-bye, but the elderly gentleman pulled him close in an embrace. His eyes were bright with unshed tears when he straightened up again.

As we turned onto the river road to join the carriers for our last trip through the jungle, Harvey's eyes scanned the trees, the birds, the river. Then he stiffened and nudged his pony forward, now looking only straight ahead.

I glanced back and saw the old white heads of the Ruckels in the distance. They stood at the gate of the white picket fence in front of their house near the river road. Mrs. Ruckel raised her hand to wave good-bye one last time, but it seemed as I watched that she stood in a mist, like a shadow-person now. I thought that I heard music, faint but dissonant and strange, like a harp strummed in anger. *Glissando.* Then the fragile silver threads of cobweb shimmered and grew tight, as one by one they snapped.

And I realized at that moment that I believed in absolutely nothing at all.

# Part Two

# Chapter Twenty-One

Philadelphia
September 1924

WE LEASED A SMALL HOUSE IN a cul-de-sac on Lantern Lane. The city was gay; compared to Nan, it sizzled and popped. Like one emerging from a dark cavern, I was dazzled by the laughter and music and light that suddenly exploded around us, by the changes that had occurred in the four years since we had left for Siam. At first I sheltered myself and watched.

"You've changed," Evie told me one day. She sat sprawled in an old blue chair in Mummy's house on Greene Street, legs dangling over the rounded arm.

"I'm four years older," I said.

"It's not that. You've always had a way of turning inside, of holding yourself very still when you have to deal with something hard. You hide behind your smile, Dad used to say."

I looked past her to the gray sky. The first cold wind of autumn was huffing in from the north. I rose to close the window. The smell of rain was in the air. This would be the end of the rainy season in Siam, I realized. I walked to the piano and played a few notes, then lifted my hand from the keyboard and rose, turning to Evie. Music has a way of unveiling truth. I wasn't in the mood for serious music. And Dad was gone, the house full of empty spaces now.

"I'm fine—just tuning the lyre," I told her in a light tone. But through the stillness of the room I heard the clock on the mantle as it ticked away the time.

Evie gave me a long look and raised her brows, then turned all her attention to a cigarette that she held in a long, delicate holder between two straight fingers.

The rainy season. It had been almost two years since Harvey left with Ai Mah and the mad Englishman during the monsoon, disappearing into the jungle for days, then weeks. Suddenly I had to talk of it to someone. I sat across from Evie, took a cigarette and a light from her, and told her everything—of how I had been so sure that Harvey would return when the monsoon struck, of the isolation and the fear, of how in the end he had pushed ahead instead.

"It's not the fear that changed me, Evie. I could have handled that alone." I heard the catch in my voice and looked away. "It's the futility of it all—the mission, the time wasted at Nan trying to change things that can't be changed. And the price we paid for that."

"Don't be silly," Evie said with impatience. "Harvey was raised to act according to duty, and you married him that way. Don't try that metaphysical mumbo jumbo on him. He doesn't think of those four years at Nan as time wasted, you know. His point of view is the same. It's you who've changed."

The truth of her words jolted me. It *was* my own point of view that had changed. I was no longer comforted by the idea that sacrifice and duty is rewarded in a next life, that life extends beyond the finite number of years allotted to us on this earth. It's *time* that's the problem, I decided. If this is all there is, each moment we're alive should be spectacular. Like Phaëton, I wanted to blaze across the sky in the sun god's golden chariot.

But Harvey's duty as a doctor, his work, simple belief, and honor—these things were still first in Harvey's life. *And where does that leave Barby Jeanne and me?* I asked myself. I did not dare to stand between Harvey and his goals. I loved him too much to risk the loss.

*Well then, it's all up to you,* whispered my inner voice. *Make the most of what you have. Fill each moment with the best things. Seize each moment.*

❧

We put off our return to Summit Church. "There's plenty of time for that," I answered vaguely when Mummy brought the subject up. "We need to get settled first."

Harvey soon found that, by virtue of our time at Nan, he was considered an expert on tropical medicine. Jefferson Medical School in Philadelphia asked him to teach. A pattern began to emerge. Each morning he disappeared and each evening, when he returned from the school and hospital, he strolled in, placed his walking stick in the porcelain stand by the front door, and carefully hung his hat on a rack nearby.

"Good evening, dear," he would say as he sank into a comfortable chair in the parlor and disappeared into his medical books. His eyes no longer seemed to linger on me.

One morning after Harvey left, I gazed into the mirror and grimaced at my reflection. We had lived with missionaries too long. My dresses still brushed my ankles, and my long hair was pulled into the knot that curled on the top of my head. I leaned close to the mirror to inspect my reflection, pulled back and frowned at myself, loosened my hair, and smoothed the skin on my cheeks with both hands. Then I phoned Evie and Alice and asked them to come right over.

"We need to get to work," I said when they arrived. "I want my hair bobbed, Alice, just like yours."

Alice was no longer the child I had left behind. She was a fashionable young woman now, married to a smooth, wealthy man, a book publisher who gratified her every wish. She had developed a sharp edge and an ironic sense of humor. Alice assessed the long hair curling down my back. "It's about time," she laughed. "Grab the scissors, Babs. Let's see what you're really made of."

I sat in front of the mirror and adopted an expression of nonchalance while my pulse raced. Evie plopped onto the edge of the bed, crossed her legs, lit a cigarette, and leaned back, dangling one foot to the beat of an internal tune while she watched. Alice began to snip, stepping back from time to time to observe her work. As my hair dropped from her scissors to the floor, I looked at the chopped locks with growing despair. Finally I turned my eyes away. I couldn't watch.

"You've never worn it short before," Evie reflected as Alice snipped. A lump grew in my throat. Harvey had always loved my hair . . . perhaps this was a mistake.

Finally the scissors were stilled and Alice stepped back. She nudged me. I took a deep breath and raised my eyes to the mirror. The face that looked back at me was framed with soft amber-colored curls that bounced when I tilted my head and swung it from side to side. The woman I saw in the mirror was me, but younger, flushed and smiling.

I preened and glanced at Alice and Evie for the verdict.

"It's the bee's knees," Evie said with a slow nod.

Alice gave a sly smile, then pulled a dress from the armoire. I stared in astonishment as the scissors began snipping again across the bottom of my dress. Evie sat up, looking at this with interest.

"What are you doing?" I exclaimed, making a grab for the scissors.

She jerked her hand away. "We have to finish what we've started now. Just wait and see. No one wears long dresses any more."

I watched in silence as she cut again into the dress with a determined snip, and after she had finished, she folded up a hem and whipped it with a quick stitch. Finally she handed me the dress. I pulled it on and my eyes grew wide as I turned to the mirror. It fell to just above my knees. A wave of triumphant, pagan joy rushed through me.

I fluffed my hair, and Alice handed me some bright red lipstick. While I put it on, she moved behind me to view her work. "Jazz baby," Alice said with an approving laugh.

Evie blew a column of smoke at me and said, "You look slick."

That evening when the front door opened, Harvey almost collided with me. He stepped back and his eyes widened as he took in the loose short hair and the raised hem of my dress. I laughed with delight as his look traveled slowly from my head to my feet in stunned silence. Then I tilted my head with a coy smile and let my hair fall over one eye.

He grinned and flung his hat to a chair, letting it spin through the air. It fell on the floor, but he left it there. He jammed his stick into the stand and, elated, I swung my arm through his. He stopped for a long look, then pulled me with him up the stairs and into our bedroom, leaving his medical books behind in the parlor.

Our second daughter was born on June 12, 1925, approximately nine months later. We named her Harriet June and called her June. She was soft and round and merry. June had a deep chuckle that was surprising to hear from a brand-new baby.

I spent my days with friends and sisters. We smoked cigarettes, raced through the streets of Philadelphia in fast, sleek cars, ate what we wanted, drank what we wanted, went where we wanted to go, and—with no apologies to Emery Breeden—thought what we wanted to think. I relished the sudden freedom I found in Philadelphia, a complete contrast to Nan.

On occasional weekends we all hopped on the train to New York to make the rounds of speakeasies, to visit Broadway, the Hippodrome, and the Midnight Follies. In smoky rooms we drank bootleg whiskey, and Alice and Evie taught me the wild, loose Charleston and, after a few drinks, the shimmy—moves that were old hat in Philadelphia but new to me.

Entertainment is not cheap and money was always a small problem. I didn't really give it much thought, however. There was always enough cash around to do what we wanted to do, though Harvey worried about the expense of things from time to time.

"We're slightly strapped," he said one evening when Alice and Evie proposed another trip to New York.

Alice gave him a humorous look. "For heaven's sake, don't be so gloomy, Harvey. I distrust practicality at this time of night. Anyway," she gave a careless shrug and leaned into her handsome husband, Dick, "the stock market's up."

It was past midnight and we sat in a speakeasy in downtown Philadelphia. Prohibition was still the law, but I noticed that no one seemed overly concerned. Across the close, crowded room a band was warming up after a short break.

Evie took a drag on her cigarette and watched us in silence.

"Well, look here," Harvey answered in a dry tone, "that doesn't help us. We have nothing to invest." His words were almost lost as the band struck up "Hard-Hearted Hannah." The crowd went wild as the music began to throb.

"That's a dreary proposition," Alice shouted over the blare.

The singer's smoky voice crawled across the room. Evie tapped her fingers on the small round table between us in time to the drummer's beat. A *strong* beat. My whole body moved with the sensual, freewheeling music that would have been banned at Nan. I threw back my head and laughed. "*Leather is tough, but Hannah's heart is tougher*," growled the singer. "*The vamp of Sa-vann-ahhh, the meanest gal in town . . .*" I mugged a face for my sisters, rose from the chair and swiveled toward Harvey, shifting my weight to one hip, and held out my arm. "C'mon Harvey. Let's dance!"

Harvey's eyes grew wide, and he exploded with laughter as I strutted in a circle before him, eyeing him over my shoulders while I turned and belted out the words: "*An ev'ning spent with Hannah sitting on your knees . . .*"

"*. . . Is like trav'ling through Alaska in your Bee Vee Dee's!*"
Dick roared as he raised his glass and pounded the table with
his other hand.

Harvey pulled himself up. "A fellow would be crazy to
turn down an offer like that," he said with a grin. I hooked my
hands with his behind my back and led him onto the dance
floor.

"Red hot mama!" someone yelled from across the room.

It didn't take long to see that the changes that had occurred
while we were gone went deeper than the garish colors splashed
onto the new pumps for gasoline, the glitz of honky-tonk, jazz,
and gin fizz, the Charleston and the shimmy and boop-boop-
a-doop. It seemed to me that the whole world had suddenly
turned upside down. The forces of science and religion now
clashed in every part of our lives. Albert Einstein's new general
theory of relativity had become cocktail party conversation
for ordinary people who knew nothing of science. *Facts* were
revered. Science had replaced religion, I decided.

The new songs and jazz suited my mood. I packed away
my old phonographs of opera and classical music that brought
unwanted memories—of Dad, of my old dreams of singing—
and bought some new ones: the hot licks of the new jazz with its
syncopated riffs, hard notes, blue notes, freed now from the old
form and structure. There were no rules left, it seemed.

One day Miss Josephine Baker of St. Louis, Missouri,
Charlestoned onto the stage of the Folies Bergeré in Paris clad
only in rhinestone-studded bananas and three bracelets.

"Did you read what she was wearing?" I asked Evie in astonishment as I scanned the story in the newspaper. "Do you suppose this is acceptable now in Paris?"

Evie shrugged. "Well, I suppose that everything is relative."

But it was a rebellion by thirteen hundred ministers of our own Presbyterian Church shortly after our arrival in Philadelphia that finally illuminated the *sine qua non* of my new view that there are no answers, that there is really nothing that we can count on to endure. I read the story one morning in the newspaper, feeling a strange sense of imbalance and a flash of vertigo—the sensation of a rug being pulled from under my feet.

Nothing. There is nothing more than this. If the elders can't agree, how are we to know? The Auburn Affirmation, signed by these men, refuted everything that Emery Breeden had insisted on at Nan—the infallibility of the Scriptures, predestination—everything he'd taught in the little mission church Sunday after Sunday. For a fleeting moment I could once again feel his hand pressing down upon my head in the empty church, my knees grinding into the hard wood floor, the humiliation of it all.

But Harvey would never know of that. "Well," I said, handing the paper to Harvey, "look at this. I could have sung any song I wanted after all at Nan." And I'd been right, I thought. Nan from start to finish was a futile mistake.

Soon after, in July of 1925, the Monkey Trial finished things off. The trial held in Dayton, Tennessee, to decide whether a teacher, Mr. Thomas Scopes, could teach the theory of evolution in his classroom, had turned into a circus. Our neighbors invited us to a loudspeaker party to listen in on their new radio as reporters in Tennessee described events as they unfolded.

Someone had shipped in a truckload of stuffed monkeys with long tails for the children of the city. Hundreds of merrymakers had arrived to watch the show: flim-flammers, photographers, reporters, peanut vendors, curious bystanders parading with signs on their backs warning everyone to read the Bible or proclaiming prophesies.

One evening as we sat quietly in our yard, I noticed a large, unusual star in the sky. Barby Jeanne and June were already asleep. I pointed it out to Harvey, but he had never noticed it before. The next day's news explained the phenomena. The planets Venus, Mars, and Mercury were in such close proximity to each other that they appeared to the naked eye as a single giant star.

"Perhaps it's the sign of a great event," I said to Harvey. "Like the star of Bethlehem."

"The light that you see was created billions of years ago, Babs," Harvey said in an offhand way. "For all we know those stars no longer exist—they've died."

I was stunned by the information that the stars were not real—nothing more than light. "False stars?" I complained. "That too?"

One morning a crisp, white business envelope arrived for Harvey from New York City. Full of curiosity, I held it up to the light but couldn't make out the words. For some reason the letter, with its embossed return address, seemed formidable, as though it had some strange power to change our lives. I placed it carefully in the center of the small, round mahogany table by the front door.

Harvey spotted it the moment he came in. I waited with impatience as he dropped his stick into the stand and hung his hat carefully on the rack. Taking the letter into the parlor, he lowered himself into a chair by the fire, tore it open, and began to read. As I watched, a smile crept across his face. When he looked up, he was transformed—he positively beamed. It was an invitation from the Rockefeller Institute, a medical research facility founded in 1901 by John D. Rockefeller, to come to their offices in New York to discuss the possibility of a teaching position at Chulalongkorn University in Bangkok. The assignment was to help establish the first medical school in Siam.

"What an opportunity!" he exclaimed.

The idea took me by surprise, but when I saw the excitement shining in his eyes, I knew that, once again, I didn't have a choice. Besides, Bangkok was a sure thing this time. I squared my shoulders and smiled back at him. And this time, I resolved, we would do things my way. Then I leapt into the sun god's chariot, grabbed the reins of those wing-footed steeds, and headed up through that golden fire.

# Chapter Twenty-Two

## Bangkok

HARVEY SIGNED A CONTRACT WITH THE Rockefeller Institute, and in the summer of 1926 we headed for Bangkok once again, this time across the Atlantic, with a short stay in Marseilles. We arrived at Port Said on the S.S. Hitano Maru after a relatively calm trip. The ship was small, with only forty-eight passengers. June kept Barby Jeanne amused during the long journey. Her little sister was just learning to get around but refused even to try to stand upright, scrambling on all fours like a baby elephant.

At Port Said the air was fetid, and we shed as many of our clothes as polite society would allow. The ship took on coal, and everything and everyone, including passengers, were immediately covered with a fine, black dust. The sun seared our skin while we hung over the rails to watch the work on the dock, peering down at the poor sailors who were coaling as they worked in the middle of a dark cloud in the blazing heat.

Once we left Port Said behind, the small but comfortable ship was thoroughly cleaned. A swimming tank on deck was filled with cool water every morning and evening. Barby Jeanne learned to swim like a fish and, in the dry heat, simply existed from one swim to the next. The journey through the Suez Canal took thirteen or fourteen hours. The canal was narrow so that when I sat on deck, I could see nothing but sand to the horizon on both sides of the ship. It was quite a new sensation, as if we were sailing on sand.

When we finally arrived at Bangkok, disembarking was easy; the Rockefeller Institute had arranged our arrival to the last detail. A home was soon to be put at our disposal for a reasonable rent, and we were to live at the Hotel Royal until it was ready. In the meantime I commissioned beds and mattresses to be made.

The expatriate community in Bangkok in 1926, made up primarily of American, British, and continental Europeans, was an intimate group engaged chiefly in the pleasurable enjoyment of life. The British, of course, had a club, which was the center of activity during the daytime for Brits and non-Brits alike, but at night everyone dressed for dinner and fanned out across the city for more spectacular entertainment.

We ran into Judith at the club almost immediately. She had married and stopped teaching and had a daughter, named Suzanne, who was about June's age. Her husband, Cyril James, was a mining engineer from England. A dignified man with bushy gray brows, he appeared to be somewhat older than Judith. She was as sensible and lively as she had been at Nan, and our friendship was quickly revived.

Harvey and I were the "new people," bearers of the latest fashions and dances and rude stories from home, and we were swept into a whirl of parties. The Charleston may have already become *passé* in Philadelphia, but I was delighted to learn that no one in Bangkok had yet mastered the dance. After a few glasses of champagne, and if the music was right, I was always asked to demonstrate.

After the tedium of our long passage from home, I found the frenetic pace of Bangkok life exciting. Each evening the children were given an early dinner at the hotel by an ayah. Afterwards, with Barby Jeanne on his knee and June on the floor with her thumb in her mouth and one arm wrapped around his long leg, Harvey read stories out loud while I dressed. At eight o'clock we tucked them into their beds in care of the ayah, who slept in their room, and departed for the evening.

Bangkok is built around a river, the Chao Phraya, locally known as the Menam. Most of the palaces, hotels, and consulate buildings fronted the river, and all provided convenient landings for boats. Sometimes we traveled by motorboat, skimming across the water through the velvet darkness, up and down the Menam with the hot colors of the city streaking by in streams of light. The small craft darted in and out of the klongs, or canals, as the wind blew against our faces and the laughter trailed behind us. I loved the free feel of the wind as it whipped through my short loose hair, and I loved that our dinner conversations never included religious matters.

After a few weeks we moved into our rented home, a large, two-story house made of wood, of a style traditional in Bangkok. Everything was light and airy, newly painted. Wooden shutters opened up the rooms to the outdoors, and when they were closed they could be adjusted to permit a cool breeze through the slats. The red-tiled roof peaked on either side of a long, enclosed porch that ran the length of the house. On the ground floor beneath, white columns surrounded an open, tiled veranda, and one portion was enclosed with lattice and mosquito screening to create a small dining room. To protect against fire, the kitchen and laundry room were separated from the house by a short, curved walkway covered with a lattice and flowering vines. The house was situated on a large property shaded by many trees so tall that they almost gave the effect of a forest.

Spiked ferns and soft ones that looked like lace, banana plants, elephant ears, and every sort of shrub and flower were spread across the broad lawn in no semblance of order. Water trickled from a fountain in a small, square pond under a tree in back near the walkway to the kitchen, and the light, musical sound of the water could be heard throughout the house.

Running water and electricity were available in Bangkok, an enormous improvement over Nan. Here we had fans on blistering hot evenings and lighting without the heat of a kerosene lamp. Ice was available and we drank cool lemon squashes in the afternoon under the shade trees.

But the best thing was an old piano. Harvey surprised me with it. It was slightly out of tune and the wood was worn, but I loved it. We placed it near a window where I could look out over the garden in the back while I played and sang.

*There's nothing I can't do here,* I thought joyfully. *Nothing I can't accomplish—anything is possible.* As I played, I resolved to take up serious singing again. The British Club had music, I knew. In this glorious, vibrant city, it would just be a matter of sifting through the alternatives. My heart swelled with love for Harvey and Barby Jeanne and June. I was riding that glimmering chariot now, forgetting altogether the sun god's warning: *Keep to the middle course.*

⌒✍

Harvey was teaching at Chulalongkorn University, and he also began taking on a few private patients to shore up our funds. The Rockefeller Institute's involvement with the new medical school was primarily due to the interest of the royal family, especially the king's half-brother, His Royal Highness Prince Mahidol of Songkla, who had befriended Harvey. Prince Mahidol was revered in Bangkok for his tireless work on behalf of the poor. As a Chakri Prince of First Rank, he mobilized tremendous resources, including his own personal fortune, to help establish the new school of medicine.

Bangkok was expensive, however. Again we found ourselves required to maintain an enormous staff of servants. Two ayahs were required for Barby Jeanne and June, one for each child. Of course, the motives for hiring them differed from those at Nan.

"Surely one ayah is enough for two such small children," Harvey observed.

"It's not done, Harvey," I said firmly. "The ladies at the club have discussed this with me, and it will look strange to hire only one." At his skeptical look I added, "This is a matter of first impressions."

But instead of the worried response that I had expected, Harvey's lips twitched and his eyes smiled at my words. "I'll leave that sort of thing to you, Babs," he said. He'd changed since Nan, as I had, I thought. So we also hired a houseboy, who doubled as a gardener and a driver, as well as a cook, a maid, and a part-time laundress. And we bought a Chevrolet touring car, shiny and black, with running boards along the side. Harvey watched my face when he showed it to me.

"How much did it cost?" I asked.

"Don't worry about that," he told me. "This isn't Nan. Besides," he added, in a reasonable tone, "it's the best way to get around. We can't take a rickshaw to the palace, can we?" He patted the hood of the car. "Hop in," he said. I grinned and did, and as we turned into the street, I slid over close to him.

Our lives soon settled into a routine. The houseboy was very organized and saw that things occurred approximately on schedule. Each morning Harvey left for work just after dawn, strolling down the lane and swinging his walking stick, over a bridge at the nearest klong, then through city streets to the Menam. A boat took him to the university hospital on the other side of the river where he taught his medical students.

Shortly after breakfast the ayahs disappeared with the children to a park nearby, along with all of the other ayahs in the neighborhood. Usually they sat together in the shade on the ground and fanned themselves with palm leaves, gossiping while the children romped. By the time they returned hours later, the children were exhausted, ready for lunch and naps.

Because of our busy evening schedule—or so I told myself— it was my habit to sleep until after Harvey and the children had gone. Usually the maid brought a tray to my bed, with letters if any had arrived, a cup of coffee or tea, and some fruit, but sometimes I carried my cup down to the garden where a small rattan chair and table were placed under a shady tree just for this purpose. Each time I was conscious of how comfortable and secure we were now, how pleasant our life was compared to our time in Nan. Judith said that the Breedens were still in Bangkok, but they might as well have been in New York for all I cared. My days were full, and I was thrilled with this exotic new life.

By midmorning each day I was off with the driver to golf, or Alliance Francaise for lessons in French, or the British Club, which turned out to have few opportunities to actually sing but did offer lectures and studies in the history of music.

"No one comes to Bangkok to learn to sing serious Western music," I was told. "One goes to Europe for that."

"Ah," I said in a light, dismissive tone to hide my disappointment. "Perhaps I'll give that some thought."

Afternoons were taken up by excursions through the city to explore temples and palaces and shops, or with luncheons or garden parties or tea or cocktails at one of the glorious hotels. When nothing was planned, there was always something going at the British Club. During the day the ladies of the club wore fashionable hats adorned with tulle and ribbons, white gloves and dresses made of fine, delicate fabrics that kept us cool in the heat—sheer lawn and linen and soft cottons trimmed with lace, all carefully washed and pressed each day by the laundress.

Dinner was almost always formal and was seldom served before ten o'clock to permit time for the children to be put in their beds. The late hour also allowed time for the extra preparation required to appear always in formal dress. After dinner we lingered in the warm night air in terraced gardens and discussed the events of the day, or we danced in the moonlight with the fragrance of jasmine floating around us. Sometimes I was asked to play a piano and sing, and everyone loved the lively tunes, the new songs we had brought from home.

Even the children entered into a veritable stream of constant social occasions. Parties were held for the celebration of birthdays and holidays every week. Clowns and balloons and kites painted with faces of tigers and dragons colored the lawns of magnificent houses. Sometimes elephants were provided for rides, and the children were piled on top into gaily-striped howdahs. I was amused that there were always as many ayahs present as children, and guests often included the young royal children. Barby Jeanne and June were given exquisite toys as party favors—dolls, miniature tea sets, colorful tops, toy monkeys.

Early one evening not long after our arrival, we sat with guests in our garden. Lanterns hung from branches of trees, casting a soft glow around us. The children tore across the lawn and scampered in and out of a copse of trees, rolling and tumbling on the damp, fragrant grass beneath our feet like small, round puppies. Their high-pitched laughter mingled with the music of the night, the hum of cicadas and crickets and the chirps and croaks of the night frogs.

I smiled with delight as I watched them play.

"Ah, what I would give for that fresh view of life," one of our guests sighed.

"What do you mean?" I said. "How can you be jaded in this exciting city?"

She looked amused. "There's a lot of activity here, I'll grant you," she said. "But the truth is that eventually it becomes tedious." She gave me a veiled look. "A few months from now you'll find that out for yourself."

I started to ask what she meant, but just then the muffled clang of temple gongs in the distance rang through the trees and I was distracted, intoxicated with the city and the night.

By November, the social season was in full swing. The king held his first court of the season at the Throne Hall in the royal palace, the most important event of the year. Harvey and I attended, as we were to be presented to the king and queen.

The palace was white with a high-spired roof laid in swirls of green and gold tile. Upon arrival we strolled across inlaid marble floors through a vestibule hung with black and gold armor of ancient Siamese warriors, until finally we came to an immense reception room of European design. Gilded carvings on the high ceiling gleamed, and beneath it all the assembly of diplomats and officials of the kingdom milled about in their uniforms, splendid with gold and silver braid, while the silks and satins of the ladies were a kaleidoscope of colors under the brilliant lights.

On the far side of the vestibule was the Throne Hall, where the king received guests. As we entered, I gazed in wonder. An immense, jewel-like mosaic ceiling was illuminated for the evening, and just below, three enormous chandeliers sparkled like large clusters of diamonds.

A steady murmur hummed through the elegant crowd, and from time to time a burst of laughter would erupt and be quickly controlled. At the far end of the vast room, Prajadhipok, Rama VII, the new king of Siam, brother of Rama VI who had been on the throne when we arrived in Nan, sat under tiers of royal umbrellas on a raised platform and a splendid throne of gold and silver and blazing gems. His queen, Rhampai Parni, sat next to him, and from time to time she turned at something he said, dipping her sleek, dark head in a charming way to listen.

The royal couple stood as the crowd formed to move past. When we were presented, the king paused to talk to Harvey of his work. He was a slight man with a dignified and commanding presence. Because the university where Harvey taught was named for his father, and because of Harvey's acquaintance with Prince Mahidol, it seemed to me as they talked that the king took a special interest in Harvey.

Queen Rhampai Parni was delicate and doll-like. Her gold tissue gown shimmered under the bright lights of the Throne Hall when she moved. She smiled and exclaimed, full of life as she greeted us, to my surprise, in fluent English.

Toward the end of the evening, Judith and Cyril James arrived, and immediately the men wandered off for a smoke. A waiter arrived with glasses of white wine on a silver tray. Judith shook her head, but I took one and thanked him. A small orchestra began to play, and a few people began to dance.

I lifted my glass and gave Judith a sly look. "Remember the last time we had a drink together?" We both laughed, remembering the brooding Danish manager of the logging company we'd met on the way to Chiang Mai.

"He'd been in the jungle too long," Judith said.

I nodded and smiled as I sipped the wine. "It was a close call," I agreed.

We watched the circling mass of people in the room. "I'm ready for something new," Judith said. "Cyril's home is England. We might be leaving soon. There's a cottage waiting for us in Cookham Dean."

"But you can't leave!" I exclaimed. "I've only just arrived. And what would you do there?"

"I miss teaching. There's a small school near the village that needs someone next year." She shrugged. "And I'll garden.

We'll have horses." She looked at me. "What will you do while you're here in Bangkok?"

"Wait for Harvey. What else?"

"Wait for him!" she said. "You'll need a better plan than that." She cocked her head and studied me. "Haven't you spent enough time waiting for things to happen? And what about your singing? Time's passing, my girl. How much longer will you wait?"

As Harvey and I drove home that night, I looked out at the moon and thought of Judith's words. Bangkok was beautiful and busy, filled with things I'd missed at Nan—glittering electric lights, parties, drinks with ice, interesting people who never mentioned religion, and—I smiled to myself—a piano of my own. *I can wait,* I thought. For Harvey I can wait. *I'll practice playing, and singing, and when we return to Philadelphia . . .*

*And when will that be?* asked my inner voice. *Every minute gone is lost forever.*

# Chapter Twenty-Three

HARVEY WAS ASKED TO ATTEND SEVERAL members of the royal family as a personal physician. He was therefore one of the few adult males in Bangkok allowed to enter the "forbidden area," the women's quarters of the palace where the young princesses and older ladies of the royal family still resided with their female attendants, although they were no longer prevented by law from socializing on the outside. Within the palace walls, Harvey was required to carry a yellow umbrella that signaled his authority as the physician.

Soon Harvey was also asked to provide medical care for the king's sacred white elephants. The luxurious royal elephant stables were also within the palace walls. The elephants were spoiled and could be quite savage, even though they had been held in captivity for many years.

Very few people in the kingdom were permitted to touch the elephants. A white elephant is the king of all elephants, as I had learned from the story of the Rachasee told to us by the Chow Luang at Nan. The king of Siam owns all white elephants, whether they are held in captivity or wild.

As the elephants' physician, however, Harvey was required to touch them, and one day he asked for my help. A huge bull elephant had developed a boil on its stomach that required lancing. Of course, the animal could not just be turned over on its back for the operation, and it could not be tied or held by others, so Harvey had devised a great scheme by which the surgery could be accomplished.

"You will stand on the balcony, Babs," he said casually. "And when I give you a signal, you'll feed bananas to the elephant."

"And then what?"

"When it's fully distracted, I'll run quickly underneath to lance the boil."

"What!"

"It will be perfectly safe, Babs. All you have to do is feed the animal. I'll take care of the rest."

"I'll be *killed*. When he feels the pain, he'll swipe me with his trunk."

"No, he won't," Harvey's voice took on a wheedling tone. "It will be perfectly safe. I promise you." He tilted my head up and kissed my cheek.

"Oh . . . well . . . all right," I said against my better judgment.

The elephant was brought outside to an open area beneath a balcony. A young Siamese boy led me, clutching a bouquet of ripe bananas in my hand, through the building, up the stairs, and out onto the balcony. The elephant stood below, his head did not quite reach to the floor on which I stood. I was disappointed to find that the animal was not really white, although it was clearly an albino. His rough, sagging skin was a light gray but still much lighter than other elephants that I had seen. The eyes, the edges of his huge ears, and his tail were pale.

A small audience of caretakers and mahouts had gathered to view the operation in the dusty courtyard below. On the edge of the crowd I recognized Princess Poon Pissa Mai Dissakul, a young royal princess about my age whom I had met at several gatherings. We had become quite fond of one another. Her outward aspect was serene and gentle, but I had learned in conversation that Princess Poon was very intelligent with a quick, dry wit and a mischievous streak. She was small, delicately built, and stood apart from the group with an attendant. When I caught her eye, she waved.

Harvey disappeared, and for a moment the elephant eyed me with a placid, uninterested expression. I stared back at him. He stood still, clothed with the dignity of his royal status. The pachyderm was the center of all attention.

Finally Harvey emerged again, and everyone moved aside. I began to peel one of the bananas, as Harvey had instructed me to do, and when I'd finished, I dropped the skin behind me on the floor of the balcony. The elephant was instantly alert to the new smell of the fruit. Harvey pulled a sharp knife from his medical bag, and holding it up in one hand like a scepter, he walked around to the other side of the animal where I could see him.

Harvey looked up at me and crouched into a runner's stance. For a moment all was silent, then he shouted, "Now!"

I dangled the banana over the side of the railing, leaning down to meet the top of the elephant's head. Before I knew what had happened, the trunk reached up, curled around the fruit, and it disappeared into his mouth. I blinked in surprise, then looked into the courtyard, searching for Harvey. To my dismay, he had not moved.

The elephant eyed me again, with more interest this time. His trunk began to curl toward me and his ears flicked. There was no need to peel the next banana, the animal now fully knew what it was that I held. My heart pounded as the trunk reached toward me, but I steeled myself and waited, alert for Harvey's signal.

When Harvey looked up, I took a deep breath. His face was tense, but he gave me an encouraging smile. Then he entered the crouched stance once more. Again the crowd below was silent.

Harvey's voice rang out. "Now!"

I danced back from the fat trunk already exploring the rail, then I leaned forward, dangling the banana to give him the scent. This time the elephant was certain of his reward and, fully distracted, he reached for the fruit.

Harvey saw his chance. With lightning speed he dashed beneath the body of the elephant, slicing through the boil as he raced out the other side and away. The elephant, just reaching for the fruit, gave a start, then—feeling the sudden pain—forgot the banana, arched the great trunk high over its head and let out an angry, trumpeting roar so loud that I thought it must have shaken the entire city of Bangkok.

Harvey was well away by now. I pushed back, pressing myself into the wall, staring at the enraged elephant, and for a split second I froze. Then I wheeled and fled through the long open window behind me. The trumpeting of the furious animal continued while I ran, at last sinking breathless against the far wall of the room. I slid to the floor, keeping an eye on the window, and tried to catch my breath. Outside, laughter rose from the courtyard, and I realized that the beast had calmed. But I waited, skirt billowing and heart pounding, until the Siamese escort returned to fetch me.

As Harvey and I left the courtyard, I heard a soft voice whisper, "Missus Perkins."

Princess Poon stepped around the corner of the building. She was dressed in a colorful silk panung and a short white lace blouse that was a stark contrast to her midnight hair. Her lips curved into an impish smile. Pulling her hand from behind her back, with a secretive gesture, she handed me something. It resembled a thin piece of silver wire.

Seconds passed while I stared, slowly realizing what it was that I held. Her eyes sparkled as she laughed and walked sedately from the courtyard.

A few weeks later Harvey surprised me with a beautiful gold-link bracelet as a gift. A topaz was set in the center of a circled hair from the royal white elephant that no one in Siam, but the king, Harvey, and the royal beast's mahout, was allowed to touch. Princess Poon had plucked it from the tail. I wore it always after that, and Princess Poon giggled every time she caught sight of it.

One day Luang Prachaup, a Siamese friend of Harvey's, invited us to accompany him on a boat trip up the Menam to see Ayuthaya, the ancient capital of Siam, and to visit some ruins with a group composed of Margaret Hunter; Harlson Leland, a handsome young businessman who had just arrived from the United States; Mr. Green, the American Charge d'Affairs; and Edward Scholtz, an outrageous Californian who always made me laugh. The boat was marvelous, large and comfortable, with every necessary convenience. The trip to Ayuthaya would take nine hours, so we decided to leave at night in order to arrive in the morning. The ayahs could manage the children while we were gone.

Margaret Hunter was young and pretty, vivacious, with a worldly air. "Call me Margaret," she had said in a breezy way when we first met at the club. I was entranced by her easy familiarity. Margaret was a seductive whirlwind of energy. Her lively face was framed by short dark hair that had the sheen of silk as it fell flat against her pale skin. Gray eyes gleamed as they sized everyone up in the first instant of a meeting. Her lips were curved at the top in a tiny bow that I envied. She and her husband had been in Bangkok for more than a year, and he traveled frequently for extended periods—unwisely, I thought, stealing a look at her shapely figure. In some places she seemed ready to burst from her dress.

We set sail at nine o'clock in the evening, trailing the moon's white path in the dark water. The deck, which our host had covered with a beautiful carpet for his guests, was broad, with plenty of room to move about. As we got underway, Mr. Prachaup provided champagne, although as a Buddhist, he abstained. Margaret was amusing, and our laughter floated across the Menam as we glided along, listening to music from an old gramophone while the lights of Bangkok flickered and dimmed behind us. After about an hour, Mr. Leland moved close to Margaret and leaned over to light her cigarette. Soon they were engaged in an animated, whispered conversation. As they talked, she looked up at him and, from time to time, threw back her head with a throaty laugh.

Mr. Prachaup told us of Ayuthaya, which is eighty-five kilometers from Bangkok at the junction of the Lopburi, Pa Sak, and Chao Phraya Rivers. "Until it was sacked by Burmese invaders in the seventeenth century," he said, "Ayuthaya was a dazzling city with more than a thousand temples covered in gold. The Burmese were cruel; it was a bloody invasion."

Margaret leaned her head on Mr. Leland's shoulder and blew wisps of smoke into the night. "I suppose that sort of thing doesn't happen anymore," she said.

"But they do," I said and told them about the bloody uprising of the Northern Shan at Phrae not many years before we had passed through on our way to Nan.

"What were you doing in that area?" Mr. Leland asked.

Mr. Scholtz plucked a cigar from his mouth with a grin. "Dr. Perkins was a missionary once," he drawled.

Harvey nodded. "We had a hospital in the Nan Valley near the Laos border. Barbara was there as well."

"Well," Mr. Leland said, looking from Harvey to me, "I'd have never taken either of you for missionaries."

Margaret gaped at me. "Weren't you terrified, living in such a remote place? There must be all sorts of things to worry about in the middle of a jungle." Her look turned sly. "But then, I don't suppose you were alone much. You had Harvey with you."

I turned cold at her words. Against my will, memories that I'd locked away emerged from some dark place, images of being trapped by the fury of the monsoon, surrounded by a sea of wind-whipped water. All at once I again heard the shrieking, howling wind, saw the undulating worms translucent in the rain, saw the tokay spit, and remembered the snakes, coiling, writhing in the attic while I waited in vain for Harvey to return from Ai Mah's village.

Mr. Green rose. A part of me watched as he picked up the champagne bottle, and then I held up my glass. "Just a bit more," I called to him, thinking that my voice sounded far away and somehow unfamiliar. While he poured the champagne into my glass, I turned my head to Margaret, and said with a bright, stiff smile, "Of course I wasn't frightened, silly. Nan was charming."

Mr. Green moved away with the bottle and I took a sip from my glass. "Why, once we were even visited by Prince Nakawn Sawan," I went on, "and he mentioned to me how lovely he thought the roses in the north."

From across the deck, Harvey looked at me. Suddenly the boat lurched, spilling champagne all over Margaret, who shrieked with laughter. Mr. Leland immediately drew out his handkerchief and made a fuss over her. She took the hand kerchief and Harvey reached to hold her glass while she patted her skirt.

Mr. Prachaup gripped the wheel until we settled back into an easy glide. "It must have been a small log," he announced in a tone of relief.

As the champagne flowed, Scholtz turned up the music and tried to pull me from my chair. "Teach me that silly dance you're always doing," he demanded.

"The Charleston?" I laughed, drawing back. My voice ascended the scale. "We can't Charleston on this boat. It will rock . . . the whole thing will sink!"

"You're a sketch, Mr. Scholtz," Margaret called. "Let's sing."

Scholtz began to croon, and Mr. Green slapped his hands over his ears as if they hurt. I sipped my champagne and moved to the railing, watching moon shadows flutter as the boat skimmed beneath thin branches of trees arched over the water. Once I heard myself laughing at something but couldn't think what was so amusing. The champagne bubbled through me, and my thoughts jumped from one thing to another.

Harvey slipped up behind and put his hands on my shoulders. I straightened and turned to him. "What's bothering you, Babs?" he asked in a low voice, looking down into my eyes.

I gazed at him a moment. *You* weren't *there when we needed you*, I thought. Dangerous thoughts. A shadow crossed his face. "Come on," I laughed and spun away from him. "Let's sing. I'm fine. Right side up and spinning like a top!"

He smiled. But it was a wistful look.

The next morning we woke to find ourselves docked at Ayuthaya. The river was jammed with sampans and small floating shops, creating a city on the water. After a late breakfast on deck, we climbed ashore and explored the market, finally wandering off into a forest of tall thin trees at the edge of town. Mr. Leland held Margaret's arm as we walked.

After an easy hike of twenty or thirty minutes, we halted in astonishment. Towering before us in the forest, plain and unprotected, was a huge bronze Buddha. From our vantage point it stood in a gashed opening of a jagged piece of crumbling brick wall, all that was left of an ancient temple. No one spoke as we stared in silence. Black and brooding, it was hemmed in by trees covered with dark-green creeping vines.

We climbed up the stone rubble beneath the frozen giant and rested. The place looked as though it had been left undisturbed for centuries. Here the forest was thick and overgrown. Harvey spotted several beautiful little pitta birds, plump with dazzling iridescent red and yellow markings.

Margaret quickly grew bored. "It's awfully grimy here," she complained, fanning herself with a handkerchief. "What I wouldn't give for a lemon squash."

Mr. Leland squeezed her arm. "Or a good scotch."

"I'm tired of looking at old things," Margaret said petulantly, slipping off the stones.

"Well then—to the docks! First one back mixes the drinks," Mr. Leland said cheerfully.

Margaret giggled, then whirled and grabbed my arm, pulling me with her in the direction of the boat. "A gin would be appreciated if you get there first," Scholtz called from behind.

Some instinct tugged at me. I stopped abruptly, throwing Margaret off balance, and looked back. Through the trees I could see Harvey. He still sat where we had left him, watching the pittas as they hopped on the forest floor, hunting for food. "I'll meet you at the boat," I told Margaret. "I'll wait for my husband." She shrugged and disappeared.

I waited for Harvey in the stillness of the forest. Mr. Prachaup stood near him, and for a while neither one noticed me. Both were completely absorbed in the movements of the little birds. From a distance Margaret's laughter mingled with Mr. Leland's and floated back through the trees.

Margaret was careless, I realized later. She was doomed, as surely as if she'd been marked by Zeus, god of storm and thunder.

# Chapter Twenty-Four

CLOUDS BEGAN TO MASS AROUND MARGARET a few weeks after our trip to Ayuthaya.

I first became conscious that her flirtation with Mr. Leland had become public knowledge when she joined Harvey and me on a trip to Hua Hin, a small fishing village south of Bangkok on the Gulf of Siam. Harvey seemed to need a respite, and so did I—time to think. I wanted a rest from the endless social whirl. With the children, one ayah, and a laundress, we took the new train for Hua Hin and its lovely beaches. The king had just completed a summer palace he named Klai Klangwon, or "Remote from Care," located on the north end of the beach facing the sea. It was built in a meadow of fragrant flowers, and the architecture gave it a light, airy look, as if it had dropped right out of the *Arabian Nights*. Hua Hin was a popular escape from Bangkok, and a new golf course right behind the train station completed its transition to a royal resort.

About mid-afternoon the train rattled through groves of cocopalm trees into the station at Hua Hin, where we alighted onto a platform next to the royal waiting room. After much commotion over her luggage with porters moving at a fast clip,

Margaret went off in search of a car that was to have been sent by the hotel. Harvey and I had taken a small bungalow on the beach.

Barby Jeanne and June were bursting with excitement and seemed to bounce in every direction at once with surprising bursts of speed. While Harvey struggled with our baggage, negotiating the transfer with a local porter, I held onto the girls, lurching after them when one or the other slipped from my grasp. We sent the ayah and the laundress ahead of us to the rented bungalow.

The small wooden cottage was one of several built in a cluster on the edge of the beach. The sand was fine white powder, and the sea was pale green in the shallow parts, gradually turning a deeper shade farther out. The beach rose to a bank of grass and flowers above the area where the bungalows were perched, and tall, feathery casuarina trees and lovely cocopalms shaded it. As soon as we were settled, Barby Jeanne and June scampered through the sand, June in a bright green bathing suit and Barby Jeanne in one with blue and white stripes.

The children shrieked and laughed as they searched for seashells and played games, running to the water's edge to catch the waves, then following the backwash into the sea. Harvey spread a blanket beneath a tree, and we dropped upon it to recuperate in the cool shade as we watched the children frolic. When the ayah came out of the cottage, I allowed myself to doze.

At dusk, after the children had been bathed and fed, Harvey and I strolled down the beach to the glorious new Railway Hotel where we expected to find many of our friends from the city.

We took off our shoes and strolled along the cool, shingled sand near the water, letting the lacy silver foam on the last sliver of each wave curl around our feet. In the fading light, the sky and water had turned to shades of sapphire.

The Railway Hotel was built in an elegant colonial style that dominated the beach and the small fishing village around it. The gardens were terraced down to a low wall near the water's edge. Beyond that was a rocky area that led to our bathing beach, clean and smooth, easy to walk upon. Hua Hin was nestled in a long protected cove with large jetties at each end of a crescent and not one unauthorized pebble in between. About one mile distant were hills of cool lavender.

I took off my hat and the white ribbons rippled in the soft breeze as we left the beach and climbed up to the hotel through the lovely formal gardens. Water flowed over smooth marble fountains and small glass-and-bamboo chimes tinkled, the musical sounds blending with the sound of the waves lapping at the shore below. As we neared a covered veranda, we spotted Mr. Green, Mr. Leland, and Mr. Scholtz reclining on rattan chairs.

"Hoy there!" Harvey called.

Scholtz opened one eye. "Come on up," he shouted when he saw us. Mr. Green and Mr. Leland jumped to their feet with evident delight as we neared.

I sat in the breeze stirred by the ceiling fans that circled slowly overhead and placed my hat on the table nearby. All of us came to Hua Hin to relax, so the conversation was confined to things that required little energy or thought—the weather, the train trip south from Bangkok, a hike planned in the hills nearby. Waiters glided soundlessly around us, taking our orders and bringing back cocktails. After about an hour, Margaret appeared, frowning.

Her husband had been detained, as usual, by business but was expected to arrive on the morning train.

She waved the waiter away when he drifted over. "Nothing for me," she said in a firm, discontented voice. She seemed uneasy as she took a chair next to mine. "I've had a difficult afternoon. Had to manage transport from the train, then unpacking . . . all alone." She glanced at Mr. Leland with glittering eyes. "Hello. I expected to run into you before this, I suppose."

Mr. Leland flushed and shifted in his chair. I looked at him with surprise.

"Have a sherry," Mr. Leland urged in a confidential tone, leaning toward her. "Here, take a taste; it's really fine, nice and dry."

She took the glass and with a flick of her wrist, downed it in one gulp. Mr. Leland stared. He was so startled that I began to laugh. Scholtz and Mr. Green chuckled, too. Harvey smiled with a dry, reserved expression.

"I thought I heard you tell the waiter that you wanted nothing to drink," Mr. Leland exclaimed.

"You heard correctly, Harlson . . . Mister Leland. But I've changed my mind." Ignoring everyone, she searched out the waiter and signaled him over. "Scotch," she ordered, when he arrived. "Johnny Walker. Straight up."

*This is interesting,* I thought, and turned my eyes to Mr. Leland. He looked distinctly uncomfortable at the turn of events.

"What shall we do about dinner?" Mr. Green asked with a note of false cheer, interrupting the strained silence. He and Scholtz and Harvey began an intense discussion on the relative merits of dining rooms. I glimpsed Mr. Leland giving Margaret a significant look.

After a few minutes she stood. "I think I'll skip dinner this evening," she said in a casual tone, avoiding my eyes.

Involuntarily, we all looked from her to Mr. Leland.

He rose. "Ah . . . me too, I'm afraid," he murmured. "I've already made other plans." Then he coughed into his knotted hand and looked away.

A smile flicked across Margaret's face, then disappeared. She stood in a bored slouch as Mr. Leland picked up his straw hat. His nose shone with a new ruddy glow.

"Upon my word, I do believe she's gone and parked her corset," Scholtz observed at dinner. Harvey and Mr. Green choked with laughter.

"Oh bother!" I snapped. "She's a grown woman . . . and her husband is always gone. What does he expect?"

"She's his wife," Mr. Green said mildly.

"A wife is not chattel."

Harvey looked surprised. Scholtz grinned and tipped his glass to me, then swallowed a long drink.

"Besides," I added, "it's a known fact that people who are bored *will* fill their time."

"Perhaps she needs a hobby," Harvey suggested. "Something to occupy her mind."

I looked up and our eyes met briefly, before we each looked away.

"No conviction," Mr. Green said. "She's empty-headed."

"Her husband's square cut, though," Scholtz said. "Good man. Engineer. Solid. Has to be to build those railroads through Burma."

"Well, his wife's gone off the tracks," Mr. Green said, signaling the waiter.

"She's a loose caboose," Scholtz snorted.

"Good heavens!" I exclaimed. "Fresh air certainly hasn't done much for your dispositions. If you're going to go on like this about *that* old code, the least you could do is wait until I've got some reinforcements."

"What *code*?" Mr. Green asked curiously.

"She means the old view of things, Green," Scholtz announced with amusement, as he picked up his napkin and carefully wiped his mouth.

Harvey smiled. "You gentlemen don't know what you're up against," he said. "My wife was a suffragette." Beneath the table his hand reached for mine and he squeezed.

Our bungalow was next to a larger one occupied by the royal family of Prince Damrong. As I lounged beneath a casuarina tree watching the children and the ayah one morning, Mr. Green strolled down the beach from the direction of the hotel. When he grew close, I saw that his bath suit and shirt were wet, and a jaunty new straw hat was perched at an angle on his head.

"Been swimming?" I asked as he plopped down beside me on the sand. It was still early, and I was surprised at his appearance.

"Yes, I've been up since the sun rose," he answered. "The water's cold this time of morning when you get into the deeper part."

We sat companionably, watching as one child after the other emerged from the royal bungalow next door and ran to the water, each one followed frantically by an ayah.

"It's marvelous—the number of people that pour forth from that house," he finally observed.

I laughed. "But they're all so pretty and lively and small." Several royal ladies now emerged, and I waved to them. Harvey was physician to many of them.

"They're quite beautiful," Mr. Green observed as they strolled slowly in the direction of the hotel. They moved together in a tight cluster down the beach.

I nodded. "Most of them speak excellent English and all play golf—they're very good company." I nodded toward one walking in front of the others. "The king's sister. She's one of Harvey's favorite patients."

"She looks a little older than the others."

I nodded. "She's the maiden aunt of the royal household. Princess Poon says that she's not permitted to marry. There's no one in the kingdom of proper age and station for a match, and a foreigner would be unacceptable."

Just then a striking woman came into view, walking in our direction. She stopped to speak to the princesses and their attendants before continuing toward us. Her black hair was slicked into a chignon at the nape of a long, graceful neck. She was slender and wore simple clothes with elegance. A small girl who looked about six years old accompanied her. My eyes lit up. The child would make an excellent playmate for Barby Jeanne.

Mr. Green followed the direction of my gaze. "Signora De Rossi," he informed me, as she grew close. "She's the wife of the Italian minister. They've taken a cottage near the hotel." He smiled and waved as she spotted us, then rose.

Mrs. De Rossi joined us under the tree, while her daughter, Paola, stood to one side with her finger in her mouth and watched Barby Jeanne and June splash in the water. Paola was thin, with small bones and a delicate face. Her huge dark eyes were fixed on the children.

"Eh, this place is so *marvelous*," Mrs. De Rossi exclaimed, as she made herself comfortable on the blanket.

I led Paola over to the children and made introductions. Barby Jeanne had already spotted the visitor and watched our progress intently. The two girls were almost the same age and, after an initial cautious examination, they became immediate friends. Barby Jeanne grasped Paola's hand and urged her out to the point in the water where the waves began to break. By the time I returned to the tree, all three were shrieking as the waves splashed over them.

"I believe I've met your husband," I said, as I sat on the edge of the blanket and drew my knees to my chest. Signore De Rossi, the Italian minister, was rumored to be minor royalty of some sort—a count, I thought. He was tall and slim with slicked black hair parted in the middle, a diplomat who peered through his monocle and bowed to kiss my hand when we were introduced.

"Yes, I'm sure," she chuckled good-naturedly. I envied her low, husky voice. "He's met every pretty woman in town. I never know where he is. Sometimes I roam through our house for hours calling, '*Paolo, Paolo!*'" She spoke English with only a slight Italian accent.

"The only women who know where their husbands are all of the time are widows," I laughed.

"Mrs. Perkins is married to Professor Perkins—at Chulalongkorn University," Mr. Green interjected.

"Ah, yes. You've just arrived." She stretched out and leaned back upon her elbows to watch the children. Her olive skin was smooth and unlined, her smile a bright streak of red lipstick over even, white teeth. "Your husband must be busy," she said. "Do you find yourself alone much of the time?"

"Often," I said, shrugging.

"Then we must be friends," she said. "We'll keep each other company."

"Please call me Barbara," I said, imitating Margaret's cool tone.

"Viola," she answered lazily, closing her eyes and turning her face toward the sun.

Mr. Green seemed to have fallen asleep. After a while I pulled a packet of cards from a basket nearby. Viola opened one eye, sat up, and we passed the morning playing gin rummy in the sand under the casuarina tree.

In the evenings, when the children were asleep, Harvey and I dined at the hotel with our friends, drinking and laughing and dancing on the veranda that overlooked the garden and the water. Often we all sauntered down the beach around midnight, Harvey and me, Mr. Green, the De Rossis, Mr. Leland, Margaret, and occasionally her husband, when he was around, and Scholtz. When we wanted to swim in the moonlight, the men changed into their bathing suits in the darkness behind a cluster of trees. The ladies used our bungalow or the De Rossi's. The warm salt water held us up as we floated on our backs and gazed at the stars in the tropical sky. At night the foam of the waves as they broke near the shore was luminous with phosphorescence.

At Hua Hin ice was sent to us from Bangkok twice a week, along with butter and meat, and local women brought us baskets of succulent mangoes, bananas, venison, eggs, and oranges. In the morning when the children woke, they simply tumbled off the veranda onto the sand and into the water. Viola and Paola De Rossi joined us each morning, and the mothers played cards while the children romped.

Margaret's husband came down to Hua Hin for short visits now and again. He was on the pudgy side, and I thought him quite dull, except that he was known to be very good at golf. When he was there, we put together small groups to play on the new nine-hole course across from the train station. Margaret professed not to enjoy the game, however, and often stayed behind.

"You should play with them, you know," Mr. Leland said to me one day, just after Mr. Hunter had first arrived. "It's an opportunity. . . . Hunter is an expert."

"I would love to," I said, "but Harvey is going and it's a day off for the ayah. I have to stay with the girls."

"Well, go along with them," he urged, "I'll take care of the girls."

I looked at him in surprise, then noticed that Margaret had parked herself under the casuarina tree.

"I'd better not," I said, feeling vaguely uncomfortable. He looked hurt, as though he could read my thoughts, so I gave him my splashiest smile. "I've already made plans with them," I said, nodding toward Barby Jeanne and June.

He recognized the falsehood and shrugged. Margaret threw me an irritated look.

Mr. Leland took my place at golf, and later in the afternoon while the girls played in the garden, Margaret and I sat on the veranda of the Railway Hotel drinking lemonade. The sea was flat, and the air was hot and humid. It was obvious that Margaret was still annoyed. I picked up a fan from a table nearby and began fanning myself in the silence. "Your husband must be exhausted from his travels," I found myself saying. "Do you find it hard . . . with him gone so often?"

She gave me a shrewd glance. "I have my enjoyments," she said.

Perversely I realized that I liked Margaret. I let a minute go by. "Is that prudent, do you think?" I asked. "I don't usually offer unsolicited advice . . . but, Margaret . . . as a friend, I think I should warn you. The ladies at the club will talk if you're not careful."

"They're perfect frumps," she said with a careless flick of the wrist. She wore a diamond bracelet that sparkled with the movement.

Diamonds before dark—I registered the fleeting thought.

She saw my glance and looked down at her bracelet then back at me. "He's got the benefit of his bargain, you know. Women have rights today as well, and I'm used to doing as I please." She lit a cigarette and blew smoke at the sky. "Besides. I like a faster pace . . . parties, dancing. I like to have a good time."

"You don't have to explain to—"

"Look," she said, interrupting me. "I know I don't live up to high morals. But it's all so boring otherwise, and I just can't seem to find it in myself to waste time pretending." Her voice faltered, but she quickly masked her feelings with a smile. "Anyway, I've decided that . . . as the man said, it's better to reign in hell than serve in heaven."

The words seemed familiar. "Who wrote that?" I queried.

"It's from *Paradise Lost*." She shook her head. "What a poem that is."

"Milton?" I asked in astonishment.

She laughed at my tone. "Yes. I thought that was the best line in the whole thing." She slanted her eyes at me. "You thought I was a dumb Dora, didn't you?"

"Heavens, no," I said. "You're lots of fun. And anyway, I admire you for remembering anything from *Paradise Lost.* I thought it fairly difficult."

"Well, keep it under your hat," she said dryly. "Men don't like girls who read books."

"Harvey's never felt that way," I said. Neither had Dad. "I suppose it depends upon the man."

"I suppose," Margaret said in a bored tone. She studied her bracelet, then lifted her forearm a bit and jiggled it to catch the light.

After the calm of Hua Hin, our social obligations in Bangkok began to seem relentless, never ending, like waves in the sea rolling toward shore. When Harvey began excusing himself on account of work, often I attended parties and events with Judith and Cyril or Viola, or on occasion, with Scholtz.

I noticed that Harvey still enjoyed parties with his Siamese friends, though I didn't know them well. Prince Nakawn Sawan held a lovely soiree one evening, and I was amazed to find that he remembered us from his visit to Nan years before. We dined on silver plates while servants glided silently around the tables, and we were entertained by music and pantomimes in the garden, and by delicate Siamese dancers in costumes made of gold and silver leaf. These dancers were trained from childhood to bend their hands and feet at astounding angles. I watched as Harvey took on a new animation that evening. *This is a part of his life that doesn't include me,* I realized, feeling a bit like an intruder.

One morning early in 1928, I woke to a quiet house. Harvey was off to the hospital, I knew, and the children were gone with their ayahs. Morning sounds drifted in through the open windows—temple bells from far across the city, birdsongs, horns honking, motorboats cutting along the klong nearby, pots and pans clattering in the kitchen. A breakfast tray holding a silver pot, a cup and saucer, and toast with marmalade was placed on the bedroom floor just inside the closed door. I rose, stretched and yawned, and slipped into a robe of pale yellow silk. The coffee was still warm. Ignoring the toast, I poured it into the delicate china cup, added a lump of sugar, and walked with lazy steps down to the garden.

Still strangely exhausted, I sank onto the rattan chair that was soft from frequent use. With a vague, unsettled feeling, I recalled the warning I'd been given when we first arrived, that expatriate life in Bangkok would soon become tedious. My eyes slid over the broad green lawn, past the trees, the pond, and the walkway to the kitchen almost hidden in thick, twisting vines, on to the gardens. Mere scenery, I told myself. Why is it that the moment and space we occupy sometimes seem so trivial, so unimportant? I looked off. It also occurred to me that I'd felt that way much of the time at Nan, in spite of my love for Harvey.

What was wrong with me?

I slumped in the chair, tilted my head back and watched gauzy white clouds drift across the clear blue sky. Harvey may be deluding himself about what he accomplished at Nan, I reflected, but his work here was important and he loved every minute. He was so engrossed in medicine, his students, patients, and his new friends, that most of the time I wasn't so sure he even knew I was around.

I certainly was tired of waiting for things to change! I sighed. I'd hung a few spangles on things, but all in all, I still wore the same old hat. My thoughts turned to the old dreams of singing, the music I'd given up long ago for life with Harvey. The thought slipped in unbidden—I had expected more in the bargain. At Nan I had yearned for something more. Well, Bangkok offered more, but something was still missing that I couldn't quite identify.

"Yoo hoo!" I was startled from my reverie to see Judith marching across the lawn toward me, shading her eyes and waving. Her motor was parked in front of our house, the driver waiting patiently, elbow crooked on the windowsill, cheek propped on his knuckles. I sat up, groaning as I glanced down at my robe. Judith, my conscience, would not approve, I knew. And I'd forgotten our luncheon plans. As I put on a smile and waited, a whisper came from deep within, soft and breathy, like the rustle of the wind it reminded me of the question that she'd asked.

*Time's passing, my girl. How much longer will you wait?*

# Chapter Twenty-Five

THE *DAILY MAIL* WAS A NEW American newspaper in Bangkok printed by a lively young couple by the name of Freeman. They were New Yorkers and we all thought them quite amusing. The newspaper created quite a stir. Everyone was taken aback when photographs were instituted on the back page and short, newsy stories covering people and parties and events were printed. The *Daily Mail* in this respect was unique among newspapers in the city, which, until then, had presented information in a flat, uninteresting way.

At first the stories, really no more than gossip, intrigued us all. But of course to remain interesting, sensational secrets must be told. One day a wicked little piece appeared on the front page about a certain lady, unnamed, who was spending considerable time with a certain gentleman, unnamed, when her husband was out of town. A ditty was spun—they had been spotted together, it seemed, "to the north, at Ayuthaya, and then again on the sugared white sands at the town of Hua Hin."

When I arrived at the club that morning, ladies whispered in small groups gathered around copies of the *Daily Mail*. They clucked at the newspaper and shook their heads with disapproval. Judith handed one to me.

"Ah, poor woman," I said sadly as I read about Margaret and Mr. Leland. I dropped into a chair next to Judith.

Judith was of the opinion that Margaret was a fool. "It's her own fault. Regardless of the modern view, a lady can't be indiscreet. Once the secret's out, the woman pays the price." She leaned back, crossed her legs, and observed the crowd. "I'm inclined to think she's an idiot."

"She's not a cut-and-dried idiot," I said. "She's intelligent and her husband's a bore. Margaret just has too much time on her hands and nothing to do all day." I watched the club ladies snicker. "Anyway, it'll blow over and next week we'll be talking about a new scandal."

"Don't be so sure," Judith murmured.

I gazed at the room full of ladies in summer dresses and, despite the heat, hats and gloves. "Well, I do pity Margaret," I said. "She's a free spirit."

"She's free all right. She's got no direction—just blows where the best wind takes her," Judith replied. She shot me a worried look. "There are still rules, even out here. One can't just *float* through life, old dear."

I looked down at the article again. Judith was right, I knew. I tossed the *Daily Mail* aside, knowing what Mummy, Evie, and Alice would think of Margaret.

At the time of Chinese New Year in the spring of 1928, Harvey and I hired a launch to take us upriver past the summer palace of the king with Judith, Viola De Rossi, and a newcomer to

Bangkok, a young British gentleman named Julius Fotherman. Viola's husband was working, and Cyril James was in Burma on business.

From the river, just beyond the city, we spotted a clearing for our picnic. Nearby was a temple. The boatman, assisted by Harvey and Mr. Fotherman, pulled the launch onto the bank of the river, and we disembarked. While Viola wandered at the edge of the river, Judith and I picked out a patch of soft grass and spread a white tablecloth upon it. We set the picnic baskets down, one on each side of the cloth to hold it in the unlikely event of a breeze.

We reclined at the water's edge and ate cold chicken and juicy, sweet fruit as we sipped wine from crystal glasses Judith brought. The river was a swarm of constantly moving, medieval-style Chinese junks, all hung with bright, new banners of scarlet and crimson that ruffled as they moved. Each boat was decorated with huge bouquets of white dahlias and yellow marigolds tied to the prows with colored ribbons.

Afterward we sprawled on the ground in languid splendor around the remains of our lunch—chicken bones and crumbs of bread and several empty bottles of wine.

"Did you see the bit in the *Daily Mail* this morning?" Viola asked in a lazy tone, breaking the comfortable silence as she eyed the boats navigating the river.

"No," I said, reaching for the wine glass that I had placed on a flat area I'd found on the ground. "What now?"

"Margaret Hunter is leaving for Lausanne."

My wine glass hovered halfway to my lips. "Margaret is leaving?"

Harvey nodded. "Yes, she's been in the hospital. I saw her yesterday."

"But why is she going to Lausanne?" I asked.

"To recuperate," Harvey said.

I lowered the glass. "Do you mean that she *wants* to go?"

"Hardly," Judith replied.

"What is she recuperating from?" I asked Harvey. He looked uncomfortable.

"Nerves," Judith broke in with an ironic smile. "People say it's her husband's idea. He wants to get her out of Bangkok."

"Margaret's never had a nervous minute in her life," I said. With a surge of anger I turned to Harvey. "Can he get away with that, Harvey? Can he *banish* Margaret from Bangkok?" I spat out the words.

Harvey grimaced and shook his head.

"She's a party girl," Mr. Fotherman said, drawing out the words and digging at his teeth with his pinky. "I'd heard she was fast. Harlson Leland, wasn't it?" When he saw my eyes on him, he dropped his hand from his mouth and gazed off.

"Nonsense!" I snapped. "What of Mr. Leland? Doesn't he bear any responsibility?"

"What's that got to do with it?" Mr. Fotherman gave me a puzzled look. "She's *married* to Hunter, isn't she?"

"Well, I doubt she's leaving Bangkok against her will," Harvey said in a soothing tone. "There's no point of law I know of, at least not these days, that gives a man the right—"

"He's the husband, and he controls the accounts. That gives him the right," Mr. Fotherman interrupted, nodding. "Indeed, she should go. This isn't Paris." He gave the women in our party a furtive glance. Viola looked amused. The pinky went back to work on his teeth. "She's lucky old Hunter doesn't demand a divorce."

Harvey looked at me and lifted his eyes to heaven.

"Divorce is out of the question," Judith said.

"If you ask me, reporters should be banned from society," I said, picturing the ladies at the club gathered around the newspaper.

"I didn't know Margaret Hunter was a particular friend of yours." Viola raised her eyebrows as she looked at me.

"Yes, she was . . . is."

"In that case, perhaps we should change the subject."

"Good idea," Judith murmured.

"But really," Viola murmured, "it's more a question of style."

Margaret was soon forgotten. When the sun rose to its highest point and the air was still and hot, we splashed into the cool river water in our clothes. In Bangkok we learned to deal with the heat in unconventional ways.

At the end of the day, as we were packing our things to leave, the royal barge glided down the Menam like a dragon drifting through a dream. We all stopped to watch as the last sunlight glittered on the gilded hull and on the inlaid chips of colored glass and gems that decorated it. Over one hundred fifty feet long, it was narrowed at each end so that the bow and stern curved upward, like the fingers of the Buddha on Ai Mah's temple in Nan. White silk tassels hung from each end.

Seventy oarsmen in scarlet livery rowed the royal barge past us through the twilight in perfect unison. At the center the king sat on a throne covered by a canopy, veiled from our eyes by sheer gold curtains that rippled as the barge moved slowly forward. Guard boats preceded him, and many private barges and small boats trailed in the royal transport's wake. It was a splendid sight with which to end the day.

❦

Harvey and Scholtz and I attended the opening night of a series of symphony concerts performed by the Royal Orchestra at the theater at Dusit Park. The concerts were a new idea, an introduction of occidental music to Bangkok. Siamese music always sounded dissonant to me; it is complex and lovely, but to untrained Western ears, it lacks a discernible melody.

Our seats weren't far from the stage. Perspiration slid down the musicians' faces as they settled into their seats under the hot lights and began tuning their instruments. There is something about this moment before the music begins that excites me— I love the sharp, raw, practice notes from the orchestra that break off and repeat, the shuffling and muffled sounds behind the curtains, the whispers and rustle of silk in the audience. With a rush of emotion, I leaned forward to watch and listen, and when the conductor, Phra Chen Duriyang, stepped onto the stage, I rose with Harvey and Scholtz and the audience to pay homage.

Scholtz leaned close and whispered from behind his hand, "Do you know that the conductor has never been outside of Siam? In fact, it's said he's never even heard another orchestra play the music on the program."

"What's the program?" Harvey asked.

Scholtz pulled a tissue-thin, folded piece of paper from his pocket and read from it aloud. "Beethoven, Schubert, Saint-Saëns, Rossini."

The audience settled down, hushed, and the lights dimmed. A strange emotion rose inside my chest while we waited, and I could barely breathe when the orchestra began. This was music that I had left behind long ago. My throat tightened, and something stirred—something old and lost and essential. I sat back and braced myself.

As the music swelled and tugged at me, despite every effort, I was transported back to Philadelphia. I was never able to listen to classical music without being drawn into the emotion of the piece. Once again I felt the cool, damp air in Miss McGregor's studio on a fall day, saw the reflection of the piano on the gleaming wooden floor, watched as she mouthed for me the words of "Cara Nome." Miss Mary Garden shimmered in a stream of sunlight. With rising exhilaration I felt again the thrill of perfecting a musical phrase, or even a single note—the thrill of creating something beautiful and perfect of my own. I closed my eyes, giving in, feeling the music, absorbing the pain of the loss. *It is mine*, I thought, *mine, mine, mine*. . . . An oboe groaned, the flutes laughed, drums thundered, rupturing the armor that I'd built over the years. A sob rose, but I fought it back.

"Is something wrong, Babs?" Harvey whispered.

I struggled for control. "No, I'm fine," I managed to say. Satisfied, he leaned back.

What had I done? I wondered, suddenly consumed with fierce longing. I tried but could not recall the moment when the center of my life had shifted from music to Harvey. Instead, I realized now that day by day my young girl's dreams had been slowly eclipsed by something else—by my growing love for Harvey, by a sense of duty, by unchallenged expectations. What could I have accomplished had I joined the Chicago Opera? I would never know. I had never given myself the right to choose. And as I listened and fought against the searing memories, the question repeated in my mind: *What have I done?*

When the last notes faded away, the crowd let loose a roar of approval, and the sound snatched me from the reverie. I took a deep breath and rose with Harvey and Scholtz.

"Bravo! Bravo!" Scholtz called. "Remarkable feat, eh?" he shouted over the noise.

*Smile. Actions have power. A smile can make you happy.*

"Yes," I said to Scholtz, applauding. "It's astounding to think they created that lovely music without ever having heard it played!"

Harvey gave a hearty assent.

Around us the enthusiastic noise grew rhythmic, like the ticking of a clock.

I must have a plan, I knew. "One can't just float through life," Judith had said. But day after day I put off facing the questions the concert had raised: What had I done? What should I do?

One day, not long after the concert, Dr. Carter of the Rockefeller Institute arrived in Bangkok and, with a small contingent of gentlemen all dressed in suits and ties, closeted with Harvey in his study. When they emerged, Harvey had committed us to stay yet another year in Siam, through 1929. I was stunned to learn that the decision had been made without any discussion between us.

"There wasn't really time, darling," Harvey whispered. "I couldn't excuse myself in the middle of the conversation to go talk to my wife, could I?"

His tone was reasonable, but I was furious. "You might have done just exactly that," I exclaimed, glaring at him.

Harvey flushed.

Everyone else took my pleasure at the announcement for granted, however, and insisted on celebrating at the Phya Thai. Harvey seemed so pleased that, despite my anger, I found myself smiling, too. What's done is done, I told myself.

"Nothing's real. I feel as though I'm encased in glass," I confessed to Judith the next day. "Or perhaps I'm just transparent—everyone looks right through me to Harvey."

She gave me a sharp look. "Just be careful you don't shatter," she said.

Viola De Rossi came to tell me good-bye. She and Paolo were returning to Italy for a short stay, then they were off to Paris for a year. "You must come to us for a visit, my dear," she said, preparing to leave. She gave me a hug and kissed the air near each ear.

"Harvey has just renewed his contract," I sighed.

"Well, Bangkok has limited appeal. You must simply come alone. Why not? Paolo and I will care for you." She posed in front of a mirror and placed her hat on her head, adjusting it carefully so that not one strand of hair was displaced. White gloves were pulled up and smoothed, and she turned to me. Her arm curled around my shoulders in a sisterly way as we walked together to the door. "We can introduce you to some fascinating people on the continent," she said.

I smiled. The idea of Europe made me happy. I imagined Paris and Rome, thought of Margaret in Lausanne and of her absent golfing husband, and decided she was almost fortunate. Visions formed in my mind of fashionable clothes and city streets rather than canals, cars instead of rickshaws and bicycles or elephants and long-tailed boats.

"I insist that you come," Viola said. "You will begin to *mildew* if you stay in this steam bath much longer."

*Italy!* I pictured myself in Rome, training with a serious singing teacher and living a life of radishes and lettuce and garlic. What would it be like to have something special of my own? What would it be like to sing in Europe, perhaps in Rome?

"How lucky you are," I told Viola.

# Chapter Twenty-Six

BANGKOK. STEAMY. WHITE-HOT SUN AND ELECTRIC lights. Searing heat and ice. Temple bells and dissonance, elephants and insects. Automobiles, rickshaws, motorcycles, bicycles, fast boats and slow boats. A city teeming with people moving, circling, whispering, laughing. As months passed, a vague desire for something more transformed into an obsession.

One evening Harvey returned to find the house in turmoil. "What's going on?" he asked as he watched me fold clothes and place them into a large square suitcase. One of the ayahs squeezed past him to hand me more things, and I put these in as well.

"I've decided to retreat from the city—for a while."

He looked puzzled. "Where to?"

"Hua Hin. Judith has taken a cottage and invited us to stay with her before she returns to England." He was silent. I averted my eyes and sorted quickly through handy excuses for leaving Bangkok.

"You know I can't possibly leave right now. It's practically the end of term."

I continued folding the clothes, placing them in the suitcase with particular care as I formed the words. I nodded. "I know. I thought I would just take the girls, alone."

The room was still as I continued packing. "When are you leaving?" he finally asked in a strange, tight voice.

"Judith will go tomorrow. She's offered to take Barby Jeanne with her. Then I'll leave by the end of the week."

He didn't respond. I looked up at him and my heart softened. He stood in the door without moving. I put down the clothes that were in my hands and walked over to him. He winced, as if in pain, when I put my arms around him. Gently I massaged the back of his neck.

"It won't be so bad," I whispered. "You're busy here during the week. And perhaps you can come down to us on the weekends."

He lifted both my hands, clasping them between his in front of his chest while he searched my eyes. Suddenly, with a strange smile, he released them and walked to the window. It was late. His white suit was a stark silhouette against the darkness as he stood staring into the night. Slowly, as if distracted, he fumbled in his pocket for his pipe. I watched while he lit it and took a deep draw. He continued puffing, standing with his back to me and very still.

"This is awfully sudden. How long will you be gone?" he asked after a moment.

"A few weeks, perhaps." Something about his posture roused my apprehension. "Would you rather we didn't go?"

"No." His shoulders rose, but his voice was level as he spoke. "I won't be your keeper, Babs." He turned and his eyes were steady. "Go to Hua Hin and think things out."

I stared at him, stricken at the words. A look of compassion crossed his face. "Don't you understand?" he said. "Talking about it right now would be a mistake."

"What is it we have to talk about?"

He removed his pipe and started toward me, then hesitated and drew back. "That's up to you, isn't it?" he said, dropping his hand. His voice had an odd catch to it, but before I could say anything more he was gone.

I stared at the empty doorway. Harvey had never needed anyone to complete his life. Medicine, his work . . . that was enough for Harvey. Nan had taught me that. Tears threatened. Once I'd thought we'd only need each other. *He also expected more*, whispered my inner voice. I sighed, knowing this was right. I remembered the admiration in his eyes when he had spotted me marching with the suffragettes. "It's nice to see a girl that has beauty and spunk," he'd said when he first came calling. "You're not afraid of much, I imagine."

But I had failed him. Harvey had never made demands on me; instead, he ruled by the perfection of his example. Harvey measured the *right thing* by some internal yardstick that I had never fully understood. He had expected me to be as courageous as he at Nan, as selfless, as strong, and I had fallen apart like a small child at the end. I turned back to packing, realizing that I was destined always to disappoint him in that way.

A steady sea breeze kept us cool every day at Hua Hin. Again the casuarina trees provided peace and green shade as Judith and I dozed while the children splashed in the water with the ayah. Cyril James had arranged for us to have the use of a small motorboat, the only one at Hua Hin. It sped along, dipping down into the waves with a smack, then flying up over the crest again and again, each time leaving us soaked and shrieking with laughter. The days passed in a pleasant, monotonous way, interrupted by nothing more than the passage of time. The problems of the city began to melt away.

Once again, our cottage was right on the beach. It was small, with rooms divided by rough wooden partitions that reached to a height about two feet from the ceiling, leaving a clear space just below the roof. Judith and Suzanne, with their ayah, slept on one side. Barby Jeanne and June and I, with our ayah, slept on the other. Each room had large windows facing the sea that we left unshuttered at night.

Every morning sunbeams woke us as they struck the water and danced across the glistening sand. As the light streamed in the windows and we lay in bed looking out over the azure sea, Judith sang out, "Oh, *how* is the weary world today?"

Each morning I answered with mock dismay, *"It's moldering to decay!"* The children always laughed with glee at this, recognizing the signal to begin scrambling about for bath suits and slippers and toys for the beach.

Day after day, as I ambled down the beach gathering shells with the children or lay in the shade or flew over the waves in the boat, the music that I'd left behind in Philadelphia played through my mind. Slowly the arias emerged, the songs—bits and pieces, here and there at first—beautiful reflections from the past, and gradually I realized that these dreams still held power.

In the evenings a chorus of frogs and cicadas and the sound of the waves lulled us all. One night, after the children were asleep, Judith and I sat on the beach digging our fingers and toes into the cool, wet sand and watching the stars. I almost forgot that the stars we saw in the night sky weren't really there at all.

"I do love Hua Hin. It's so peaceful, as though we're caught in another world," I said to Judith. "I believe I'm dreading our return to Bangkok."

She studied me with a thoughtful air. "Why don't you think of coming to stay with us in England for a while?" she finally said. "I'm taking Suzanne back soon, you know."

"I'd love to," I admitted. "Life is just too short. I find I need more time."

"What would you do with it?"

I shrugged, hesitating, then the words rushed out. "I want to sing. That's all . . . just sing." I turned my head to Judith. "It will soon be too late, you know. I'll be too old. Time is *racing* by."

She stretched out, crossed her feet, and looked out over the water. "Then why don't you go on to Europe, while Harvey finishes up here, and see what you find. Isn't Rome the place to train for opera?"

I shook my head. "I can't just pick up and leave Harvey alone. Besides, we can't afford that."

"Of course you can." She picked up a handful of sand and let it drizzle between her fingers. "Cyril says the American dollar is strong on the Continent; there's a very favorable exchange rate right now."

I watched her sifting sand while I turned this new idea over slowly in my mind. I'd never looked at things this way before. "In fact, it may be that we could save money in Europe," I said slowly. "There'd be no expenses for parties and dinners and such."

"You don't have to worry over Harvey," Judith said. "He's the smartest man I know, and he's perfectly capable of taking care of himself. He'd make out just fine on his own for a while."

I gazed up at the stars that pricked the black dome of the earth, sharp points of glittering silver. False stars. Suddenly I knew what I would do. The decision flashed and burned on the tinder of my almost forgotten dreams. I would put the girls in school in Europe and go to Rome to sing and wait for Harvey.

I told Judith of my plan and she beamed. "It's about time," she said.

I nodded, excited. "I'll sing, and eat garlic and lettuce and radishes," I laughed.

Later, as I lay in bed with everyone else asleep, Harvey's face rose before me, concentrated and disciplined, lit with curiosity and satisfaction as he worked. His life had meaning; people would remember him when he was gone. That's what I wanted to find for myself—that elusive thing, the thing that would light up my life and give it purpose. I was safe with Harvey, I knew; I had leaned on his gentle strength and loved him in a way that I would never love another man. But if I had learned one lesson from Nan and the monsoon, it was that I couldn't continue to exist on bits and pieces of someone else's life. For years I had refused to face the truth. It wasn't enough—love was not enough.

A haze of dark clouds tarnished the moon and stars, leaving me in darkness. I lay awake for hours after that, listening to the sea and thinking of Harvey and the girls, frightened at the enormity of my decision.

Harvey met us at the station three weeks from the day that we had left, and as we scrambled off the train he gathered all three of us into his arms at once. On the ride home we chattered about small, unimportant things while my heart raced at the thought of confronting him with my decision.

The children were noisy that afternoon, excited at being home. It was too late for naps, so we let them play on the parlor floor, where they shrieked and scattered toys in every direction. Soon I noticed that Harvey had slipped away. Dreading what was to come but wanting to get it over, I searched him out.

I found him sitting in a cool, dark corner of his study with his eyes closed. He looked to be asleep. But when I tiptoed into the room, he seemed to sense my presence and glanced up. His eyes were deep green, darker than usual, and I was startled to see in them a sorrowful understanding—a recognition of words that were not yet spoken.

I sank to the floor near his feet, leaning my head on his knee. The moment seemed almost peaceful, but I knew this to be a deceitful illusion. He began to stroke my hair in an absent, rhythmic manner. Birds sang to each other in trees outside the window; the children's voices rang with joy from another part of the house. But the sounds were muffled, as if they came from a great distance. Thin slits of hard light slipped through the half-closed shutters, throwing a ladder of short, straight, bright lines before us on the polished floor.

Finally I broke the silence. As I spoke the words, a sudden wave of despair washed over me. My voice broke. "I cannot go on here, you know. I can't bear it."

He didn't speak. His hand continued to move across my hair. Long, patient strokes.

"I thought this is what I wanted—the parties, the fun. But I was wrong. I feel as though life is passing me by, Harvey. *Our time is limited.* Each minute ticks past before we realize that it's gone. And I'm afraid . . . that this is all we have."

He was silent.

"We've spent almost our entire married lives in this country, you know. For your choices—your career, your medicine." I swallowed, attempting to smother the rising note of defiance I heard in my voice.

"I know."

"All those years at Nan . . . wasted." My eyes swam with tears and angrily I blinked them back.

Harvey began to object, but I interrupted. "No. Don't bother. It was pointless. Nothing ever changed because of us in the Nan Valley." Now I found myself unable to stop the flow of words. "You still have medicine. Your life is full, exciting, but my days are empty. Each one is as meaningless as the next, and now they all seem to run together."

"I don't understand," Harvey said impatiently. "This isn't realistic, isn't useful? What is it you want to accomplish? It seems to me that the remedy for boredom is to first decide exactly what it is you want and then put your energy into the solution of the thing. Meet it square on, treat it like a problem, and work to solve it."

"It's not that simple for me, Harvey. I don't yet know what the one important thing is in my life—like medicine is for you. Maybe it's singing, but I don't know; I haven't had the choice. So far, I only know the *little* things." Filled with that desperate longing, I swiveled and looked up at him. "I love you, Harvey, but love isn't enough. I want to find out if I can still sing. I want to be able to choose." I paused and took a deep breath. "I want to wait for you in Rome and study singing while I wait." And I want to know that you love me as much as you love medicine, I wanted to say, but did not.

His hand grew still. The room was silent as snowflakes on the wind.

"Why don't you come with me? Just leave!" I braced my hands on his thighs as I urged him. "Think about it."

He gave a sharp little laugh. "You know I can't just walk out," he said, jutting out his chin and fixing his eyes on me. "We're starting a new term at the university. I've just renewed my contract with the Rockefeller group, and I have *patients* here who need me." He glanced around and picked up his pipe. He tapped the pipe against an ashtray, then lit it, taking deep draws, like sighs.

I glanced up and saw that his eyes shone in the dim light. Could this possibly be tears? But then he blinked, and the gleam disappeared.

I was mistaken, I realized, slumping against his leg. Harvey didn't need me here at all. My heart contracted. A terrible foreboding, a sense of dread, crept over me. I was walking through a door that could close him off forever—but I had already gone too far. And for some reason I was unable to stop careening down this path.

"It may be too late, but I have to find out," I said with finality.

Suddenly, he grasped my shoulders, holding them in a firm grip. His voice was low and urgent. "My God, Babs, I don't know what is going on in your mind, but this isn't right. You must come to your senses. I can't keep you if you're determined to go. I want to, but I won't. *I won't!*" His fingers dug into my skin. "But I can't leave with you. I have obligations. That's what we came here for."

I grew cold as I heard the hateful, familiar words. *That's what we came here for.*

"They're your obligations, Harvey. Why is it that all our plans center around your work—*your* needs and obligations, never mine?" I demanded in a savage tone. Angry tears slipped from my eyes, and I brushed them away. "I gave up a singing career because of your sense of obligation."

Harvey sat very still.

My voice rose. "You're not coming with me." It was a statement, not a question.

"No." His voice was flat.

My chest tightened. I longed to cradle in his lap, to let my eyes close and think of something else. I wanted to explain, wanted him to understand. "It's the light," I cried. "It's the light. I want my life to matter! I *must* have something of my own."

"What light . . . what do you mean?" he asked roughly, pushing me away.

My hands dropped into my lap. "Think of the stars, Harvey. Remember when you told me they've all died? The only way we know those stars have lived is by their light. Don't you see?" I tilted my head, looking up into his eyes. "I want to be a good wife. But I have no light of my own. Dad used to say, 'Shine out, Babs!' But my life is secondhand. I am . . ." I looked past him, searching for the words. "I am *bereft* of light," I said. "When I'm gone, no one will even remember that I existed."

I dropped my head onto his knee, and my sobs broke through the stillness of the room. Harvey said nothing until gradually they subsided, but he stroked my hair gently, with tenderness. Minutes passed.

"It's your choice," he finally said.

"I'll take the girls and wait for you in Europe," I whispered.

"I knew something like this was coming." He lifted his hand and sat back in the chair. "Wish I could make things right. Keep you here somehow."

I lifted my head from his knee, wiped the tears, and looked up. "It was simpler for our parents, wasn't it? Mummy never knew that she had a choice."

"Perhaps she didn't want to know. You have to give something up when you choose between two things, you know." He shook his head. "But then, knowing you, Babs, you'll try to have it all."

I was silent. "I'll be fine," he said, looking away abruptly. "It's clear you've made up your mind to leave, and I won't be the one to change it."

I trembled, sensing that a force had been put in motion that I might later regret . . . when it would be too late. But I knew that if I did not reach for something of my own right now, unless I followed that lodestar that winked and glittered, always dancing, darting just beyond my grasp, drawing me ever forward, I would never know what I could do. Now, I resolved, I would *catch* that star, take hold, and shine. And then . . . and then . . .

The room had grown dark except for the yellow glow of a lamp on the table nearby. Harvey's face was hidden in shadows. After a moment I picked myself up and walked from the room. My feet seemed to drag across the floor. Every nerve in my body was tuned for his call to return, to hear that he loved me and needed me and couldn't live without me. But these words did not come.

Our departure wasn't easy. Harvey's work became more demanding, it seemed, and when at home he closeted himself in his study, working sometimes late into the evening. The university announced that they were happy to provide accommodations for his residence at the new Siriraj Hospital across the river. As we began the seemingly endless task of closing up a household, June and Barby Jeanne watched with wide eyes while the ayahs and I sorted through their clothes and toys, discarding things better left behind. Once, when I threw out an old doll of Barby Jeanne's, she scrambled through the boxes and pulled it out, hugging it to her. Its hair was almost gone, and one arm was missing. "Barby Jeanne?" I said.

She ignored me and looked down at her dress, seemingly distracted by a piece of fluff. She began picking it off the material.

"Barby Jeanne," I said again. "Look at me." I slipped my hand under her chin and tilted her face up. "Are you sure that you want to take this one with you?" I nodded to the doll. "It's broken."

"Yes, but it's Daddy's," she said in a firm voice. Harvey had given it to her as a surprise, I recalled, a reward for good behavior.

Once I caught Harvey studying me, as I imagined one might observe a small animal in a laboratory. His expression was mild, but his gaze was intent.

"How can you be so hard?" I asked with a flash of anger. It was late and I was exhausted. Startled, he seemed to shake himself back to the moment.

"I certainly don't mean to be, Babs," he said in a cordial tone that chilled me. "I'm just distracted by things at the hospital. Why don't you go along to bed, and I'll be there soon." He picked up a book and the glasses he'd been wearing for reading, tucked his pipe into his pocket, and walked carefully to the door of his study. As with every other night, I was well asleep by the time he turned off the lights and retired.

On the morning of our departure I awoke suddenly with a sense of dread. *It would be so easy not to go,* my inner voice wheedled. *Suppose you fail . . . make a mess of things?*

I thrust the fear aside, determined not to let it drag me down. There was no light or air left in Harvey's shadow now. I lay very still, feeling Harvey beside me in the soft bed, then I curled against him as he slept. For the last time I listened to the sounds of early morning in Siam, felt the shafts of warm, golden light reaching to us through the window. One of the ayahs called to someone, and the cook began the clattering and clanking that accompanied his preparation for breakfast each day.

*It's only for a short time,* I told myself, *and Harvey's so involved with work that he won't even notice we're gone.* When he woke up, Harvey found me smiling.

# Chapter Twenty-Seven

## Paris

THE ANTENOR STEAMED INTO MARSEILLES, HOME of the French Foreign Legion, on Christmas day, 1928. From Marseilles to Lyon and on to Paris, Barby Jeanne, June, and I traveled by steam locomotive. I had read and dreamed of Paris all my life, of flower carts, bookstalls, of bright cafés and the strange, muted light that bathes the city at certain times of day. I believe I will know it as one recognizes a dear friend, I reflected, savoring the rush of anticipation.

Viola De Rossi had suggested a reasonably priced pension on the left bank, known to be favored by ladies traveling alone. A quick exchange of telegrams had confirmed reservations. The Rockefeller Institute maintained offices in Paris—some of our belongings had been shipped there in advance and were to be transferred to the pension ahead of our arrival.

At Harvey's insistence we traveled in first-class train compartments that held about eight passengers. They were small and cramped, with wooden partitions to the side corridor that led to the water closet. As we rolled through the small French villages and zipped past larger towns, every hedge was green and trimmed. Gardens were manicured and the farmland carved into neat, plowed squares. Trees planted in perfectly straight lines flashed past our windows. Fine strong roads tamed hillsides and forests, a contrast to the wild sprawl of jungles in Siam barely held back by city walls.

As dawn broke the train slowed, and I saw by the signs that we were entering the city of Paris. I pressed my face to the window and watched while we rolled past heavy old stone buildings. Then, for one instant, we were covered in darkness before the train emerged into an enormous depot, a vast glittering dome of light and glass and steel. With a final heave the train jolted to a stop. I unlatched the window, leaning out in my excitement. The air was bright and cold. Barby Jeanne and June stood on the seat beside me and squeezed their shoulders through the window.

The door to our compartment was pulled open, and quickly I gathered our belongings, toys, jackets, mittens, and shoes. After a short wait a porter appeared, and I gestured to him to take our bags. I grasped Barby Jeanne and June, each by one arm as they wiggled, eager to be free. We negotiated our way through the carriage door, down the steel steps, and onto the cement platform. As my feet touched the ground, an electric current seemed to shoot from the soles of my feet to the top of my head. I laughed out loud, and the children turned to see what was funny.

The pension was on a narrow street with rows of horse chestnut trees near the sidewalks. They'd been stripped by nature for the winter, but in the springtime when green leaves sprouted, I knew that they would provide lovely shade. The place was just off the Boulevard Raspail, not far from the Luxembourg gardens. Viola had written that it was within a stone's throw of the Faubourg St. Germain, where stylish people lived. Many of the residents of the pension were married women traveling without their husbands.

The proprietress was a tawny-skinned woman of about forty years, fashionably thin, with a smooth face set off by high cheekbones. She wore her hair, brown with a tinge of auburn, short and close to her head and curled on each cheek like a comma, her long straight nose forming an exclamation mark in the center of her face. She welcomed us with the *sang-froid* that is always admired in French women.

We were given two clean rooms on the third floor, with a bath of our own and hot-and-cold running water. Our windows overlooked a quiet courtyard with a small marble fountain in the center. The day had turned overcast, and the gray light that filtered in through the glass was now dim. I lowered myself into a chair near the windows to catch my breath while the girls explored the rooms.

After a quick inspection, Barby Jeanne looked solemn.

"It's awfully small," she finally said.

"It will be a cozy place, like a cocoon for you and me and Junie—we'll be together in a nice little cocoon," I said, keeping my tone light. She gave me a tentative smile. June was scampering from one room to another. "We'll all sleep together in this room," I said.

Her face brightened. "I will sleep with you?"

"Yes, with me and with June."

"Will the ayah mind?"

I was startled but made a quick recovery. "There is no ayah here, Barby Jeanne. It's just us." She climbed onto my lap and curled into me while I held her tight, awash with guilt as I thought of the home that we had left behind, and of Harvey.

June seemed to be transfixed by a plump wood pigeon that perched near our window on a shallow ledge. I watched the fog spread in a circle around her nose as she pressed it against the glass, then moved back quickly as the bird cocked its head in her direction. I felt tired.

The penetrating cold was surprising. Somehow I had always imagined that Paris existed in perpetual spring. "Has the weather been like this for long?" I asked the proprietress later.

She shrugged. "You never know. Tomorrow may be sunny and warm."

"Ah, wonderful!" I took her at her word and smiled happily.

That night the wind whistled through the cracks around the frame of the windows. The children and I snuggled against each other under a thick quilt for warmth. I drifted into a drowsy, dreamlike state and wondered what Harvey was doing right at that moment. An image of our house in Bangkok, empty of furniture and life, worked its way into my thoughts. I shut my eyes to blot the picture out.

Wind and sleet greeted us the next morning, and the day ahead loomed lonely and depressing. Our rooms were cold and the children shivered as they dressed. After breakfast, I took a seat in a soft chair in the parlor in front of the fire while the children sprawled at my feet and played games. Black branches from trees near the sidewalk in front of the building beat against the windows in the gray light. The sleet had turned to rain that looked as though it would last for days. I sighed. This was certainly not how I had imagined Paris. I leaned back and closed my eyes.

Days passed with no change in the weather. The wind and rain continued. But the children were wild to get out, and I was anxious to visit Viola. One morning, three days after our arrival, a rush of energy propelled me from the chair by the fire, and I went in search of the proprietress. I located her in a small office at the end of the hall behind the stairs. She looked up without expression at my entrance, clearly distracted by some problem of her own. With my Alliance Française-tutored accent, I asked if she had a map. When I read out the address from my book, however, she knew it at once.

"Near the Italian embassy, on Rue de Varenne," she said. "Only a few blocks away."

The storm raged until late afternoon. Even then, when the rain had gone and the wind died, the day was bleak and clouds hung low over the city. I drummed my fingers on the chair in boredom and thought of the cold, damp air outside. Finally I bundled the children into their warmest clothes for the walk to the De Rossi residence. I couldn't wait to see a friendly face.

Nothing would be lost if she wasn't there, I told myself as we walked along. I enjoyed the pull of muscles as I stretched my legs. The children ran in circles around me on the wet sidewalks, splashing through an occasional puddle. Despite the cold I laughed at their excitement and, as we walked, the lethargy began to disappear.

A damp breeze blew around us as we scurried down the street, turning right onto Boulevard Raspail. I hurried the girls along, walking briskly past crowded old apartment buildings, cafés that were almost empty because of the weather, tobacco shops, and bookshops, their mullioned panes of dusty glass reflecting a soft, yellow glow. We walked in and out of the dull light flecked with shadows that shifted with the movement of branches in the tall, slender trees. Rising in the distance, over acres of rough-hewn limestone buildings, was the tallest structure in the world, the Eiffel Tower, made of iron latticework that appeared fragile from where we stood. The children scampered along beside me, energized by the cold. My skin was raw, and my nose and ears burned.

I rang the bell to the De Rossi apartment and waited. After a moment the door clicked and opened, and I stared with delight into Viola's lovely face.

She shrieked with surprise. "Come in, come in at once!" she demanded as she pulled us into the hall. "Poor dears! You are freezing. You're shivering!"

Barby Jeanne and June whooped and threw their arms around her neck. "You can't imagine how wonderful it is to see someone that I know," I exclaimed in a rush of words.

She laughed again and fluttered her hands as the children hung onto her. "Well, here you are at last! And how is Dr. Perkins doing?" she asked.

I hesitated. No mail had been waiting when we arrived. "I haven't heard from him yet."

Her eyes crinkled with understanding. "He's a busy man, of course."

We climbed a wide, curved staircase to the first floor and entered a vast room that was grand, with tall ceilings trimmed with carved wood moldings painted blue, gold, and white. A round table in the center held a vase of fresh-cut flowers on the marble top. On this winter day they already smelled of spring. Long glass doors, with breezy white curtains tied to one side with a sash, opened to a balcony in warm weather. The wide plank floors were of dark polished wood, smooth and worn. In a huge stone fireplace a fire blazed and crackled, throwing off light that washed everything in a yellow hue.

Paola, hearing the noise of our arrival, ran into the room. The children laughed and hugged each other, then disappeared. I took off my hat, unbuttoned my coat, and a butler promptly appeared to take them away.

"You look wonderful!" I said, turning to Viola. "It's hard to believe that we're really here."

She smiled and grimaced at the window. "Really, it's *too* bad that you've been greeted by such foul weather. What's hard to believe is that either of us was foolish enough to leave lovely Bangkok at all." We both looked at the window and gray city beyond.

"I can't say I miss Siam," I admitted, not mentioning Harvey. "But I have certainly been freezing ever since we got off the train."

"Well, you've arrived just in time, darling." She put her arm around my shoulders and led me to a chair placed on a small, thick rug near the fire. I sank into velvet cushions and leaned forward as she offered me a cigarette from a silver box. I lit it and inhaled, enjoying the taste.

Viola inspected me and smiled, then tilted her head back and gently released a pale blue curl of smoke. "Paolo is expecting me any moment for drinks and dinner. My dear," she said. "You must come."

"Now?" I exclaimed. I shook my head. "I can't. I haven't the proper clothes."

She rolled her eyes. "Barbara, certainly you can. You are like a fine bird—your natural feathers are beautiful. I insist that you come; the girls can stay here with Paola and the nurse."

I laughed at her demanding tone. "Why not!" I said, feeling carefree.

It wasn't until much later, when I was comfortably seated beside her in the bar of a small hotel, glass of Vichy in hand, that I realized other guests were included. The walls of the room were covered with polished wood paneling that gave it a cozy feel. Signore De Rossi soon arrived and greeted me with delight.

Gradually a large group of people gathered in our corner. I was introduced to everyone as an exotic new surprise, recently arrived from the Far East. Everyone used Christian names, and I was entranced by the immediate familiarity this produced. The Vichy was soon replaced with gin and tonic by an American man who hovered over Viola's shoulder as she introduced us. He was tall, but not so tall as Harvey. He wore a mustache, and unkempt dark hair curled over his ears and down on the back of his neck. His tweed jacket was worn, but his cravat was made of good silk, and he did not have an air of poverty.

"Ben's a writer . . . I think that's right. Am I right, Ben?" Viola's tone was lively and bright, but her eyes roved past him as she spoke.

He watched her for a moment. "That's right . . . at times."

"Darling!" Viola waved gaily and rose. We watched her work her way into the crowd.

I ducked my head, and my hair swung into my face. I blew it away and looked up to catch Ben staring at me.

"Have you really just arrived from Bangkok, lovely Barbara?" he asked, pulling out the chair that Viola had vacated. "Or is that just one of Viola's stories?" He sat, sprawling beside me. I explained that Viola and I had met in Bangkok. He set his drink down on the table and hunched over a cigarette to light it, then looked at me.

I picked up the cocktail he had brought and sipped it. "What sort of things do you write?" I asked, raising my voice to be heard over the din of conversation around us.

"This and that." I was taken aback by his offhand tone.

"Ah." I looked for Viola, not knowing what to say, but she had disappeared.

"Poetry."

"How interesting. I love poetry."

"Who do you like to read?"

I gave a light shrug. "Tennyson, Shelley. But my favorite is Emily Dickinson."

He looked amused. "Dickinson's for little girls in love."

I lifted my brows. "Let me hear something better then. Something of yours."

"Now?"

"Well, yes. Why not?"

His face tightened. "I'm a writer, not an entertainer." He glowered as he picked up a small glass ashtray and ground out his cigarette. "What about you? What brings you to this city?" He watched the crowd as he spoke.

"I'm . . . here to place my daughters in school." Something told me not to mention singing.

"Oh." His eyes grew bored. "Well," he drawled. "I wouldn't know anything about that." A gentleman from across the room called to him. He rose, mumbling an excuse, and was absorbed into the crowd.

The small bar grew heavy with smoke and warm from the heat of so many bodies. By the time that we finally bundled into cars and raced through the wide boulevards and small twisted streets to the restaurant, our party had grown to twelve in number.

Fog diffused the light of street lamps as we stepped from the cars onto wet cobblestones. We hurried into a small corner building, climbing down worn stairs to a level below the sidewalk. An open fire blazed at the far end of a large room, its light flickering in the row of leaded glass windows that curved across the front at the top, near the ceiling.

The proprietor greeted the De Rossis as old friends and led us back to a long table made of old, thick, glossed boards placed directly in front of the fireplace. The wood gleamed like honey in the soft light. The warmth of the fire cast a rosy glow over everyone as we arranged ourselves around the table. Carriage lamps flickered on the walls, and large, thick candles, lacy with wax drippings, were set at each end of the table.

After a serious discussion with Signore De Rossi, the proprietor sent the waiters dashing in every direction. Cocktails were served, then bottles of old red wine arrived, mellow and full flavored, and also a fruity white, with course after course of fine things to eat—small birds roasted crisp, beef so tender that it melted as I bit into it, bowls of hot vegetables that we passed around family style, and spiced fruit and sharp cheese.

The candles burned, dimming as the noise increased. Our voices grew louder with each new bottle of wine, and Viola and

I laughed until everything seemed absurd. Once I saw Ben watching me from the other end of the table. I smiled, and he frowned and looked away. In the corner of the room, a piano played and a chanteuse sang.

So, I thought, *this* is Paris.

Around midnight we headed for the door. I joined the De Rossis and a smaller group headed for La Coupoule, a new place in Montparnasse with a dance hall in the basement. I found myself squeezed into the back seat of the car between Ben and a gentleman who appeared to speak only Italian. As we pulled away from the restaurant, the pale moon shone over the trees. Fog still hovered around the street lamps. We rounded a sharp corner, and I was thrown against Ben.

"Whoa!" he laughed, holding out his arm to steady me. When I straightened, the arm lifted and dropped down over the back of the seat behind me.

"I do hope that you're not just passing through," he said in a low voice. He smelled of wine and cheese and smoke. "I would like you to stay around for a while."

"Do you have cigarettes?" I asked Viola.

She twisted around from the front seat and held out an open pack "Sure," she said, glancing at Ben's fingertips brushing my shoulder.

I bent forward and took one. Ben struck a match and lit it, leaning close as he cupped his hand over mine. I stared at our hands and the cigarette slipped from my fingers onto the floor. A smile played around his mouth as he blew out the flame, scooped the cigarette up, rolled down the window a couple of inches, and flipped it into the night. Viola turned back to the driver and said something that made him chuckle. I watched the back of her head, feeling my cheeks grow hot.

The car rolled to a stop, and Viola instructed the driver to wait. Ben led the way through a long bar and a large, crowded restaurant, then down some stairs into a mirrored dance hall festooned in bright, garish colors. A small band at the opposite end of the room played loud, pulsing music, and dancers in the center of the room churned with the beat. We squeezed through the small tables crammed with people perched precariously on the edges of their chairs, twitching as if ready any second to bolt for the dance floor, until finally we reached an empty one. I glanced around for Viola, but she and Paolo had disappeared.

Ben pulled out a chair for me and promptly ordered drinks for us from a waiter. I scanned the room, taking in the short stylish dresses and high heels of the women with sleek hair and scarlet lips and ropes of pearls. Bangkok was a bit behind the times, I observed.

When the tempo of the music slowed, a hand touched my shoulder. "Have a go, kiddo?" Ben asked.

Without waiting for an answer, he pulled me up from the chair and onto the dance floor, catching me in his arms. I laughed, and we did a tentative fox trot. He said something rude and smart, shouting over the music, and when I laughed again, he pulled me close. I stiffened, but suddenly the band struck up the Charleston.

Ben released me with a grin and a snap of his fingers, while I raked my own through my hair. Horns blared, drums rolled, and the piano and ukulele took off as our legs and arms began to fly with those kicks and bends and swivels and struts that made you dance like bubbles in champagne. This was not the sedate coupling that the Charleston had become by now in Philadelphia. In 1928, in Paris, the Charleston was still sheer effervescence.

*"Charleston! Charleston!"* The crowd sang out as the band wailed and the walls shook. Ben threw back his head with a wild laugh.

"Yes! Oh baby, yes!" he shouted through the clamor.

*"Lord, how you can shuffle. Ev'ry step you do, leads to something new!"* The band played on for hours while we danced—faster, wilder, more frantic as the night wore on until at last the whole room throbbed. *"Ain't she sweet? See her coming down the street!"* Side by side, thighs spread, hands on knees, arms crossed, uncrossed. *"And I ask you very confidentially, Ain't she sweet?"* A singing, laughing, whirling smear of happy faces, flying legs, bare shoulders and arms, all gleaming from heat and perspiration. *"Two left feet, but oh so neat . . . sweet Georgia Brown!"* Partners swung on to someone new—it didn't matter who. Champagne flowed amid rivers of bourbon, gin, and scotch. No prohibition here.

"Wanna sit?" Ben shouted once, reaching for me through the fizzy, foaming, sweating, swirling mob.

I shook off his hand, laughing, and tossed my head. "I'm having too much fun!"

Ben grinned. "You *are* a wild thing, pretty lady. I think you've been cooped up too long." And then the band delivered a shimmy that took my breath away. *"Wish I could shimmy like my sister Kate."* We stretched out our arms, bent back, and shook like jelly.

In the early hours of the morning I collapsed, falling into a chair. I glanced at my watch and was startled to see the time—half past three. Ben was still dancing, and Viola was nowhere in sight. I leaned my head against the back of the chair, letting the breeze from an overhead fan cool my skin.

The music slowed, and a long blue note sliding from major to minor key drifted through the room. Lights dimmed. Only a few people were left on the dance floor now. Ben sauntered over and touched my shoulder, then dragged a chair close, straddling it with great effort. His cravat was loose, thrown back over his shoulder.

He spoke softly. I bent my head close to hear him. "Let's get out of this place," he said. "I'll take you to my hole-in-the-wall."

I stared as he pushed back his chair and rose, towering over me. "It's not far. We can walk." He held out his hand and fixed his eyes on mine. "It's really not far. I might even read a few of my poems for you."

"What did you say?" I asked, conscious that my voice was shrill. I glanced around for Viola.

With an impatient grunt, he reached for me. "I said, let's go. I'm taking you home with me."

"Are you *mad*?" I stammered, pressing against the back of the chair as I shrugged out of his grasp. Viola! Where was Viola?! With a sinking feeling, I realized she'd gone.

"You've made a terrible mistake," I said, as Ben's face turned to stone. "I can't possibly go home with you. What on earth do you take me for?"

As he dropped his hand, Ben's eyes flickered with contempt. He took one step back, observing me. "Perhaps I should ask you that," he finally said. "Correct me if I'm wrong, Madame. But I believe that you've just spent an entire evening asking for this invite."

I drew in my breath and held it.

His hooded eyes ran from my own startled ones down to my feet and back up again as he pulled a stick of chewing gum from a side pocket of his jacket. Slowly he unwrapped it. "I thought you might be different," he murmured with a shrug.

"But it seems I was wrong." He popped the gum into his mouth and, with a short laugh, rolled the paper into a ball between his fingers. His eyes narrowed. "You're a pretty little package, Barbara. All shiny paper and curly ribbons on the outside. But I suspect that if I unwrapped you, all I'd find inside is bonbons after all."

I wanted to disappear.

Ben chewed his gum, glaring down at me for what seemed like ten minutes, then he flipped the balled-up wrapper onto the floor, shoved his hands into his pockets, and strode away.

I stared after him. "Where is Viola!" I hissed under my breath, twisting around to search the crowd again. My face burned, scorched with humiliation. The tables around me were empty now; only a few stragglers remained on the dance floor. Viola was nowhere to be found. I slumped in the chair.

"Harvey," I whimpered, longing to feel his arms around me.

Across the room a bartender leaned on his elbows, surveying the crowd. I studied him a moment, then lifted my chin, rose, and began working my way toward him through the empty tables and chairs. He looked up as I put the question to him.

"A taxi? Certainly. One moment." His neutral expression did not change. He wiped his hands with a small white towel that he folded and laid carefully upon the bar, then disappeared through a door while I took a seat at an empty table nearby, composing a smile for anyone watching. I scanned the blur of dancers in the center of the room once more for Viola.

In the taxi I leaned back in the darkness with relief. Some instinct asserted itself, and I gave the driver the address of the pension rather than that of the De Rossi house. The girls would be better off with a sound sleep, I told myself.

As the cold light of the morning sun slid through the parlor window, I sipped a steaming cup of black coffee. My mood was pensive, but I pushed away the slight depression that hovered this morning and refused to think of Ben. But for some strange reason, an image of phosphorous in the froth of the waves at Hua Hin formed in my mind.

Viola was at her desk surrounded by notepaper and envelopes when I arrived for the girls. "There you are," she said in a business-like tone as she gave me a quick glance before returning to the sorting of papers in front of her. "Paolo is so impulsive. He insisted that we go on to another party last night." She looked again at me from the corners of her eyes. "But you were taken care of by Ben?"

"Yes, of course. I had a wonderful time." I kept my tone light as I moved to the fire to wait for the children to arrive.

"Well?"

I was startled. "Well?" I repeated without comprehension.

"What did you think of our Ben?" she asked with a chuckle. She gave me a reflective look. "He's intense . . . no?"

I shrugged. "He's a good dancer." As I spoke I was conscious of her amusement and prickled with discomfort.

Viola gave an impatient shrug and lit a cigarette. "Would you like to join us this evening? It's just a small party." Without waiting for an answer, she inhaled smoke and returned to her work.

Just then the door opened and the nurse herded Barby Jeanne and June into the room. The elderly woman's hair was covered in a white linen scarf, and she wore a long black dress of heavy linen, like a nun's habit. The girls rushed to me and buried their sleepy heads in my skirt. I smoothed the backs of their small heads, feeling the curve of their necks and the fine silky hair, suddenly feeling happy. "Not tonight," I said to Viola, smiling. "Another time perhaps."

"Ah!" Viola exclaimed as she looked at her watch, jabbed the cigarette into a crystal ashtray, and rose. "You must excuse me, Barbara, I have an engagement just now . . . I'm late." Setting sail for the door, she blew a kiss from her lips with the tips of her fingers and disappeared. I knew that we were already forgotten. But as I held my daughters' hands, glanced through the window and saw that the morning fog had begun to lift and that the street below was awash in sunshine, I knew that I didn't really care.

On New Year's Eve at the pension, I sat alone in the parlor writing a letter to Harvey. A vision of my husband celebrating the holiday at the club in Bangkok popped into my mind, and I forced the thought away. "I wish you were here and we could sit by the fire and talk," I wrote. I stared at the words, then tore the page in two and scribbled a brief note that we'd arrived intact, finishing with a flourish. "Happy New Year, Harvey!" The clock in the hall struck midnight. The year 1929 had begun its march through time.

The weather remained cold, but after a few days the rain and sleet finally stopped. I was determined to see all of the sights in Paris that I had read about for so many years and to show everything to the children. With that in mind, I drew up a plan for our limited budget, with a bit thrown in for ice cream, balloons, and such. Paris was full of wonderful things that didn't cost one franc—parks and Punch and Judy shows, carousels and bands, and ponds for sailing small wooden boats. Day by day we carried through the schedule while I tried to banish from my thoughts the increasing worry over Harvey's silence. Perhaps he was too busy to write, I told myself.

The girls and I raced through the Louvre, then strolled across the gardens of the Tuileries to the Place de la Concord where the children dutifully fed the pigeons. Down the Champs-Élysées we walked through rows of bare-boned trees, past glittering shops and expensive cafés crowded with men in business suits, until we reached the Arc d'Triomphe and turned back again.

The children scampered down broken stone steps worn smooth by feet and water for hundreds of years, to the quays that run along the Seine, past moored barges that housed families. Gleeful with each new discovery, we strolled under the bridges, across the Pont Neuf, and through the narrow streets of the Ile de la Cité for ice cream, then to Notre Dame.

One cold, sunny morning we met Viola and Paola for hot chocolate at a café near the Seine. We sat near a window and watched a group of schoolgirls skip past. Frost puffed from their mouths as they talked and laughed, giving the impression of steam erupting from many tiny engines. They were all about the age of Barby Jeanne.

"I suppose it's time to get the children in school," I murmured.

"You should consider Geneva," Viola advised. "It's a lovely city for children and less expensive than Paris."

"I'm thinking of Lausanne," I said.

"Ah. Margaret's living there, isn't she?" She picked up her coffee and took a sip.

I nodded. "I assume so."

"Well, I don't see *Margaret* as a reason to go," she said, looking off. "But Lausanne does have a wonderful boarding school, run by Americans, I think."

I glanced up with surprise, remembering that several of our acquaintances from home had sent their children to the Fellowship School in Lausanne. "It's run by Quakers," I recalled with a tinge of excitement. "The students keep gardens and pets, and it's a healthy environment."

"Yes, that sounds like the one. It's supposed to be lovely." Viola frowned and dabbed chocolate from the front of Paola's dress with her napkin. "It's built near the lake." Leaning back, she looked at me and raised her brows. "Boarding school might be a good idea. Children cannot be dragged around Europe from city to city like baggage."

"It would certainly be best if the girls were in one place for a few months," I agreed. Suddenly I was impatient to leave. Paris was cold and gray, and Rome awaited. I decided to investigate the school in Lausanne right away.

# Chapter Twenty-Eight

## Lausanne

AFTER A BRIEF STOP IN GENEVA, we moved on to Lausanne. Our rooms at the Pension Florissant, where Margaret lived, faced such a beautiful view of the lake and snow-powdered mountains from the windows of our rooms that I almost could not tear myself away. Lausanne had a special charm, as if frozen in parallel time from another century. A watchman's call each night was carried up the hill to us on the cold breeze from the lake.

A majority of residents at the pension were young women of my age, including some besides Margaret that I had known briefly in Bangkok. This was a favorite spot for young wives of diplomats and officers, waiting out their tours of duty in the Far East. The girls and I arrived in the early spring of 1929. Margaret greeted me with surprise, a cool kiss, and a watchful eye that became less guarded as the first day passed without any mention of her abrupt departure. That evening as she handed me a glass of wine before dinner, her red lips curled into that heart-shaped smile and her eyes danced. "Beats the British Club, doesn't it?" she drawled. Margaret was back in form.

I sent a wireless to the hospital in Bangkok advising Harvey of our new address and promised a letter as soon as we were settled. Conscious that I still had not received a word from him since our departure, I began to wonder if he was angry. *Would you really blame him?* asked my inner voice. Depression descended as I realized that I secretly wished that this might be the case. At least anger would show that he cared. *Harvey's never needed anyone*, I thought. I shook myself from the rumination, told myself that I was being unreasonable. Ten years of marriage had taught me that Harvey was perfectly capable of forgetting everything, including his own family, when he was engrossed in something having to do with medicine.

But Mummy was another matter, I mused. I had not heard from her either, not since she had admonished me to remain in Bangkok with Harvey. "The woman holds the family together; she's the spirit of the home," she had written again. With a sense of foreboding, I wrote to her, working to keep the tone of the letter light.

After initial inquiries, I was invited out to the Fellowship School to make an inspection. It was cheerful and clean, surrounded by a wood of tall trees, with a private beach on the shore of the lake where the children could learn to swim and row. The main building was a large house with an enormous kitchen that was the central gathering point for everyone. It was a homey place that emphasized a wholesome, healthy view of life.

I fenced with my conscience as I enrolled the girls. They were both so young. How could I leave them here?

"They will be fine," the headmistress said in a consoling tone. Miss Thomas had a great sense of authority and a lively, humorous personality. The girls took to her immediately.

"I don't suppose they'll be here longer than about two months," I said.

She nodded.

On the first morning at the pension without the children, I awoke in a gloomy mood. After breakfast I sat on a porch overlooking the hills and lake and thought how much had changed in the few months since I'd left Bangkok. Yet here I was, alone, having accomplished nothing.

About midmorning, a young woman wandered out and took a chair nearby. She carried a drawing pad and, after a great commotion over the organization of pens and paper, began sketching the view, glancing at me occasionally as I strained to see what she was doing. Finally, overcome with admiration, I complimented her picture, which was developing into an almost perfect rendition of the vista. She smiled, pleased, and responded in English. To my delight, I realized that she was an American.

"Gertrude Edmonson," she said when I introduced myself. She was waiting for her husband who was traveling through the Far East on business. I studied her while she sketched. She was plain in looks, but her tweed skirt and fitted jacket were the latest fashion.

"How long until he returns?" I asked.

Her answer was nonchalant. "About a year or so," she said without looking up. "But the time will fly," she added. "I intend to get some work done while he's gone . . . drawing . . . and I'll learn to paint as well, if I can find a teacher that I like." While she spoke, her attention remained riveted on the picture, her hand moving quickly with short, brisk strokes over the paper.

"What about you?" she asked after a moment.

"My plans aren't set," I answered, gazing at the reflections of white clouds in the blue water of the lake below. I told her about Harvey in Bangkok, and the children now in school.

She shot me a knowing look. "So. The children are boarding and now you're free. You'll join the wandering wives of Europe." Her chuckle was unnerving.

I frowned. "Is that how we're thought of . . . *wandering wives*?" I asked, drawing out the words.

"Well, that's up to us, isn't it?" she responded without looking up.

I found Gertrude refreshing. She was from Washington, DC, where her father was—in her words—a mid-level employee in the State Department, and where she had met her husband, George. There was an assured, continental air about Gertrude, the result, I supposed, of growing up with people who viewed an assignment across the globe in the same manner that I would have accepted an invitation to afternoon tea on the other side of Philadelphia.

One day, in a blatant attempt to establish my own credentials, I mentioned the suffragettes. Her customary look of indifference was replaced at once with one of surprise, and a slight smile broke through her reserve. The common interest soon forged a bond of friendship between us.

Over time I noticed that Gertrude's pictures were all precise replications of exactly what stood in front of her. They were bold, neat and orderly, always done in black and white.

"Why don't you try using some color?" I asked curiously one day.

"It's a question of being ready," she answered. "Technique is important to art . . . to perfection." She glanced at me. "Isn't it the same in music? Discipline requires you to concentrate on the routine at first, scales and such, instead of moving right into the pretty arias."

I shook my head. "You're describing a formula," I objected. "In music, technique is just a tool, not a substitute for emotion. Technique only gives the music shape."

Gertrude gave me a patient look. "It *is* a formula," she insisted. "Think of how you build anything. A stone wall, for example. You have to take things one step at a time to achieve artistic expression—like building a wall one stone at a time."

I thought that pictures created in that way were more likely to hang in her mother's parlor than a museum. It's only when the imagination takes wings and soars that creativity occurs. "Well, Gertrude," I finally said. "Perhaps you should just consider splashing a little bit of color on that wall."

"I will, once I've built it," she assured me.

Life at the pension was casual and lively. Each evening the friendly buzz of conversation rose from every corner of the parlor in English, German, and French, and rumbles of laughter and tunes from a piano in the corner, a baby grand that was always the main focus of attention.

The room was bright and warm and cheerful, decorated in an extravagant style, with soft chintz-covered couches and chairs that had fringes around the bottoms in startling shades of cerise and blue and yellow that matched nothing else. Cherubs and flowers and scrolls, carved on the ceiling, over the doors, and around the mirrors, were gilded with gold paint that gleamed from the illumination of many small electric lamps. The fire blazed and warmed us as we gathered there before the evening meal.

One evening after dinner I sat down at the piano, which I had been eyeing for some time. Now as my fingers touched the ivory keyboard, the warmth in that room struck me full force, and I began to play a rollicking rendition of "Breezin' Along with the Breeze," a popular tune that everyone knew, singing along as my fingers jumped over the keys. Margaret and Gertrude joined in and soon others, laughing as they tried the words in different languages. After that night this became our evening ritual.

An old gentleman, an elderly American boarder, told me one night that I should consider singing professionally. "You have good musical intuition," he said. "A clear soprano sound. Very pure."

I took a seat in an overstuffed chair beside him in front of the fire and picked a cigarette out of the box on a table between us. He rose and hunched to light it, then backed into his seat.

"Thanks. I'm hoping to get to Rome for lessons one day soon," I said as I took a long draw and slowly released the smoke. Margaret came into the room. I watched her absently as she paused to chatter with everyone, making her way toward us.

"Yes, that's the place to be," he said. "I heard the great Claudia Muzio last year in Rome. She sang Violetta in a very modern production of *La Traviata*. It was dramatic . . . her voice was surprising, unexpected."

He looked off with a thoughtful expression, then pulled a piece of paper and a pen from a pocket inside his jacket and scribbled something. "If you decide to follow up on training, here's a name. A maestro who is known everywhere. An excellent teacher."

I looked down at the note he handed to me. On it he'd written an address in Rome, a name—Ferrati—and an introduction, saying he'd suggested that I call upon the maestro. A thrill shot through me. I glanced at the signature on the bottom, but could not read it.

"Rome," I murmured.

"Yes," he said. "Ferrati once taught Enrico Caruso. This teacher can provide you a solid technique if he takes you on. If you're ever in the city, you should visit his studio in Trastevere. Just show this to him."

"Do you think that he would take an American housewife as a student?" I asked.

"You should not be coy, Mrs. Perkins," he reproved. His tone grew impatient. "The great roles require maturity. Think of Tosca or Aida." He studied the flickering fire. "Besides, housewives who sing are no longer just housewives. Ernestine Schumann-Heink used to pretend that she was nothing but a housewife."

I was embarrassed and hurried to redirect the conversation. "Ah, yes. I have some of her recordings."

"Schumann-Heink was a mezzo-soprano, wonderful with the colorful parts. She was from Austria, but she became an American citizen and during the war she sang out her heart for the country."

"That must have been hard for her."

"The war was hard on everyone, there's no doubt." He paused then went on. "During that time Schumann-Heink was already too old for the difficult parts, but she was beloved. When she sang "The Star-Spangled Banner," it made you weep. Soldiers adored her. No one ever suspected that she had a secret—sons fighting on both sides in the war."

I shook my head slowly, unable to imagine such a situation. The idea left me almost breathless. "I wonder how she lived with that?"

"It was difficult. One son was killed in combat, fighting on the German side. It tore her apart, broke her heart." His voice caught.

I glanced at him. His eyes swam with unshed tears. He looked down at the floor. "I was young when I first heard her sing," he said in a low voice. "In Dresden in 1909 or 1910, I forget the date . . . but it was *Carmen* she sang. She was magnificent. What passion! What fire . . . " His voice trailed off.

I was silent.

He pushed himself up from the chair and nodded toward the letter of introduction that he had handed me. "She knew him well," he said after a moment. "Ferrati. She took on one of his students."

Margaret arrived and took the gentleman's chair. "Do you know him?" I asked, watching the retreating figure.

She glanced at him then shook her head. "No," she answered. "But I've heard that he was once a great impresario. I think he was married to some famous singer."

I looked again at the piece of paper that he had handed to me and felt a rush of excitement.

One morning I sat in bed propped up with soft pillows, facing the window and the beautiful view with a breakfast tray on my lap. On the tray were several letters forwarded to me from Paris, among them one from Harvey. This was the first that I had received from him since leaving Bangkok four months ago. I opened it eagerly, picturing Harvey's smile as it reached his eyes.

"Dear Barbara," the letter began. I paused with a vague sense of unease. Not Babs. *Barbara.*

Slowly I continued reading. He had moved into the hospital immediately after we left and was managing well. He wrote of his work, the new class of medical students and nurses, the weather, Prince Nakawn Sawan, the old princess, and told a few stories saved from visits to the club.

When I reached the end, I put the dutiful letter down and gazed out the window. The words were civil, courteous sentinels that held me gently at a distance, sheltering his thoughts. Startled, I realized this was a letter from a stranger. Anger, loneliness, any emotion in fact, would have been preferable. With deliberation I shook the thought away and smiled at the unlikely idea. It's a fact that a smile, even an artificial one, can sometimes change your whole outlook.

Harvey's contract would be up at the end of the year, I reflected, folding the letter and tucking it away on a bedside table. If Rome was in the cards, I'd better get on with it. My gloomy mood began to dissolve as I thought of the recommendation I'd been given to Maestro Ferrati. Later that morning I scribbled a gay note to Judith who had returned to her home at Cookham Dean, in England. "I'm considering that life of radishes, lettuce, and garlic again. What do you think?" I asked.

That afternoon I found Gertrude sitting in the garden and wearing a distracted look. Her sketchpad lay across her lap. When I greeted her in a happy tone, she gave me a tight smile and ducked her head.

"What's wrong?" I asked immediately.

She was silent, so I sat quietly beside her, watching her work. Her hand began moving over the paper with those brisk little strokes. "It seems I don't need to wait any longer for George," she finally said in a hard voice.

"He's returning?"

"No. He's found someone else. He's met a woman from Canada and intends to marry her after we're divorced."

I sucked in my breath.

"Don't waste your pity," she said, with a quick glance at me before bending over the sketchpad. "Who needs him anyway?" Her expression was hidden, but the crayon now fluttered across the picture like butterfly wings.

"Have you thought of going to India? Perhaps if you were together . . ."

She interrupted me. "I prefer to face things as they are, you know."

I was shaken by her words. Divorce was becoming acceptable in fast society, I knew, but not in my circle of friends, and not in my family. My thoughts jumped to Harvey's cool letter. What if Harvey had written such a thing—what would I have left? Nonsense, I told myself. Nevertheless, my plans suddenly crystallized.

"Well, then. Come with me to Rome."

"Rome!" She turned to stare. "What on earth are you talking about?"

After several days of urging, Gertrude agreed to accompany me. "Why not?" she said. "I'll lose myself in art." She gave a short laugh. "*Pictures* can take his place!"

I wrote a letter to Harvey to let him know, assuring him that I'd send an address as soon as I was settled in Italy.

Gertrude had many acquaintances in Rome. The bitterness of her situation resolved itself in the form of tremendous energy. She mailed announcements to everyone that she knew in the city, telling them of our pending arrival.

I went out to see the children before leaving. Barby Jeanne and June seemed to radiate happiness and good health and were generally doing well. I enrolled them for eight more months, until the end of the year. Miss Thomas gave them leave to stay with me at the pension for a few days before my departure. We had a glorious time. A gypsy circus was in town, so we sat in the grandstand under a big tattered, red-and-white-striped tent, eating peanuts and dropping the shells on the trampled ground below as the animals and clowns spun around the ring. We read stories by Hans Christian Anderson for hours and sewed clothes for their dolls.

In the late afternoons the children played in the gardens, while Margaret and Gertrude and I watched from the terrace sipping dry sherry. The air was so clear that in the evenings we often saw shooting stars, silver streaks of fire streaming through the dark.

Another letter arrived from Harvey. "As to your inquiry," he wrote, "you mustn't worry over me. Some interesting news: You may remember that Prince Mahidol received his medical degree from Harvard and has been teaching at Siriraj. He's now with your own Dr. Cord in Chiang Mai working as a resident. Mr. Breeden is there as well, on a short teaching assignment for the mission. His wife is waiting here for him, I understand." I gazed at the lake through the window, surprised. I'd almost forgotten that the Breedens were in Bangkok. Amalie Breeden must enjoy her temporary freedom, I reflected.

"In any event," the letter continued, "I'm extremely busy now. I can't say that I see much of our old crowd, but as an extra man at table, between Prince Nakawn Sawan and occasionally Princess Poon's set, I find myself being well fed most evenings. She sends her regards, by the way, and plans to write soon."

Once again I was conscious that the letter was cool and impersonal. He was fatigued, he said, but not in ill health. A nurse at the hospital had found a Chinese houseboy to cook and clean for Harvey. Only later did I realize that Harvey had not asked about my immediate plans.

# Chapter Twenty-Nine

## Rome

ON MAY 15, 1929, GERTRUDE AND I embarked on a train for Rome, with a changeover in Geneva. As we descended from the Swiss Alps in the early light of dawn, rolling past the lakes of northern Italy, we found ourselves gradually moving through shades of lighter green and the yellow haze of a relentless sun. Gertrude chattered as the bright light began to warm her spirits, but my thoughts drifted as I mulled over the perplexing letters I had received from Harvey at Lausanne. The click of the wheels on the tracks eventually drowned out her words.

For ten years Harvey had been my rock, my comfort, my strength. But ever since the rainy season at Nan when he'd disappeared on that fruitless mission into Ai Mah's village, I had been vaguely aware that I needed him more than he needed me, that his first love was medicine. I thought of my days and nights of terror waiting for him during the monsoon, certain each day that he would return from the Village of the Beautiful God to take care of Barby Jeanne and me. *What could have been important enough to desert us? I asked myself once again.*

As the train rocked on, somewhere along the way I faced the hard, sad truth: Regardless of the outcome, Harvey's patients came first. He didn't need me now any more than he had needed me at Nan, I concluded with a lump in my throat. His letters proved that. He had not tried to stop my leaving for Europe. I rested my head against the seat cushion, feeling somewhat like a hatchling that's just spotted the first crack in the shell.

*Perhaps now's the time to learn how to fly*, soothed my inner voice.

I gazed out the window, and my spirits gradually rose as I took in the beauty of the countryside. It was a day glossed with sunshine. Now patchworks of bright colors marked terraced hills. Finally, as we neared Rome the vista changed to umber shades—old buildings and flags of laundry and signs in faded rich colors lined the tracks.

Suddenly, almost without warning, the train slowed and with a screech it lurched to a stop. After gathering our belongings, Gertrude and I climbed down from our car, dragging our luggage behind us until we located a porter. He loaded our bags onto a trolley and took off, leaving us trailing behind as he hurried down long raised bridges of concrete between the tracks, then through the center of the bustling terminal and outside, where a row of taxis waited. As we emerged, drivers surrounded us, all speaking at once as they vied for our luggage. After a confusing discussion, we negotiated the price of a ride to our hotel.

As we left the station and the taxi began to weave through narrow, twisting streets and over broad, paved boulevards, crossing piazzas in a wild free-for-all, I was stunned by the ancient beauty of the city. Almost every corner held a marvelous surprise—an ornate church, palaces and parks, roundabouts with fountains and sculptures in the center, works of art plastered on the outside of buildings where they were exposed to the weather. Every street was its own marvel.

Finally, with the horn blaring, our taxi raced across the red-gold Piazza Barberini while we gaped at Bernini's Fountain of the Triton, where a whimsical Bacchus at the center of the pond leered as he blew into his conch. With a swerve we entered the Via Veneto, a wide boulevard lined on either side by tall, slender trees that created a tunnel of shade for the sidewalks and the street. It was well past noon, the sun was high, and the air was no longer cool.

The chairs in the empty cafés were still tipped against the tables on the sidewalks. A man wearing a bibbed apron and stooped with age swept the pavement with his old, wide broom, using a lazy back-and-forth motion as he shuffled forward. Behind him, a flight of stairs was lined with flowerpots and vendors who leaned against the wall, half asleep. The wide stone stairs led to a street higher up, on a different level. We passed an old church, hotels, bookstores, and shops until, a few blocks farther on, we reached the Hotel Excelsior, where the taxi swooped into the *porte-cochère* at the main entrance on a corner. We would stay here until we could find a small apartment.

Gertrude paid the fare while I gazed at the parade of people rushing in and out of the hotel. The bellman hefted our bags onto a pushcart, and we followed him inside. The lobby expanded to a long, elegant parlor, with archways into open areas bathed in light that streamed through tall windows on the far side. Sofas covered in silk and brocade and comfortable chairs placed around small marble tables gave the place an air of opulent hospitality, of wealth and convenience—the things money could buy.

"We'd better find a place quickly," Gertrude said in an undertone as we looked around.

I nodded; my handbag suddenly felt light.

The room we were given faced onto the Via Veneto. White walls and high ceilings gave it a spacious feel. Long double doors opened to a white stone balcony that hung over the sidewalk. Outside, lemon-yellow sunshine flooded the scene under a blue sky. A table of polished dark wood with a marble top separated two small beds covered with blue satin quilts. There was a small desk with writing paper, a pen, and an inkwell in one corner. In another corner were two overstuffed, but elegant, comfortable chairs and a low table. Soon a maid appeared to hang our clothes in a tall mahogany armoire.

After we were settled and the porter and the maid had gone, I threw open the glass doors and stepped onto the balcony. Across the street a row of small hotels and shops faced us. Below, automobiles and motorbikes raced by, honking and swerving madly around one another. Occasionally a Victoria, an open carriage pulled by one horse, rolled past, the hooves clopping with a hollow sound on the neat pavement.

On both sides of the street were sidewalk cafés. Waiters wearing black and green aprons with red letters across the front pulled back chairs and shoved them beneath the rows of empty tables. Clean white linen cloths and silverware were dropped expertly on each one as they moved past. The cafés would soon to be open for business.

I took a deep breath of the warm, sultry air and soaked in the noise and color of the ancient city.

Gertrude emerged from the room. "What is that smell?" she asked, wrinkling her nose as she sniffed the air.

"Garlic," I told her with a smile.

We soon found a furnished apartment in a gray stone building on a side street near the Piazza Barberini, not far from the
Trevi Fountain. Built slightly below the street, it was small but
comfortable, with a parlor, a bedroom for each of us, and a tiny
kitchen. More like alleyways, the streets in that area were paved
with red bricks, worn and rounded at the edges and crumbled in
places. The streets were too narrow for sidewalks and were kept
constantly in the shadows because the buildings on each side hid
the sun. At night, the streets were brightly lit by sagging rows of
lanterns overhead strung on thin black cables latched to buildings on either side. But even this modest neighborhood seemed
to radiate a classical sort of elegance.

I sent my address to Harvey and told him of my recommendation to Maestro Ferrati. "He has an international reputation as
one of the best singing teachers on the continent," I wrote. "His
students are taken seriously; one was taken on by Schumann-
Heink. And many of them have gone on to great success."

With Mummy, my spirit deflated. "Please don't be horrified,
and don't tell anyone how silly I am," I wrote. "I hate leaving the
children in school, but don't you think it would be foolish not
to take this opportunity?" She didn't answer.

But a week and a half later, a response from Harvey arrived.
I was amazed, remembering the days at Nan when letters took
months to reach us. With a pleasant feeling of comfort at this
evidence of Harvey's attention, I opened the letter.

"It sounds as though you're getting established now, and
I shall forward funds through Thomas Cook in Rome,"
he wrote in his neat, precise hand. It seemed he was quite
concerned about Prince Mahidol, who was returning from

Chiang Mai because of illness. Things were much the same otherwise. An ominous chill ran through me; once again, I was conscious that the letter was cool and remote. It was signed impersonally: "Fondly, Harvey."

I frowned as I put it aside, disquieted by the complacent picture that Harvey had presented, his apparent satisfaction with the new arrangement in our lives. Once again, I realized with a sharp little pang that his life had not changed one whit as a result of my departure.

One early evening Gertrude and I headed on foot to the Piazza Navona to meet an old friend of hers from the United States, Ted Jordan. They had grown up together in Washington, where her father had worked for his in the State Department. Ted was an attaché at the American Embassy in Rome. "He's easygoing. You'll like him," Gertrude promised.

It took us only a few minutes to reach the lively Trevi Fountain, which was on the way. Neptune spewed clear water into a large pool in the center of the piazza facing rows of small bright shops and already crowded cafés. In contrast, in one corner stood an old dark church. We stopped at a cart for a raspberry gelato, amusing the vendor as we struggled with the language and the count of money.

When the ice cream was finished, we dipped our hands into the pool and cleaned off the sticky stuff, then continued on until a few blocks farther we crossed in front of the bulky, elegant Pantheon. The sky was now dark, but everywhere the city was lit with artificial lights and seething with people on the move, a cast of characters that never seemed to change—students, gypsies, beggars, and businessmen with women who looked beautiful and rich. Every piazza was crowded with people speaking different languages, drinking carafes of wine at small iron tables that rocked on uneven legs. We stepped around a man squatting on the ground to feed a mongrel dog. Through narrow streets strung with bare yellow bulbs, we finally came to the Piazza Navona.

At the juncture where the street entered the large, rectangled piazza, we halted, staring with admiration. The white fountain by Bernini in the center, four figures representing the four great rivers—the Danube, Ganges, de la Plata, and Nile—drew our eyes right to it. Buildings that Gertrude remarked were palaces enclosed the piazza, although I observed that they looked suspiciously bourgeois, to me—like apartments. Crowded cafés lined the central open area. Less-commanding and smaller fountains stood at each end of the piazza.

We crossed the center of the piazza, weaving around artists seated before easels, dogs, students, musicians, acrobats, jugglers, dancing monkeys, and magicians—a mosaic of people and cultures. Gertrude eyed the canvases propped up for sale and strung across makeshift lines as we strolled past, commenting on each one, *sotto voce*, "Too flat . . . good . . . good lines, good perspective." She scattered criticism with the ease of one who was unaccountable. As if reading my thoughts, she muttered, "I know, I know. It's time to get started."

Just then I was distracted by a handsome young man sitting at a table in a café nearby. He seemed to be waving in our direction. Gertrude gave a cry of delight and waved to the same young man. "It's Ted!" she exclaimed, pulling me toward him.

He stood as we approached and embraced Gertrude. He was solidly built, with a light suntan, and just a few inches taller than me. His face was friendly; the lines around his eyes crinkled as he gave us both a breezy smile. Light-brown hair curled on his neck but was still trim, and he wore it parted on the side. I studied him while they talked. With his healthy good looks, I could have picked him out from any crowd as an American. He had the easy familiarity and confidence of a man who is comfortable, who does not take life too seriously, and is quick to form friendships.

He turned to me. "Ted Jordan," he said, holding out his hand. He quickly realized that I had been sizing him up and grinned as he grasped my hand, shook, and dropped it. "From Boston," he added. But his look held mine as he pulled out two chairs. Gertrude slid into one, and I collapsed into the other. I'd worn the wrong shoes, and my feet hurt.

"Ted's been in Rome for a year," Gertrude said, removing her hat and shaking her hair loose. She glanced at me, then at Ted, and gave him a mocking look. "Why are you leering at Barbara?"

"I'm not leering," he laughed, caught off guard. "I'm just completely charmed to find two American roses in my garden."

"He's a bit rough around the edges, but I love him," she said to me in a sorrowful tone. Leaning back in the chair, she added, "Barbara's already taken, Ted. Her husband is very smart and good looking." Gertrude had never laid eyes on Harvey, but she was right.

He drooped with a stricken look and chuckled. It wasn't that amusing, but Ted had an easy laugh.

I was exhausted from our long walk, but as I brushed stray curls back from my face and looked around, I felt a rush of exhilaration. Suddenly the fatigue seemed to melt away. A waiter hovered nearby, and Ted motioned him over.

"I understand you're at the embassy," I said, watching him from the corner of my eye as he looked toward the waiter. His patrician nose was nice, I thought. His profile was even more striking than his features had appeared at first. He had a ruddy face, however, and I wondered, was this from heat or too much wine? I glanced around at the piazza surrounded by cafes and thought it could be either one in this fascinating city.

"I'm just a minor bureaucrat," he replied in a distracted manner.

"He really is . . . *very* minor," Gertrude said in a loud whisper for me, as the waiter advanced. Ted ordered two more glasses and a bottle of white Italian wine and entered into a friendly discussion with the waiter over the difficulty of finding something dry, until finally they came to agreement. "And make sure it's cool," he added as the waiter started away, then he turned his attention back to us.

"My position at the embassy *is* perhaps somewhat unimpressive at the moment," he went on. He leaned across the table and stretched his mouth into a grin that showed his teeth. "But you must understand, Barbara, that . . . *I*—am—a—rich—man—in—waiting."

"He's a trust-fund baby," Gertrude said, laughing with the familiarity of a sister, "so we'll be kind and let him pay the check."

We bantered while the evening turned to night, and gas lamps and electric lights on posts around the cafés and throughout the piazza glimmered. Ted ordered another bottle of wine and plates of hot, light, and buttered pasta. Ted had to bargain for the butter; our waiter made it plain that olive oil would be the better choice.

"Tell me about this beautiful place," I said, waving my glass over the vast expanse of the piazza.

"Do I look like a tour guide?" he drawled.

"Yes, actually," I said. He laughed.

"Well, let's see." He wrinkled his brow, leaned forward on his elbows, rested his chin on his knuckles, and looked at me. "I am not the ordinary tour guide, please understand. But here's a surprising bit of information to ponder."

"Let's hear it, Ted," Gertrude said, taking a sip of wine.

He glanced at Gertrude, lowered his chin, and raised his brows. "Don't badger the help." He sat upright and turned to me. "Did you know that hundreds of years ago chariot races were held in this piazza?"

"I did not." I shrugged. "But a tour guide should do better than that."

"I'm coming to it," he said. He glanced over his shoulder and jerked his thumb toward a street that entered the piazza between two buildings. "Over there. During the races when the first stallion—the winner—crossed the finish line," he paused for a beat, "just at the moment he'd won, his head was lopped off. " He paused. "And while still dripping fresh blood, the severed head was carried by runners to the Temple of the Vestal Virgins."

I masked my thoughts and curled my lips into a smile. "I've heard worse," I said.

He gave me a sly look, leaned forward, and pushed his face closer to mine. "That's not the point, Barbara." He looked off and back again. "What does this say about a culture? Imagine that split-second when the stallion is conscious of winning, when he's just begun to slow his pace, but his heart still pumps from the effort and his blood is rushing through his veins and he can hear the crowd cheering all around him . . . and suddenly," Ted's hand knifed down through the air, "in the midst

of triumph he feels that searing pain, that burn, and . . . *blotto!*"
he slapped the table with the flat of his hand and straightened,
"it's over." He shifted back and slid down in his chair, slouching.
"He feels nothing at all." Picking up his wine, he sipped, watching me over the rim. "Or so we're led to believe."

I was silent, picturing the scene. "Well," I said, after a
moment, "only the Romans could think of that. But least he
died a champion. If he'd lived, he might have lost the next
race."

Ted threw me a curious look. "So what? He'd be alive."

"Yes," Gertrude snorted, "and we'd be discussing something
pleasant."

Ted reached for the wine bottle, and she covered her glass
with her hand. "No more tonight for me," she said. He topped
off his own, poured some in mine, and still watching me, set
down the bottle.

I picked up the glass and sipped the wine. "As it is, though,"
I said, "the race was won, and we only remember the winners.
The stallion made his mark, but the others are dust, gone and
forgotten."

"I give," Ted laughed, throwing up his hands. "I suppose
you're right. There's nothing to remember if you lose. Winning's
the thing." He braced his hands on the edge of the table and
tipped back his chair. "You're very philosophical," he said.

Ironically, I thought of Margaret's words: Boys don't like
girls that read books. Too bad. "It's late, I'm tired, and my life is
chaos," I told him, smiling. "Wasn't it Socrates who said confusion provides fertile soil for philosophy?"

He grinned and lifted his glass. "To confusion, then. *Salute*,"
he said.

"*Salute.*" A crystal tone, a bell-like sound, cracked the air as my glass met his. He studied my face, and quickly I glanced away. Suddenly, a wave of excitement stirred the crowd around us.

"What is it?" Gertrude asked.

"A celebration," an elderly man at the next table answered. "At the center of town."

"It's in the Piazza Venezia," Ted told us. "Let's go. Every visitor in Rome must see the wedding cake monument; it's the only thing in the city that's not old." He drained his glass, and we prepared to leave. "You're not allowed to admire it though—that would be in poor taste."

We located a taxi on one of the dark, narrow streets surrounding Piazza Navona and headed for the center of Rome. The taxi driver let us out at the edge of a packed crowd on a large, bright square where we were instantly immobilized by the large number of people. High above everything stood the new white monument building with its long pyramid of wide steps that directed my gaze up, up toward the white figures at the pinnacle, a horseman and his mount. The whole thing blazed with fierce white lights. Dark flags that pictured bundled rods, the *fasces* that were once the symbol of glory for the Roman Empire, and other flags, black and bearing pictures of a white skull and bones, hung from windows all around the square.

Suddenly, with one voice, the crowd began to chant, "Duce! Duce!" The sound was ugly, somehow, and it grew, taking on the spirit of a living thing as the words were repeated over and over, until all that I could hear at last was the frightening, rhythmic tempo.

"What is happening?" I whispered.

"Just watch," Ted answered.

A cordon of soldiers now moved in quickstep down the stairs of the monument and formed a sharp, straight line in front of the crowd and along one side of the wide piazza. After a minute, a stout figure materialized on a balcony above the square behind the line of soldiers. From a distance the man looked short and heavy, but as soon as he appeared the crowd fell silent and not a sound was heard while he stood before us, waiting. He was bald, dressed in the uniform of a soldier, and he stood in a solid and powerful stance with his chest thrust out. His face was square and hard, his jaw jutted forward.

He began to speak, slowly at first, but soon with loud vigor in short, staccato bursts. His left arm was held straight and motionless at his side, but his right stabbed the air like a piston, punctuating his words as his voice rose with growing passion. Almost with contempt he commanded the mood of the crowd, stopping for cheers and silencing them with an imperious gesture when he became impatient.

Suddenly he finished and raised one stiff arm. The crowd broke into a roar. I blinked and he disappeared.

"Who was that?" Gertrude asked, nodding toward the now empty balcony.

"Benito Mussolini," Ted answered slowly. "We're not sure yet just what to make of him."

His voice was grave. I gave him a sharp look. "The prime minister? Isn't he an anarchist?"

Ted's eyes darted to the side. "He's Fascist," he corrected, cutting his words. "Right now he seems to be one of the most popular figures in the world. Statesmen from all over have come to visit him in Rome over the past year."

The voices around us rose again to a senseless frenzy.

"*Duce! Duce!*" they screamed, and the animalistic roar clawed through the night. Flags whipped in the breeze, lights on the monument glowed, competing with the full moon above. I shivered, hearing in the noise an ominous pulse of something that I did not yet understand.

Ted noticed. "Come," he said pleasantly, putting his arms around Gertrude and me as he steered us away from the crowd. "Let's get out of here. This has nothing to do with us. The prime minister knows how to put on a good show, but the Italians are too lighthearted to take this man seriously for long. It will all soon blow over."

I swung through the patterned morning light along a broken paved walk that was separated from the brown Tiber River by a low stone wall and a drop of about twenty feet. Below, along the banks of the river, hard earth was overgrown with patches of wild grass, not at all like the paved, well-traveled quays of the Seine in Paris. Across the river, on my right, was the old section of the city known as Trastevere. The address given to me for the maestro who claimed to have taught Caruso was located in this district.

As I looked up, sun flickered through the leaves of tall trees that lined the street. Rooted in the grassy area between the sidewalk and the street, their thin, smooth, white branches arched toward the river over the wall, as if seeking water. Birdsongs broke through the sound of automobile horns, motorbikes, and carriages passing by on my left. On the other side of the street, elegant townhouses and apartments faced the river.

I crossed the Tiber near the little island that divides its waters, the Isola Tiberina, and found myself in Trastevere.

The day was hot, and I was already damp from perspiration. Reaching into my handbag, I pulled out a slip of paper with the address and checked the directions against a rough map that Ted had drawn. Crossing the broad boulevard along the river, I headed through a small square of shops, then into lanes narrowed by two- and three-story buildings of muted shades of yellow, brown, and rust, streaked with the grime of age. Finally I came to a wide, busy street.

Between the sidewalks and the street were enormous stands, carts loaded with fresh fruit, vegetables, and flowers. There was an open-air market hung with old clothes, and a child's tiny white lace umbrella was propped open in the midst of odds and ends jumbled on a table. Everywhere were people with laughing eyes, talking with large, dramatic gestures, voices rising in the excitement of negotiations over the price of a thing or the latest news.

Cafés were filled with people, many still drinking their morning coffee as they scanned newspapers and books; others were lovers, heads close together as they whispered secrets. Here and there clumps of round balloons in a riot of flat, bright colors—red and blue, yellow, green, and white—were tied in bunches to legs of the tables. The child's lace umbrella and balloons brought poignant thoughts of Barby Jeanne and June. The day was burnished gold, however, and the scent of lemon was in the air. I quickly brushed away the melancholy thoughts, refusing to succumb.

Nearby were shops with long glass doors propped open to the street. Beyond the market and cafés, high, flat, mustard-colored walls covered with graffiti curved around open areas. Here Ted's map became somewhat vague, and I stopped to ask directions from an old woman with a soft, folded face. She sat on a high stool near a flower cart and pointed to a small alley nearby as she spoke. I was elated that I understood her. Picking up the Italian language was proving to be easier than I'd expected.

Following the woman's directions, I turned right onto a cobblestone lane with no sidewalk, and after dodging wooden carts, ice wagons, and three men playing dice who called out to me, laughing, I turned yet another corner. A few blocks farther on brought me to the address I sought. It was a three-story apartment building, situated so that the entrance faced the tip of a small triangular park with grass and trees. The second block of the triangle was a commercial place, a store made of large granite blocks; and a sidewalk café with an interior just big enough for a counter and a newsstand formed the third. Double glass doors on the second floor of the apartment building also faced the park, and these were open to a small, iron-railed balcony. Piano music drifted through the open doors.

I hesitated, suddenly afraid. Then I smoothed my skirt, adjusted the bag on my shoulder in which I carried some music scores, and climbed the stairs from the street to the wooden front door. There was no bell, only a handle, so I opened the heavy door and stepped into a dim room with a rough stone floor. It was empty of furniture and opened on one side to a bare, sunny walled courtyard. On my left, the name *M. Ferrati* was engraved in scrolled metal beside another door. I knocked and waited in the gloom.

The music above stopped abruptly. After a moment a door opened and slammed closed, then I heard the shuffle of shoes on the stairs. I waited.

Finally the door opened, and I was startled by the face that greeted me, as I had expected someone older. His bones were fine and sharp. Dark eyes scowled under fierce, unruly brows.

He looked to be about sixty years, but the maestro was not at all the kindly, gray-haired gentleman I had pictured. His head was larger than normal and covered with thick dark hair combed back from a high forehead. His height was medium, but he had presence that exuded authority.

"Si?" he demanded, adjusting the buttons on a sagging brown sweater as his eyes traveled over me.

I employed my most engaging smile, but he did not respond. Quickly, before he could close the door, I handed him the note of introduction from my acquaintance in Geneva and gave my name, suddenly struggling with the language.

Muscles near his eyes flinched as he listened to my linguistic fumbling. He took the note, glanced at the signature, and read. When he'd finished, he frowned and inspected me while his eyebrows drew together to form a single line. I lifted my chin and waited in silence. After a moment of consideration, he held the door open and stepped aside, looking down and gesturing. He spoke in broken English. "Come in, come in," he said with impatience, as he turned back to the stairs.

I closed the door behind me and followed him. The stairwell was dark, but at the next landing we entered a large room with high ceilings and wooden floors that reflected light from the tall windows on either side. Summer smells breezed through the open doors that I'd seen from below—odors of hot tar, wilting vegetables and pungent fruit, old damp stone. A grand piano polished to a high ebony gloss stood alone in the center of the room. A small table that held an ashtray filled with cigarette stubs, and three chairs that stood in a circle near the balcony, were the only other furnishings. The room was stark. The walls were painted white, bare of pictures, curtains, or any sort of decoration.

Signore Ferrati took a seat at the piano, settling himself while I stood in the middle of the room. Finally he looked at me. "Stand up straight," he admonished, as if I were a child.

I pulled my torso up and took a deep breath to stretch my diaphragm.

He sounded the notes of a chord on the piano one at a time in rapid succession, *arpeggio*, then nodded. "With me," he commanded.

He began playing again and I sang with the music, still contained and shying from risk, repeating the sequence of brief notes over and over as he tested my range. As I sang, I grew conscious of my lack of power and projection, of how much effort it took from me. It had been a long time. When we finished he looked into the distance for a moment, then swung his legs around the end of the bench, straddling it so that he faced me and asked, "What do you want from me? Do you want to study for the opera?" He beetled his brows and watched.

"I just want to learn to sing."

"Ah, an after-dinner singer. You would sing at soirees? Art songs?" He folded his arms and glanced at the ring on my finger. His tone was mocking. "Or do you just want to sing for your husband?"

I felt my face flush and looked away, out the window. The street noises that were muffled when I first entered the room now sounded loud and jarring. "I don't know. But I'd like to learn the basic technique—breath control, how to put light and shade into the notes."

After a moment he nodded. "At least you are honest." He turned back to the piano. "Let us try again."

As he hit the first note, I began to sing again. My throat was tight with tension, thin and reedy—but then, I hit one rounded note that was sweet and full and clear.

He stopped playing abruptly. "Let me hear that one once more," he said. "Try to sustain it."

I took a deep breath and sang the note again, drawing it out.

"Ah," he murmured with a small nod to himself, and the word released me. When he hit the next key my voice was loose, flexible, and relaxed.

Eventually he stopped playing and I found myself exhausted. The maestro ignored me. After a moment I brushed back my hair with a flip of my hand, feeling foolish, then stalked across the room and sank into a chair. He ran his fingers lightly over the tops of the white keys, deep in thought. When he spoke, it was without looking up, "It was a little breathy."

My heart pounded and my eyes stung while I struggled not to let him see them fill with tears. The room was quiet now. I shifted my canvas bag to the other hand and moved, preparing to leave.

But as I opened my mouth to thank him for his time, he interrupted. "We will have to work on the breath control, the evenness of tone, phrasing. But you have a feel for the music." I glanced up and he gave me a hard look. "I do not waste my time. You will have to start at the beginning, you know. It will seem difficult . . . tiresome at first."

It took a moment for his words to register. Then I gaped at him and caught my breath. "I'll work hard, Signore Ferrati," I blurted, trying to hide my surprise and delight.

"All right then, I will charge you $1.50 for each lesson. In lira. Let us begin."

"You mean, a lesson right now?"

"Yes, of course," he answered. Then, almost as an afterthought, "Have you brought the money with you to pay, Mrs. Perkins?"

I pulled the lira from my handbag. He placed it on the top of the piano, and we began with scales.

# Chapter Thirty

"THAT IS QUITE GOOD," I SAID, peering over Gertrude's shoulder as she sketched. She was taking lessons with Baron Meyer de Scha, one of the best-known artists in Rome.

She held the black-and-white sketchbook out before her. After a moment she frowned and put it down. "It's boring," she pronounced. "I've bought some paints, oils, and canvas and an easel. I'm dying to learn to use colors."

I took off my straw hat, threw it onto a table, and fell into the nearest chair. I had walked all the way from the gallery at Borghese Villa. It was a long walk, and I was tired and hot and irritable. "Has the mail arrived?" I asked. It had been several weeks since I had received a letter from Harvey. I dismissed a flutter of concern.

"There's something from Bangkok for you on the table," she said.

The letter was from Princess Poon. She wrote of all the latest news with a witty flare. I scanned the page with delight until I reached the last paragraph. Then, as I read, I drew in my breath.

*I look forward to your return, Barbara; your depar-*
*ture has taken some of the sparkle from our town. Your*
*husband has become quite a prominent figure in Bangkok,*
*as he is attending physician for Prince Mahidol, whom*
*you may know, has returned from Chiang Mai gravely ill.*
*Dr. Perkins is required to make daily reports to the news-*
*papers and, I'm told, personally to Their Majesties, our*
*King and Queen. Recalling your concern that he might*
*bury himself in work, however, you will be interested to*
*know that Prince Nakawn Sawan seems to have solved*
*that problem. Indeed, at one recent soiree, I was amazed*
*to see him actually dancing. Someone you both knew from*
*Nan, I believe, Amalie Breeden.*

I paused. The words cut through me as I recalled that the
Breedens were still in Bangkok. I read Princess Poon's words
again, trying to determine whether they were meant as reassur-
ance or an oblique warning. Was it possible that Harvey was
spending time with Amalie Breeden while her husband was in
Chiang Mai? Unwanted images of Amalie with Harvey rose in
my mind. Harvey in his dapper white suit, with his stick and
straw hat, as he dallied on the terrace of the Phya Thai with
someone like Amalie, someone happy to make life easy for the
royal physician, especially after so many years of marriage to
a monster.

Like skeins of colored yarn, my hopes and plans began
to come unraveled. Harvey was in Bangkok, the girls were in
Lausanne, and here I was in Italy just beginning to stand on
my own. I checked the thought. There was no time for envy
or suspicion or self-pity right now; there was too much to lose
through foolish, girlish fears. Still, thinking of Amalie Breeden,

my heart raced as I tossed the letter onto a table and struggled
to turn my attention to other things, to the maestro and singing.
When a few minutes later Gertrude gathered up her new easel
and paints and suggested that we meet Ted at a nearby café,
I was more than happy to accompany her.

It was already September but still hot in Rome. We found
Ted at an outside table, under the shade of an umbrella, drinking a cool gin fizz. His feet were propped up on a chair as he idly
surveyed the passersby. He gave us an insolent grin and pushed
out a chair with his foot. The thought crossed my mind that
Harvey would have stood for us. I sat down while Gertrude busied herself with the folded easel and paints that she had brought
along. Ted and I watched with amusement as she attempted to
store her things in the crowded space between the tables. Finally
she gave up in frustration and held them in her lap.

We ordered lemonade for ourselves, and Ted took another
gin. As we lolled in the warmth of the sun, a group of four or
five young toughs dressed in black with knee boots and baggy
pants strutted past our table. Their aggressive manner halted our
conversation. Wide-eyed, we watched them pass and knock into
an elderly woman just emerging from a shop next door. Her bag
fell to the ground, and vegetables rolled toward our table. I rose
to help, but Ted's hand shot out to pull me back. I looked at him
in surprise. Just then, the young men stopped and turned, apolo-
gizing as they picked up her things and placed them in the bag.

"Why did you stop me?" I said with a flash of anger.

Ted's eyes were puzzled as he followed their passage down the
narrow street. "They're blackshirts," he finally said. "Fascists."

Gertrude followed his gaze. "They seem perfectly nice to
me," she said, turning to Ted with a questioning look. "You
heard them apologize."

He frowned, then shook his head and raised the glass to his lips. "It's just that I'm not sure what to think about these people around the prime minister. He may be well thought of in the international community, but he's also a man who says that blood moves the wheels of history."

Gertrude gave a nervous laugh. "You're exaggerating!"

Ted shrugged. "Things are unsettled. The embassy received a report only yesterday of an incident near Venice where local fascists ordered all shops selling alcohol to display a pint of castor oil in their windows."

He saw our confusion. "It's a warning for drunks. If they're found on the streets in an inebriated state, a pint of castor oil is poured down their throats," he explained.

Memories of the taste of only a spoonful of the nasty stuff, a childhood remedy for a variety of illnesses, gave me an involuntary shudder.

"That's horrible," Gertrude complained. "You're going to ruin this lovely afternoon with such maudlin talk."

"You're right, Gertrude." He dismissed the subject with a laugh. "It's an Italian problem, not ours. What can we do with this day to cheer things up?"

"Let's go to the most beautiful spot in Rome, and Gertrude can paint it for us," I suggested.

"Well, why not?" Ted said gaily. Gertrude's eyes lit up and Ted motioned to the waiter for the bill. "We'll leave right now if you'd like. You can paint to your heart's content." He handed a fistful of lira to the waiter and, with a warning not to move, disappeared around the corner, leaving Gertrude and me at the table.

Gertrude looked at me and raised her eyebrows. I laughed and shook my head. We finished our lemonade, and a few minutes later we heard the clop of a horse's hooves on the street behind us, and an open black buggy with red wheels rounded the corner. It was a small Victoria pulled by one horse, like the ones that carried tourists all over Rome. Ted was perched next to the driver. We looked at him with surprise, then Gertrude and I piled into the carriage with her easel and paints, and off we went.

"Piazza de Spagna," Ted instructed the driver.

The carriage wound its way to the piazza and stopped near a lovely fountain just below the long flight of stairs known as the Spanish Steps. We scrambled down while Ted paid the fare. Gertrude gathered up her art supplies, and I looked around in awe at the wide, beautiful piazza. Five- and six-story buildings washed in soft colors of ochre, pink, and yellow gave the scene a mellow, aged look. Carts brimmed with flowers; gelato vendors were everywhere, and gypsies were selling trinkets.

I was thirsty, and Ted assured me that the clear, cool water from the fountain was clean. As I cupped my hands and dipped them under the flowing stream, I glanced up at the sculpture in the center. "Bernini again?"

"The father," Ted said.

"This place was made to be painted," Gertrude said, gazing about wide-eyed.

"It has bccn." Ted laughed. "Thousands of times."

The Spanish Steps stretched across and up a steep hill. Colorful flowers and lace ferns spilled from planters and heavy pots placed along the stairs, and more flowers hung over a white stone balustrade across a broad terrace near the top. To the right of the terrace the stairs narrowed and continued to a higher level and a second balustrade. There, set back from a small piazza, was an ancient gray church with clock and bell towers.

We each bought a gelato, licking the ice cream before it could melt, and climbed up the worn steps past beautiful sculptured women and men with shirts open to the waist, standing in poses that could only be feigned. "Here are some models, Gertrude," Ted whispered as we passed them. "They're waiting to be chosen by artists at the top of the steps."

Crossing the terrace and climbing more stairs, we reached the sun-drenched square in front of the old church. Here, artists had set up easels, and people browsed among them. Some sat patiently for portraits. We rested, leaning against the white railing over the long steps to catch our breath.

Spread before us and beyond the piazza below, split down the center by the street of dreams—the Via Condotti—was the city of Rome. In the distance the dome of St. Peter's Basilica rose above every building. The sky was clear and bright and blue. In the afternoon light the whole scene shimmered in an umber haze of heat and action. It was Sunday afternoon, and the streets leading away from the piazza were jammed with people and carriages, motorcycles and cars.

"Here's your subject," Ted announced, waving his hand across the vista. Gertrude smiled with delight.

While she set up her easel and paints, I turned and, resting on my elbows, leaned against the balustrade with my back to the city as I gazed at the old stone church.

"It's the Church of Trinita dei Monti," Ted said, leaning beside me.

The sun warmed us, soaking into our bare skin. People milled about, inspecting the pictures. As my gaze wandered, a movement in the shadows at the side of the church caught my attention. I watched as a priest in a black frock emerged from a door in the far corner. He closed it behind him with care and turned in my direction, fingering the edges of his flat, black hat.

Strange. There was something familiar about him, but I couldn't retrieve the memory. He seemed to feel my stare and, as he turned, his eyes met mine. For an instant he hesitated, then he hunched his shoulders, slapped his hat on his head, and walked away. I wondered if I had seen him before, then shook myself, and the fleeting thought disappeared.

For a long time I sat on the balustrade with my feet dangling over the side as Gertrude painted me into the scene. After a while some students from her art class appeared—two men who were locals, and one woman just arrived from Amsterdam. They had brought two bottles of Frascati, a slightly sweet wine grown in vineyards not far from Rome, but had only three glasses. While Gertrude continued to paint, we sprawled on the ground around her and shared the glasses and wine until the sky turned a darker blue and streaked with purple and yellow and gold.

In the twilight, Ted and I wandered down the Spanish Steps to the piazza below, leaving Gertrude with her friends. We sat on the edge of the boat-shaped fountain and grew quiet, watching the constant movement of flower vendors, couples, children, old sellers of odd things, while lights winked on around us.

I trailed my fingers through the clear, cool water in the fountain pool. A young man at the top of the steps threw a ball that his dog chased as it bounced down to the piazza, repeating the game over and over while the tireless animal ran after it. Neither of us spoke while the noises of the city wound down at the end of a weekend.

"Hungry?" Ted finally asked.

"Starved," I said, looking up for Gertrude. She had disappeared.

Ted followed my eyes, then turned to me. "Looks like we're on our own."

We strolled along until we found a small but lively café near the piazza. The doors were thrown back so that it was open to the street. Gas lamps on the wall and candles on the tables provided cheery light, and a trio of musicians in one corner played the mandolin, a guitar, and an accordion.

We ordered pasta that came piled upon the plates and salads just touched with garlic, basil, and fine olive oil. Ted smiled as I took a hungry bite of the noodles, so soft and delicate they seemed to slide down my throat.

Afterward we ate Parmesan served in great chunks, sweet and sharp and crunchy. We washed the cheese down with glasses of chilled white wine, until at last we were sated. As the night wore on, the music turned mellow. Ted rested his hand on my arm while we talked. When I turned my head and the room moved, I grew conscious that my thoughts were jumbled and slow. The glow of alcohol and food and music created a gold-brushed intimacy that was far too seductive, I realized.

"We'd better go," I murmured, rising abruptly. I stumbled against the table and Ted caught my waist. His hands were warm, almost electric. I pulled away.

"Can you walk?" he asked in an amused tone, pushing back from the table. He stood, waiting.

"Certainly," I replied. As we left the café, Ted pulled my arm through his, and we sauntered in silence in the general direction of my apartment, away from the noise and bright lights. After a few blocks, we turned onto a short, dark and narrow, closed-in street. A full yellow moon hung in the space straight ahead between low buildings. Above the moon, a thousand stars scattered across the indigo sky.

We walked on toward the moon as a man sitting on a stoop down the street began plucking haunting notes of the "Moonlight Sonata" from his guitar. He sat under a streetlight, caressing his instrument. The slow, simple melody echoed from the ancient stone buildings. Ted pulled me close so that we touched as we walked, and a forbidden thrill rose inside. The music seduced; it was hot yet soft, like a sensual wave of molten glass.

He slid his arm around my shoulders, and we slowed our steps, suspended in the magical moment, neither daring to glance at the other. The guitar player did not look up when we passed. As we wound our way through the old city, buildings soon hid the moon and the music faded.

With a turn in the narrow street, a carnival of light and sound and color fractured the spell. I halted, looking about in surprise, and Ted's arm dropped from my shoulders. We had come to the piazza of the Trevi Fountain, not far from my apartment. A group of barefoot men and women sat on a ledge at the edge of the pool. A woman cried out as her toes touched the cold water, while the men laughed. Lights blazed and searched out the shadowed places.

My eyes met Ted's. "I have to go home," I said.

Ted smiled down at me and nodded. "All right. We'll leave our business unfinished, for now," he said.

Lessons with Signore Ferrati continued, and I turned all of my energy and attention to them. Four days a week I walked to his studio in Trastevere where we worked, the one-hour lessons extending into two, then sometimes three hours.

"Every voice has its own nature, its strength and weakness," he told me. "Down, lower!" he said when I reached too high. "Stay in a range that is comfortable for you."

Sometimes the entire lesson was occupied practicing scales. Ferrati listened for breaks in tone as I pushed my voice up and down the ladder of sound, over and over.

He often became impatient. "I cannot do this if you refuse to control your breathing," he exclaimed. I pulled myself up, and my shoulders rose with the movement.

"No, no. Not like that." He placed one hand on my diaphragm and the other pressed my shoulders down. "You must keep your breath deep, gentle. You must relax." He waited to emphasize his point. "When you release the air you must remain relaxed; the emission must be smooth . . . smooth . . . smooth . . . while you finish the phrase."

Over and over he drilled me in the basics. Every day I practiced at home, usually when Gertrude was not around.

"It must be seamless, Mrs. Perkins," the maestro said. "The voice must be even all the way through the range. You must work on the passage notes, this . . . this . . . and this." He sang the notes for me. I started over again, but he pressed his palm to his forehead in exasperation.

One day I arrived late and breathless. I hurried to the piano, prepared for the usual drills when Signore Ferrati surprised me. He handed me something. I looked down and was stunned to find myself holding a score.

"We will begin to work on this," he said with no further explanation.

The passage he handed to me was from *La Traviata*, a heartbreaking, haunting piece sung by the courtesan Violetta. *"Amami Alfredo,"* she cries. *"Love me as I love you!"* It is short, quick as a breath, but the soprano's grief arcs through the music and soars to cold, clear heights that turn the voice to steel, or break it.

He saw my excitement. "Do not get your hopes up." he warned. "You will never sing grand opera. This is for practice only. It is too late . . . one must begin that sort of training at a younger age, you know."

My exultant mood vanished, and my throat tightened. I nodded, willing myself to relax and tried to mask my disappointment.

"But you have something," he added, smiling in an uncharacteristic but kind manner. "Learning to sing music like this will give you adequate technique for melodies, recitals . . . perhaps even for character appearances, small parts, where it is not necessary to have the full range." He turned to the piano. "After we are through, you will be able to sing for your supper."

A letter from Mummy arrived full of recrimination regarding the singing lessons. I wrote back: "I suppose you think that I'm quite wild and irresponsible, like those waltzing mice that go round and round when part of the brain is removed. I suppose I've no business spending money on music lessons, but maybe someone will want to hear me sing someday."

"That was flat, Barbara."

Abruptly I stopped. Signore Ferrati stood on the balcony facing the street as he smoked his cigarette. I watched him from the interior of the room—a dark figure against the bright sunlight.

I began again. His fingers drummed on the balcony railing, and then he whirled around and strode back inside to the piano.

He sat down on the bench with a thud, still holding the ciga-rette, and plunked the note. "That is the key—*that* is the key." The note rang out again as he hit it harder. "Try it!"

I drew in my breath, then started to sing as he played the melody with one hand, studying my throat, my posture, my face. When I had finished, he sighed.

"You must work harder—still the problem is the breathing. You are nervous and the sound comes out thrusting, grabbing . . . so!" He struck a firm note on the piano. "*Free* the music. It is inside of you. Let it flow from within. *You* are the instrument. Come! We must begin again."

With each lesson Ferrati pushed me harder, farther, and each day I sank deeper into a place that I had never known, another universe that seemed to exist parallel to my own—an ambient musical world with a lyrical, dreamlike quality. Walking to his studio induced a fantastical transposition: the narrow street that led to Ferrati's studio transformed, becom-ing a passage to an enchanted place. When I opened the heavy wooden doors and stepped into the cool, dim entry hall below his studio, the real world melted away. To this day the musky odor of old wood and damp stone recalls that stairwell and brings back the thrill, a rush of excitement and expectation, of drama and magic, of crystalline light. An apricot glow washed Trastevere.

"It's as if I've shed a layer of old, hard skin," I tried to explain to Gertrude. "As if I'm new and everything that touches me tingles."

Gertrude gave me a worried look. "Have you heard from Harvey lately?"

I looked away. "No," I said lightly. "But he's terribly busy."

When I was with Ferrati, thoughts of Harvey, even those forbidden thoughts of Amalie Breeden, faded. "Cleaner, cleaner . . . clear the upper voice! Do it again!" the maestro demanded. My stamina increased day by day, and my voice grew strong and clear. "I wish to hear exquisite notes, like pearls," Ferrati shouted.

But when he was silent and smiled, I was exultant.

"This is Rome!" I thought each day, feeling the joy. "And I am singing."

I dragged Gertrude and Ted to the opera, to concerts and chorales, to hear choirs in the multitude of churches in the city. If they could not attend, I went alone. Each time when the lights dimmed, I drifted into the glorious, enthralling music. I *became* Mimi or Floria or Norma. It no longer mattered that I was past the time for training. The maestro's warning was now just so much dust. I studied the voices of the singers on the stage, their articulation of words and notes, the timbre, the breath control, the accuracy of pitch.

The days passed, and weeks turned into months. As I worked with Ferrati to create pure, lyrical sound, the old restless feeling was replaced with a gradual sense of accomplishment that poured into each moment, a feeling that I was creating something of my own. Now it seemed to me that for the first time since Harvey and I were married, I was more than just a wife.

Since the evening that Ted and I had walked home together from the Piazza de Spagna, he had begun spending much of his free time with Gertrude and me. He seemed to sense my need to keep things as they were, however. With the exception of an amused smile that played around the corners of his mouth at times, to my relief, he managed to avoid the subject.

*Compared to Harvey, he has no ballast,* warned my inner voice.

I chased the thought away. Ted was fun, just a friend, I told myself. But Harvey's letters were now few and far between. Princess Poon had written again to let me know that, despite everything, Prince Mahidol had died. Harvey must have been downcast, I knew, but still he did not write.

One afternoon in early November, Ted arrived at our front door looking exhausted. His face had lost its healthy glow, his eyes shadowed with rings. We hadn't seen him for several days. "What on earth has happened?" I cried as I pulled him into our parlor. Gertrude popped her head in, took the measure of things, and returned with a highball that she handed to Ted.

He took it gratefully. "Terrible news from home," he finally said after gulping half the drink. He shook his head.

"Well, what is it?" Gertrude demanded impatiently.

"The market has crashed," he said simply.

Gertrude and I both stared at him in bewilderment.

"Stocks," he explained. "The stock market is in ruins. Banks are going under, speculators are rioting on Wall Street—it's a nightmare come true."

"How could such a thing happen?" I asked. "What does it mean? How long will it last?"

"Whoa!" Ted raised his hands. "We've been trying at the embassy to get those answers for two days and nights, Barbara. It's not simple. Inflation, rising prices, overconfidence, speculation, all mixed up together. It'll take years to sort out, I imagine." He raked his fingers through his hair, then picked up his glass and finished the drink.

I wondered if this would hurt Mummy. Harvey and I had never invested in stocks, and neither had Dad, I believed. As I watched Ted, I suddenly remembered his jest that he was a rich man in waiting. As if reading my mind, he glanced at me. "I received a wireless from my father last night," he said. "He sold out months ago. Says he always thought there was too much gas in the balloon."

I sent a wireless to Alice, and she answered right away. Mummy was fine, she said. Dick was managing their money, and Dad's pension appeared to be safe. Gertrude's family lost some of their holdings, though, and her face took on a worried look. After a few weeks, things returned to normal so far as I could tell. The market rumble at home did not seem to have an effect on day-to-day life in Rome. My lessons with Ferrati continued.

A letter arrived from Harvey. With barely concealed excitement, he wrote that he was to be decorated by the king of Siam with the Order of the White Elephant, the greatest honor bestowed to the farang, for services to the country and to the royal family. Stunned by the news, I put the letter down carefully upon my lap and smoothed it with my hand.

When I picked it up again, the question was put squarely: Would I retrieve the children from boarding school and return in time for the ceremony? It was to be held at the royal palace on December tenth, a month away. A response was required immediately, by return mail if possible, in order to permit him to make the necessary arrangements.

I felt a stab of fear, knowing that I would not return to Bangkok yet wanting him to understand. Violetta's haunting song rose in my mind as I composed my answer, a plea: *Love me as I love you*, she cried. But I had given up singing once for Harvey; I could not do it again, not now. Not just yet. An overwhelming sense of sorrow settled on me at the thought of what Harvey might conclude when he realized that I wasn't coming. I knew that I must let him know how important the lessons were to me. But this was a lesson day, and if I didn't hurry I would be late. There was only just time to send an answer. So with a stab of anxiety, I picked up a pen. My heart welled with pride and love for Harvey, and silently I begged him to understand.

"You make me so proud," I wrote with large, careful strokes, knowing that when he read my answer, it would convey to him a meaning far beyond the words, knowing that Mummy would rage. I hesitated. Then I shook myself, and like a moth dancing too near the flame, I slowly continued.

> *I recall that the Prince of Wales was given the Order of the White Elephant, so he can now consider himself in good company. No one deserves this more than you. Unfortunately, I cannot get away at this time.*

I bore down on the pen so that the letters were thick with ink, then paused, letting my thoughts settle before going on.

> *You must understand. It is absolutely impossible for me to return right now. I've begun working on serious music. Music that I never believed I would sing again. And I can do it, Harvey!*

I stopped to underline the last words.

> *Maestro Ferrati thinks that I can do it. My heart is with you, but I cannot leave—please understand.*

I picked up the letter and ran my thumb gently down the edge of the page, then hesitated. Would I lose him now? I wondered, suddenly gripped with the terror of this risk. I pushed away poisoned thoughts of the unsaid things in Princess Poon's letters, of Amalie Breeden, of dreary, long, empty days without Harvey's love, and set my mind instead on Ferrati, on the music. To return right now would be sheer martyrdom, I argued, as I sealed the envelope.

*Just a little longer. Please understand.* I dropped off the letter to be mailed from Thomas Cook & Sons, then continued on to Ferrati's studio.

# Chapter Thirty-One

CHRISTMAS WAS COMING. I BOOKED PASSAGE to Lausanne to celebrate the holiday with the children. Gertrude accompanied me as far as Geneva, then continued on to visit friends in Gstaad.

Lausanne was gray, and a sharp wind blew off the lake. I took a lovely big room with a fireplace at the Pension Florissant. After unpacking, I hurried out to the Fellowship School. When I arrived, the parlor was empty except for a young girl curled with a book in an overstuffed chair in front of the fire. She looked up as I walked in, marking her place with her finger as I asked where the children could be found.

"I believe they're playing in the woods," she said, pointing in the direction of the forest near the school. "We play hide and seek there."

A light crust of snow covered the ground, and it crunched beneath my boots as I crossed the meadow. The air was cold and crisp, and as I entered the forest it was pungent with the fragrance of fir trees. There was no undergrowth, and it was easy to walk. Thin, high voices like barbs of silver pierced the frigid air with shouts and gales of laughter. I drew closer to the sounds, huddling into myself for warmth, then caught a glimpse of color and movement as the children flashed back and forth among the trees ahead.

Suddenly I spotted Barby Jeanne and June standing together in a clearing with a group waiting for their turns in the game. I stopped to watch; they had not yet seen me. They looked so small, but their cheeks glowed with health, and they hopped from one foot to the other with excitement as they chattered with the other girls. I smiled at the thought of my surprise and quickly ducked behind a tree where I could watch without being seen.

After a few minutes, the group broke up as the children spread out, looking for places to hide, I suppose. Barby Jeanne turned and looked my way. I peeked around the trunk and waved. She froze and stared in disbelief. I grinned, then waved again as she moved closer with her eyes fixed on me. Then she gave a yelp and broke into a run that ended with a leap and a hug. "Mummy!"

June turned and seeing me, raced to us too.

I gathered them into my arms and held them tight, fighting a hint of sadness that cast a shadow on our glee. Baby arms and legs wrapped around me as I pressed their soft bodies into mine. I carried June while Barby Jeanne clung to me, and we walked back to the parlor. I was surprised to find that June had grown heavy. I had to set her down to climb the stairs.

We found Miss Thomas in the kitchen, just beyond the parlor. She was making tea and asked us to join her, but I shook my head, anxious to return with the girls to the pension.

"They are a joy," the headmistress said as we departed, pulling the girls close and stroking their heads. They snuggled against her with obvious fondness. "Everyone loves them."

The pension was still full of women waiting for their husbands working abroad. Once again the great number of such women in Europe struck me.

"When will Daddy come?" June asked that evening.

My voice wavered as I answered. "He has to spend Christmas at the hospital this year, Junie."

"Oh." Her eyes were puzzled.

One night I heard quiet weeping. I tiptoed through the darkness, not sure of the sound. It was Barby Jeanne.

"What's the matter?" I asked as I turned her to me and wiped tears from her cheeks.

"I miss him," she sobbed.

I didn't have to ask whom; the child adored her father. The words pierced my soul, and my throat grew thick and tight as I looked down at her. Children need their fathers and mothers nearby, to hold and kiss them goodnight, to listen to stories of their day, to laugh with them and wipe their tears and share their triumphs. Barby Jeanne shuddered. I pulled her onto my lap, feeling her warmth, and rocked back and forth, humming softly until, at last, she fell asleep.

But then the strange, tight expression long ago on Mummy's face came to mind. She had told me to forget my dreams of music, that my duty as a wife was to support my husband's decisions. Children need parents that are joyful and strong, satisfied with their own accomplishments, as well, I mused. Tears spilled onto my cheeks. Cold, soft moonlight bathed my daughters' faces. *The old code is not for you*, I resolved, wiping my tears with a fierce swipe. *Trudging that dreary path through the world in someone else's shadow in the name of duty is not for you.*

It was not a matter of love, I brooded. True love requires strength, not weakness, as a partner. It was a matter of being complete, especially for my daughters. But would they ever understand? And was I right? I fell asleep as slivers of morning light crept in through the frosted windowpanes.

On Christmas Eve, as the children slept, I hung stockings at the foot of my bed and filled them with candy and toys and small stuffed animals that peeked over the tops. They laughed with glee when they discovered the surprise. As they tore the treats from the stockings, I watched in a pensive mood with sharp little jabs at my conscience each time they looked up at me with their bright eyes.

I had heard no more from Harvey. For weeks after sending my last letter I had waited for a response, but none came. Christmas presents had arrived in Lausanne with letters for each child, but the brief note to me that accompanied them was cool, no more than a polite and uninformative recitation of facts.

I wavered. Perhaps, after all, I should wait for Harvey in Lausanne.

*Good diversionary tactic,* whispered my scornful inner voice.

I watched the girls carefully. They seemed happy at the thought of returning to school. Only a bit more time, I told myself as the holiday neared its end. Odd, I thought, how the promise of a beginning seems, at times, like the beginning of the end. Like the evening star and morning star, they're one and the same, but meaning is determined by the beholder.

The day before I was to leave, the girls and I were sitting on the floor playing our own version of the card game called Hearts. I glanced up to see Barby Jeanne's face shining, her eyes locked on something behind me. June looked up and her mouth dropped open. I turned my head.

Harvey stood in the doorway. He held his hat in his hands and smiled, then dropped the hat, laughing as Barby Jeanne and June flew into his arms. I sat watching them, unable to move. My heart seemed to stop, and my thoughts roiled. Rome, Harvey, my lessons, Bangkok, the children—nothing made sense.

"Hello, darling," he said in a polite tone.

I stared at him. He walked over to me, stooped down, and kissed my cheek, then straightened. The girls curled around him again, hanging onto his long legs and giving me time to stand, smooth my hair, and gather my thoughts.

"What a wonderful surprise," I said gaily, moving toward him.

"Didn't you get my letter?" he asked, turning from me to sink into a chair. I halted. The girls immediately climbed upon his lap. His tone as he spoke reflected the distance in his letters. It was the voice of a stranger.

"No," I said, but he was already distracted by the girls.

We spent the evening together in the parlor with the girls. He told me of the royal ceremony, without spending much time on the details, and grew vague when I pressed him. When Barby Jeanne and June went to bed and we were finally alone, I looked at him with a sudden, deep longing. "Are you . . ."

He stood and gazed down at me, poised to leave. "I've taken a room near the station," he said.

I felt myself flush.

Harvey moved close, and his arms circled me. Time stopped as we stood together, his forehead resting atop my head. We were one for an instant, until he pulled away and, still holding me, looked down. "I'm not here to force you to change your mind," he began. His voice caught and he cleared his throat, "You know, about this arrangement. But I want you to know that I'd like you to come back to Bangkok with me. You and the girls." With a slight smile, almost one of embarrassment, he released me and stepped back.

"Do you *need* for me to return?" I held my breath, not sure what answer I wished to hear.

"No." His voice was flat as he looked past me. "I'm doing fine. You mustn't view things from that angle. You see, I believe that a marriage, without choice, is drudgery." His eyes met mine, then slid away. "Actually, I'm only here for a few days."

Drudgery. I hesitated, focused on the word. Amalie Breeden slipped into my mind, and my heart plummeted as the thought grew. Harvey had always admired the headmaster's wife. Marriage with someone like her would not be drudgery. I lifted my chin, determined not to show Harvey how his words had hurt. "This is a long way to come for a few days," I said with an aching heart.

"Yes . . . well." He shrugged and offered no explanation. He was only here for the girls.

I nodded and veiled my eyes. "If I had known . . ."

"Yes, of course." His back stiffened. I watched as he walked to the door. "Don't change your plans." He picked up the hat from the floor where it had fallen and turned. "When are you set to leave?"

"I was to leave tomorrow."

"Well, you must do that."

I felt cold and sick, wanted to cling to him and weep. "The girls were to return to school," I said, working for a casual tone. "But . . . I could stay a bit longer if you'd like. That shouldn't be a problem to arrange."

He shook his head. "Not necessary, Babs. This is just a short trip. The girls can stay with me, and I'll take them back to school."

His tone was dispassionate, brisk. Tears swelled in my throat.

He opened the door, then turned around. "My contract's up at the end of March, you know." His voice took on that distant tone again. "We'll have some decisions to make, I suppose."

"Harvey?"

I saw a flicker in his eyes, then his expression went blank, "Yes, Babs?"

"Is . . ." My mouth was dry. My heart pounded. I didn't know if I could bear to hear the answer, but I had to ask the question. "Is there . . . someone else?"

He stared at me and seconds passed. His eyes drew together, his lips tightened, and he turned and walked through the door, closing it quietly behind him.

I stood rigid, listening as his footsteps faded down the hallway and, despite my pride and Rome and Ferrati, I fought to contain a desperate urge to run after him, to call out to him, to throw myself at him. This took all my strength. Through a bleak haze I heard voices at the end of the hall. His laughter. The front door closing. And at last, only silence.

I turned away from the door, determined not to think. In the silence, I said aloud to myself, "Well, Babs, did you expect him to play the *Cavaliere* to your Floria?" And then I began to cry. A radio set was on a table nearby, and I switched it on as I lowered myself into a straight-backed wooden chair, moving slowly, knowing Harvey's love for me was finished, with or without a divorce. Static came through the radio, and I was leaning across to switch it off when I heard the orchestra begin and then a woman's voice—Schumann-Heink's voice—and the dark beauty of Mozart's *Requiem*.

A requiem is appropriate, I thought, listening to the velvet sound—blue, I thought—of a great coloratura mezzo. I dried my tears, forcing my thoughts to the music. I'd been given a second chance to sing—a last chance, I told myself as the diva's voice penetrated, filling me with determination. This is what I'd wanted for so many years. And, Harvey certainly didn't care. Whatever was to come, it made no difference to him now.

I returned to Rome alone, ahead of Gertrude. The train arrived on December 31, 1929, a dark, cold, blustery day. If the sign on the wall had not said Roma, I would not have believed that we had arrived. I left the train and walked down an almost deserted platform toward the terminal, wrapping my coat tight against the damp cold. Ahead, occasional wisps of smoke and steam from the big engine on the tracks curled through the cold gray air. Yanking a felt cloche below my ears, I continued through the terminal and into the parking lot where taxis waited, their drivers huddled down behind frosted glass.

The apartment was chilled. The empty rooms were stark, bare and lonely. The tap of my soles on the hardwood floor rang hollow as I walked through the parlor to deposit my valise in the bedroom. Moodily, I wondered what the children were doing just now. They had clung to me before I left. Harvey had been withdrawn, polite.

I wandered aimlessly through the rooms, then back into the parlor. The last cold light of day streaked across the floor from the windows that looked out onto the street. It was New Year's Eve. I wanted to be angry with Harvey but found myself wondering how he and the girls were celebrating the evening.

I shook off the dark mood and spun around for my coat. Closing the door carefully behind me, I walked to the café at

Trevi Fountain where I thought I might find Ted. Outside, the chairs were tipped against the tables. It was growing dark, but inside the room glowed with bright, welcome light. Without giving myself time to think, I pulled the door open and walked in.

Every table was filled. I quickly scanned the room, then spotted him. Ted sat with a group of friends near the back, almost hidden in a bay window. A quick flood of happiness was instantly replaced with a strange, uneasy feeling. I hesitated.

A waiter approached. "I'm afraid we're full at the moment. Are you looking for someone in particular?" he asked in a polite tone. Just then Ted glanced up and saw me. His eyes widened in surprise, then he grinned and jumped up, shoving the chair aside. "Barbara!" he called, waving me over. As I reached the table, he gave me a hug and introduced everyone.

"Have some champy," a woman called across the table as she pushed a glass toward me.

The room was noisy, and a group nearby began to sing a raucous, bawdy song. I hesitated, then made up my mind. "I really can't stay," I said. "I'm exhausted from my trip. Just stopped by to say 'Happy New Year' to Ted."

"What the devil?" Ted exclaimed. "Well, hold on a moment while I get my coat, and I'll walk you home."

The night was brilliant, deliciously cold. Leaving the café, my spirits immediately lifted, and Ted soon had me laughing as we romped arm in arm through crowded streets. He pulled me toward an American bar that he said served hot sausage and beer. As he steered me through the door, his hand gripped my shoulder in a possessive manner, and I shrugged it off. Just then the piano player struck up "The Star Spangled Banner," and the crowd grew wild as everyone began to sing. Ted handed me a foaming glass of beer, and we joined the merriment.

At midnight we found ourselves in the center of the city. The Colosseum was flooded with harsh, bright lights. "It looks like a dance hall," I cried, feeling lighthearted.

"Then let's dance," Ted laughed, and he took me in his arms. Sorrows were erased in the enchantment of the evening— Harvey, Amalie Breeden, the girls. Only the moment remained. We waltzed a few steps down the street, then as the bells began to toll for midnight, ran past the ruins of the Forum toward the bright lights of the Piazza Venezia.

We pushed our way into the crowded square. Faint strands of "Auld Lang Syne" drifted from an open window above a balcony nearby. Someone shoved a party hat onto my head, and whistles and horns and cheerful shouts rang from every direction while the bells of Rome continued to hail the arrival of 1930.

Ted turned to me and, in an instant, I understood that things had changed. The bells continued to clang their greeting, and as the deep, solemn tones echoed from the walls of old stone buildings around us, he leaned down and slowly brushed his lips over mine. In a mellow glow that lingered from the champagne and wine and beer, I felt the warmth of this man and softened. His arms slid around me. He tilted his head back and looked into my eyes, then pressed his body into mine, leaned down, and kissed me again, harder, hungry now.

Suddenly I pulled away, trembling as Harvey's face swam before me.

"It's late," I laughed, affecting a casual air as I turned away from Ted. The pleasant cold had somehow become a damp chill that seemed to penetrate to my bones. I tucked my coat closer around and shivered. People poured into the piazza from a narrow street nearby. From a small café a few doors down, raucous laughter shot into the street, then drunken voices singing.

The yellow light reflecting from the small square windows was somehow safe and reassuring.

"Let's go have coffee," I said. My voice sounded strange, I thought, thin and strained. I glanced at Ted.

A sardonic smile creased his face. "Don't run away just yet." He looked down at me and cupped my face in his hands. "I have something to say. I think . . . well," he gave a short laugh, "I suppose I have to admit that I'm in love with you." He paused, dropped his arms to his sides, and the words came out in a rush. "The truth of it is, Barbara, I fell for you the first time we met, in Piazza Navona."

"Not now." I fumbled with the collar on my coat. "Let's have some coffee. I've had too much to drink."

"No." Ted's voice rasped with emotion. He reached for my arm, but I shoved my hands down into my pockets, creating a wedge that eluded his grasp. He gazed at me a moment, then seemed to come to a decision and shrugged.

"All right," he said lightly. "Let's have some coffee."

I felt a surge of relief and smiled. "Here." I gestured to the small café that looked so cheerful. "Let's go in this one." I started forward, but he grasped my shoulders and spun me back toward him.

"I want more from you than friendship," he said in a low, husky voice, holding his face just inches from mine.

"I'm married, Ted. I have two children."

"Get a divorce." His tone was preemptory, commanding. "Don't you understand? I love you."

I stared at him without moving.

He looked into my eyes, and as he tightened his grip, his shone. "And you feel something for me . . . don't deny it. There's something there for me." Suddenly his manner changed.

He tapped his forefinger lightly on the tip of my nose and grinned.

I was silent, at once apprehensive and confused and excited as his words swirled around me. I looked at his handsome, ruddy face framed by ragged hair that somehow always fell into place. His even white teeth shone against his healthy complexion. His knee-length cashmere chesterfield coat hung open, and a burgundy silk scarf was thrown around his neck, giving him a worldly and prosperous look.

Like lightning, a feeling of power, of exhilaration and confidence, shot through me. It was intoxicating to know that Ted loved me, not as someone's wife or mother or daughter, but as me, independent and on my own. I tossed my head and smiled, hiding my thoughts. I would have to mull this over later when I was alone.

"I have friends in Rome and Paris and Vienna who can be helpful with your singing," he murmured, still holding onto my shoulders.

"I don't have big ambitions," I reproached him, shrugging from under his grip. I didn't want to owe Ted anything, didn't want to be in his debt. "I just need time to think things through."

"There's nothing wrong with ambition," he laughed, back to his usual carefree manner, as he linked his arm through mine and swung me toward the well-lit café. "Just don't wait too long. I'm not a saint."

I glanced sideways at him. He caught my look and gave me a breezy smile.

# Chapter Thirty-Two

SIGNORE FERRATI'S ENTIRE DEMEANOR HAD UNDER-GONE a startling change. The intense training now reached new levels. We extended the length of the lessons and began working every day instead of four times a week.

Each day I sorted through the mail in vain, hoping to find a letter from Harvey. Princess Poon wrote again, and this time she failed to mention Harvey at all, a glaring omission given her detailed description of the social season. It was almost as if he'd dropped off the earth. I scribbled a gay little missive back to her and turned my thoughts quickly to the music.

Ted was annoyed at my distraction, but I found that all of my energy was focused on the music. "I can't think clearly now," I told him. "First, I must find how singing fits into my life. Other decisions have to wait a bit."

"Life's short, Barbara," he said with half-closed eyes.

Near the end of February, Gertrude returned from Gstaad, and with her was Margaret. "I found her on the slopes," Gertrude said, and Margaret laughed at my expression.

"Not likely, darling," she drawled, and her sensuous mouth curled up slightly in an enigmatic way. "I'm better at warming the hearth." She gave me a sly look and twisted a long strand of milky pearls around her finger.

One afternoon a rapid succession of knocks sounded on the front door of our apartment, and before we could answer, it swung open and Ted walked in. His face was browner than usual and flushed from a walk. He had just come from the embassy. His hair was blown, giving him a roguish appearance, and he was careless and confident as he strode over to greet Gertrude with a hug, throwing me a wry smile at the same time.

Just then Margaret entered the parlor. Her gray eyes turned on Ted, and she gave him a long look, with a flicker of a smile as her bold gaze traveled from his head to his toes. She smoothed the back of her hair, then raised her brows in a question as she sank into a chair.

Ted stopped short and returned her gaze. "Now here's a pretty lady," he murmured. Gertrude watched with obvious humor.

Margaret stretched her arm across the back of the chair and crossed her long legs, a move that caused her short skirt to inch farther up her thighs. Her eyes remained fixed on Ted, but she didn't say a word. I introduced them and told her that he was with the American Embassy.

Ted was tantalized. He shrugged out of his coat and threw it across a chair, then began prowling around the room like a panther, keeping up a stream of conversation with Gertrude as he picked things up and put them down, rearranging them, all the while continuing a covert examination of Margaret. His look traced her profile when she turned away. Strangely, though, I found I didn't care.

"And what do you do at the embassy?" she finally asked. She lowered her dark, gleaming head as she spoke, watching him beneath her lids.

"I make sure that Americans don't get into trouble over here," he answered with a grin. "Are you perhaps in need of assistance? You do sound like an American." He let the sentence dangle.

She laughed, a gay, tinkling sound. "I left America almost ten years ago when prohibition arrived." She drummed her fingers on the back of the chair and tilted her head as she looked at Ted. "Haven't been back since."

"You left just about the time that women got the vote," I said.

"An empty victory, my dear." She gave me a bored look.

I flushed with annoyance. "Why do you say that?"

She laughed again. "What a joke. Do you know that for a while the vote turned on the whim of a twenty-four-year-old boy from the Tennessee mountains?"

"That's nonsense," I said.

"Actually, that's about right," Ted interjected, still gazing at Margaret. "It was a kid named Harry Burn. He had the deciding vote. His mother made him change his vote to yes so the amendment could be ratified."

"His mother made him do it?" I was astounded.

"Mothers are like that," Margaret said without taking her eyes off of Ted.

"Is prohibition really why you left?" Ted asked with amusement.

"That, and the fact that in Europe a girl can have her own party . . . in a manner of speaking."

"I see." Ted's eyes gleamed. "Would you care to have a party?"

"A woman needs a reason for a party."

"Perhaps I can think of one."

I rolled my eyes and turned to leave. As I walked past, Ted said under his breath, "Don't wait too long, Barbara."

One day a letter from Harvey arrived. I was on my way out the door for a lesson with Ferrati when I saw it on a table where Gertrude had carefully placed it, face up so that I would notice it. A premonition of disaster sent a chill through me.

I sat down and closed my eyes. When I opened them, the letter was still there. I glanced away. The window was open and I concentrated on the sounds outside. In the branches of a nearby tree, a bird sang all alone in high, shrill notes. I remembered that Harvey had once said the high-pitched calls were for sounding an alarm. Finally my eyes were drawn back to the envelope and, without further reflection, I picked it up and tore it open.

The handwriting was neat and even, with no flourishes— like the words.

> *I hope this letter finds you well. I'll get right to the point. As you know, I'm a plain man. I found it difficult to talk to you in Lausanne—too painful. I had come to ask you to return but found I couldn't argue my case. I was terrified that you would choose music over me.*

I stopped breathing and looked down at the paper to see if it was real. The writing was smudged and I had to strain to read the rest.

> *I can't speak or write poetic words. So I'll just say this simply: I miss you, Babs. And the girls. I'm lonely,*

*and the raw truth is that life without you, even my work,
seems terrible and empty. I love you. There is no one else
who matters.*

I gripped the letter and forced myself to continue reading.

*But it's time now for you to choose.*

A bright, searing pain shot from the base of my spine.

*My contract is almost up and I could leave for
Lausanne, then Philadelphia, in a matter of weeks.*

So soon! The pain exploded like shattered glass from my spine
through my chest, into my lungs. I stopped reading and bent
forward to catch my breath, feeling curiously weightless. After
a moment I forced myself to look back down at the letter.

*If you don't wish to return to America with me, I'll
extend my contract here, or perhaps I'll take up an offer
to go to Africa, then on to Buenos Aires. The Rockefeller
people are here now and they are pressing me for a com-
mitment. It's difficult to write these words because I don't
want to lose you, and I find that my hands are like ice.
Perhaps you have already given your answer, but I can't
give up without one last try.*

*Only one thing more: If you choose to stay in Rome,
you mustn't worry over me. I'll get on with things, as we
all must do. If that's the case, be assured that you and the
children will have no financial worries. It's been so difficult not to impose my desires upon you, to leave you free
to choose. But as I've said before, love without choice is
drudgery, not love.*

I froze, returned to that last line, and when I'd read it over again, I gazed through the window at the sunlight dancing through the tree, at the new buds ready to burst from the tips of the branches, like the fireworks in Chiang Mai. Had I misunderstood Harvey in Lausanne?

Something moved inside. I looked down at the letter in my hands with a confusing mix of desperate fear and joy. He was giving me the chance to choose, I realized. I could gather the children from school in Lausanne and go home to America with Harvey, or remain in Italy to sing, to find out what this new life offered. But inside I felt the chips of glass each time I took a breath. As Harvey had warned, when you choose between two things you love, one of them is lost.

*"So know that you are free, if that's what you really want,"* Harvey finished. *"If I haven't heard from you before the end of March, I'll understand you've made your choice and will finalize my plans. But my heart will always be with you, and Barby Jeanne and June."*

I glanced at the postmark and my heart skipped a beat. The letter had been mailed weeks ago, and he must be wondering why I had not answered. Frantically I searched through the things that lay on the table until I found the morning paper, then caught my breath. This was Thursday, the twenty-ninth of March. A letter would take too long, I knew. A cable would have to be wired from Thomas Cook by tomorrow evening, before they closed for the weekend. I knew Harvey too well—by Monday he'd be committed to another life.

The house rang with silence. The glass ground in my chest. I placed the letter on the table where I'd found it, grabbed my coat, and fled. I was late for my lesson.

I lay my coat across the back of a chair. Signore Ferrati was already at the piano, picking out a melody, his eyes on the score as his fingers stretched across the keys. I smoothed my dress and then, with great effort, walked to a place behind him. He was playing something new.

"What is that?" I asked.

"It's from the last act of *Traviata*. Muzio sang it with the Rome opera last year—it is a classic. 'Addio del passato.'" He played a few bars, then looked at me. "Here Violetta is full of passion, full of grief for her lost love. She is dying . . . all hope is gone. It is too late. When you sing this—"

"When *I* sing this?"

"Si. Si. Perhaps," he answered with impatience. "Let me finish, please."

I waited.

"When you sing this," he waited, but I did not interrupt, "you must let go. Here is *fate*. Short breaths . . . like so." He drew a quick intake of air, let it out slowly, then looked at me. His voice was low, controlled. "Can you do this?"

I nodded. He handed me the sheets of music. I held them with a shaking hand as he began to play. I was too late. He stopped, then without a word, started over. Finally we were together, my voice, tremulous at first, gained strength. His fingers on the piano guided me through the notes . . . a constant shifting, back and forth, up and down, *crescendo, diminuendo*, the music feverish with grief, single notes, full phrases. I sang and suspended my dread, letting the music flow from me, from the husk that was my self.

"No, no!" He stopped. "Like this. *Le rose del volto*," he sang. "Short spasms of breath . . . repeat . . . repeat . . . *pull* the sorrow from here." He tapped his chest. "And at the end . . . Ah! *Tutto fini*." He stared at me, his voice rose, "Into a cry . . . an arc of pain to break the heart . . . all is over now. It is too late, too late. Here! And here!" His wide hands struck the keys with force, his head bowed over the keyboard as he played.

We began again. And again. For hours we worked. I became absorbed, and Violetta's song became my song. I wept inside as the music swept me onto a ghost ship of grief. *All is over now,* I sang with Violetta. *All is over now.*

When finally Ferrati's hands struck a chord and the notes faded away, I looked up in surprise, dazzled by the abrupt change. He sat without moving. I swallowed my tears, but he did not speak. The score was still clutched in my hand. Quietly I placed it on top of the piano.

My movement broke the spell. He turned to look at me. "Perhaps you are not too old, Barbara," he said in a tired voice. The corners of his mouth flicked up for an instant, giving the fleeting impression of a smile before it disappeared.

He turned back to the piano. "Tomorrow then."

His tone was abrupt. I was dismissed.

I took a taxi home, feeling as though I had woken from a happy dream, only to be faced with the reality of some terrible sorrow that had been there all the while. It was late in the afternoon and I had no energy left to walk, but as I faced the door to our apartment and thought of the letter waiting on the table just inside, I turned away.

Blindly I stumbled through the narrow streets, across the Piazza Barberini and left onto the Via Veneto. Neither the trees with silver bark nor the lace patterns of sun and shadow on the walkway warmed my heart. The normally animated flower vendors and bustling cafés seemed to stand still. I passed the Hotel Excelsior and continued walking until I emerged through the arched opening in the Aurelian Wall that surrounded the ancient part of Rome. I crossed the street to the Borghese Gardens.

Without thinking I took a turn to the right, moving deeper into the park down a shaded lane, under a canopy of tall elegant trees that arced together over the road. Wooden benches were set against raised mounds of grass on each side of the walkway. Crumbled brick steps embedded in the soil led up to the well-kept lawn. Recent rain had left behind the fragrance of damp wood and green moss and fresh-cut grass.

I turned to the left before reaching the enormous white villa, the art gallery, to avoid seeing anyone, yet I soon happened upon a tree with an enormous trunk and children climbing over its limbs, a gelato stand with advertisements painted gaily in red and white and blue, and a small carousel. The lane continued through rows of rough, uneven hedges and crossed a small square. In the center was a fountain where clear water slid in smooth sheets over four white marble horses, almost life-sized. In frozen motion they reared, nostrils flared, mouths wide. I took a seat on an iron bench and allowed my thoughts to drift.

The air was crisp and cool, but not cold. Beyond the fountain and the hedge across the way stretched a field with thick patches of tiny scarlet and yellow flowers peeking through the grass. I watched a bird with sleek black feathers move on the edge of the fountain with small, sharp hops from one spot to another as he kept up a constant song. Suddenly he stopped and cocked his head, one small round eye fixed in my direction, as if to inquire, "What are *you* looking at, signora?" I remained still until he resumed his song and dance. The muted laughter of the children climbing the tree filtered from afar, muffled but pitched with joy, making me think of Barby Jeanne and June. I dropped my head as tears threatened and I fought them back.

A shadow crossed the path in front of me. Startled, I glanced up into eyes that were dark and familiar. For a moment I was confused and my thoughts scattered. A remembrance of the old stone church above Piazza de Spagna came to mind, images of a priest gazing from the shadows of Trinita dei Monti.

A priest? The man before me wore a black cassock and the collar of a Catholic priest. I closed my eyes and opened them again. Looking down at me was the mysterious Englishman that I had known in Nan so many years ago, Joshua Smithers.

"So it *was* you," he said, holding a flat black hat in his hand, fingering it into circles as if it were the wheel of life. "I thought I knew you a few months ago, but I wasn't sure. Now here you are again. I called when you entered the park, tried to catch up, but you were too far ahead."

As he spoke, memories of Nan overwhelmed me—the despair, the gradual shriveling of my spirit, the joyless doctrine that had parched my soul, the weeks of isolation when Harvey left us to attend to the jungle villages. The futility of it all, and the singing I had lost. Bitterness washed over me, and suddenly I was fatigued. I began to cry.

Joshua Smithers sat down. It took him a moment. He moved in a heavy manner, as though the action weighed on him. Then he waited.

"What are you doing here?" I finally asked. My voice broke. "And why are you wearing those clothes?"

"I live in Rome. I am a priest—a Jesuit."

"And at Nan?"

After a brief pause, he nodded. "Yes, at Nan as well. But there I was running away—or perhaps I was searching." He changed the subject abruptly. "Where is Doctor Perkins? I would like to see him again."

"He's in Bangkok," I answered and drew a shuddered breath. He fixed his look on me. I hurried to explain. "There are many demands on his time. And the children . . . well, the children needed more, you see." My voice drifted off, and to my horror I began to cry again. I covered my face with my hands.

He was quiet. Finally my sobs subsided, but I felt his gaze. A clean, white handkerchief was placed in my lap. I stared for a moment, then picked it up and wiped the tears away.

I could not look at him. "You never seemed to me to be a man with a folded, white handkerchief for a lady." I forced a wooden smile, humiliated at my weakness.

"I never had the room to carry a handkerchief before. Too much baggage in those days, Mrs. Perkins."

I looked away and remembered the priest as a shoeless vagabond, his only possessions a few books and a small box that contained a piece of wood—a piece of the true cross, he had said. I began to smile, then pressed my lips together.

"Baggage, Reverend Smithers?" I looked directly at him now. "I remember that you traveled very light. You came and left like a forest spirit."

He chuckled—a deep, friendly sound. This was the first time that I had ever heard him laugh. "The burdens I carried at Nan were much heavier, much bulkier, than mere belongings."

I waited for him to continue; after a moment he seemed to make up his mind.

"I was a priest of the Catholic Church, you see. For thirty years. But . . . " He stopped again. Still I waited. "This new age of science that we occupy—it finally sowed the seeds of doubt, of cynicism. It threw me into a turmoil."

"But why were you there—at Nan—in the jungle?"

"I suppose I was looking for meaning, for purpose. For something of value."

"Wasted years," I said. "I'll bet a hat you didn't find it there."

"You're wrong." The vehemence of his words startled me. "I found the answers I sought at Nan."

I looked hard at him. His face was grave. He watched me with a sorrowful expression.

My throat grew dry. "What do you mean?" I asked, afraid now of what I would hear.

"I was lost in those days," he said. "But I found the meaning of life at Nan in your husband's work. God was there with him, in that jungle, in Ai Mah's village."

"What are you talking about? God—religion—had nothing to do with it," I cried. Furious anger coursed through me. "It was all hopeless. *Nothing* changed at Nan because of Harvey's work. It cost me ten years of life—and a marriage." I caught my breath. "Religion is nothing but lies. Rules and barren, frozen dogma."

"Mrs. Perkins. Christianity only requires that you give your best. Do you remember the story of the Good Samaritan in the Scriptures?"

I nodded dumbly, struggling not to cry again.

"A lawyer asked what must be done to win eternal life, and Jesus answered simply that he must love God and care for those less fortunate. The example he gave was a man of Samaria, a man who knew nothing of the Hebrew law or rules or religion or even of the Scriptures. He just did the right thing. Dogma—doctrine—is not religion. Our God is not so small as that."

The hat went round again. Then in a low, strong voice, he began to tell me what I had never known—of the time that he had accompanied Harvey and Ai Mah to the Village of the Beautiful God. I remembered that I had never asked what happened at that time. I had never even wondered what caused Ai Mah's desertion, his flight to seek refuge with the Buddha. I had been consumed by my own misery . . . the constant rain, the cant of Emery Breeden, the loneliness and sense of failure.

The priest continued. "We arrived at the village late in the evening, exhausted and hungry. Our path through the jungle, the most traveled way to and from the village, had not been used in weeks. It was so overgrown with weeds and thick vines that we were forced to hack our way through. Even far away, however, we could smell the smoke."

"I don't want to hear," I said in a low voice.

"I tried to tell you then, you know. At Nan." He paused, and when I didn't speak, he continued. "Just outside the village we saw bodies being burned by those who were still alive—barely alive. The smell of death was in the smoke, so strong that we were forced to cover our faces with handkerchiefs. The village was being destroyed by dysentery and famine." He stopped, took a deep breath, and shuddered. "It was appalling.

"Ai Mah was with us. He was so young." He shook his head. "Too young to see such evil. He clapped his hands over his ears at the cries of his friends . . . friends who were like his own family. Their bowels were eroded; they writhed in pain from the bloody flux. Ai Mah froze when he saw the blood, when the cries turned to screams.

"I stopped at first—it was too much. I could go no farther. But your husband kept going until he reached the clearing. Like a man possessed he climbed the ladder of each hut, one after the other—never stopping—to let the ones still alive know that he had come.

"Spirit charms surrounded every house, and they were placed all along the paths. Streamers of colored paper had been hung—pitiful attempts to appease the spirits, they sagged on bamboo poles stuck in the bare ground before the temple. But the cleared area between the huts where the wells were dug, the areas where animals should have been—those were deserted. Filth covered everything. There were scarlet heaps of waste beneath the houses." He ran his hand over his eyes and looked down. "Do you remember how the wood and bamboo were separated from each other on the floors of the huts?"

I nodded. They had all been built high off the ground.

"Well," he continued in a voice full of pain. "So much blood had seeped to the ground between those spaces that the edges of the wood were tinted dark, almost black. Flies swarmed in clustered masses beneath the floors . . . and below on the ground their larvae churned in the wet dirt, so that the dirt and the blood and the droppings were whipped together into a frothy paste."

I stared at him in horror, but still he continued.

"That is what dysentery does. I was terrified, and so was Ai Mah. But your husband kept on going. He boiled water and brought it to each person still alive, holding the dipper to their cracked lips, opening their mouths and forcing it in. He tended the fires of the dead and cleaned the waste of the living.

"Dr. Perkins consoled them, he wept with them, but he never stopped. Then the rain began. He kept working day and night in the rain until he was almost skin and bones. I wondered how he kept going. No one would have blamed him for leaving—the village was decimated, and there was almost nothing that any human could do.

"But he stayed. He had no time to pray, but I prayed. For the first time in years, I prayed." His eyes filled with tears. I looked away.

"There was nothing left to eat. We sent Ai Mah to another village for food, but he returned with only a small amount of rice. The water had to be boiled; it was contaminated. But I never heard your husband complain, not even once. Then he became ill. Malaria, probably, or dengue." Joshua Smithers glanced at me, then away. "But still he kept moving—going from one hut to the other in the rain, from one person who looked like the living dead to the next, hardly sleeping, barely eating . . . for days and days and days." He shook his head. "Finally . . . he collapsed. I don't know how he lived. It was a week before he gained the strength to walk. He was in no condition to make the trip back through the jungle, but he insisted that he must return to you and the child to make sure that you were safe."

I was rigid as I listened. Tears rolled down my cheeks. It had been the monsoon season when I had thought he'd deserted us, thought he'd chosen strangers over Barby Jeanne and me.

"I saw your struggle then," he said. "Ask yourself this question, Mrs. Perkins," Joshua Smithers looked over the field of flowers, "the question that everyone asks when faith is gone: If I died tomorrow, what difference did my life make to the world?

"Your husband showed me the answer. The value of life is not measured by success—neither ours, nor others—nor by happiness or tranquility, nor by what people think of us. There are right actions and wrong ones. It's not decided by how we obey men's rules, sometimes even the rules of a church. It's neither simple nor easy." He looked off. "Faith is grace. But the value of our lives is measured by what we do, by how we live." The hat went around again. "The words are nineteen hundred years old: 'Ye shall know them by their fruits.'"

I couldn't speak.

He shuddered. "You think that life is tenuous, elusive, that nothing has meaning beyond the moment of death, so that time and pleasure are the driving forces. Tell me," he turned his head and looked at me, "do you think your husband found pleasure in those days at the Village of the Beautiful God?"

I could only shake my head.

"Of course not. But what he did for those people made a difference. But for your husband's efforts, more would have perished. Yet some of them lived. Some were children who grew up and today have children—because of your husband. They laugh, they sing, they love—because of your husband. He was not chasing an abstract ideal, Mrs. Perkins. He changed lives. . . . God lived in him then, whether he knew that or not. God ceased to be an abstraction when he dwelt within your husband's spirit. His life has meaning."

As he spoke, I felt once more the white-hot light of Siam burning into my skin. I heard the rumble of the evening temple drums; saw the still, dark eyes of Ai Mah, full of pride. I saw the moon rising over the Nan Valley.

He added softly. "Your husband loved his work at Nan." The priest turned his eyes to me. "He loved the jungle and the people, even the animals and the birds. But I knew before I left that he would give it up for you."

I stiffened but could not respond. We sat in silence as the light began to fade. The children had left long ago; the little blackbird was nowhere to be seen.

After a long pause, I asked Reverend Smithers why he had carried around the piece of wood that he claimed was from the true cross. "I thought perhaps you were demented," I said.

"For me, at that time—it was the one true thing."

"What do you mean?"

"It was a reminder that there is something more than I can see or feel or touch. You can find out for yourself, if you search. The answers are all around you. That little piece of wood helped carry me through the darkness."

We sat shrouded in silence. "I wish I had that kind of faith," I sighed.

"The Scriptures tell us that love is greater than faith," he answered.

I looked at him with surprise.

"Those are the words of the apostle Paul," he said, smiling. "We can't understand everything yet. But we have faith, hope, love . . . these three. And the greatest of these is love." His smile disappeared, and he gave me an intent look. "With love, faith will follow."

After a moment he braced his hands on his knees and pushed himself up. Patches of fog had drifted through the park and hovered low, just above the ground. He placed his hat upon his head, pulled it down, then turned to look at me and nodded. I watched him walk away, our mysterious Englishman, until he was only a shadow in the mist.

# Chapter Thirty-Three

"WHY DON'T YOU COME WITH US to Frascati for the day?" Gertrude asked for the third time as she watched me. I slouched in my chair, sipping black coffee. An English newspaper was spread before me on the table.

I shook my head. She started to speak again and I interrupted. "No, I really can't." I had tossed and turned all night, thinking of Joshua Smithers' story, of Harvey's courage in the Village of the Beautiful God and the strength that I had never understood, of his letter and my music and Ferrati. By the time the sun rose and the moon disappeared, I knew that I could no longer put off the inevitable decision. This was Friday, the end of March, and once Harvey was committed to a course of action, I knew, my choice would already have been made.

Seeing Gertrude's worried look, I added, "I have a lesson. And if I have time, I'm going to a concert."

She frowned in disbelief. I pushed the newspaper to her. "Bach: *Mass in B Minor*, Basilica of St. Peter, 4:30 PM" was circled in pencil. Harvey loved the mathematical quality, the complexity of Bach's music. "It's mathematics, art, and religion all mixed into one," he had once told me.

"Ted's coming with us," Gertrude tried again. "He's got the use of an embassy car for the day."

I shook my head and took a sip of coffee, suddenly realizing that I had no real interest in Ted. The choice I had to make was much larger than a possible relationship with him. Ted's character paled next to Harvey's strength and his simple, straightforward view of life. In comparison, Ted seemed to have all the substance of bubbles in champagne. But music . . . that was something else again. I knew that Ferrati had changed his mind about my prospects; grand opera might actually be open to me now—once again. The painful decision seemed to have resolved itself around my love for Harvey or seizing the last opportunity to sing.

"Margaret will keep him company," I said with a dismissive wave.

When they had gone, I sat at the table, aimless and moody. The morning sun disappeared, and light rain began to fall. For an hour I watched the water roll down the windowpane, creating translucent waves and ridges on the glass. Finally I grabbed my coat, opened the door, and walked up the few steps to the wet street. The rain had turned into soft mist, and my shoes slipped on the slick, uneven surface. Street lamps glowed in the dim, gray light.

For hours I walked through the ancient city, thinking of Harvey's letter and of what Joshua Smithers had told me. When I reached the Tiber and the bridge near the small island in the middle, I stopped and leaned against the rail, watching the water below. The river was opaque and brown, rushing in swift currents toward the sea. The wind swept through my hair; Violetta called.

So many years spent trying to make sense of things, to find the point of life, I reflected. How could I know which choice was right? Either way I would lose something that I loved, something essential. The old monk's words in the ruins of the temple at Nan long ago came back to me. Perhaps he was right and life is like a rainbow, each person seeing its colors, its promise, from a different perspective. There was no map for me to follow. Bells peeled in the distance, breaking through my reverie.

As if in a dream, and conscious that not much time was left to send the cable, I crossed the river into Trastevere. A half hour later I found myself standing alone in the small triangular park in front of the maestro's studio. I listened as music from his piano floated through the open doors, crisp notes, like lemon drops falling through the air, sweet, pungent reminders of the life that Rome now offered. The music clashed with the sounds of the street, the rolling wheels of carts nearby, the sharp clink of bottles, the wet whoosh of a broom upon the pavement. I stood staring at the balcony for a long time, but instead of going in, I turned and walked away. Tomorrow I could tell him that the rain had held me up.

I glanced down at my watch and saw that it was half past three. A fresh rush of anxiety assaulted me. The offices of Thomas Cook & Sons would close at six-thirty. I continued on, until at last I found myself standing before St. Peter's Square in front of the huge basilica. The wide expanse was almost empty, except for birds. Feeling depressed, I crossed the piazza and entered through the big open doors in front. I walked past the guards into the wondrous, cavernous interior. Ahead and to my left were rows of chairs set up in preparation for the concert I had planned to attend, before the letter came.

Pamphlets describing the performance were on a table near the door. Absently I picked one up. The room was dark and cool, almost empty at this time of day. Suddenly I was fatigued; the muscles in my legs began to ache. I took a seat and forced myself to look around and admire the beauty of the art and architecture, the rich colors all around me—bright gold, the deepest blue, and crimson. In the silence I heard only echoes of sound from a distance, the heavy clunk of furniture being dragged across a floor, footsteps, doors opening and closing—firm, solid sounds, with intervals as quiet as the universe must be, way out beyond the stars that are no more.

An hour passed and still I sat alone in the church, wrapped in the heavy, languorous darkness. Faint lights on the walls began to flicker, then steadied themselves and glowed. People drifted in around me, ones and twos speaking in whispers, until finally a crowd had gathered. I watched with detachment while the seats began to fill, and then, when no more were vacant, the people stood leaning against the walls.

I opened the folded sheet in my hand. The *Mass in B Minor* by Johann Sebastian Bach is music created for eternity, it said. Forty musicians and singers would celebrate the gift of living water, the passion of Christ nineteen hundred years earlier that promised that life has meaning, that we will live on beyond our time on earth.

Promises. But, I thought of Joshua Smithers' words: *There is something more than I can see or feel or touch.*

My inner voice whispered, *What if it is true?*

I started to rise, conscious of the time, then some inner urge held me back. Harvey's fascination with Bach's music had once puzzled me. "His compositions are so complex they suggest a kind of mathematical intuition not yet explained by modern science. It's perplexing," he had said. "A form of mental activity that we don't understand, that doesn't seem to result from physical processes."

Everyone was seated. Voices hushed, then rustling and whispers faded to silence.

Then the air was pierced by voices sharp and strong and urgent—a clear chorus that dropped at once to hover in the minor key before starting an ascent, a twisting, pulsing climb weaving a pattern of hope and love and life over a staccato current of despair. The voices crossed, turned back and blended, then escalated as one, filled with the counterpoints of passion and emptiness, hope and despair, light and shadow.

The chorus soared. I closed my eyes and heard music so beautiful that it defied all limitations, growing, reaching for infinity. Harvey had been right. This music accomplished something greater than the human mind could create. For an hour I did not move.

And while the music circled—a glorious passage of life and love and death, then life again—my heart unfolded and began to turn. I closed my eyes and heard the laughter of the children in the Nan Valley, saw the beauty of the roses in the north, the moon as it shone through the mango tree, dusting its limbs with gold. I felt Harvey's love, saw the faces of my children, sweet and trusting. These things, like love, are gifts, the voices sang in different words. They are the mysteries of our minds that transcend flesh, transcend our mortal bounds.

The music swelled. Through space and time I heard the drum, faint but triumphant as it beat against the last few chords, grace notes filled with faith and hope. *Messiah.* The music lifted me with it in that instant, coursing up through the veil that conceals the timeless realm where Harvey's love, and Barby Jeanne's and June's . . . and something else—a greater love—spread as light, mingling with my own and filling me.

*Love is not measured by time*, whispered my inner voice. *This is what endures.* I rested in this place for minutes, hours, days, for years. In the past, present, future. In eternity.

When the last notes faded, no one moved. The great basilica was utterly still. I listened to the silence. For the first time in years I ceased to hear the ticking of the universal clock that measures out our lives. The wheel of life had slowed. It trembled . . . then it shuddered to a stop.

I could not move when the audience rose to applaud, softly at first, then bolder when the choir appeared. Suddenly I remembered and glanced down at my watch. A chill rushed through me when I saw the time. It was late—already five past six. Frantically I stood, stumbling in haste and mumbling, "Excuse me, please, excuse me," as I worked my way through the crowd. As I burst through the great double doors past the guards and hurried away from the cathedral, the applause faded. Crossing the piazza, I began to run—fast, then faster—as fast as I have ever run, I flew through the square and down the street.

A taxi was parked one block away. I ran toward it, but my legs moved slowly now, dreamlike, as if I ran through water. Time seemed to slow. I gathered all of my strength and . . . *willed it . . . willed* myself to run, to move forward. Far away I heard shoes clattering on the pavement and realized they were mine. When at last I reached the corner and the taxi, I found the driver slumped in the front seat with his head resting on the steering wheel, dozing.

"Are you free?" I gasped through the window. He jerked his head up in surprise.

"Si." But before he could move I yanked open the back door and climbed in, breathless.

"Where to, Signora?"

I gave him directions to the offices of Thomas Cook & Sons and looked again at my watch. It was six-fifteen—the office would close in fifteen minutes.

"Please hurry," I begged as we pulled away from the curve and began winding our way through the city. "It's an emergency." But as soon as we crossed the river the car slowed. The streets had filled with evening traffic. I leaned forward as we rolled to a stop. The driver ignored me. He propped his elbow on the windowsill and glanced away, apparently content to wait. It was six-twenty.

"Double fare if you can get me there in ten minutes," I said.

He nodded, and I saw his smile reflected in the rearview mirror. But still we sat, trapped in the jammed traffic. Slowly we inched forward. Six twenty-five, my watch read.

Suddenly, with a burst of speed the taxi swerved sharply to the right, into an alley. The walls of the buildings on each side closed around us, and I braced for the harsh sound of a collision as we flew through. I closed my eyes. When I opened them again, we were almost through the narrow gap.

We burst into the street, and a sharp left turn threw me to the seat. I pulled myself up and braced as we shot forward and out onto another road that was clear and free of traffic. Once again I looked down at my watch, and this time, as I stared at the minute hand, my breath stopped. The office of Thomas Cook & Sons was closed for the weekend.

In despair, I sank back in the taxi, and thin fingers of ice clawed their way into my chest. It would be Monday before

I could send the cable, and Harvey would assume the worst. He would set his other plans in motion, make commitments that he would have to keep . . . might even leave. I squeezed shut my eyes, wanting not to think of what I had done. Still the taxi raced on, down the crowded boulevards, through tiny lanes, through roundabouts and across piazzas.

At last the car slowed and my watch blurred as I looked down. It was six forty-five. But as we rolled to a stop, I glanced up and my heart jumped. A clerk was fumbling with a key, locking the doors. Behind him the office was in darkness. Frantically I dug into my handbag for lira and dropped double the fare into the driver's hands, thanking him as I shoved open the door.

I called out wildly to the clerk to wait. He stopped, looked around, then turned and frowned as I slid from the taxi.

"Please," I begged, rushing to him, "I must send a cable right away."

My words weren't clear. His eyes were puzzled. He didn't understand and moved with impatience, as if to leave.

"A wireless!" Deliberately, I calmed my voice. "*Please!* It's an urgent matter."

My eyes swam with tears that I knew he saw, but still he didn't move. He pursed his lips and shook his head, clearly anxious to leave. But I lifted my chin and planted my feet; I've always had success with my blue eyes. Our eyes locked. Finally he smiled in defeat and shrugged.

"Of course," he said, opening the door once again and stepping aside to let me in. He turned on the lights and went around the counter to the other side. After a search he pulled a slip of paper from a box and held it out to me. "Write what you want to say. I will send it now."

My hand shook as I took the piece of paper and his pen. For an instant, the maestro's fairy dust glittered around me, clouding my sight. I hesitated, thinking of singing, of Violetta, and of Rome. Then once again I felt that love, saw Harvey's smile and felt his strength, thought of my children's faces on the day that I surprised them in the woods.

Suddenly I was liberated—free, warmed, happy, and filled with light. I had found the purpose that I'd sought so long. The pieces in the shifting, changing mosaic of my life were joined now, complete—daughter, wife, mother, woman. And the last, woman, was whole and greater than the sum of all the other parts.

*But what about the music?* asked my inner voice.

I smiled to myself. I had made the choice—Harvey and the girls. But the music still lived within. It was sufficient to know that I *could* sing, that the choice was mine to make. The maestro had been right: *I* am the instrument.

No. No regrets. As I wrote these words to Harvey, my hand grew firm and strong.

*"I'll meet you in Lausanne. Let's go home."*

# Epilogue

MUSIC WAKES ME, AS IT OFTEN does in my grandparents' house. I yawn and stretch my legs until my eight-year-old toes hit the tucked end of the blanket at the foot of the bed. My grandmother is playing the piano downstairs, softly, softly, because it is early and everyone is asleep.

The window is open, and I take a deep breath. The air here in Philadelphia is cool and fresh, even in the summer, and there are different smells here, unlike those at home in New Orleans. My grandfather keeps the windows open; he says it's good for me, and he's a doctor, so he's right. I roll my head on the pillow and gaze through the window at the tops of trees in the back yard. At the bottom of the terrace, below my window, there is a secret path twisting through my grandfather's rose gardens. It ends at a stone fishpond that marks the dead center of the universe. He marked the spot that way himself, my grandmother says. Turtles live in that pond. There is a big stone wall around the back yard, but I have made some friends on our visit this summer, and my grandfather leaves the back gate unlocked for them to come in and play.

The piano stops. I hear my grandfather's voice and my grandmother's soft laugh, like a shower of musical notes. Pushing the blanket aside, I slide from the bed and, still in my nightgown, open the door very slowly so as not to let it creak and wake the parents. I tiptoe down the long hallway to the stairs, down the stairs through a smaller hall, into an enormous, high-ceilinged room. This room is flooded with morning sunshine from a row of long windows that lead to a front terrace and a broad front lawn.

Near the piano my grandparents stand close together, and he is looking down at her, smiling as she whispers. He tips up her chin and gives her a little kiss. He says something, and she makes that little sound that I've heard before—a slip of laughter in the back of her throat that tells you the rest of that laugh is in there, boxed up, and she'll just keep it to herself for now.

I halt in the doorway, suddenly shy. She is small standing next to him. He's tall and thin, and even though he's as old as anyone can be and his mustache is getting gray and he says his hair is disappearing, when he's in a room everyone turns to him and listens to every word he says.

I shuffle my feet and they spot me. Granddaddy picks up his hat from the top of the piano, kisses my grandmother's cheek. He says "Good-bye, Babs, I'll be home around five or so," and walks over to me. He stoops to my level, sitting on his heels because there is pain in his neck and shoulders and he cannot bend over, and sometimes, when I forget and reach out for a hug, his eyes almost close and I can see the muscles jump around them. He's still carrying a burden on his shoulders, my grandmother told me once—something he caught in the jungle long ago in that magic land across the world where they lived when they were young.

"Will you take me to the zoo?" I have to tilt my head back to see his expression when he's this close to me.

He nods, kisses my cheek, smiling as he rises. "On Saturday," he says. He's repeated this promise every day this week and I'm testing, checking. This is Thursday. I'm counting too.

"And to your place for ice cream."

"The Harvey House?"

I nod.

The Harvey House is everywhere in Philadelphia—restaurants that my grandfather has assured me are named for him.

"Harvey," my grandmother says in a strange, warning tone.

He laughs. I turn and watch as he walks to the door, picks up his walking stick, and sets his hat on his head. With a wink he says to me, "Ice cream, too. On Saturday." I hear my grandmother chuckling to herself. The music starts up again as I watch him walk down the sidewalk. He turns, salutes me with his stick, and opens the front gate. He is an important man, my grandmother says—the dean of Jefferson Medical School in Philadelphia.

I go to the piano. My grandmother slides over to make room for me as she always does and pats the piano bench. I sit, watching. Her hands fluttering across the keys are like little birds, and she begins to play a tune that brings down my mood. "What is the name of this?" I ask again. I never can remember. She plays this often. Whenever I hear it, I think of her and this big stone house and my grandfather.

"'Liebestraum,'" she says, with a glance at me. When she plays this one, her chin sometimes drops a bit and her shoulders move with the music. There is something sweet and private and maybe sad between my grandmother and this tune.

Sometimes she sings. Once she took me to a movie, and if I'd known what she would do before we went, I can tell you right now that I wouldn't have gone. In the dark theater, just as I'd settled down into my seat with a box of Good & Plenty, a picture of the American flag popped onto the screen and a band began to play the national anthem. I know the name of this song because we sing it at school. My grandmother suddenly rose from her chair. I shot a look at her, then at the silent, seated crowd around us and, holding my breath, shrank back into my seat. You never know what my grandmother will do. But she tapped my shoulder, so I had to stand up too, and we both put our hands over our hearts while she began to sing.

I'd never heard her sing full out like that before. With the flag waving on the screen, her voice soared through that theater, filling it. I have to say it made me proud. I stood beside her, stunned into silence as she sang every verse of that song by herself, right along with the band. At the end she turned to me and said, "You may sit now," in a tight, clipped tone. We sat down, straight-backed, chins up, and I stared at the waving flag on the screen, praying for the movie to start. For a split-second the theater was absolutely silent. The sudden roar startled me and I looked around to see people beginning to stand, clapping and shouting and stamping their feet, turning toward my grandmother. The screen in front went dark, and the lights came on as people cheered. My grandmother stood, smiled all around, and dipped her head.

Later I asked her why.

"The flag stands for something important," she said. "It stands for something right and good."

I lean against her now while she plays. Sunbeams slant across the wooden floor. She is playing a song that I know, and I struggle to sing along with her, missing some of the words. She supplies them for me though and tells me to play the piano with her, down at the far end. I do and the high, tinkling noise seems to me to add quite a bit to the tune. But then I grow bored, and I slide my fingers down the keyboard a little way until I can touch the top of her hand.

She lifts her hands above the keys and holds them there for just one instant as she turns to me, waiting. "Tell me," I say, looking up. Her eyes are blue, blue as the sky in spring. Her hair is a cloud of soft, white waves that frame her face. She is beautiful.

She laughs with that tinkling laugh and drops her hands to the piano keys once more. "Again?" she says as she resumes playing, softly, muted, as if she's speaking just to me through the music.

"Yes," I say, snuggling close to her. She stretches her hands over the keys.

"Princess Poon and the white elephant?"

I think for a second and shake my head.

"Your mother in the lion cage?"

Again, I shake my head.

"Gibbon?"

I think about that and say, "Tell me about the tiger and the farmer and the man with the umbrella." I giggle at the thought of that umbrella.

"All right." And while she plays, she tells the story as she always does, and I half close my eyes and look through the mist to that magical place where my mother was born all those years ago. Once my mother read me a story from the *Times-Picayune* newspaper in New Orleans where they lived when she was my age and my grandfather taught medicine at Tulane Medical School. It was a story of my grandparents in the jungle. Beside the story was a picture of my grandmother standing next to a tiger on a pole. She wore a long dress and a strange hat.

So my grandmother plays and tells me the tales of faraway places, of silver moons, gilded temples flashing in the sun, dark green jungles, elephants and monkeys and tigers in the dusk, princes and priests in yellow robes. She has pictures in albums, too. I love to look at them—all so long ago and far away.

Upstairs I hear the hollow sound of my mother's shoes in the hallway. She's calling my name, searching for me.

"She's down here, Barby Jeanne," my grandmother calls, still playing the piano.

My mother says, "Oh, well, that's all right," and her voice fades. I hear her talking to her sister, June, who has a studio for her paints and clay up on the third floor. Aunt June has just married a war hero with one real leg and one made of wood. He sticks pins in the wooden leg and I shiver. My father was a hero in that war, too, I know. He was captain of a fast little boat way out in the ocean.

I wonder about my uncle's leg. I ask my grandmother how he lost it.

"He lost it in the last war. At a place called Iwo Jima."

"Why?"

"Hmmm." She looks at me from the corners of her eyes, lifts her hands from the keyboard, and rests them on her lap. "If your friend Paul tried to hurt one of the turtles in our pond, would you let him?"

"No."

"But he might become angry and leave. You'd have no one to play with then."

I wind a strand of hair around my finger and think about that. "I'd stop him anyway," I say. "I wouldn't want the turtles to be hurt."

She nods and I watch her carefully. "Good choice. Then the turtles can swim and grow, and pretty soon there will be happy babies in that pond, all because you did the right thing."

She pushes back the piano bench and stands. Reaching down for my hand, she pulls me to my feet. "Your uncle and father chose to fight for something right and good. And your grandfather did too. That's why you and I are here right now, safe and sound."

We head for the kitchen, and I realize that I'm hungry. "We all have to make hard choices sometimes, and our decisions have consequences."

I frown, struggling to pretend that I understand.

"It's the 'but for' rule," she says, looking down at me. "The past becomes the future, little one."

A familiar sound comes from upstairs. It is the *thump, thump* of my uncle's wooden leg on the floor. I know nothing of wars, nothing of burdens like the one that causes my grandfather pain when he bends, sometimes even when he walks.

But I am here, now in Philadelphia because of the past, and it is 1954, and today the world to me seems right and good. I steal a look at my grandmother and see the smile on her face and feel her love. I can feel it in the music that pours forth from her. I can sense it in the sun-filled room, the roses in the garden, the velvet moss that coats the old damp stone on the terrace and the pond.

Just to think of all of this now makes my thoughts spin round and round. I am here walking beside my grandmother, feeling the warmth of the sun shining through the windows and counting the hours until Saturday rolls around and my grandfather will take me to the zoo. And it's all because of the "but for" rule, I suppose.

# Author's Note

THE MOON IN THE MANGO TREE is based on my grandmother's life during the decade of the Roaring Twenties. When I was a child, she spun for me fantastical stories of faraway places. Years later, when she was gone, I found letters, journals, and old photographs sepia with age that told me the stories were true. Together they formed a rich narrative of her struggle with faith during her time in Siam and Europe—her search for meaning and purpose. Finally she was forced to choose between love and a deep desire for independence. The story is not invented, but I have fictionalized some elements because I've learned that sometimes fiction reveals the deeper truth.

In connection with the language of Theravada Buddhism that was practiced in Siam in the early nineteenth century, I have sometimes used terms from the Mahayana school that are more familiar to Westerners, such as "nirvana" rather than "nibbana." The influence of the spirit world on Buddhist practice and lore as set forth in *The Moon in the Mango Tree* was described by my grandmother and grandfather as pervasive in the jungles of Siam during their time there.

The names of some characters in this story have been changed. My grandfather described the character of Ai Mah in stories that he wrote and told, and I believe that Ai Mah is a composite of several young men to whom my grandfather taught basic medicine while at Nan.

Princess Poon and my grandmother remained friends, and after my grandmother left Siam, they corresponded until her death. Prince Mahidol was a particular friend of my grandparents, and it was under his influence that they returned to Bangkok in 1926 with the Rockefeller Institute. My grandfather received the Order of the White Elephant from the king of Siam as described in the book.

I would like to thank David Webb, my editor, and the team at B&H Publishing Group, not only for their professionalism in shepherding this book through publication, but also for their friendship. Thank you, David, for caring about the book and for your considerate and thoughtful editing. I hope the result will make all of you proud.

Special thanks go to my agent, Peter Rubie. I am especially indebted for his insight that led me to fictionalize the story and probe beneath the surface for substance.

Thanks also to Camille Cline for her inspiration, editorial advice over the years, and her love for this story. I have come to think of Camille as a muse.

Thanks to my mother and her sister for sharing their memories, for their laughter and, sometimes, bittersweet tears as they read and reread drafts. The responsibility of writing about their lives and their parents and getting it right was a heavy weight. I thank them for their trust and hope they will feel that it was justified. As my grandmother would have said—to both of them—*salute!*

And finally, my thanks go to two very special people. To my husband, Jimmy, love and gratitude. You are my *listener*. Your love sustains me every day. And for Muriel, whose friendship, joy, and enthusiasm while reading draft after draft kept me writing even on the dark days: Here's to you, Muriel! Thank you for the sunshine.

# Glossary

**ayah**—(n.) a native nursemaid

**catafalque**—(n.) a decorated platform or framework on which a coffin rests in state during a funeral

**chedi**—(n.) a domelike structure used to house sacred artifacts

**Chow Luang**—the title attributed to local, royal rulers in certain northern provinces of Siam.

**farang**—(n.) a foreigner

**howdah**—(n.) an ornate carriage positioned on the back of an elephant

**klong**—(n.) a canal

**mahout**—(n.) one who drives an elephant

**naga**—(n.) a Buddhist spirit taking the form of a very large, Cobra-like snake

**panung**—(n.) a traditional garment consisting of a long piece of cloth passed between the legs, hanging loose between the knee and ankle, and held at the waist with a belt

**rachasee**—mythical animals, similar to lions in appearance, which, according to lore, ruled all animals at one time

**sala nam**—(n.) open pavilions where river travelers can rest and sleep

**samsara**—(n.) the cycle of reincarnation and rebirth in the Buddhist religion

**syse**—(n.) one who cares for horses

**tical**—(n.) the currency of Siam, now known as a *baht*

**tokay**—(n.) a gecko native to southeast Asia, usually 7 to 15 inches in length

**topi**—(n.) also known as a pith helmet, it's designed to protect one's head from the sun

**viharn**—the hall in a temple that visually holds the Buddha image